FLIGHT OF THE DESTINED

—BOOK 2—

of the

CLAIMING DESTINATION

SERIES

By

Colleen A. Parkinson

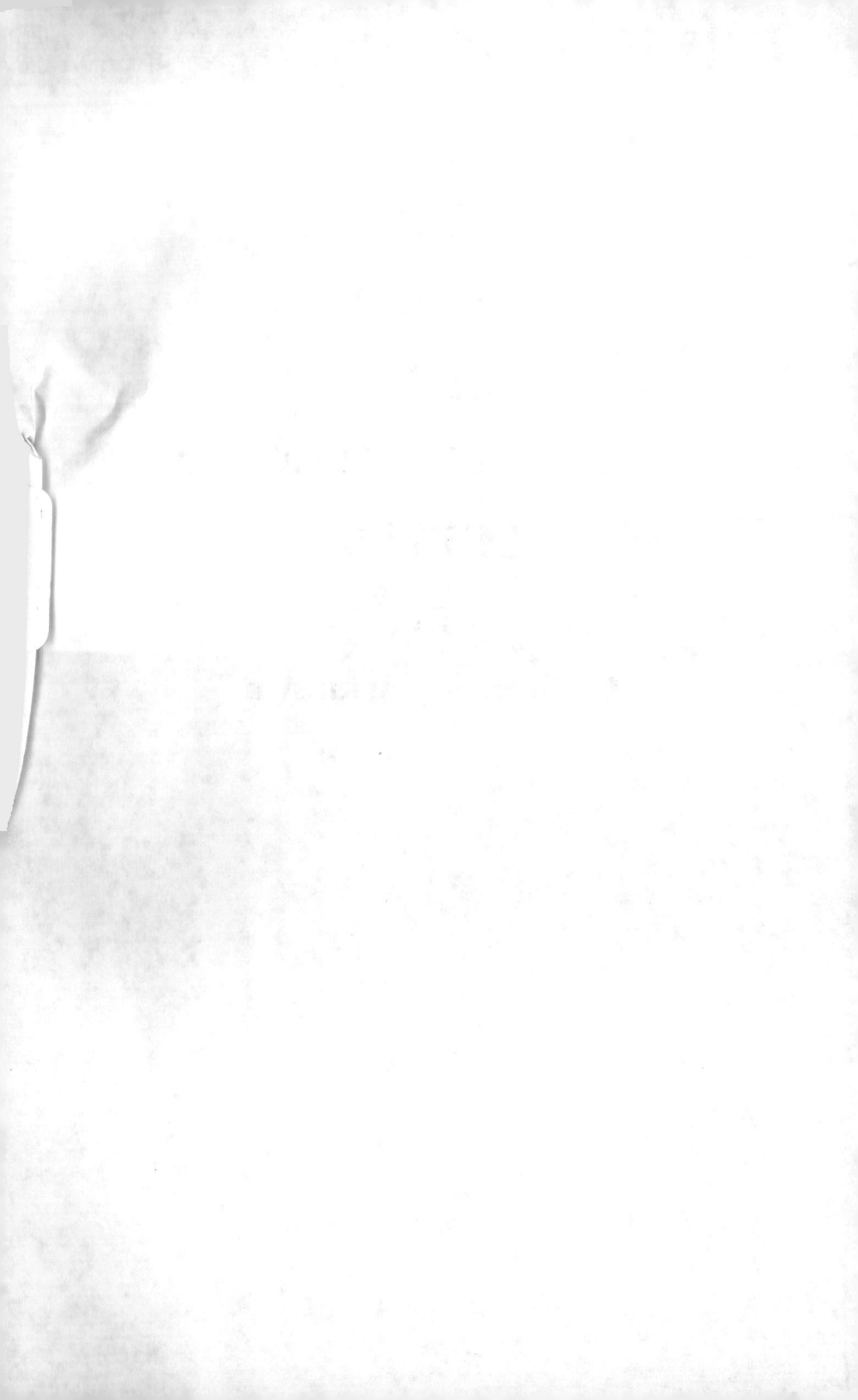

CHAPTER 1

THE WRECKAGE WITHOUT AND WITHIN

Mario took Rosa's hand and led her out of the Bujjet Mart stockroom and out to the deserted rear of the building. They were hungry, and both sniffed the air to pick up the scent of a living, breathing meal. The only aromas that filled the air were the odors of decaying corpses, vehicle exhaust and some rotting garbage near the dumpsters. Noises assaulted their ears from near and far, noises of machinery, gunfire, barking dogs and the faint voices of men and women. They sniffed the air again. The humans were too far away.

Mario took into account the noises of gunfire, and he sensed the humans were armed and hunting for him and the little girl. A vague flash of memory showed the child on his lap with a picture book. A second flash showed her laughing, which stirred a strong feeling of love for her and his compulsion to protect her from the humans with the guns and the noisy, growling machines.

Overhead, a helicopter puttered, and its searchlight swept over the vacant lot to his right. Mario jerked the little girl to his side and took cover behind one of the pallets of flattened cardboard boxes. He watched the helicopter veer away and cast its light northwestward where it followed the ribbon of interstate freeway. The girl bared her teeth and growled at the giant black insect with the big bright eye.

Although it was pitch black with the absence of electrical power to light the loading docks, Mario could see clearly across the lot as if it was noontime. He wanted to escape this place, escape without their predators' detection. But... how? The entire massive square of pavement around the building was wide open to the sky, wide open for the things in the air to spot them.

He scanned the pavement again, recalling there was something, some way to get under the pavement.

It began to rain. He remembered rain. He remembered the time it rained so hard the store flooded because the storm drains clogged.

He grinned then, and a low rumble of satisfaction rolled up his throat. He tightened his grip of the girl's hand, tugged on it to get her attention. When she looked up at him inquiringly, he grunted and pointed at the manhole cover. She smiled and nodded.

NATALIE HAD NOT SLEPT. She'd lain in the darkness listening to the rain and mourning for her parents. She knew her grief was causing her insomnia, that and her fear regarding her situation and her future.

Coltan tossed and turned most of the night. He had been talking in his sleep, sometimes yelling at someone, other times pleading and whimpering in a child-like voice. Natalie listened closely, but could not understand a word of it. The only thing she understood was the language he spoke in these dreams was not English, but French. At one point during the night, he experienced a particularly bad nightmare in which he began pleading while shielding his face and head from imaginary assault. His voice was so loud, she was compelled to shush him and calm him, and he never awakened during that episode.

He was quiet now and sleeping peacefully. She turned on her side and observed him, wondering about his secret conflicts and torments. A part of her wondered if he would be able to hold it together over the next few months of hiding. If his nightmares became worse and more frequent, and if it began to affect his waking behavior, she would have to encourage him to talk about it, or things would only worsen.

Natalie gave up on the idea of sleep and started a pot of coffee. She put the scanner on low volume and watched the channel numbers blink by as it scanned for transmissions. The minutes went by without a single voice. It seemed all human life had disappeared from her town and the surrounding communities. It was eerie.

She switched off the scanner and turned on the television, flipped through the channels. As usual, all were dark except SWNS. The usual news anchors and correspondents were not there. Instead, three soldiers from the new military were at the anchor desk. They took turns reading evacuation information off the teleprompter. They encouraged viewers to fully cooperate with all authorities during the ongoing urban, suburban and rural sweeps. Natalie noticed they repeated the phrases, "for your safety and that of your loved ones," and "throughout the duration of this global crisis." For a few minutes, they reported some non-connected stories about environmental disasters: two large earthquakes on the west coast between Washington and southern Canada, a monster 8.7 magnitude quake off New Zealand; an F-3 hurricane threatening the gulf coast; and record snowfall in the Midwest northern states and the East Coast. Following those reports, the anchors briefly discussed the record low temperatures throughout the North American continent during the summer and through the waning days of fall and how those temperatures could affect spring crops if the forecasted extreme winter proved correct.

She wearily shut off the television and sat there in the silence. The only thing good about this morning so far was the coffee.

The wafting odor of cigarette smoke caused her to look Coltan's way. Not fully awake yet, he smoked and peered blearily across at the stack of mattresses, obviously considering a return to the escape of sleep.

Natalie poured a cup of coffee and offered it to him. He smiled and took it from her.

"Hungry?" she asked.

"No..." His voice was soft. He didn't seem completely in the moment.

She decided to have a smoke too, and they sat next to each other, smoking and enjoying the sound of the rain. She thought about his nightmares and wanted to discuss it with him. "Are you awake yet?"

"Uh-huh."

"You had nightmares all night."

"Gee... I wonder why?" He was being a smartass.

"Do you remember?"

"Nope."

If he actually did remember, he obviously didn't want to talk about it. She decided not to press the issue.

"There's nothing on the scanner," she remarked. "The military's taken over SWNS."

"That figures." He took big sips of his coffee before he paused long enough to tell her, "You sure make good coffee. You gotta show me what you do different."

"It's just making the right measurement, that's all."

"Your Dad always made it too strong, and your Mom always made it too weak."

"So, I'm Goldilocks, and I make it just right?"

"Yeah." He tilted his face sideways at her and grinned, "Commando Goldilocks..."

She grinned back at him, happy he was in a fairly good mood. If all it took was a properly measured brew of coffee to lift his mood, life couldn't be all that bad.

"We should start on that exercise and weight training regimen today." He was thinking aloud.

"I guess we should be up and at 'em." she replied.

"In a while." He adjusted the sleeping bag around him. Mister Dolce was wide-awake and he didn't want her to see it. He regretted not wearing a bulky pair of sweat pants to bed instead of just his boxer shorts. It would take some planning to get from his bed to the downstairs bathroom without her noticing the morning bulge. Until he could figure something out, he opted to stay hidden under the cover of the sleeping bag.

Natalie blurted, "I didn't know you spoke French."

"I picked it up from my tormenters." It was a shot at droll humor that didn't work. "Richard insisted we spoke it at home."

"Richard?"

"My stepdad."

"Oh..." She had always assumed the Squirrel on Speed was Coltan's father. "Where's your real dad?"

"Hell if I know. I don't even know who he is."

"Oh..." This was getting awkward.

"And, I don't wanna know, either." In case that was Natalie's next question.

"Well..." She grasped for conversation. Nothing came to mind. "Guess I'll grab a quick shower."

He was relieved; it would buy a little time for Mister Dolce to settle down and for him to put on some sweats.

Later that morning they set up a workout area in the basement and utilized the equipment. Coltan set her up with some weights appropriate for her size and strength to start her on a gradual strengthening regimen. He had no trouble with the larger weights, and was looking forward to increasing his strength. They couldn't know for certain what the future held, but they wanted to be ready for every possible scenario.

Natalie knew hand-to-hand combat and self-defense techniques.

She had learned most of it from Dad, and the rest from classes. She took Coltan through some of the basics, and progressed into the more advanced, at first placing him in the role of adversary so he could see her defensive strategies. After tossing him to the mat three times, she encouraged him to be rougher and try to subdue her. He did so, and she defeated him again. It frustrated him he couldn't restrain and conquer someone as small as her. She knew he was getting angry, and it gave her another lesson to teach him. After encouraging his rage, she taunted him into attacking her. He gave it his all. However, his rage caused him to be careless, and she easily matted him again. Humiliated and angry, he lied there trying to catch his breath and retrieve whatever shred of dignity remained within him.

She had hardly broken a sweat.

"I hate you," he stated.

She sat down on the mat with him. "You let your anger make you careless. Never let your emotions get in the way of common sense."

He struggled for breath as he repeated, "I hate you."

"We'll try this again tomorrow," she said. "I'll show you how to disable an opponent. I'll teach you each move, step by step. Okay?"

He knew unless he learned to control his temper, he would end up putting them both in jeopardy. "I shouldn't have got mad. I'm sorry."

"It was my fault. I was showing off."

He agreed, but forgave her with a smile and a casual shrug. He was too tired for a discussion about the evils of ego. Once they returned to the attic, he went directly to his mattress where he snuggled under the sleeping bag for a nap.

She hadn't expected him to return to bed. "Aren't you going to study today?"

"Maybe later." He closed his eyes. This indicated all further communication was on hold for the time being.

Something thumped and crashed on the rear porch below. Natalie looked through the window as Coltan shot up. A woman, a man and a child, all infected with the virus, were examining the items on the porch, sniffing like dogs for a trace of scent. Natalie moved to the wall and retrieved a rifle and silencer.

Coltan rushed beside her and saw their visitors, and she preparing to eliminate them. "No!" he whispered.

"What do you mean, 'no'?"

"Who's gonna dispose of the bodies? You? It sure won't be me!"

"They could get in!"

"They'd have to try real hard." He cornered her. "Put the gun away. Let's watch them and see what they do. Let's watch them."

"Are you nuts?"

"The more we learn about them, the better for us."

He made a good point. She reluctantly set the rifle aside, but where it was still accessible.

The three mords continued investigating and sniffing. The female zeroed in on the chair Coltan had been sitting in the day before. She panted and grunted at the male and the child, who was a little boy of about four. Natalie saw the boy's leg had turned gangrenous from his bite wound where his shorts exposed the infected skin. He limped painfully as he came up beside the woman and sniffed the seat of the chair. The man sniffed the air in all directions. As he did this, the woman went down on all fours and began sniffing the deck, crawling on her hands and knees, following the trail of scent to the rear security door. From there, she knelt and sniffed the doorknob. The discovery now a certainty, she let out a shrill sound that was a combination of a growl and a shriek, and the man and boy quickly joined her. The three of them began to rattle the doorknob and pound on the door. It made a horrible racket.

"Are you sure they can't get in?" Natalie asked softly.

"I'm sure." Coltan stated. "See? They're concentrating on the door, not the windows. I never touched the outside of the windows. I guess they're following my scent. I was at that chair the longest. The last thing I touched was that doorknob. Remember?"

"I don't know," Natalie said.

Attracted by the noise, two more infected men appeared from the east corner of the house. They were a hideous sight, full of festering wounds that leaked pus upon their tattered, bloodstained clothing. The youngest was missing two fingers and his thumb from his masticated right hand that was swollen and gray from blood loss, crushed bones, and infection.

"Shit!" Natalie reached for the rifle and attached the silencer.

"Don't do it!" Coltan warned.

Natalie calmed herself. "I won't. This is just in case."

The other two joined the first three at the door. Now, they were fighting over it.

Coltan studied them curiously. "Interesting..." When the three men began trading fists, shoves and growls, Coltan laughed softly. "Kinda like when the Gas'n Go Station had that *five-dollar gas for one hour only* sale."

The woman and child continued pounding the security door and intermittently tugging on it. The door held firm.

When Natalie failed to react to his musing, he glanced at her. She was tensely watching the mords. Coltan worried she was waiting for any excuse to start shooting. He sought to distract her. "Pull up the stairway, just in case."

"I thought you said they won't get in?"

"Just in case."

"You're so full of it. You're afraid I'll shoot at them!"

Chagrined, he shook his head, knowing she had caught him.

"You're such an ass..." She had to get the final word.

At the door, the woman and child began to tire from their useless attempts to gain entry. Their pounding slowed and finally stopped, and the woman moved away and down the steps to the garden path. The child limped behind her. The three men were still battling each other, and their fight became so intense they forgot all about their prey. One managed to throw one of the others off the porch, and the victim landed and rolled onto the gravel. He rolled into the child's legs, sweeping the child off his feet and causing him to fall, crashing onto his buttocks. The child cried out in alarm and pain. The woman turned and saw what happened. She screamed out, hissed and growled at the men. They immediately ceased their fight and stood gaping at her. She warned them with another growl and a look to kill. They carefully stepped away from her and, giving her wide berth, trudged hesitantly onto the mud of the flowerbed and headed toward the gully ahead of her.

The child sobbed and rubbed his gangrenous leg, pitifully reached out his arms to the woman. The woman regarded him compassionately, tilted her head side-to-side as she gazed at him before she bent, gently lifted the child and cuddled and soothed him. Without another sound, she turned and carried him down the garden path. Natalie and Coltan watched in stunned amazement as the woman and child disappeared over the crest of the hill.

"My God," Natalie whispered, "Compassion. Did you see that? They have compassion for each other...!"

Coltan was still gazing after them. He was aware he felt a mix of emotions good and bad he couldn't decipher, even if he wanted to. After several long moments, he finally whispered, "Love remains... How can that be?"

Her voice soft with her astonishment, Natalie stated, "I guess the bond between a mother and child... at least between those two... the love there is so strong..."

It was then she saw it in Coltan's eyes. She could read his thoughts plainly. He was thinking if that woman, that disease-infested monster out there, could still retain and demonstrate her love for her child, why couldn't his own mother possess that same love for him?

Natalie read him accurately. Coltan was completely unaware of it, though; all his attention was riveted on the infected woman and her infected and dying son. Even though they were both monsters to him, their love touched him profoundly. How strong their love must have been to thrive through all of this.

He pulled away from the window, sad and greatly disturbed. A strange and morose weariness spread within him, and he returned to the warmth of his sleeping bag. All he desired for the time being was escape from the whole wretched world. There was nothing left inside him for anything, at least nothing he could find. His mind wanted to shut down and he gave it permission to do so.

She set the rifle aside and watched him, noted his despondency. "Colt?"

He whispered, "What?"

"Are you feeling sick?"

He finally looked at her, "Just tired."

"What did they do to you?"

"Leave it," he said firmly.

"I saw what he did with your dog's chain leash. I saw the whole thing."

His voice came wearily, "Don't."

"Okay." She would give him time. He was not ready. "I just want you to know, when you feel up to it, you can tell me."

He turned over on his back and took her hands in his. "It was a long time ago, and it's over. Don't worry about me."

"I'm worried about *us*." She saw that perplexed him. "What they did to you is still affecting you. If this keeps up, you could put us both in danger."

She could be exasperating. He thought she was making a big deal out of nothing. His first impulse was to reassure her with affection.

He tugged at her hands to encourage her to lie with him.

She wasn't buying it, and resisted his patronizing display. "That won't work. You must think I'm really stupid."

"No." If anything, she was really *frustrating*.

"Alright," she told him, "I'm not going to push you."

He released her hands and turned over on his side, glad she got the message.

It began to rain again, a comforting cadence.

Natalie took to her mattress beside his and covered herself with the sleeping bag. She made eye contact with Coltan, and they stared at each other, waiting to see who would blink first. He blinked first and, just to lighten the mood, he crossed his eyes and contorted his face. She responded, laughing. Without thinking about it, he reached over and pulled her and the mattress to him so they would be closer to each other. He didn't know why, and he didn't care to know why, he just wanted to feel her close to him.

"Listen to the rain," he said, "I like the sound of the rain. Don't you?"

"I like it a lot," she replied softly.

Coltan dreamily whispered, *"Dieu chante une berceuse pour nous."*

Whatever it was he said, it certainly sounded beautiful. "What does that mean?"

He smiled and said softly, "God is singing a lullaby for us."

CHAPTER 2

J ames observed the progress of the newest volunteers. Most of
them were young men and women, and a few of them were barely
into their teens. They wanted to fight. They wanted to fight because
the Evil had spread like a cancer into the hearts and minds of the
families and friends they had fled. They wanted to fight because this
was God's war and they were God's warriors, and they loved God.

A young man of about twenty years of age took down three
opponents at once and had thrown them all to the mat. He was only
five-feet-five-inches tall, but what he lacked in height he made up
for in muscle and agility. He was fair-skinned, with blue eyes. His
expression was earnest, yet proud, as if he assumed there was none
at Alpha who could take him down. His dark, thick and wavy hair
stuck to his sweat-beaded forehead in thin wet strands.

James already pegged him as most promising. He looked over
his file, the record of personal statistics and training progress. The
young man had demonstrated astounding skill as a sharpshooter,
and comparable skill performing hand-to-hand combat. His
psychological profile revealed a cheerful temperament, compassion
for others and the ability to think on his feet. However, he was
also a skirt-chaser and sometimes too eager to prove his masculinity,
something James attributed to an underlying self-consciousness
about his short height. Looking over the personal information in the
young man's file, James learned his name was Trevor Rolardy. He was
from London, and became stranded on U.S. soil during a tour with a
small group of missionary Christian youth when all hell broke loose.

Their bus came under attack while stuck dead in a traffic jam caused by a multi-car collision out on the interstate. Most of the boys under his charge fell victim to the mords. He had led the few survivors to safety away from the interstate and into the hills surrounding the Bonito Valle area. Four of his five surviving charges suffered bites. By the next morning, he had to kill all four when they began to show symptoms of the pre-biting stage—those symptoms being a high fever, frigid skin, loss of speech and memory, and the burgeoning ability to smell human blood from a distance.

By the time he encountered James's undercover operatives, Trevor had managed to save only one under his charge: Ian, a small boy age twelve, who was still suffering from shock one month later.

James leaned into the mic, "Rolardy!"

Trevor quickly stood at attention. His lean, muscular form made him appear taller and his chest heaved for breath. He peered up into the booth, "Sir?"

"See me in my office at nineteen-hundred hours."

He saluted. "Yes, sir."

"You're dismissed. Good work."

Tomorrow, James and his team would scour the immediate area for stray mords and eliminate them before additional refugees arrived.

COLTAN HOOKED UP THE short wave and scanned the dial for transmissions. He picked up a distant and intermittently fading woman's voice pleading in what sounded like German. He did not understand German, and even if he could, he was unable to broadcast out to strike up an informative conversation with anyone.

Natalie cautioned him, "I'd be careful with that. They might be able to intercept the transmission and zero in on us."

Coltan hadn't considered it. "How else can we find out what's going on?"

"Regular radio. Has that Montana station come back?"

"No."

"We'll keep listening for it. That's all we can do." She placed another pancake on the stack and covered it with a towel to keep them warm. After spooning one more scoop of batter into the pan, she asked him, "How many do you want?"

"Six, I guess."

"I thawed some strawberries to go with mine. You want some, too?"

"That sounds good." He shut off the short wave and checked out each window, surveying for unwanted guests.

She watched him. "How's it look?"

"Maybe the rain's keeping them away."

"I wouldn't think so. Maybe what we saw last week was the last of them—at least, around here."

"Maybe." He slid one of the window blocking plywood panels back and forth, checking for smoothness of operation. "The days are getting shorter. We'll be using the lights more. Do you think it would be safe by now to use the sliders? Do you think it might give us away?"

"I'd use the sliders. We won't see any soldiers for months. They're busy everywhere else."

MARIO LIFTED THE GIRL out of the big pipe and set her down gently on the wet concrete of the spillway. There was a good two inches of standing water there, and it soaked his shoes. She was barefooted and did not seem to notice the coldness of the water. Standing there in nothing but her torn, wet and soiled nightie, she did not react to the chill in the air, either. All that seemed to matter to her was the comfort of her hand in his as she gazed up at him and grinned, a soft affectionate growl in her throat.

The bandage on his forearm had come loose with the dampness and the wound was bleeding anew. He released her hand, removed the bandage and brought his arm to his lips, tasted his blood. It did not taste good to him. She noticed a bleeding scrape on her wrist. She offered it to him and he tasted it. He spit the blood out and shook his head. She frowned worriedly. They were so hungry.

He peered up into the sky and listened for the flying things. There was only silence in the gray overcast. He sniffed the air, detected the approaching rain, but not a hint of the scent he hoped to find. This was good, and this was bad. It was good because it meant no one was hunting them; it was bad because there was no food nearby.

It was also bad the open spillway exposed them. The girl read his thoughts, tugged on his torn and filthy blue Bujjet Mart vest. As she pointed over to the ladder attached to the wall, she struggled to remember how to pronounce and form the words. Finally, her voice came.

"Yaddoo, Mahwo. Up yaddoo."

Mario could not remember how to speak, and his throat did not search for his voice. However, his sense of hearing was strong, and he vaguely understood what she was trying to say. He took her hand again and led her to the ladder, hopeful they would find a safer route and perhaps a warm, breathing meal.

"What's the word?" James asked Mitchell Fenny.

They were in the Communications, Security and Surveillance room. Mitchell was glad his expertise with the equipment came in handy. He was grateful to have a safe place to bunker down, and even more grateful to God for gifting him with the technical know-how that had seen him through four tours of duty in Iraq and Afghanistan. Up until the last five years, he ignored his friends' assertions war would spring up on their own home soil. It wasn't until his best pal Brian Danbury presented the proof when he finally took it seriously.

He wondered about the Danburys. Were they still safely bunkered at their reinforced house? Or, had they switched gears at the last minute and were now on their way to the safe zone? Brian and Beverly had not answered their portafones, and he never knew their daughter's number. Upon phoning the landline at their house, he found the lines were down. All he could do at that point was wonder and pray for them.

In answer to James's question, he told him, "They're still doing mostly search and rescue ops. They got other troops all over dedicated to nothing else but eliminating mords. So far, there've been no more reports from the camps."

"What about Sillessi?"

"They killed him."

"Man..." James felt sad about Sillessi, and at the same time worried.

"He got careless."

"Did they torture him?" If so, Sillessi might have caved and revealed information.

"I don't know. All I heard was they killed him."

"What about Franks?"

"He's on his way back. Should be here by midnight. He'll have more info on Sillessi."

"Leave word to wake me the minute he gets back." James patted his shoulder and turned to leave.

Mitchell remembered something. "Say, James?"

"Yo, man?"

"I heard you were in Bonito Valle."

"Yeah?"

"Search and recovery and clean-up teams, right?"

"Yeah."

"Did they put you on house search?"

"Yeah. Why?"

"Did you happen to come across a big, boarded up house with a giant garden in the back?"

"You're the second one that's asked me that."

"Who's the first?"

"Some kid I picked up. A girl."

Mitchell's eyes brightened with hope. "A petite teenage girl with dark hair?"

"Naw, man. Some blonde fat chick. Why?"

"I got friends who might still be bunkered down there. I've been wondering." He studied James's expression for a hint of recollection or recognition.

"I've been in a lot of boarded-up houses, man..."

"This one was on a hill at the east side; a little neighborhood in the higher valley just below the foothills. Nice homes. Like I said, this place has a huge garden in the back. They boarded up the windows from the inside, not shit-slapped together, either. It was well thought out." Mitchell paused and waited for James to perform reconnaissance on his memory.

James tried to think back. Something came to mind, but he couldn't remember in what part of town it was located. He had too many things to think about, and his memory was still fuzzy about the search operation. In truth, he blocked a lot of it out, mostly those incidences involving the terrified civilians he found hiding and surrendered to his commanding officers. In order to maintain his cover, he had no choice but to turn them over to the authorities. If he had been alone during those discoveries, he would have let them go;

but there was always a partner accompanying him, and the partners assigned to him worked for the Evil Ones. His regret shadowed him then and now.

After a minute or so, he told Mitchell, "I don't know, man. If something comes to mind..." He shrugged. "Sorry, bro."

COLTAN SPED THE HARLEY to crest the hill and slowed for the curving downgrade ahead. The weather was cold and it rained persistently. The blacktop sparkled with the downpour, and the tires splashed through the puddles and soaked his bare feet.

Seated behind him, Richard's icy hands clung to Coltan's bare wet chest. His fingernails dug into his flesh like the razor-sharp teeth of a bear trap.

"Get off me!" Coltan demanded through the wind in his face.

The beast laughed raucously.

It took all Coltan's concentration to keep the bike on the road. The curves were increasing in number. "You're gonna cause me to crash!"

Richard cackled and screamed in his ear, "I want you to crash!"

He lost control of the bike and skidded sideways. The vehicle toppled over and scraped the pavement, trapping his leg and one-half of his body between the bike and the road. He could feel the flesh peel away from his bones, and his bones began scraping and splintering as his body skidded over the wet blacktop.

Richard was still laughing as they flew into a tree and bounced back onto the road from the force of the impact. They tumbled together and rolled, Richard stubbornly clinging to him, his legs wrapped around Coltan's waist like a vise. Richard disengaged when they finally came to a stop and both spilled face up upon the muddy roadside. Coltan saw the Harley fly into the gully, and then he felt his skull split open and the wet heat of his brains spill down his shoulders and back. Richard's insane laughter rang in his ears with a tauntingly unrelenting echo.

Coltan screamed, "Shut up, shut up, *shut up*!"

Richard sprang upon his chest and sat there as if riding a horse. He bent his face inches from Coltan's. "Jesus is gonna send you to hell, send you to hell! Burn you in hell!"

Coltan felt suffocated by the man's weight, felt terrified because the Harley had sailed into the gully thus leaving him no means of escape, and he felt his childhood hopelessness return as Richard pinned him and damned him to hell.

Richard's spit landed on Coltan's cheeks as he warned him, "You're gonna lick up those brains you just puked, and you're gonna like it, you weak little piece of shit Jesus hates."

Coltan screamed for God to help him.

His screaming finally delivered him from the horrifying nightmare. He discovered he was sitting bent forward, covering his ears with his hands. A clicking sound and then slight illumination beyond his closed eyelids brought him into a strange awareness that he was straddling dimensions.

Natalie's voice came muffled, but he fully felt the jostling as she shook him. "Wake up!"

Is he gone? Am I safe? What's Nat doing here?

Something caressed his back. He cringed at the sensation, expecting to next feel pain.

He's trying to trick me. He's still here.

He moaned softly, still in a dream state, "Oh, Jesus Christ! Help me!" In the next moment, he wiped at his face and his chest, "Oh, no. The blood! The blood! I gotta wash it off! Gotta wash..."

"There is no blood," Natalie told him. "You're clean."

When he spoke, his voice did not sound like his own voice; it was otherworldly and full of foreboding, "I'll never be clean! He's gonna burn me! I can't be cleaned! They gotta burn it off!"

"No, no! No, Colt. There's no blood on you. Look at yourself. Look at your hands. There's no blood." She took his hands in hers and brought them up where he could see them, "See? There's no blood." He examined his hands, his arms, his chest and belly. Confused, he gazed at her for an explanation. She soothed him, "It was a nightmare, that's all. You're okay."

The curtain between the nightmare world of his mind and the nightmarish world of his reality finally lifted. Reality, although frightening in itself, was somehow a relief compared to where he had just been. He could recall the dream in its entirety. He wished he couldn't remember it.

"I must have scared you," he said, his voice shaky.

"Not as scared as you were," she replied. "What were you dreaming about?"

He looked away from her, stubbornly silent.

"Colt, you've got to talk about—"

He responded fiercely and with finality, "No!"

"Do you have any idea how loud you were screaming? If someone had been out there, you would have blown it for both of us. Think about that! Next time, we might not be so lucky!" She waited for a response. When he offered none, she softened her voice and her approach, "If you really care about me and about our safety..." Her point made, she let it end there.

He took the coward's way out, "Everything over the past couple of months... you know. The disease, all the people dying, the camps, the military—it's gotten to me, I guess. And, your mom and dad—I miss them."

"Your nightmares are about something else. You talk in your sleep. Mostly in French, but a lot in English, too." She tried to peer into his face, but he stubbornly avoided her. "I know now when you talk in French, you're dreaming about that Richard guy and your mom. Those are the dreams where you try to protect yourself from being hit. We both know what that's about, don't we?"

His only response to this was an angry and defeated sigh.

She persisted, "You need to talk it out. Will you trust me?"

He still avoided her gaze, and his tone of voice was just as evasive. "I don't want to go back to all that. I just want to forget it."

"You can't forget it unless you release it; that's why you keep having nightmares."

He delivered the warning in a whisper. "Leave it."

"I won't. You can't go on like this."

His eyes were pinpoints of fire when they met hers. "You just won't leave it alone, will you?"

"No. I won't. I won't leave it alone."

She took his hand and she looked down at it as he unconsciously tightened his grip around hers before releasing it. He knew she caught a glimpse of some of the scars inside his arms from his self-inflicted cuts and cigarette burns. He expected it all made sense to her, that the demons in his dreams were the source of his shame and inner turmoil.

She confirmed his expectation as she surmised, "That's why you kept burning yourself. Is that also why you tried to kill yourself?"

He bent and rested his face in his hands. Reconciliation with God, with his tormented conscience seemed impossible.

He answered before he realized the ramifications. "It was the only thing I knew."

Her brow furrowed as she peered bewilderedly into his eyes. "What...?"

He was tired of carrying it, tired of the turmoil it created within him. He wanted to tell Natalie, but was unsure how to begin and unsure how she would react once he told her.

She gazed at him expectantly, her downturned lips displaying her disappointment as well as her simmering anger with him. However, in all of that he sensed she desired his explanation would somehow alleviate those emotions and reinstate her trust in him. He wanted the same, *needed* the same. His defenses fell away with his determination to make her understand the root of his shame.

"That's what they taught me," he began hesitantly. "That's how they controlled me."

"Who?"

"Mom and Richard."

IT WAS AFTER ONE IN the morning when James got the wake-up call to meet with Franks. They sipped herbal tea in James's office, and Franks lit a smoke, hoping the nicotine would jump-start his nearly depleted reserve of energy. Although James was not a smoker, he allowed Franks the luxury and slid him an empty soft drink can to use as an ashtray.

"What happened with Sillessi?" It was the first thing James wanted to know about.

"They caught him trying to help a guy with a kid escape the camp. Found out he wasn't chipped. They put two and two together." Franks inhaled deeply. His scarred and weathered hands trembled, a result of exhaustion and psychological trauma.

"What'd they do to him?"

"When they caught him, he went for the fence. They shot him in the leg. They could have killed him, but they wanted information. The bullet wound would have been a great place to start with the torture." A long ash fell from the cigarette onto James's desk. Franks immediately swept it into the can and continued. "I've seen what they do to resisters, even the ones who aren't with *us*. So, Sillessi and I had an agreement. When he went for the fence a second time, I shot him in the head."

"Man..."

"I told the brass it was a reflex action. They yelled a lot and slapped me around. But that was all they did. There was too much turmoil among the refugees at that point. Just as quick, they had a riot on their hands; made it easy for me to slip out of there." The cigarette shook between his fingers. He took another long drag and dropped it into the can. "They killed the guy and his kid as an example. Bastards... The kid was only six, same age as my daughter. *Bastards...!*"

"They're looking for you." James assumed.

"I got out okay. They were busy dealing with the riot. I don't think they noticed for hours."

"What's it like there?"

"Very regimented. They're chipping everyone while they vaccinate. They make it mandatory for all refugees. If they refuse the chip and the vaccination, the Elimination Squads take them out to some soundproof concrete building off the main compound. No one ever sees them again." Franks paused and thought about it. "There's a rumor they're keeping a few mords around as insurance to keep the people scared. Someone thought they might be feeding the executed to them. I heard they also use them as a means of torture. But, I didn't get a chance to verify that.

"They're also using brainwashing techniques to get the people to cooperate, making themselves out to be the good guys and the chips as some kind of lifetime protection against the infection and everything else. Nothing new there. You know the drill."

"Did you find out anything on the top brass? The leader?"

"Nothing, man. I couldn't get access to the higher-ups. I don't think the camps are where you're gonna find that info. I don't think even they know who they're working for. It's like they're hypnotized."

"Do you think the chips are programmed to control them?"

"Maybe. I don't know."

James leaned back in his chair, frustrated. He had hoped for more information than this. He observed Franks, noted the tremors and the rock-hard tension in his face. Obviously, Franks was just as frustrated and more than a little affected by what he'd witnessed.

"We just got another Chaplain," James offered, "Brother has a degree in psychology. He's helped a lot of the refugees and our troops. I want you to meet with him."

"No need, sir. I'm fine."

James sat forward, "That's an order, Franks!"

"Yes, sir."

"I want you to take a week off. Chill out." James sipped his tea, wondered what to do with this guy. He didn't want to send him back out in the field. "After that, we'll talk about reassignment."

"I can go back out. If I can get to—"

"Not a chance, man." He saw the disappointment in the young man's face. Franks was a farm kid, rugged, strong, and eager to please. He had served one tour of duty with the Army overseas, but he didn't have the stomach for the horrors of war. But he possessed good weapons skills, and would come in handy as a trainer. The more James considered it, the more he thought it right to keep Franks in the compound where he could do more good and at less cost to his psyche. "We got some new volunteers who'd benefit from your training. I want you to consider it."

"I could've stayed and tried for more info. I got scared. Shit..."

James leaned into him, regarded him in a fatherly way, "You protected us, Franks. That counts for a lot. Go get some sleep."

CHAPTER 3

"They made me dirty, and they kept me dirty," Coltan continued. "Richard used it to keep me in line, to keep me scared, keep me... obedient. I knew it was wrong, but I didn't know anything else."

Natalie's heart sunk. "Are you telling me he raped you?"

Coltan nodded heavily and looked away from her, his eyes welling.

Her face reddened and her jaw tightened with a combination of rage and sadness. "How old were you when he raped you?"

After hesitating a few moments, he answered with lingering shame, "I was eight years old."

Natalie nodded slightly and stared at the floor. Coltan saw tears wet her cheeks. She lit a cigarette for each of them and offered Coltan his. They said nothing for a while; they smoked and privately sifted through their churning emotions. Finally, Natalie broke the silence. "Was it only one time, or was it ongoing?"

He avoided looking at her as he answered in a whisper through his tight throat, "Ongoing." There came another silence between them, not an awkward silence, but a reflective interlude. Coltan spoke again, his voice stronger, "At first he was nice to me, used to set me on his lap after Mom passed out—which was often. He used to cuddle me, something I really needed and wanted 'cause Mom never did that with me. She never did it—ever. It wasn't long before he started touching me where he shouldn't have. At first, I let him. I let him because it felt good and I was curious, and I liked the affection. When he started wanting me to touch him, I begged off.

He got real mad and pushed me off his lap onto the floor. He kicked me. He kicked me so hard he broke one of my ribs. That was the first time he ever showed me his temper. I started crying and tried to crawl away from him. He pinned me onto the floor, said I was a tease—practically *spit* the words at me. That was the first time he raped me."

"Did you tell your mother?"

Coltan looked sideways at Natalie and said matter-of-factly, "When she finally found out, caught him in the act, she didn't do anything. She sat down and watched. She liked to watch. She got off on it. Richard wasn't the first one she let... that she..." Natalie responded with an expression of shock and bewilderment. Coltan expected that response, and he glanced away from her, stared down at nothing in particular. His eyes were not seeing the present, but experiencing the past. He paused and remembered, let the memories and disturbing fragmented images crowd forth. His voice was soft, strained, as he described it all. "We were homeless for a long time. Sometimes the men wanted me and not her. But she never let them violate me in the way Richard did. She let Richard do what he wanted because he supplied her drugs. She was an addict by then. That's how they met. I guess you could say I was her insurance, and he knew it. When he first started, I tried like hell to fight him off. He'd beat the shit out of me with a strap. He always kept that strap nearby, always warning me what I'd get if I... He thought I was sissy, punished me if I cried. He always called me *pretty*. His *pretty little boy*. And, I fought him. Fought like hell with everything I had. I was so small, no match for him. After him beating me so many times, I finally just... cooperated. It was easier." His voice broke, and he wiped away the tears streaming down his face. He took a final drag off his smoke and extinguished it. He slouched against the pillow and pulled the sleeping bag up against his chest.

Natalie found the entire scenario too disturbing to fathom.

"How on earth did you manage to live through it? How could you stand it?"

"I learned to block out most of the physical pain. I learned how to zone out and leave my body. That's how I coped with it."

"What about the neighbors? Somebody must have heard."

"Richard always made sure we lived out in the boonies. We moved around a lot. Never in the same place very long. I think someone might have been after him. He made sure we were isolated."

"Did you ever try to run away from home?"

"Once. I didn't get very far. We were out in the middle of nowhere."

"What happened?"

"He came after me and dragged me into the car. Once he got me home, he gave me the worst beating I'd ever had in my life. He didn't miss a single place on my body. It wasn't just the strap this time; he used other things on me. I couldn't walk for days. It was that bad." Coltan paused, and his brow furrowed, "I never ran away again." He shivered under the sleeping bag and curled up beneath it. "It's cold in here."

Natalie retrieved her sleeping bag and covered them both with it. As she curled beside him, she placed her arm protectively over his chest. "What about school? You must have gone. Didn't anyone notice anything?"

"I attended... like a good boy. It got me away from him for a while. I hid the welts and stuff with long sleeves, coats, jackets... whatever. I didn't talk to anyone. Didn't make friends. I felt like an alien. Everyone else seemed so normal. I wasn't normal." His tears were becoming more of an irritation and an embarrassment to him. He wiped them away impatiently. "The school library was my escape. I lost myself in books. I read everything I could get my hands on. That's another way I coped. I also drank a lot, smoked a lot of pot; that helped dull some of the pain. I took other drugs when I could get them—stole most of it from Mom and Richard.

"By the time I was thirteen, the only thing I felt anymore was rage. And, I had to stuff that. He made sure of that. He tried to beat it out of me, decided he wanted that passive and scared little boy back—that same little boy he hated, that same little boy he... Just to spite him, I got real tough. I took it without a sound. How much more could he do to me, anyway?" At this point, Coltan felt sick with it all and fell silent for a few moments. He wiped away more tears.

"What about STD's?"

"I got tested. I'm clear. He always used a condom. Looking back, I don't think it was for health reasons. I think he wanted to make sure he didn't leave any evidence, in case someone found out. Like I was gonna tell anybody. He finally stopped when I was fourteen. I think I was too old for him by then."

He took a deep, quavering breath. His lips and his chin trembled quickly and forcefully, and he could not control it. After a long moment, he said, "I felt like a monster! I hated that I went along with it for so long. Even though I knew I was too young and small and powerless, I still blamed myself for him doing that to me." His throat hurt and felt constricted to where he could barely swallow. He sniffed as more tears ran down his cheeks. His tears seemed endless, and he felt humiliated by them. "Some tough guy, huh? Now you know."

She stroked his hair and the side of his face. "Don't be ashamed. It takes such strength to deal with the hell you've lived through. You're so strong, Colt. I wish I were as strong as you."

He wiped her tears and kissed her lips. She sat up and invited him to curl up in the safety of her embrace. He accepted and rested his head upon her shoulder as she wrapped her arms around him, tenderly caressed his back.

She was caring for him, comforting him as her mother Beverly did after his suicidal dive off the bridge. Years of experience in the medical profession gave Beverly the wisdom to recognize the psychological signs of sexual abuse. He steadfastly denied anyone ever sexually assaulted him. Although he never confessed the truth to her, Beverly's respect for his privacy became a bridge of trust between them. He loved her. He never told her how much he loved her. Maybe she knew. He hoped she knew.

Natalie's voice swept him into present time, "Are you falling asleep?"

"No," he whispered contentedly.

"You'll be okay," she said.

He thought Natalie had inherited all the best of Beverly's traits and instincts. "Can I tell you something?"

"Sure."

"You're a lot like your mom. You are." Maybe it wasn't the right thing to say. Looking back on all the battles between Natalie and Bev, he realized Natalie would probably interpret it wrongly. However, it was too late to take it back. "She wouldn't let me get away with anything," Coltan explained, "She wouldn't give up on me, either. You're like that."

"Did my mom know about what you...? Did you tell her?"

"No, but I'm sure she had it figured out."

"Mom was abused as a kid. Did she ever tell you?"

"Yeah." That was one of the many reasons he trusted Beverly. She understood him.

"You really loved her, didn't you?"

"I still do."

"Did you have a crush on her?"

He grinned and chuckled at the idea. It would have been easy to feel that way towards her. However, their relationship was one of trust between mother and son. He sensed Natalie got the wrong idea when she caught his grin, which compelled him to snuff out any misunderstanding immediately. "It wasn't like that. She was a mother to me, and a friend, too."

They spent the remainder of the night in deep and revealing conversation. Natalie revealed some of her own baggage. Her revelation about sometimes feeling abandoned by her parents was something he already suspected. Although she understood their work required them to spend long hours away from home, their absence left her feeling secondary and resentful. She regretted she never resolved this with them, and she feared it would haunt her for the rest of her life.

It surprised Coltan when she revealed she once carved a cross into her skin as an effort to atone for an evening of sexual self-exploration during an overnighter with Carolyn. Carolyn had introduced her to the pleasures of masturbation and, after they each pleasured themselves, they experimented further by pleasuring each other. Ever since that incident, Natalie never touched herself in that way again. She wondered aloud to Coltan if that was why she never felt any attraction towards boys in the past. When, on instinct, he questioned her as to when this happened, she answered it had been about two years before. This gave him an opportunity to counsel her, when he surmised that was probably the reason she tried to make herself unattractive; in reality, she felt ugly on the inside, not the outside. The realization made her cry. That led to a great deal of discussion about guilt and remorse, which led to a discussion about forgiveness of self.

The hours of revelation and sharing cemented their bond of trust. Natalie viewed their long, intimate discussion as confirmation they would be able to handle anything the future had in store, as long as they handled it together.

For Coltan, it produced more hope than confirmation. Although it helped him immensely to unload the bulk of his turbulence, too much remained. He secretly accepted the fact his anguish would continue to wear him down. He wanted to tell Natalie, but he could not tell her.

Coltan cast his concerns aside and tried hard to focus on the beauty of the dawn. Brian once told him the sunrise itself was a gift from God, assurance his Holy Father was indeed still watching, still aware of each stirring upon the Earth. Coltan knew God was aware of his battles, and he considered the sunrise a promise that, one day, God would step forward and help him slay his demons. Today, he would rest from his lingering conflicts. Today, he would appreciate the little things, the little gifts of God. He called Natalie over to the window and they stood there and admired the sunrise. He draped his arms around her as she stood in front of him to take in the view.

"Keep in mind," she advised him, "The Devil will find your weaknesses and your conflicts and will use them to turn you away from God. Those nightmares were part of his work. Don't let him get away with it. Fight him. Call on Jesus to help you."

It was good advice. "That will be my first plan of action," he promised. "The same goes for you whenever you begin to lose faith."

CHAPTER 4

Rosa stopped suddenly on the muddy trail and sniffed the air. In the next moment, she opened her mouth slightly, directed the scented air to the roof of her mouth, panted, tasted the scent. Food... She looked up at Mario and saw he also tasted the air.

They followed the scent to a small clearing among the pines and brush, paused and crouched at the discovery beyond. Five people just like them feasted on freshly killed prey. They had torn the clothing from the bodies of the man and woman. Blood and drag indentations in the mud led from the toppled tent to the circle of feasting mords. All at once, the diners stopped eating and sniffed the air. They detected the scents of the two young intruders.

Mario stood and emitted a staccato whine, begged them to share their spoils. The little girl stood next and also whined, her eyes painful with hunger.

There was only one woman with this group, a slightly overweight, dark-skinned woman about the same age as Mario and Rosa's mother. The woman's appearance stirred a vague recollection in Rosa, and she responsively longed for her mother's touch and voice. The woman stood and, when she stood, the two saw she wore no shoes or trousers; all she wore was a torn summer blouse. Bruises, bites, scrapes and scratch marks riddled her dirty bare legs. The woman remained erect, her face pinched in concentration. Her facial muscles relaxed with a smile of pleasure as a stream of brown urine cascaded down her legs. When she finished urinating, she eyed the girl and reached out her hand.

The little girl stepped forward, and the men growled at her.

The woman hissed at them and slapped one on the back of his head, sent him reeling forward on his knees. The others immediately submitted to her authority and made space for the newcomers.

In a whisper, Rosa implored the woman, "Hep... peeze." She caressed her aching belly. Tears rolled down her cheeks. "Peeze... food..."

The woman reached out to Rosa again as she limped over to Mario and stretched out her other hand. The siblings took her hands and allowed her to lead them to the warm feast. Mario and the girl bent over the body of the male prey and reached into the ravaged abdominal cavity.

At last, they ate.

THERE WERE STILL HUNDREDS of books to be unpacked, boxes and boxes of them on the floor of the library at the Alpha Base refuge. In addition to the general assortment were marked cases of Bibles in all translations and languages.

Carolyn had never seen so many different Bibles in one place. She sat on the floor and began the task of sorting. They gave her the assignment when her lack of expertise with anything else made her useless for most of the other duties there. However, she enjoyed working at the library because she loved sorting and organizing things. This project was something she could do well, and they appreciated her enthusiasm.

A boy came up and squatted next to her. His freckled face reminded her of a boy she knew from school, although this kid was smaller.

"Hi!" she said.

"Hullo..." His voice was soft, shy and deeper than she expected. "They sent me to assist you if you don't mind me bein' 'ere."

"My name's Carolyn." She offered her hand in welcome.

He timidly shook her hand. "Ian."

"Ian...," she repeated. "That's a nice name."

"After me uncle," he said.

She detected his accent. "Where are you from?"

"Outside London." He figured if he named his town, she wouldn't know where it was, and would probably forget, anyhow.

She tried to emulate the accent, "From across the Pond, are we?"

He grinned. "Yes. The Pond. You're the first Yank I 'eard refer to it like that. They usually say, *'Oh, you're from England. How charming!'*"

"What are you doing here in the States?"

"The same as you. Survivin'."

"Alright, smartass...," she whispered. "What brought you here in the first place?"

"A missionary group. We were visitin' on mission." He pulled a fat Bible out of the box and placed it on his lap. "What we got 'ere? An Oxford Edition."

"If you want to keep it, they might let you."

"I 'ave me own." He hoisted it up and down in his hands. "This is very 'eavy. Quite much to lug about, y'know."

"Are your folks here with you?"

"No. It was just us boys with a chaperone. You might've met 'im. Good fellow. Name of Trevor."

"Nope," she replied. "I haven't met any Trevors yet."

Confidentially, he said, "The birds all potty for 'im!"

She laughed, imagining birds defecating on some strange faceless, man. "What?"

"Birds..." he said, "They like 'im. Got the look, y'know, an' muscles, too."

"Oh. You mean all the girls."

"They go potty for 'im." To demonstrate, he playacted like a girl, making sarcastic squealing noises and kissing his fingertips. "Potty! Bloody 'ell..."

She found him amusing. "You sound a little bit jealous, Ian."

"Jealous? Per'aps... But, 'e saved me life."

"Where's the rest of your group?"

He thought she was daft. With he and Trevor the only British residents there, how could she not realize the fate of his mates? "Dead... Don't ask 'ow."

"I got an idea," she commiserated. "My folks, too. I'm the only one left."

"I'm sorry, mum." He said it bravely and sincerely.

"I'm sorry for your loss, too." She had thirteen assorted stacks by now, and pulled over the next box.

Ian helped her. "I've got it there."

"Any word on your family back home?" she asked.

"No ringers, no telly."

She had no idea what that meant. "Do you have a large family?"

"Just me, Mum, Dad an' me older brother Cedric. Got a dog named Wheezer."

"What kind of dog?"

"Big, clumsy mongrel. Who knows? All 'e knows is food."

"Maybe they're all okay."

He became quiet and resumed unloading the Bibles. He saw she was trying to sort them into some kind of order, but left it to her to decide.

"How old's your brother?" Carolyn asked.

"Seven'een. Used to pummel me. Never thought I'd miss 'im, but I do." He stopped and sat back, his head bowed. Carolyn wondered if he was praying, and gave him a minute of personal space. After a while, he looked up and said morosely, "The sickness is there, too."

She felt sorry for him. Although she assumed his family was dead like so many others, she wanted to give him hope. "Maybe they're okay. Maybe they're in a safe place where the sickness won't get them."

"If they're in the safest place, I won't 'ave to worry, then, will I?"

"The safest place?"

"Our Lord's 'ouse in 'eaven. What could be safer, eh?" He managed a smile, and somehow it comforted her, which was his intention.

AFTER BREAKFAST, NATALIE and Coltan worked out in the basement and continued reviewing and practicing self-defense moves. They made some progress, and felt more confident in their abilities to stay alive when the time came to leave for the Christian refuge in late spring.

Natalie found a local map in the den that included the three mountain ranges surrounding Bonito Valle. Unfortunately, the map was not detailed enough to show them the exact longitude and latitude that would pinpoint the location of the refuge. They discussed looking it up on the Internet, but dismissed the idea when they considered the new government was probably monitoring the Internet; it would give them away and bring soldiers to their door.

Coltan had just finished microwaving a dish of frozen mixed vegetables in the kitchen when the power went out. Now in total darkness because of the sliders covering the windows, he reached for his flashlight on the counter and flipped it on.

"Guess that's the end of that," he remarked. "It lasted longer than I thought it would."

Natalie removed the battery-powered lantern and some candles from the utility closet and set them on the table. "There's still meat in the freezer downstairs. It'll keep for a few days, but we'll have to cook it or waste it. If we let it rot down there, it's gonna stink."

"Guess we'll have to cook it and hope the smell doesn't attract mords," Coltan replied,

"At least we'll eat good for the next few days." She switched on the lantern and set it on the table. "What's left in the fridge?"

He opened it and shined the flashlight over the contents, "Barbeque sauce, pickle relish, something with green fuzzy stuff on it, a bottle of apple juice."

"Is the apple juice opened?"

"Doesn't look like it." He took it out and spied something else, "Parmesan cheese and a tub of butter."

"Those are still good. Take those out, all of it." And on second thought, "You can leave the green fuzzy stuff, though." She made a face and grinned at him.

He found a paper bag stuffed between the refrigerator and the counter and put the items in it. "I was gonna use the cheese and butter on the veggies, anyway," Coltan said. He removed the bowl of mixed vegetables from the microwave and set it on the table with a fork for each of them. "Have you ever put butter and parmesan on your veggies?"

"Yeah." She smiled at him, thinking he would be a good cook someday.

They shared the bowl and ate.

"There's got to be another map around here," Coltan said. He mulled it over, thinking about what agencies in town would offer a detailed map like the one they needed. It occurred to him medical personnel would have access because of their role in disaster response and civil defense. "Do you think there'd be one in your Mom's office?"

She hadn't thought of that. "It's worth a try."

"Maybe she downloaded something on her computer." In the next second, he recalled the electricity was gone, "That was dumb! Well, maybe she printed something."

"She and Dad were working together in there sometimes back when all of this was just starting. I bet they found a map when they were considering leaving. I bet..."

He was suddenly confident. "Let's eat. We'll look after."

The wind blew something against the wall, and the noise made them both jump. They listened tensely for other sounds, particularly footsteps. After a few minutes, they relaxed; it was nothing but wind.

"We won't have any heat," Natalie said. "The central's all electric. The portable heaters in the attic are electric, too."

"We'll have to dress warm, then." Coltan mentally reviewed the wardrobe he'd brought to the house. The only warm items he brought were one set of sweats and his leather jacket. They would not do once the icy cold of winter set in. He considered a trip back to his old house to recover some winter clothing. However, the thought of setting foot there made his stomach feel queasy. There was only one alternative. "I'll need to borrow some of your dad's clothes. Would that be okay with you?"

"Yeah. That'd be fine. Dad would want you to have whatever you can use. Feel free to go in there and look."

He stared at the food but didn't see it, his thoughts taking precedence. He missed Brian, and considered it would be invasive to enter the room the man once shared with Beverly. It would not be easy to look through the man's clothing; so much of it would be items Coltan would recognize as things Brian often wore. It would be the same when he saw Beverly's things. He wasn't sure he could handle the memories triggered by the items.

Natalie understood. "Do you want me to help you with that?"

He considerately reminded her, "It's your mom's room, too."

She thought about it. "Well... we have to face it sooner or later."

"Is there something of your mom's you'd like to keep?"

"Probably. Nothing comes to mind right now. I'm sure I'll see something, though."

He referred to the food with a blasé swipe of his fingers. "Are you done eating?"

"Yeah."

"I'll finish it, I guess." He ate the rest of it, washed and dried the bowl and their forks and put it all away. "We should start in your mom's office," he suggested. "Find a good map." He took Clyde off the counter and tucked it down the front of his pants.

She put the candles in her pocket and used the lantern to light their way.

CHAPTER 5

M itchell watched the screens fed by the numerous security surveillance cameras he and his team installed. Mitchell used his expertise to convert the cameras to remote and powered them with solar. They spent the last month installing the cameras in trees along the two routes leading up to the refuge and also those trees at the perimeter of the refuge. Once in place, they camouflaged the cameras. The system was finally up and running and all the cameras were working.

He had two partners this day, and the three of them divided up surveillance duties, each taking six screens. The youngest was a fat fifteen year-old named Roger who spent his previous life attached to his computer and heavily addicted to online gaming. The kid had since gone through withdrawal from the gaming obsession, and his computer knowledge and technical skills proved handy for Mitchell's team. His other partner this day was Glenda, who once worked as a security consultant for an oil company before they outsourced her job to some guy in India. Her work with the Army of Christ was her sweet revenge against the corporate empire that tossed her out on the pavement without so much as a thank you. Mitchell especially liked Glenda. She was close to his age, intelligent and possessed a wicked sense of humor. It was also a plus she managed to retain her looks over the years; her skin only superficially wrinkled and her body strong and toned from years of working out at the gym.

"Yo-ho!" Roger exclaimed, "Camera two. Looks like refugees."

Glenda leaned sideways and peered at the screen. She saw a man, woman and three children hiking up the west trail. They appeared healthy. "Good catch, Roger!"

Mitchell left his chair and hovered over Roger's shoulder for a look. "Alrighty! Let's get them before the mords do." He went back to his station and rang James. "James... got five on the west trail about ten clicks south."

"Are they sick?" James asked.

"Doesn't look like it. Hold on." He stole another look at the monitor. "They look okay. The kids are draggin', though. We got two adults and three kids. They all got backpacks."

"Ten-four," James said, "Keep in com with us. We're going out."

James recruited Trevor Rolardy, Franks, and Suzanne Zazzakowski, a child psychologist and early supporter of the Army of Christ for the mission. He always depended on Suzanne when children were involved; there were a few cases in the past when they separated the kids from their infected parents before his team performed the necessary duty of extermination. If this proved to be the case again, Suzanne would handle the kids and get them into the refuge so they wouldn't witness their parents' fate.

They stopped the jeep at the bottom of the hill and took the rest of the way on foot. James had the scanner ready, Trevor manned the weapons as Franks and Suzanne carried water and energy bars to the refugees. They intercepted the family at the other side of the hill.

The man, woman and three children came to a dead stop when they spotted the Alpha team. All five of them were mosquito-eaten and caked with dirt and sweat. They were physically exhausted, and the eyes of the children revealed not only their weariness, but the shock of their ordeal. The two young boys resembled the woman, and the little girl inherited her father's coloring. The woman was tall and, under her open leather jacket, her summer clothing revealed the figure of a teenager, although everything about the way she carried herself, and the calm manner in which she reacted to the strangers in her path suggested years of maturity. Her face was angular with chiseled features and lightly tanned skin. The man looked to be in his early thirties, a tall, lanky yet muscular guy. A generous mop of wavy brown hair that glistened with gold in the sunlight framed his face. The sun-baked color of his tanned skin accentuated his cautious piercing light blue eyes that exhibited both a common sense and college-educated type of intelligence. As they expected, the man was armed and he pointed his rifle at the four strangers.

"Don't shoot," James shouted. "We're friends."

"There's no more friends," the man shouted back, "Stop right there."

"You got the card with you?" James asked.

"The card?" He regarded James suspiciously.

The woman removed the card from her breast pocket and held it up. "We're looking for the refuge."

The man glanced at her, exasperated. "Don't tell 'em that!"

"That's alright," James said. "You found us." He turned to Trevor and said in a low voice, "Lower your weapon before this guy shits his pants." Trevor obeyed reluctantly.

"Do you need water?" Suzanne asked them. "We have food and water." She raised two of the water bottles she carried.

"We still have some," the woman replied.

The man addressed James, "What's that in your hand?"

"A scanner," James said. "To see if you're chipped."

"What if we're not?" A brief shadow of apprehension flickered in his eyes.

"That's good news for all of us." James pressed the button on the side and scanned them all from a distance. He breathed a sigh of relief and said to them, "No chips."

Suzanne grinned. "Yay!"

"Where you from?" James asked the man.

"Bonito Valle."

45

"How's it looking there?"

"Empty except for the military. Some areas are demolished. It's a mess."

"Any of you sick?"

"No."

The woman piped up, "My youngest got blisters. They're bleeding."

"Blisters where?" Suzanne inquired.

"Feet. From walking." She referred to the girl of around five who was sitting on the dirt trail. "She's in a lot of pain. We've taken turns carrying her. That's all. No one's sick. None of us has been bitten." She scratched a mosquito bite on her neck as she added, "At least by the mords. I swear to God."

"We gotta check you," James said. "Okay if Suzanne and Franks go over there?"

"Okay," the woman said. She turned to the man. "Okay, baby?"

He stared at each of James's party individually in turn before he nodded at Suzanne. "Just the woman."

Trevor did not like that idea. The man was still pointing his weapon, still distrustful. He was sure the guy would panic and try to pull a fast one, maybe try to hold Suzanne hostage or something. He glanced at James, awaiting his decision.

James glanced at her. "Suzanne?"

"It's fine with me." Suzanne started down the hill.

"Bloody hell..." Trevor muttered.

Suzanne approached them confidently and went first to the youngest with the blistered feet. The mother encouraged all the children to sit down, and she did the same. One at a time, Suzanne examined the children. Aside from bruises and scrapes, they were fine. She took the woman behind a bush for privacy, examined her and found her free of human bites, as well.

"All clear," Suzanne announced as she emerged from the bushes with the woman.

James addressed the man, "Okay if I check you out?"

The man regarded James suspiciously again, and James assumed he was not comfortable with a black man in a position of power. The man's gaze fell upon Franks. "You. I'll let you."

James nodded at Franks, and Franks went to the man. They talked softly for a long time, before the man agreed to the exam. After he handed the woman his rifle, the man removed his shoes, socks, shirt and his denims and stood on the trail in his underwear as Franks checked him.

"He's clear." Franks said. He handed the man his clothing. "I'm Jerry Franks. You've found the Army of Christ."

"Oh, thank God!" the woman said. She extended her hand to Franks. "My name's Darla. My husband here is Joe. Please forgive his scowl."

Joe protested as he struggled into his pants, "Just don't know who to trust anymore!"

"You can trust us," Suzanne said.

Franks picked up the little girl. "What's your name, sweetie-pie?"

"Rebecca." She smiled at her father. "Jesus People, Daddy! Don't be scared."

"Quite a talker for a five-year old," Suzanne commented.

"She's six," Darla corrected. "We home school our kids."

James thought that would come in handy. They were short of teachers.

Joe reached for Rebecca., "I'll carry her." Franks relinquished her to him.

Darla introduced her two boys, "This is Randy. He's eleven. This is Joe Junior. He's thirteen."

"We got a jeep waiting up the hill," James said. "We should head up there before we lose the light."

"Where are we goin'?" Joe Junior asked.

"To the safe place," Suzanne replied. "You'll like it."

Franks grinned at Joe. "You can relax now."

Joe grinned back. "I haven't relaxed in months, man."

"Y'all can rest up," Franks told him. As an afterthought to reassure the man, he added, "And, we ain't gonna take your weapon. That's yours and we respect your right to carry it. Just keep it unloaded for safety with the ammo in your pocket. Welcome to our home, man."

Joe cast a glance at James for validation of this. James said, "That's true. We're on your side. You're one of us now."

NATALIE FOUND THE MAP they needed in a file folder marked, "Camping." It made her remember the times they went for short trips to the mountains when she was little. The outings dwindled in frequency once Mom accepted more responsibilities at the hospital and her schedule became more erratic. However, she was glad they kept the maps; the one they found showed hiking trails and other details that would come in handy. She brought the map and other items up to the attic while Coltan entered her parents' room for warm clothing.

He sat down at the edge of the bed and surveyed the room with the flashlight. The closet doors were open, two separate closets, his and hers. At least he wouldn't have to rummage through Beverly's things, but it still didn't make it any easier. He decided to wait for Natalie to return, and felt relieved when the light from her lantern illuminated the hallway.

"What are you waiting for?" she asked.

"You."

"Most of the winter stuff is probably in drawers." She pointed. "That's his dresser over there. Take everything you need."

He couldn't bring himself to do it. He stayed put.

Understanding, she went over to the dresser and removed items she thought might fit him and placed them on the bed. It was difficult for her to put aside her emotions as she did this; the entire room still held a lingering trace of their scent, and she could almost feel their presence. When she glanced through Dad's closet, she caught sight of one of his uniforms still enclosed in plastic from the cleaners. She paused and gazed at it for a long time.

"What is it?" Coltan inquired.

She left the closet and joined him at the edge of the bed. "Of all the things that belonged to him, the only thing I wish I had is his badge and police I.D. I wish I could've gotten that."

"I'm sorry." He didn't know what else to say.

"You should look around in case there's something you might want. You know, to remember him."

He touched his chest. "I remember him here."

His eyes revealed his sadness, which caused her to look away from him. Stifling her reemerging grief, she reverently lifted some of her father's clothing from the bed and clutched them to her bosom. "Do you think this will do?"

"Yeah... sure." He stood and quickly gathered the rest of the clothing. "It's too soon for us to be in here. Let's go. Unless, of course, you want something of your mom's."

"No." She stood also, avoided with obvious restraint a final visual sweep of the room. "I can't think of anything right now." Uncontainable tears slid down her cheeks, "What good would it do, anyway?"

He tried not to think about it. "You got everything from your room?" She sniffled and nodded. "Well..." he said, "Let's find those coordinates on the map."

"It's funny," Natalie began. "I don't really want to come down here anymore. The attic feels more like home, these days. That's weird, isn't it?"

"No. When you think about it, it's like we kind of made it our own little home. Like it's our space. Just ours." Before this moment, he hadn't given it much consideration, but it was true; they had begun a new life there, just the two of them.

She agreed. "Our little fortress."

"Yeah." He watched her, expecting she would break down sobbing at any moment. However, she restrained her tears and met his gaze. Her eyes were so full of love for him, the honesty of it made his heart leap in his chest. He dropped the clothing onto the bed, took the armful she had gathered and dropped it there as well. She was still gazing at him, loving him with her eyes. He touched her face with his fingertips and traced the soft contours, felt the warmth and smoothness of her skin. She offered her lips to his, and he tenderly accepted, kissing her gently and sweetly. He held her tightly and whispered, "We'll be all right. I promise."

CHAPTER 6

James decided two days was enough time for Joe and Darla Davidson to settle in and rest up with their kids. He met with Joe in the community-dining hall where they got acquainted over coffee and peasant rolls.

Joe was a paramedic in Bonito Valle for twelve years. When the first cases of the mord virus emerged seemingly out of nowhere, Joe suspected someone planted the disease among the populace. In his experience, he had never seen an illness that hit so suddenly and spread so quickly. Its violence horrified him. Once it became obvious the CDC and the Feds were either unable or unwilling to stem the epidemic, he quit his job and began preparations for eventual flight to his parents' ranch in the northwestern corner of Wyoming.

The Davidsons packed and entered the interstate in late summer, only to become stuck in a traffic jam and subsequently turned back by armed soldiers at roadblocks. After wasting precious gasoline on detours that only brought them back to Bonito Valle, Joe and Darla rethought their plan. They decided to take the back routes into the mountains and try for Wyoming that way. They scrapped that plan when the gasoline shortages caused many of the stations to close down. The military quickly took over the stations that remained open and secured all fuel for military and emergency personnel use, only.

They returned home with their car's gas gauge hovering on "E" and locked their garage door for the last time. They watched television footage of the riots and mord attacks on the south side of town with growing desperation. Three days before the mords overran their northeastern corner of Bonito Valle, the Davidsons filled their backpacks, grabbed sleeping bags, and Joe his rifle and ammo, and they began their journey on foot. At the outskirts of Bonito Valle, a young woman hiker at a burger stand called *The Dairy Delight* struck up a conversation with them and, finding they were also Christians, gave them her spare card with the coordinates for the refuge. With nothing left to trust but the grace of God, they decided to trek up the mountain with her and take a chance the refuge actually existed and was not a trap.

They had only been with the woman for one day before she came down sick. Joe knew the symptoms and, while she was unconscious during the brief stroke phase, he examined her and found the bite on her hip. After instructing Darla to take the kids down to the riverbed for some fishing, he smothered the woman and buried her in the woods. He gathered her food and supplies into his own backpack and, after spending the night along the river, they continued their journey. Darla told the kids the woman decided to return to Bonito Valle. The only one of the children who figured it out was Joe Junior, and he kept the secret.

"Did you see anybody else?" James asked.

"No," Joe answered, "No other people. We came across a lotta sick animals, though. Had to shoot 'em."

"Sick with what? Rabies?"

"Hell, no. They got the virus, too. Only, it affects 'em different. They don't go after their own kind, like in the human version." Joe shuddered and sipped his coffee, reached for another peasant roll, "They go after humans. They got that taste for human flesh. I had to shoot a lot of animals. It was either them, or us. Sure as hell wasn't gonna be us. Hated to do it, man. Little Randy—he got a heart for critters—it tore him up. He still ain't over it. Might not ever get over it. What can I do, man?"

"Have you seen any evidence the virus kills them? Have you seen any dead ones, intact? You know, not messed up like they were a meal?"

"Yeah. Found some rats, a couple of cats. Small animals. Not roadkill, either. Just dead." He lit a cigarette, leaned back in his chair and scratched his head, "You gotta watch out for the pack-type critters. They're the most dangerous. Attack in packs, like the mords. I saw it happen over in Bonito Valle on the west side. Packs of dogs came outa the hills and attacked a bunch of people at a park. Bloodiest mess I ever saw. That was when I quit my job. That was when I knew it was time to get out. I wasn't gonna let my kids end up like that." He took a drag and thought for a moment, "Randy's pretty messed up. I was thinking about that Suzanne lady. Could she meet with him and help him? Somebody said she was a kid shrink. That true?"

"Yeah. That's true," James said, "She could counsel all your kids, if you want. The kids are all having a hard time with this. We got a lot of orphans. Most of them are traumatized. It seems the older ones got the worst of it."

"Because they know what's going on," Joe stated.

James paused with an idea. Their small hospital facility was woefully understaffed, and there were a number of injured refugees. He considered Joe's paramedic skills. "Say, Joe. Would you be interested in working in our hospital? We could sure use you."

Joe nodded, "Any way I can contribute. I'll be glad to."

"We could also use a teacher. Would Darla be interested?"

"I'm sure. I'll ask her. When can we get Randy some help?"

"I'll talk to Suzanne right now. She'll probably schedule him for today."

"We appreciate that," Joe's bottom lip quivered. He tightened his jaw to make it stop.

"You need some counseling for yourself, Joe?"

"Naw, man..."

"Just so you know," James offered, "We all take advantage of it whenever we need it. There's no shame in it. We're family here. We take care of each other."

Tears slid down his reddening cheeks, "I just want my boy to be well."

"We'll do the best we can." He patted Joe's arm. "You rest up for a couple more days. Franks give you the tour yet?"

"Yeah. Nice set-up. Wish I'd known about it sooner."

"We had to be careful. The Feds—"

Joe looked up at him, met his eyes, "I know all about it, man. Do you think they did this? The disease, I mean."

"We're still trying to find out."

DURING THE DAY, THEY left the sliders open over the attic windows to enjoy what little light they could get as the days shortened. Coltan sat on the floor under the south window to take advantage of the cool gray light. He spread the map out in front of him and studied the coordinates in order to pinpoint the location of the refuge.

From what he could tell, the refuge was hidden somewhere in the eastern mountains. That area was accessible from Bonito Valle by way of the old road he and Muffy used to stroll. If the military stayed on the west side and didn't bother with the east side for at least another year, he and Natalie had a good chance of making their exodus with little problem. However, the first part of the journey would take them over wide-open country until they reached the foothills. That would be the most hazardous leg of the trip. He and Natalie had seen and heard the occasional whirlybird over their area, so they knew the military was still looking for survivors. He clung to hope they would suspend their surveillance once the winter storms moved in, and maybe by summer they would forget about this side altogether.

"Call it luck or God's blessing," he told Natalie, "The refuge isn't that far."

She joined him there. "Where is it?"

He pointed to a spot deep in the mountains, "Right about here."

"How many miles is that?"

"About eighty. Maybe a little more. We could make it easily on the bike."

"How long would it take?"

"It would depend on the weather and the road conditions." He began to fold the map, "In ideal conditions, we could get there in two hours or less. But, if the roads are clogged with slides and if there's still a lot of snow at the peaks, it's gonna take a lot longer. We also have to consider if the weather gets bad. You know, it could be fine down here, but up there's another story."

"Are we talking days?"

"Worst case scenario."

"It'd be worth it, though."

"Unless we get there and the military's waiting for us." He knew she hadn't considered it, but he had. Those birds they saw over Baker Creek made him wonder.

"You think we could be walking into a trap?"

"We won't know until we get there."

She bit her lip. "The coordinates on the card are the same as the ones Mitch gave us. I trust Mitch."

"The danger by then couldn't be any worse than if we stayed here. Eventually, they'll find us. If we stay here, I mean."

"Do you think we're safe for the winter?"

"As long as we don't get careless." He observed the shadows on the floor. They stretched out earlier every day. "We're already losing the light."

CHAPTER 7

I an pulled up some more potatoes and gently dropped them into his bucket. He looked across the garden at Carolyn and caught her eye.

She grinned and said, "My bucket's almost full. How many have you got?"

"Half that." He liked her very well. Of all the young people at the refuge, Carolyn spent the most time with him. He thought she was pretty, and funny and nice, and she paid attention to him when he spoke. She liked his accent and told him she hoped he never lost it.

"You must be working a lot slower than me."

"I'm bein' careful," he replied, "I don't want to bruise 'em."

"Peaches, you can bruise. Not potatoes."

"Not what Mum said. She insisted on care. Woulda boxed me ears, otherwise." They both heard the rumble and whir of a chopper overhead, and they paused to watch it. "Say what?" Ian exclaimed. "Friend or foe?"

"Foe, probably!" Carolyn answered.

Although the air was bitterly cold, and the rain-soaked soil even colder, the day was sunny. Storm clouds were moving in from the northwest, and that meant another cold front from Alaska would be paying a visit. They needed to get the harvest out of the ground before the freeze hit, and Carolyn and Ian volunteered to help.

It was nice to escape the underground complex for a while. Carolyn relished the fresh air and sunlight, even though the cold was beginning to turn her fingertips blue. Ian, more accustomed to a colder climate, hardly gave it notice.

He extracted a potato that had grown into a funny shape. He studied it carefully before deciding what it resembled to him. "Oy!" he called out to Carolyn and tossed it across to her, "Looks like a cat sunnin' on the window ledge."

She caught it and examined it from all angles. She agreed and said, "I'll add it to my collection!" Beside her was a smaller bucket for the interesting ones. So far, she had collected a *sunnin' cat*, an elephant with half a trunk, an oversized arrowhead, and a computer mouse. It had been Ian who started noticing the odd shapes, and Carolyn began to collect them just for fun.

Above, the copter veered and started back their way. They watched it as it came closer.

From the camouflaged doorway, Trevor popped out and hollered at them, "Inside! Now! Now, children!"

Carolyn and Ian rose, as did the younger children. All ran for the doorway.

Trevor held it open for them. "Speed up, now! Speed up."

Ian stopped to help a little girl who had tripped and fallen. He got her on her feet and took her hand. They ran together. Both he and Carolyn paused at the door to let the little ones enter first.

"Chop-chop!" Trevor ordered. "No time to waste!"

"What about our buckets?" Carolyn asked.

"Later!" Trevor replied. He gripped her arm and pulled her through the doorway. When Ian followed directly behind, Trevor lightly slapped the side of his head just over his ear. "Speed up, you!"

"Ow...!" Ian protested. "What was 'at for?"

"You're too slow, mate." He closed and locked the door.

Carolyn caught what Trevor did. She spun and told him hotly, "You didn't have to do that! He was being a gentleman! A gentleman is something you'll never be!"

Trevor laughed softly. "Saucy one, are we? So, you like Ian, do you?"

She responded by stomping on his foot.

He yelled out and lifted his sore foot. "Bloody hell! Damned kids! I hate kids!"

"Ya 'ad it comin', ya did!" Ian said. "'it me again, I'll 'ave your guts for garters! I will!"

"Oooh... I'm bloody scared," Trevor joked.

"Just you wait!" Ian warned.

"Bloody bastard..." Trevor said. "I saved your bloody worthless life. No thanks an' no respect! Ay! Ay?"

"Ay!" Ian retorted playfully.

Carolyn laughed.

Over the intercom, *"Rolardy! Report to Con One."*

"Bloody hell... what now?" Trevor muttered. He knew it had to do with the copter. The Feds, or whoever was running the world these days, was still searching the mountains for stray refugees. He knew they had apprehended a few in the foothills and returned them to the camps in the valley. It was likely the opposition had gotten hold of their coordinates through some of those unfortunates.

*T*he Communications, Retrieval and Defense teams filed in to Conference Room One in a lower level cavern. Trevor Rolardy served double duty on Retrieval and Defense as needed, depending on the situation. He took the one remaining seat at the table, between Suzanne (who he thought was hot) and pimply-faced, obese Roger (who always smelled like corn chips). He shifted the chair a bit closer to Suzanne.

Seated at the head of the table, James waited patiently as Trevor settled in.

"Alright," he began, "Now that we're all here. It looks like we got a situation coming up." He referred to Mitchell Fenny sitting at the corner closest to him, "Y'all know Mitchell Fenny, our Communications and Surveillance Leader. Mitchell, you got the floor."

Mitchell stood and addressed the group. "We've been picking up transmissions from the military in the valley. As most of you know by now, there was an incident in Oak Shores where they uncovered a large group of resisters. And... as you all know by now... not a single one has been left alive."

"What does this have to do with us?" someone asked.

"They found cards on some of the victims." Mitchell shifted uncomfortably. He was still getting used to public speaking and was nervous. The news he was about to share only added to his discomfort. "And... as most of you know, the bad guys have also intercepted some of the refugees travelling toward the mountain to our base here. Although some of the refugees had the good sense to eat the cards, the enemy recovered some from the others. In short, we've been found out."

"So, what now?" Trevor inquired, "Are we moving camp?" He knew better. His inquiry was only to move the meeting forward.

"Impossible," James said. "It took us over ten years to plan and build this. We're staying put."

Murmuring filled the room. Over the din, Trevor said loudly, "This means we have to fight. Is that it? Defend the castle?"

"That's right." James raised his arms and hollered, "Settle down, y'all! Settle down. We knew this would come eventually. Y'all knew that. Settle down." He waited until the murmuring died down before he continued. "Now, then... We have a good-sized army here." He glanced at Trevor and directed the inquiry to him, "We got—what—two hundred or so experienced men and women, right?" Trevor nodded.

"That ain't much against that friggin' army down there!" A male voice from the back of the room remarked.

"Rolardy," James continued, "How many are combat ready?"

"About one-seventy-five, give or take." Trevor's doubt regarding their odds of turning back the military in the valley was clear in his voice.

"Franks," James said, "How many sharp-shooters we got?"

"I'm not sure," Franks replied.

"Give me an estimate."

"Maybe a hundred or so." Franks grabbed that out of thin air. He had no idea. All he knew was he had been training many over the past month since his return to Base.

James turned to Mitchell. "Mitchell! Have you been able to trunk frequencies between our other bases?"

"Last night," Mitchell answered. "Me and Roger worked on it till six-thirty this morning. We contacted Denver. Our own equipment didn't intercept that transmission. Around noon, we hooked up with Montana Moses. No interception there, either. Looks good, sir."

"How many troops does Denver have?"

"Over five-hundred."

"Montana Moses?"

"Four-thirty or so."

"What about the Mohave/Death Valley Block—Whadda they call it? Mohave Cross?"

"Yes, sir. Mohave Cross. No word from them in the past two weeks before trunking."

"Lift the trunk on them and try again." James glanced around the room, made eye contact with every individual before he continued. "Alright, then. Here's the good news. The military still has their hands full dealing with the refugees in the camps and the mords who are trying to get in for food. They've also got squads still tied up in Oak Shores cleaning up that lab animal situation and all the human victims. I don't think they have much to spare at this moment, which means an attack on our base is unlikely in the immediate future. There's also a blizzard coming in by tomorrow night. That's gonna make it impossible for them to send more surveillance birds our way, much less fighting troops. In short, that gives us time for a plan of action."

James already briefed Trevor on the plan of action. However, just to be polite and set a good example, the Brit sat forward at the table and rested his chin in his hand. Beneath the table, he felt Suzanne's fingers caress his knee. They stole a sideways glance at each other. He caught the hint of a mischievous smile at the corners of her lips. Trevor reciprocated her expression.

"Denver has offered to send two-hundred combat-ready troops, plus additional weaponry to us."

"How are they gonna do that?" The same male voice from the back of the room.

"Underground railroad." James answered.

"What?" Same guy.

"We got the book in the library," James said impatiently, "Check it out and read it." He glanced again at all in turn, "There's a network of people throughout the western mountains who are working with us. These people have agreed to open their homes to all traveling Army of Christ troops enroute to our various bases. In addition to Army of Christ members, we've got almost one thousand citizen militia troops we've recruited over the years—survivalist types who are currently working within our network. They may not all be Christians, but they're just as much against this new emerging World Order as we are."

"They have no problem with us being Christians?" This came from Glenda.

"There's no problem with that." James knew it was getting a little off subject, but he felt the group should be reminded, "As Christians, we believe in giving everyone a chance to come to Christ. However, we also know not every person will accept our belief. However, Jesus himself would not turn these people away, and neither will we. I just want to remind y'all we have many among us who have not accepted Jesus Christ as Savior, and that's all right. We plant the seed; God does the rest." He took a deep breath and returned to the main subject, "Now, then... Our plan of action right now and into the next few months is to train and equip as many fighting troops as possible. We've arranged for reinforcements from Denver and Montana Moses. We've got plenty of room and plenty of provisions. I'll be interviewing and accepting volunteers for specific committees that will be responsible for assimilating the reinforcements. We also need skilled personnel for identifying and isolating in custody any spies or suspected threats. We need more volunteers to relieve our Security and Surveillance Teams on swing and graveyard shifts. We need more volunteers for a number of other teams. I am hoping someone in this group will specifically volunteer to design a committee list and oversee the leaders of each committee. Am I clear on that?"

Scattered "yes sirs" around the room.

James continued, "I know we already have something to that effect already in place. However, we need to have it fine-tuned, and we need to have it done soon. Keep your eyes and ears open for recruitment candidates from the latest batch of refugees that came in this week. With the weather turning, I expect fewer will make it here before next summer. So, keep it in mind. Now, I anticipate you have questions. However, it's close to suppertime and we're all hungry. I respectfully request we continue this meeting at oh-five-hundred tomorrow. Those in favor?" He raised his hand.

All the others did, too.

"SUBJECTS APPROACHING..." It came over the scanner. Surprised and curious, they listened. *"mords!"*

There came a long and loud hissing and crackling.

Natalie went for the scanner. "Got the squelch too high." She grabbed it and turned the squelch down.

Another voice, *"Secure the perimeter! Get those people back!"*

"Where's it coming from?" Coltan hollered.

She checked the numbers. "Oak Shores."

"I thought that was evacuated."

The first voice came back, *"Looks like someone freed the animals. Fuck! Shaunnessy, shoot 'em! Shoot 'em now!"*

Coltan listened, aghast. Why were they shooting animals?

The first voice again, *"Fuck! They got him! Sonofabitch! Jones, get your team over there. Stop fuckin' around. Kill those bastards!"*

The second voice came on, *"Did they get to the trucks?"*

The first voice, *"Not yet. They got 'em."* There came a pause, then, *"Heyheyhey! Get that fuckin' pit bull! Hardheaded bastard! Shoot 'im again! Fuckin' ay..."*

The second voice, *"Calloway! Get those people into the trucks!"*

The first voice, *"We're tryin'! What the fuck..!"* Another pause, then, *"Aw... shit... fuck... most of 'em are bit. Aw, shit! Whadaya wanna do? Base? Base? Whadaya wanna do?"*

The second voice, *"You know the procedure!"*

The first voice, *"Aw... fuck!"* The voice trailed off for a moment as the man listened to voices in the background. Natalie and Coltan could hear screams. The voice came back, *"That's Shepherd. Yeah. Kill 'im. You heard right. Do what I tell ya!"* He hesitated, stammered something they couldn't understand. His next words were clear. *"Fuckin' lab assholes! Base? Base, we just offed Shepherd. The Elimination Team's got the civvies. Aw... fuck. We got little kids here. Some of 'em won't shoot the kids."* He paused again, listening to voices in the background. He replied to someone, *"Shoot the fuckin' kids! That's an order. Kill all of 'em! Mow 'em down. You, over there! Start up the dozer! Get that pit started! You heard me!"*

Natalie and Coltan could only gaze at each other in stunned

silence.

MARIO AND ROSA ACCOMPANIED the Biting Woman and her companions through the foothills. They noticed the farther they trekked, the fewer the oak trees and the more numerous the pines. Rosa loved the scent of the pines, and she often paused to shut her eyes and sniff in three brief, but deep, inhalations of the aroma. The Biting Woman, who possessively maintained a grip on her small hand, tugged her hand and admonished her with a hiss of her tongue to keep her moving. Mario lagged two steps behind to protect them from attack at the rear of the pack. He resented the Biting Woman's possessiveness of the little girl, but he could not understand why. The only thing he did understand was the woman meant business when she glared and growled at him each time he tried to take the girl's free hand.

The Biting Woman abruptly halted and sniffed the air, and her companions followed her example. They smelled human flesh. There was the hint of death about the odor, but not enough to make it unappetizing. The unfortunate corpse was still fresh enough to nourish them. The woman led them through a tangle of manzanita and thorn bushes to a small green clearing. The meal awaited them there, laid out naked on his back upon a haphazard sprawl of thick brown rope. Delirious with the seductive odor of the feast, they pounced on it and tore into the pre-incised abdominal flesh with their fingers and teeth.

Before the soft cracking sound of it registered in their brains, the giant net enveloped them and lifted them into the air, carcass and all.

CHAPTER 8

Coltan left the house in the early afternoon. Natalie had dedicated her attention to the scanner and he expected she would continue listening to it for the rest of the day and most of the night. He wanted to go outside, not only for the blessed quiet, but to get some air and see some different scenery, even though that scenery was nothing but devastation in what used to be his neighborhood.

After a perimeter check including a quick exam of all the windows, he strolled up the damp sidewalk toward his former home. The area was dead silent. Even the birds were silent. The sky had cleared for a while, but he spotted storm clouds moving in from the west. At least the rain had washed the stench out of the air. He took a deep breath and savored the crispness and the freshness of it. A bullet casing floated downhill in the waterlogged gutter, and he watched it for a few moments until it reached the storm drain and tumbled down, clinking as it dropped.

His house was right ahead at the end of the road at the highest point.

He stopped at the battered front gate that was ajar and hanging off the top hinge. The neglected, weed invaded yard looked the same as he remembered it, except for the deep tracks created by the tank that had taken a shortcut through the property. Upon further observation, he saw the corner section of the front fence along the gateway askew, and that was what probably dislodged the gate. He pulled the gate open, and it fell off completely. He let it drop. The house seemed foreboding to him; that was normal. In all the time he had lived there, the house seemed to warn him away as if it was telling him he didn't belong there. It was a strange feeling. However, his curiosity was stronger than any fear he felt, so he continued on to the open front door.

He paused on the porch and listened. The house was silent; silent and dead like the rest of the street. Even the wet, wind-driven maple leaves under his feet made no sound. He stepped inside. The interior looked like a tornado had gone through. Overturned side tables, small furniture pieces, knickknacks and weeks' old unread mail hindered easy passage from one room to the next. Coltan pushed the big items out of his way and kicked the small items off to the side to create a path through the foyer.

In the living room, he spotted a large pool of dried blood on the sofa where his mother traditionally enjoyed her drug-induced coma. He didn't need a detective to explain what had happened to her—the bullet hole was vivid on the blood-splattered pillow. It didn't strike him as odd that he felt no grief for her. On the contrary, he was glad she was dead, and he hoped she died slowly. She deserved it.

This brought to mind his chief tormentor, Richard. What had happened to him? Coltan readied Clyde, just in case, and searched the first floor. The only evidence of Richard was a half-finished joint on the kitchen table, and a dozen or so empty beer cans on the floor there. Over by the refrigerator, an open bottle of whiskey lay on its side on the floor. What remained of the booze puddled around the bottle and disappeared under the fridge. Even the ants didn't want it. Coltan could smell the rank odor of spoiled food. He noticed dried vomit in the sink. The sight of it turned his stomach. He left the kitchen and headed for the stairs.

It was a good time to rescue some winter clothing before it became unsafe to return here. With that in mind, he headed up the stairs and tried to ignore the stench that permeated every inch of the place.

At the top of the stairs, he stopped. What if Richard was there and bitten? Enough time had passed to ensure infection. The possibility produced an ironic picture in Coltan's mind. Of all the brutal abuse he had endured at Richard's hands, the abuse he had survived—*how screwed-up it would be* if Richard overpowered him and had him for a meal!

The thought of it made him angry. He made certain Clyde was cocked and ready. Coltan sucked in a breath, called Richard's name. The only reply was a tinny vibratory echo.

Another thought came to mind. What if Richard was there and had not been bitten or infected? What then? Most likely, Richard would insist on taking shelter with him, would expect it, even. *No, no, no!* Coltan told himself, *I'll kill the motherfucker first! No cops around, no witnesses. How perfect! What a perfect opportunity!*

The brief fantasy brought him pleasure—too much pleasure. In the next moment, he felt guilty and sickened that he could—maybe even *would*—do such a thing. Coltan reeled away and collapsed at the top step. His breakfast erupted with volcanic force onto the dirty carpet. He continued heaving until there was nothing left. Sick and trembling with exhaustion, he curled up there for a long time until he could recover enough strength to stand and get the hell out of there.

He spotted a reefer in the seam where the step met the face of the step above. It was just what he needed, not only to calm him, but also to relieve his nausea. He reached for it and lit it, inhaled deeply and held the smoke in as long as he could. It gave him an immediate buzz, and he released it and took a second drag. He finally began to feel the relaxing effect of it after the third drag. He leaned back against the banister and took a fourth and closed his eyes and let the warmth of it flow through him as his nausea subsided.

"What are you doing?" The voice startled him. He realized it was his own voice.

He dropped the joint and glanced around condemningly. The place held nothing but evil. Everything there was evil and filthy, and repugnant to God. What did God do with evil? He sent it to Hell, that's what He did.

Oh... let me do it! Coltan told God, *Let me do it!*

Dazed, yet compelled by purpose, he found a full gas can in the garage and sprinkled the contents around the upper and lower floors. Next, he entered the kitchen and opened the stove. He turned on all the burners and blew out the fires, let the gas wander freely into the air. He lit a candle on the coffee table in the living room. Satisfied, he headed for the front door where he emptied the remainder of the gasoline on the floor. He lit the rest of the matchbook and tossed it into the puddle, and ran as fast as he could to the sidewalk.

From there, he waited. His heart pounded in his chest, pounded so hard he thought its power would break his ribs. He was out of breath and panting, sweat running down his face. It didn't matter. All that mattered was the explosion that finally erupted and shook even the sidewalk under his feet. The house became a giant bonfire, and it made him happy to see it finally burn to Hell where it belonged. The memories in the walls and in the floors were burning out of existence, and he felt triumphant.

"Fuck you, Richard!" Coltan shouted, "Burn in Hell! Burn in Hell! Burn in Hell!"

He sunk upon the sidewalk and watched the conflagration, the enraged and unforgiving tears of an eight-year old boy spilling down his face as he laughed and sobbed and cursed it all to Hell.

Natalie had turned the scanner volume on high in the earphones so as not to miss a word of the intermittent but continuing drama in Oak Shores. She felt the explosion, and heard it. As the smoke and burning cinders drifted across the east window, she removed her earphones and flipped the scanner off. She ran to the window and looked out.

Coltan's house...

Where's Colt? She glanced around and realized he hadn't

70

returned from downstairs.

By the time she grabbed Bonnie and a flashlight, put on her shoes and jacket and reached the front door, Coltan was on the porch. She stared at him as he silently unlocked and pulled open the security door. His eyes were strange, and he didn't acknowledge her as he entered the house. Without a word, he climbed the stairs in the semi-darkness with only the light from the open door to guide him safely.

Natalie locked both doors, double-checked the other doors and found them locked. She heard the shower come on upstairs. At the top of the stairs, the door to Coltan's old room was open and the daylight came through the window there. She entered the room and secured the door, ducked through the hidden door into the attic access room and the bathroom there.

"Colt?"

He didn't answer. She opened the bathroom door and gazed across at the shower stall. The room was filling with steam, and his shoes and clothing were scattered on the floor as if he had removed each piece en-route to the stall. She could see his shadowy form through the milky glass when she reached the stall. He was sitting in a corner, not moving. She opened the door. He sat there with his legs drawn up, his knees against his chest and his arms wrapped around his knees as the water showered upon him.

"Did you set the fire?" she asked gently.

"Sent it all to Hell," he answered with a subtle smile of satisfaction. "They belong there."

Natalie felt the water. It was almost scalding. She shut it off and knelt down in front of him on the steaming wet floor of the stall. She observed him, alarmed by the child-like appearance of his face, the terror in his eyes. "They can't hurt you anymore."

"I can't get clean..." He pulled at his lower lip. "I keep trying."

CHAPTER 9

Natalie removed the headphones and set the scanner aside in frustration. There were few transmissions in over a week. What little came through before was boring clean-up operations talk from the Oak Shores incident. That had dwindled down to nothing.

She looked over at Coltan kicked back on his mattress studying his Bible and listening to music through his earphones from his old disk player. She wondered how he could be so content while she was going crazy with hunger for outside information. Thinking about it, she remembered what he once mentioned about not wanting to know. It seemed to be his defense mechanism against the frightening world beyond their windows, and it was serving him well. She watched him as he paused and pondered something before he wrote in his journal. However, he did not have that clear, bright look to his eyes that used to be there when he studied the Scriptures. Lately, his studies had become more of a chore than a pleasure. She had noticed it, although he said little about it. He flipped shut his notebook and tossed his pen down. After a few moments, he turned his attention to the disk player and pushed a button. Satisfied with what he heard, he resumed reading.

Ever since the day he blew up his parents' house, when he experienced some kind of breakdown, he had become both physically and emotionally distant. He seemed preoccupied with his thoughts, irritable and secretive. Once, he had even slammed shut his Bible in frustration and mumbled a complaint that he could not concentrate enough to understand what he was reading. When she tried to comfort him, he yelled at her to leave him alone, only to apologize a moment later.

Now, his frustration arose once more, this time over the disk player. He ripped the earphones away and tossed them onto the floor, cussed and angrily poked off the power button. After that, he slammed his Bible shut and returned it to its protective leather carrying case. His eyes blazing, he stared off at the wall, whispered the F-Word to himself.

"What is it?" Natalie dared to ask.

He did not look at her. "The batteries wore out."

"I'll go get you some fresh ones." She moved to stand.

"Forget it," he said in a brittle voice. "It won't help anything." He sighed with genuine exhaustion and rubbed his eyes.

She noticed his hands were trembling when he did that. His hands had been trembling almost non-stop over the last many days, and Natalie had attributed the tremor to lack of sleep from his recurring nightmares. The dreams had grown more violent over the last two days, he taking swings at an imaginary attacker while screaming and pleading in French. The most unsettling thing about this was the fact that, in these dreams, his voice took on the tone of a child and he sobbed and cried as if he was a child until he finally awoke from the terrors.

Coltan refused to discuss the nightmares.

A male voice suddenly blurted from the earphones of Natalie's scanner, *"Charley Four! Saint Luke's Church at Boyd and Third! About two dozen mords in the basement, mostly kids."*

Coltan recognized Boyd and Third as a Reyton intersection. The mention of Saint Luke's Church lent certainty to the fact the troops were in Reyton. Coltan attended Saint Luke's during his short residency there when he had worked at the Reyton Theater.

A second voice answered the first, *"Roger that. What's the situation? Are the kids dead?"*

"Some of them are," the first replied, *"Looks like the mords might've*

been feeding off the dead ones." There came frantic voices speaking over each other in the background. The soldier came back briefly, *"Uh... hold on a minute."* In the next second his voice sounded as if he had turned away from his transmitter, *"What? No! Kill it! Kill it!"* He spoke directly into his radio this time, *"They know we're up here. They're trying to rush the stairs. One of 'em broke out. We got the bastard. Looks like they tried to hide the kids down there."*

Natalie thought she had shut the scanner off. She yanked the earphone plug out of the jack, and that only made the volume come out louder from the main speaker. Horrified and at the same time fascinated by the narrative, she forgot Coltan for a moment and listened spellbound to the transmission.

The second voice came back, *"Jenson wants to know if you're all wearing your hazard suits."*

"Yes, sir!"

"Have any of your men been bitten?"

"No, sir."

"These are your orders, Bradford. Eliminate every one of the mords and torch the place."

"Torch the place?"

"That's affirmative!"

Coltan lost it at that moment. His face paled and his eyes took on a wild, desperate expression. His anguished outburst echoed throughout the house, "No more!" He snatched the scanner out of Natalie's hand and tore out the batteries, all the while blurting profanities and words that ran into each other and made no sense. He flung the silenced unit and batteries against the wall with another scream of overwhelming rage.

For the longest time all Natalie could do was stare at him in stunned paralysis. She had never seen him like this, had never seen anyone act like this.

He turned on her, gripped her arms and shook her. "No more!

No more! *No fucking more!*" He flung her onto her back and pinned her to the floor. "This isn't fucking entertainment! What the hell is wrong with you? Couldn't you hear those kids screaming? Couldn't you hear them?"

She had not heard any screaming. There was no screaming from the children. Coltan heard it all in his head, and now he was screaming at her. Frozen with terror at his behavior, she could only gaze pleadingly at him as he slammed her repeatedly against the floor.

In the passion of that moment, Coltan saw the fear in her eyes. He became aware of his actions. Reason returned to him. He scolded himself for losing his temper and losing control. His behavior was that of the *old* Coltan, and he feared the phantom's reappearance. It took all his willpower to rein in his temper and regain control. Coltan released Natalie's wrists and lifted his weight from her.

Although he released her, Natalie was too afraid to move. She opened her eyes and peered into his. His love and compassion for her replaced his fury and fire. That is what scared her—his *snap of a finger* transformation from dangerous lunatic to loving soul mate. She was convinced he had gone crazy. Perhaps someday he would lose it big time, even worse than this. He could kill her or, at the least, severely injure her. Natalie knew she could not let it get that far, could not forgive him again and again only to see him repeat the same dangerous behavior. It would be safer living alone than with a man as volatile as Coltan. It broke her heart to believe it, yet she accepted it as best for them both. She tried to convince herself he would survive just fine on his own.

He slowly withdrew from her and sat, facing her. He was ashamed of his behavior and regretted there was no way to undo the damage to her trust. It was in her eyes, and it might be there forever.

"I could never hurt you." He had difficulty speaking through the lump in his throat.

She looked away and drew her knees up to her chest, hugged her legs against her chest as he had done down in the shower that day. It made her remember that, remember him saying he couldn't get clean. What was that all about? Why did he torch his parents' house? Did the soldier's order to torch the church in Reyton trigger his memory of that event? And, there was something else... kids screaming; Coltan said he heard the kids in the church screaming. Could it be what he actually heard were his own screams? Were they the screams of the little boy who relived his agony in terrifying nightmares?

Finally, she found the courage to ask, "What made you burn down your house?"

A vague recollection of the event and the reason for his actions floated back to his memory in a slow-motion wave. The subject filled him with revulsion. Regardless, he felt a need to explain, and he expected she would understand just as he so completely understood. "I had to destroy the evil there."

"The evil...?" She did not know if the evil he attempted to destroy was real or perceived. Whether real or imaginary, she wanted to know what form the evil took. How did that evil send Coltan over the edge? Why did Coltan regress to his *child self* the day he torched the house? She recalled the child's words and the confused innocence in his voice and in his eyes. "You said something down in the bathroom that day. The day you burned down your house."

That entire episode in the shower was a blank to him. The only thing he remembered was *waking up*, sort of, in the shower stall.

Natalie leaned forward, "You don't remember?"

"No."

"You told me you couldn't get clean. Why couldn't you get clean?"

"What?" He could not recall that.

"Were your mom and Richard there? Were they in the house

when you torched it?"

He couldn't speak. The lump in his throat felt bigger, and it hurt. The memories of his mother's and Richard's abuse returned to him with sudden clarity. The shame of it returned, as well.

She persisted in a hard tone of voice, "This is your last chance, Colt. Tell me the truth. Tell me all of it."

Coltan searched his memory, recovered fragments of his visit to the house. He put the fragments together, and it made sense to him. He wanted her to understand. "They were gone, but the evil was still there. It was on everything! I had to destroy it before it spread."

This was too much for her to grasp. His explanation only strengthened her fear of him. Her voice wavered with disappointment, sorrow and bitter resolve. "Pack up and leave."

He understood and would not plead his case. This wasn't the first time he had been pitched out onto the street, and he'd become an expert at packing quickly. He changed into warm clothing and put on his boots. He took one of the pre-packed bug-out backpacks and stuffed his remaining clothing, Bible and the rest of his belongings into the space remaining inside it. He rolled up the sleeping bag and tied it to the bar at the top of the pack.

They heard the sudden cloudburst of heavy rain come down, the crack and roll of thunder.

She stood her ground, resolute and strong. Once he was gone, she would cry, grieve, and pray for him. She knew in her heart she would always love him—that would never change.

He grabbed a flashlight and Clyde. "Okay if I keep the gun?"

"Keep it." She didn't look at him. "Take some extra ammo, too."

He did so, went to the retractable staircase, and eased it down. As he stood at the top step, he told her, "Lock up after me." He wanted to tell her he still loved her, would always love her, but he felt it would come across as begging for forgiveness.

She took a flashlight, stuffed Bonnie into her waistband, and followed him down to the garage. She watched him board the Harley and turn the ignition. It didn't respond the first time, or the second. It sputtered to life on the third try, and he flipped on the headlamp. Natalie lifted the big door and rolled it up. He put on his helmet and rode slowly out into the rain and the darkness. A flash of lightning illuminated his form for a moment as he rolled up the street toward the road that led into the eastern mountain range.

As she watched him get farther away, she wanted to call him back to her. However, in retrospect, she knew it would be no good. He would not change. He was too messed-up. It was better to let him go.

Coltan reached the end of the street and paused, wondering what to do, where to go. He decided to go for the refuge. If he made it there, he could tell them about Natalie, and maybe they would send someone to bring her back there. If he didn't make it, Natalie's fate was up to God. He figured if all went well he would reach the refuge by morning. If the storm got worse, or if there was trouble along the way, he would have to trust that to God.

The rain pounded heavy and cold, and the wind began to pick up. Loud bursts of thunder tumbled to his ears from far away. The voice of the thunder seemed to double-dare him to follow it into the unknown beyond. With each flash of lightning, the mountains far off appeared as sharp black shadows against the sky. Every time the lightning backlit the range, the mountains impressed Coltan as awaiting his arrival.

Coltan remembered how months ago he had mused about the road there, how it seemed so much like his life, if his life had been a road. Would he find his destination there? Would he even make it that far? Considering everything, it no longer mattered. He decided he would accept whatever God had planned for him. Even if it meant God would snatch him from the Earth that night, he would accept it. His entire life had been nothing but a battlefield, and he could anticipate more battles ahead. He was weary of the fight. Weary of the struggle. Weary of the demons that manipulated him into sabotaging his few good breaks along the way. Above all, he was weary of himself. Death would be a welcome relief. He didn't care what happened to him anymore.

He prayed for Natalie all the way to the foothills.

Up in the attic, she found his house keys on his bare mattress. She sat and cried.

CHAPTER 10

In Baker Creek, the mords growled and hissed at the thunder and lightning. They became more agitated than usual the past two days, and Guffy, their Overseer, had observed this and taken detailed notes.

He heard a new disturbance coming from a far corner in the rear of the cage. It sounded like low growls, labored breathing and moaning. He walked around to the corner and shined his light there. Two male mords had removed the clothing from another in the cage, a teenage girl. One was sniffing the ragged clothing while the other was on top of her, ramming it to her. She seemed to be enjoying it. At once fascinated and repulsed, Guffy watched. When the first one finished with her, the second abandoned the clothing and took his turn with her. In the interim while one dismounted and the other moved to mount her, Guffy noticed a lot of blood on the floor between her legs; the girl was menstruating.

Guffy unlatched his radio from his belt loop and contacted Command.

Smith answered, "What's up?"

"Got a situation here," Guffy reported.

"This better be good!" Smith sounded irritated.

"The mords are fucking."

"Fucking?"

"That's right, Smitty. They're fucking."

There was wonder and fear in Smith's voice, "Shit..." After a moment, he asked, "All of 'em?"

"Hell no!" Guffy stole a glance back at the lovers, "Two on one.

The girl's on her period. Maybe the smell of her blood made them horny. Whadaya want me to do about it?"

"Let 'em fuck. At least somebody's gettin' some around here."

"You can't be serious!"

"Guffy, your job is to observe and report. Nothin' else. Take notes and report your findings to Clausberg in the morning."

The mords on top of the girl spotted Guffy, who was standing a little too close to the cage. He stopped humping the girl, made eye contact with Guffy and growled a warning. Guffy took six steps back out of harm's way. The mord resumed his pleasurable task. The girl moaned and hissed, screamed. Her body convulsed with orgasm.

"There's already two pregnant ones," Guffy said into the radio, "One's ready to drop it any day now."

"We know about it," Smith said tiredly, "They wanna see what happens with the babies."

Guffy couldn't understand why. "What the hell for?"

"The babies might hold a cure, asshole."

"You gotta be kiddin' me!"

"That's what the brass says. I don't make the rules, man. Fuckin' scientists..."

A flash of lightning right on top of the camp lit the place up like noontime. An earsplitting roll of thunder followed two seconds later. The mords became more agitated, and many began to pound on the bars and tug at them. Guffy stared, terrified. There were twenty-seven total in there, and if they broke out, he would be dinner.

"I need backup!" Guffy demanded.

Smith found this amusing. "They're gettin' restless, huh?"

"They're trying to break out!"

"Use your cattle prod!"

""No!" Guffy pulled away further and considered retreating to the guardhouse. The sudden cloudburst that began to saturate his uniform made it easier to decide. "It's pouring! I'm heading back to the guardhouse!"

"Chicken!" Smith taunted.

"You come out here, then!"

"I can see well enough from here."

"You got the cameras working?"

"Yep. Too late, man... They're done fuckin', I see. At least you got to see the good shit."

"Good shit, my ass. These things are disgusting!" Guffy flipped off his light and entered the safety and warmth of the guardhouse. "I'm gonna write my report. Tell your scientist perverts I want backup out here from now on."

NATALIE CRIED FOR TWO hours. Now she was exhausted and could feel more tears building inside. Adding to her misery was the guilt she felt for banishing Coltan into the storm and into the frightening unknown of the world outside. She wanted to find him and bring him back, but it was night and the storm was too intense. Besides that, in two hours time, there was no telling where he could be. She prayed again for his safety and surrendered to a fresh wave of tears.

It struck her as both curious and disturbing he had not resisted leaving her and their refuge. How could he find it so easy to simply pack up and ride off into the night? Why had he not defended himself, argued his case or asked for her forgiveness? Could it be he also saw himself as a threat to her safety? Was he that screwed up and hopeless?

As she replayed the entire episode in her mind, she tried to assemble the fragments into a sensible explanation. She considered his delusion that he heard children's screams, and his sudden, unrestrained fury; his admonishment of her for seemingly *entertained* by the horror unfolding over the scanner. Natalie examined each piece separately—helpless children suffering, his enraged reaction to that, his perception someone found the terror, agony and imminent execution of those children *entertaining*.

"*I can't get clean... Mommy and him made me dirty...*"

She finally figured it out.

THE UNRELENTING RAIN obscured his vision as he rode deeper into the foothills. His jeans were soaked through to the skin, and the wind chilled his legs. Only his leather jacket kept the rest of his body warm and dry, and he hardly noticed it because his legs were so cold. He knew he needed to find shelter soon.

He slowed to a crawl when he arrived at the junction. There were three ways to go from here, the south face of the mountain at his right, the center road that led to the summit of the east face straight ahead, or Baker Creek to the left. After what he had seen that one day in Baker Creek, and what he had seen above it over the ensuing weeks, Baker Creek was out. A flash of lightning illuminated snow at the summit. It would be a foolish decision to go that way. He steered right and took the narrow disintegrating road toward the south face. It would take longer to reach the refuge by this route, but it would be the safest.

The road was heavily rutted and overgrown with brush in many places, and he had to slow and steer around all the hazards. It became curvier as he rode further uphill and into the base of the mountain, and he was having a hard time differentiating the roadway from the treacherous saturated mud on one side, and the steep slope into oblivion on the other.

He had just rounded another curve when he spotted too late the pile of rocks and debris spilled across his path. The front tire of the Harley caught the mess just right and the bike flew a few feet before it crashed on its side at the crest of the rockslide. In the moments the bike was airborne, the centrifugal force threw him sideways off the seat, only to be pinned under the whirring machine once it landed. His right lower leg screamed pain into him as the weight crashed down on him. He found himself on his back, his legs twisted and pinned under the motorcycle. He could not free himself.

While the engine sputtered, the headlamp threw light against the trunk of a fallen pine tree.

Coltan removed his helmet and tossed it to one side. The rain showered upon his face, and he hated the sensation of it; the drops were fast and heavy, and they slapped into his skin like blunt needles. He shook off his momentary shock and laboriously sat up and wiped his face. His right leg pulsated pain. He managed to free his left leg, and he carefully leaned forward, found the ignition and shut the motor off. Dizziness overcame him. He settled again on his back and caught his breath, listened to the patter of rain. In a few moments, the sound of rain subsided into silence; he could no longer feel the rain upon his face, and he could no longer see the light from the headlamp.

JOE AND DARLA DAVIDSON had just dozed off when the tap at the canvas flap separating their bedroom from the children's in their tent awakened them. Late night tappings on the flap was nothing unusual for them; with three kids of their own, and now with the latest addition of Ian to their family, one of the four was always in need of something.

"Come in," Joe called softly.

Ian parted the flap and peeked in. "Sorry to bother you. Were you sleepin'?"

Darla sat up. "What is it, Ian?"

"If you were sleepin'," Ian said hesitantly.

"No, no..." Joe waved him in, "Come in, bugger. What's up?"

Ian approached the foot of the bed as Darla clicked on the lamp. "Somethin' strange..."

"Well...?" Joe sat forward and peered at him. The boy seemed distressed.

"Me leg 'urts..."

THUNDER SHOOK THE HOUSE. Natalie poured a second glass of wine and lit a cigarette. With his absence, she felt isolated and frightened. She wished she could take back her actions. Over the hours, she anxiously tried to will him to return, and she listened for the sound of the Harley in the driveway. Vain willfulness had given way to prayer, and prayer finally gave way to a need for release from the whole thing, release from the regret, the fear, the encompassing isolation.

She gulped down the wine and refilled the glass.

THE ROLLING THUNDER brought him back to his senses. He sat up and looked around. The illuminated trunk of the pine tree stared back at him. It impressed him as a lone actor awaiting direction upon a lit stage.

"How about some Shakespeare?" Coltan suggested aloud.

The tree replied with dumb silence.

"Well... fuck you, too." Coltan said offhandedly.

The dull steady pain in his leg still pinned under the weight of the Harley reminded him of his predicament. He scooted backwards in an attempt to free his leg, and was surprised and relieved when it slid easily from under the Harley. Perhaps his weight on the mud had created a pocket under the bike while he lied unconscious there in the rain. Whatever the *how* of the miracle, Coltan decided not to question. He was grateful to finally be free.

As his brain absorbed the reality of the moment, the circumstances that brought him here eluded him. It took a few minutes to recall the events of that night and somewhat longer to accept it as fact. Self-hate and rage overcame him. Culpability accompanied the rage although he did not feel the blame was his alone. He turned it outward and cast it skyward to God.

It was *His* fault. *He* could have prevented this. *He* could have prevented everything. Instead, *He* chose to watch Coltan suffer.

"What the fuck is your problem?" Coltan screamed at God. "You just love fucking with me, don't you? Well, *fuck you!* How do you like that? *Fuck you!*"

An earthshaking thunderclap rumbled above.

Coltan decided he should have expected God to answer him with rolling thunder. He wasn't impressed or intimidated. "Well, fuck you, too!"

He fished in his breast pocket for his cigarettes, found the pack crushed, the cigarettes broken. "That figures..." One breath away from a temper tantrum, he threw the pack as far as it would fly, stood and took a few steps up the pile of rock debris to get his backpack. His leg protested. "Shut up!" He yelled at it, "Shut the fuck up!" He beat his leg with his fist, "I've had worse than you. Shut the fuck up!" Angrily enduring the pain, he reached his backpack and started to unclip the straps that held it to the rack. In those moments, he ranted to himself and his hurt leg, "Fuckin' fag baby. Just take it. Just take it. Fuckin' little fag boy. Fuckin', fuckin', fuckin' fag boy..." One clip was being stubborn, and his frozen fingers required his increased and determined effort to free the damned thing. "All I want is a fucking cigarette. Sonofabitch. Fucking cigarette. Fuckin' fag boy wants a fuckin' smoke. Have a smoke. Have a smoke when you're done. I'm done. Have a smoke. Smoke the whole fuckin', fuckin' pack... gettin' green there, little fag boy. Do you one more. You gonna cry? I'll make you cry! Gimme a fuckin' smoke. Be a man. Hold it there. Take it... take it... little fag boy... make you a man... fuckin'fag... sweet little fag boy... pretty little fag boy..."

He was oblivious to his tirade of verbal self-abuse, a repetitive voice that had grown roots inside him and always surfaced in times like this to continue his torment. Maybe it was the Monster's voice. Whoever it belonged to, Coltan had stopped wondering years ago.

The backpack came free with a final, rage-empowered tug. He fell backwards with it and landed flat on his back in the rocks and mud. The rocks dug into his back. "That fucking figures..."

He fished around inside the backpack and found cigarettes. "Whadaya know? Something's going right..." The first deep drag was satisfying, but it did nothing to relieve his hopelessness and surging temper. As he lay there on his back, smoking, he stared up into the frigid black sky. It occurred to him the rain had stopped. Maybe God had stopped it so He could get a better view of this suffering human waste.

"Kill me!" Coltan challenged Him. "If you don't do it, I will!"

The sky said nothing.

There was agony in his soul. Unbearable agony. He wanted it to end.

He considered the burning ember at the tip of his cigarette. It was tempting. It would hurt less than the pain inside him and would mask his inner pain. He sat up, removed his jacket, and rolled up his sleeve. It had helped before.

Hadn't it...?

He thought about it, tried to remember. He couldn't remember, not clearly. Still, the impulse returned, and he brought the ember closer to his skin, almost touching it. The heat stung. He didn't remember it hurting like that, and he hadn't even set it into his skin yet. To his best recollection, all the other times he had barely felt it until the burning set through the first thin layer; that was during his Days of Rage when he had built up a tolerance for it, for all pain. It made him realize he had gotten soft over the last couple of years. All that *Jesus loves you* and *you're worthy of being loved* had made him soft.

Sweet little fag boy. Gonna cry, boy? Can't be a man, boy?

He tried to press it into his skin, and he couldn't do it.

His anguished screaming rose up into the black sky.

It had to end. It had to end now.

He threw away the cigarette and removed Clyde from his pocket. Clyde would end it with one quick and, hopefully, painless bullet. *Under the chin... Pow! Up into the brain. Done deal.* He pulled the hammer back and positioned the barrel under his chin.

To God, he said, "I just can't do this anymore."

He pulled the trigger.

THE WOMAN'S GROANS became screams, and her cage mates backed away from her. They formed a semi-circle and curiously watched her. She had torn her pants off an hour ago and retreated into a corner. There she squatted, her belly straining with the contractions. She took a deep breath and pushed. The onlookers grunted, growled and hissed. Her final scream brought them all to an abrupt silence. It slid out slowly and dropped gently to the floor of the cage, the neck folding as the top of its head met the puddle of water, blood and urine on the concrete below. The baby's shoulders rolled onto the concrete and the rest of the body followed until it rested there on its back, still attached to its mother by the umbilical chord. The woman gazed down at it. Her head tilted from side to side as she regarded it. A distant memory and her instinct solved the puzzle of this thing below her parted legs. She shortly forgot the pain of delivery, and she lifted her baby boy and examined him. She felt the tugging of the umbilical chord and it told her what to do next. She rested the child upon her knees and chewed through the chord until it severed. The afterbirth followed. After examining it and sniffing it, she took it into her mouth and began to eat it.

Her companions squatted before her and stared. One reached to steal the afterbirth from her hands. She growled and hissed.

The baby began to cry.

COLTAN EXPECTED THE last thing he would hear would be the shattering pop of the bullet before it seared into his brain. However, all he heard was a clicking noise. There was no pain, no ear-shattering pop, nothing he had expected.

He pulled the gun away and stared at it. "What the hell?" Without thinking about his next action, he pointed it at the tree trunk and pulled the trigger again. It fired. The blast made his ears ring. It almost made him laugh. "Shit..." He shook his head, reset the hammer and placed the barrel below his chin once more. "Try number two... Fuck you..." He pressed the trigger.

Click...

COMPLETELY ENRAGED and at the same time amused, he peered up into the sky. *What kind of a game is this? Can't I do one thing right?*

He pulled back the hammer and tried a third time.
Click.

He couldn't see God, but he could imagine Him laughing.

"Aw... fuck you!" Coltan shouted.

A subtle humming of many voices behind him caused him to startle and turn around. He saw the shadows of many figures standing there, watching him.

Mords!

He figured God had decided to have the final word by feeding him to the mords. Coltan laughed uproariously at the irony.

Completely unafraid, and even feeling relieved, Coltan stood and limped toward the shadow figures. "Come and get your supper! Get it while it's still warm!"

One figure stepped away from the others and approached him. It walked slowly and stopped about two feet away from him. When it stopped, a tiny beam of faint light began at its heart. The light gradually spread and became brighter until it illuminated the entire from the inside out.

A thin sleeveless white undershirt exposed his upper body and lean muscular arms to the elements. Years of filth soiled the undershirt, jeans and boots, the skin and the hair. He took another step forward and stopped again, his face fixed in an expression of hatred and violent intent, his jaw set tightly. His eyes peered into Coltan's eyes with fiery rage. Their faces were only inches apart.

Coltan stood paralyzed. He stared at himself.

Without warning, his duplicate attacked him and began to fiercely beat him. Unprepared for this, Coltan found he was unable to defend himself. The boy was on top of him, pounding him with his fists, pounding him rapidly and viciously. He made no sound at all as he delivered the beating; there was not even the sound of breathing. The face was twisted and insane with wrathful hatred for the target of his assault.

Overpowered, Coltan curled up and attempted to shield himself from the hard and painful blows. There had been no time to think of what to do, or even where this assailant had come from or why he was doing this. The only thing of which Coltan was aware was the fact his tormentor was himself. The moment that awareness opened fully into his consciousness, the duplicate faded away into nothing.

Coltan sat up quickly and gave himself a cursory exam for injuries. He was not hurt. The attacker had done no damage other than to fill him with terror.

It couldn't have been real.

The footsteps of a second figure approaching seized his attention. Like the first one, this one lit up from the inside out until the features became clear.

Her skin was as white as he remembered it. Coltan saw a remnant of innocence in her eyes, innocence he viciously stole from her. His mortification over the violence he committed against her body and spirit returned.

"I beg you..." he began in a tight, wavering voice, "I'm so sorry for what I did to you. You never deserved it. No one deserves it. I'm so sorry... I'm—"

She knelt in front of him and gazed sadly into his eyes. "I forgave you a long time ago," she whispered, "Forgive yourself. Forgive them, too."

"I can't," he told her.

"You have to. If you don't, this will never end." She took his hands in hers, "Release me, Coltan. Release us both."

She faded away, leaving the way free for the next figure already coming forward. This person was not someone he wanted to see.

Her black hair hung straight and limp over her emaciated frame. Her eyes were deep blue, like his.

"Pray for me."

He hated her, and would always hate her. "No."

The eyes were intent, full of pain. "Pray for me."

"Burn in Hell."

"Pray for me." Tears raced down her cheeks. She faded into darkness.

He needed to vomit. He fought it.

One more figure stood far away. It was tall, bulky, a dark giant. It came closer, but it did not walk; it seemed to float toward him. There was still no light in it as it stopped and hovered in front of him. Coltan felt frightened and tried to back away, but he could not move. He sat there and wondered at it, tried to understand what it could be and what it wanted with him. The authority emanating from it made him tremble from head to toe. A gradually increasing light filled the entity. Coltan saw it was standing there observing him. It cradled something indiscernible in its arms. The figure's inner light became complete and the warmth of it enveloped him.

Its face alternated from male to female, as did the imposing form of its body. The clothing seemed draped over and inside it, all one piece. The white was so pure the color of it was almost blinding to behold. It drifted down to his level in the mud and rested on its knees before him. Coltan saw its eyes were gold as amber and firelight.

It presented something wrapped in a soiled pallid blanket. When it spoke to him, its voice was both masculine and feminine at the same time. "Hold him in your arms, Coltan."

He didn't want to take it. Whatever was inside the blanket was something he couldn't confront; he knew it. He knew it without a doubt.

The female voice said gently, "Take him."

"I can't." Yet, his arms opened to accept the strange offering. His arms opened to accept it under their own power. He had no control over his actions.

The entity placed the bundle in his arms and, through the masculine voice, commanded, "Open the blanket."

The bundle was heavier than he expected. It felt like a small human body, a small and lifeless human body. He opened the blanket and looked. It was a child, a boy. A light shone upon him, exposed the bruises, scrapes, lacerations, burns and dried blood. The child was limp and dead, yet still warm. He wondered how a dead body could still be so warm. He recognized the hair, the shape of the face, the softly curved jaw line and the delicate chin that would square slightly in maturity.

Compassion and grief overwhelmed him. His sudden uncontrollable tears flooded down his face and dropped onto the face of the boy in his arms. Sobbing, he brought the child tenderly to his chest and rested the small face against his shoulder. He rested his cheek upon the child's brow and began to rock him.

"Why...?" Coltan questioned the suffering, the life of undeserved misery.

The boy took a breath and opened his eyes. He gazed at Coltan, and Coltan returned his gaze. Their eyes were the same.

The child whispered in a plaintive voice, "Let me go." His eyes closed, and he fell limp in Coltan's embrace, the life gone once more.

The entity reached for the boy. Coltan closed the blanket around the small battered body with paternal tenderness. As he transferred the child into the waiting arms, he felt peace slowly rise and grow within him.

The entity faded away.

Coltan sat there for a while, crying and praying, needing and wanting to release it all. He prayed for his mother. He forgave her and wished her peace. He reviewed his own crimes and sins and the circumstances behind it all. It was difficult, but he forgave himself. With this forgiveness, he also released the girl, a fellow casualty of his hellish existence, to complete her journey into the glory of God's embrace.

He didn't know what to think or say concerning the duplicate Self that attacked him. Another half hour's worth of pondering revealed to him the other Self was his rage. Still, he was at a loss as to what to do about it. As he ruminated over this, he saw an image of Jesus extending his hands to take it. Confident it was the only thing to do, he placed this other miserable Self into his Savior's hands.

The rain soaked through his clothing and chilled him. His drenched hair dropped icy water down his face and neck. He became aware of it gradually, as if he was awakening from a dream. The reality of the rain and cold helped him return to full lucidity. Physically, it was not pleasant. He was freezing. As much as he wanted to stand and find his jacket, he couldn't move. His legs were weak and refused to follow his brain's instructions. The cold settled into his bones and caused him to shiver uncontrollably. Still, he could not move.

He thought about what he had just experienced; the surreal world from which he'd seemingly awakened. In comparison to his present reality of the icy storm and the smell of pine, his dreamlike encounter with these strange spirits couldn't have happened. The logical part of him insisted he most likely hurt his head in the crash and suffered a temporary hallucination as a result. He remembered the gun, remembered pulling the trigger three times, only to have the damned thing jam each time. That could not have been real, either.

The events that brought him to this mountain returned to his memory. Natalie threw him out; she had done it for a good reason. He couldn't blame her. Now, he wondered what to do next.

His leather jacket landed in his lap, and it made him jump, startled. Before he could react or even consider the how of it, someone gripped his arm and pulled him up on his feet. That same someone spun him around to confront him.

Coltan met the stern gaze of his own eyes.

"Are you the Monster?" Coltan asked him.

The other Self paused before answering, and Coltan noticed the rage had vanished from his face. "Not anymore." He draped the jacket over Coltan's shoulders. "You made a promise to Brian."

In his self-absorption, Coltan had forgotten his promise. Now he thought Brian was a fool to ever depend on him to keep his daughter safe. After what happened tonight, how could Natalie ever trust him? Numbly and automatically, he put the jacket on and zipped it up as all his excuses not to return to her tumbled through his mind.

"For once in your life, focus on someone besides yourself!" His twin roughly turned him again in the direction of the spilled motorcycle.

He saw the Harley parked upright and facing the road in the direction of Bonito Valle. Coltan discovered his backpack still in its place secured to the luggage frame, and his helmet hung from the left handlebar. The headlamp illuminated the road.

Self gave him a gentle shove toward the bike, "She needs you."

Coltan looked back to tell him he would follow through. He was gone.

The air became still and quiet as death. Snowflakes began to drift down, lightly at first. After another minute, the flakes increased until it became a steady sprinkling of powder, as if someone had opened a shaker and turned it upside-down upon the earth.

He boarded the bike, took his helmet from the handlebar and put it on. The sight of the snow and its accompanying silence comforted him and filled him with serenity. He wanted to experience it a while longer and he hesitated to pull down the helmet's face shield. His glance caught sight of the key in the ignition. Yes, it was time to consider someone else's needs. He lowered the face shield and started the ignition. The Harley rumbled to life.

As he headed down the mountain in the silent, gently falling snow, he noticed his leg no longer hurt. His surroundings gradually felt eerily intangible, and he continued on his way in autopilot. Nothing seemed real except his desire to return to Natalie. He prayed she would accept him with forgiveness.

By the time he reached the bottom of the foothills and the dawn sent light into the gray-clouded sky, the events of that night had settled into him with certainty. It had all been real. God had heard him and healed him. God had forced him to confront his lingering demons and helped him settle it once and for all.

Coltan knew there would be more battles ahead, but these battles would not be personal; they would be on God's behalf. The knowing didn't frighten him or worry him. He understood God's reason for allowing him to endure the suffering of the past. He was ready for anything, now.

The snow became rain as he descended closer to the valley below. The rain came down harder. The wind picked up, blowing at his back.

Bonito Valle unfolded in the distance.

CHAPTER 11

D octor Renée Clausberg started the *Sesame Street* disk and powered the screen with the remote. As the theme music began, she observed the children in the cage. Their reactions to this vaguely familiar experience from their past would tell her if they could recall anything of their former lives before the mord virus.

Of the four children, the first to react to the music was the child she named Isabelle. Clausberg noted her initial reaction was to the sound of the familiar song, as Isabelle had her back turned away from the screen and had not seen the video yet. The doctor estimated this child to be about five years old. Isabelle suffered two bite wounds, one on her knee and the other on her buttocks. Blood stained her muddy and ragged flannel nightgown. She was among a group of seven others captured just outside Bonito Valle. There was a woman with her that had held her hand and tried to protect her after capture; this woman later died of infection from her many bite wounds and other injuries. Clausberg assumed the woman had been her mother, and they had escaped the *Mordant Rage* (as the eggheads called it), only to later become what they had fled.

Isabelle stood from her crouching position in the wall corner of the cage and nodded her head to the music. She began to hum along, not well, but she hummed what she remembered. When her wide brown eyes saw the image on the screen, she smiled and murmured a low growl. She stood watching for a while before she decided to sit Indian Style and enjoy the show for the duration. The sight of her made Clausberg recall her own childhood, sitting just that way on the carpet in front of the television while Mom made lunch.

The other three children were a little older.

Hans, an overweight, fair-skinned, blue-eyed boy with blond hair, Clausberg estimated at close to eleven years old. Clausberg named him Hans because he reminded her of a beer-guzzling boyfriend she had dated on holiday in Germany. Hans suffered a vicious bite on the back of his neck, the skin torn away. The wound now gaped with pus and an awful odor despite the antibiotics she had injected into him. By the reddish hue of his skin, the doctor could tell he was running a fever and would die soon. He had been lethargic ever since they had separated him from the adults. As Clausberg expected, Hans was not impressed with *Sesame Street* and remained lying on his belly near the front of the cage, tracing the cracks in the cement floor with his blood-encrusted fingers.

Rita Reynolds was ten years old, and captured with her brother Ryan, who was seven. Their mother or father had written their names and ages in permanent ink on their t-shirts. Each child had a note pinned into their pockets, the notes a pathetic request for someone to take them to the nearest shelter in the event they were orphaned. Apparently orphaned, Rita and Ryan were the only African Americans in the captured group, and the home address listed in their notes was in the south end of Bonito Valle where the population was predominantly people of color.

These two were interesting to Doctor Clausberg in that they arrived with something of a history. In addition to the notes, each child carried identical photographs of them with their parents, and someone had written on the back of the photos, *Ray and Jeanne with Rita and Ryan. These children have no other living relatives. Please try to keep them together.*

Upon arrival, the Reynolds children proved to be the most docile of the bunch and were easy to sedate for examination. It appeared one of the predatory mords who zeroed in on the two children bit Ryan first, crushed the boy's wrist while it feasted on his arm. Bruises on his left arm and scrapes on both his knees hinted at his attempt to escape. The doctors surmised the mords attacked Ryan and his sister in a crowd of refugees heading for the Red Cross Shelter by Bonito Valle Medical Center near the south end. Maybe some adult had managed to wrench the boy out of the grip of one or more of the monsters, and his sister took his hand and fled with him. The boy's bite wounds were old and highly infected. He had been in and out of a high fever for two days, now. His sister Rita had a bite wound on her hand, the small teeth imprints evidence another child bit her. The doctors figured most likely her little brother had delivered the bite a few days into their ordeal on the road. Rita's wound had not festered yet, but the telltale red line that followed an artery from the bite wound had already completed its journey to her brain where the virus did its damage erasing humanity from the unfortunate victim.

Rita ceased being human well over a week ago. Television and *Sesame Street* no longer impressed her in any way. She knelt at the front of the cage and put her hand through the bars, her palm upright, begging for food.

Hans saw this and did the same.

Doctor Clausberg retrieved a snack from the warmer for them. She dropped one tasty morsel into each upturned palm, one human finger for each. The doctor told them in a *baby voice*, "People Fingers...!" They ate voraciously.

She observed Ryan as the music caught his attention and he crawled on his hands and knees to sit beside Isabelle. He watched the screen.

Today's lesson was the letter B, as in *b...a...l...l...*, with a scene of a child bouncing a ball.

Isabelle pointed at the screen, "Ba..." She clapped and grinned. "Ba...!"

Clausberg turned to the two-way mirror on the wall behind her,

"Morris! You're getting this, I hope!"

Morris's deep voice came back over the intercom, "I've got it."

She glanced back at Isabelle, "She's the first one who's tried to talk."

"Get the ball out of the toy box," Morris suggested, "See if she'll play with it."

Clausberg found the small red ball and rolled it to Isabelle through the bars. Isabelle watched the ball bounce lightly against her knees and stop. She put her hand on it and looked at Clausberg with a perplexed expression. "Ball!" Clausberg said. Isabelle responded by snarling, drooling, smacking her lips and growling at her. The doctor walked away out of her view. Isabelle returned to watching *Sesame Street*.

Little Ryan crawled to the side of the cage and thrust his upturned hand through the bars. He screeched at the doctor to get her attention. When she looked at him, he wobbled his hand up and down and flexed his fingers, the palm upturned. He wanted a *People Finger*.

Doctor Clausberg told Morris through the two-way mirror, "I still think they can be trained."

She retrieved a People Finger from the warmer, and another ball from the toy box. When she returned to Ryan at the cage, she presented the finger in one hand, and the ball in the other. Ryan reached for the food. Clausberg pulled the treat away from his reach and offered him the ball. He screeched and leaned through the bars, tried to grab for the food. Clausberg rolled the ball to him. He pushed it back, and it rolled to her.

"Good!" the doctor said sweetly, "Good boy!"

She broke the finger in half. The overlaying skin stretched some and held the bones together at the second joint, and she had to tear at it to break it away into two pieces. The finger bled a little. She dropped one of the halves into Ryan's hand and watched him eat.

When he was done, he begged for the remaining half. She rolled the ball to him. He stopped the ball and stared at her dumbly. She stared back, wondering if he would get the idea. He came up on his knees and reached through the bars again for the treat, wobbling his upturned palm.

Clausberg again kept the treat out of reach but plainly visible. She pointed at the ball, "Ball, Ryan. Roll the ball to me."

He screeched angrily.

"Ball, Ryan. Ball!" She pointed again.

He gazed down at the ball, and then at her.

She patted her chest and pointed to the ball once more. "Give me the ball. Ball..."

He rolled the ball to her and watched her curiously, his eyes darting from her to the treat and back again. She offered him the treat, held it up to give it to him. He held out his hand for it. She dropped it into his hand. The whole thing went into his mouth, and he chewed it up and demanded another. She took another from the warmer and returned to him, held up the treat so he could see it. He reached. She rolled him the ball. He stopped it and rolled it back to her. When his eyes met hers, he grinned smugly and emitted a low growl.

"Good boy!" She exclaimed. She gave him the entire finger as a reward.

"Well, I'll be damned!" Morris said from behind the mirror.

Isabelle's ball came rolling out onto the floor beside Clausberg. Clausberg intercepted the ball and looked at Isabelle. Isabelle presented her hand for a reward.

Clausberg laughed.

"Well, I'll be *double* damned!" Morris remarked appreciatively.

"Told you!" Clausberg declared.

Morris entered the lab. He was a slight, thin man with a receding hairline and thick wire-rimmed glasses. Not as comfortable as the doctor with the grisly task of feeding "*the kids*," he used the set of tongs to retrieve a finger from the warmer. "We're getting low on these," he said.

"There's plenty more," the doctor assured him, "They killed two more prisoners this morning." She scooted over to Isabelle and sat before her on the floor, feeling protected by the bars and the distance between herself and the cannibal child. "Isabelle? Do you want to play ball with me?"

"Ba!" Isabelle uttered, "Ba! Ba! Ba!"

Without looking away from her subject, she ordered urgently, "Bring it to me, Morris." Morris handed it to her, keeping a safe distance. "Are the cameras still rolling?"

It was a stupid and insulting question. "Yeah," Morris replied.

She held up the bait and rolled the ball to Isabelle. Isabelle stopped it with both her little hands and gazed at the doctor. There was a strange glint in her eyes, as if she knew a secret and wouldn't reveal it. Not taking her eyes off the doctor, she rolled the ball through the bars to her.

Clausberg caught it as it rolled into her lap. "Good girl! Good girl, Isabelle!"

Isabelle scooted on her knees against the bars and presented her hand for her reward.

The doctor was impressed. "You're a smart one, aren't you...?" She leaned forward to drop the treat into the girl's hand.

Isabelle took the treat, but dropped it, just out of her reach. She looked up at Clausberg, sad and pleading. "Peep fing! Oh, no...! Peep fing!" She began to cry, gazing at the doctor with tragic and pitiful sorrow. "Peep fing. Gib. Peeze gib?" She pleaded with her big brown eyes fixed on Clausberg's. "Peeze...?"

Morris shook his head, "I'll be damned..."

Doctor Clausberg sat up on her knees, leaned forward and retrieved the People Finger. She held it up and showed it to Isabelle.

"Here it is, baby."

Isabelle smiled and clapped. She fixed her eyes on the doctor again and asked sweetly, "Peep fing, peeze? Gib? Peeze?"

Clausberg inched closer to the girl. She tried unsuccessfully not to grimace as the child's sulfurous stench assaulted her nostrils and stung her eyes. "Give me your hand."

Isabelle, with pleading eyes and pitifully quivering lips, stuck her hand halfway through the bars. She intoned softly and timidly, "Peeze? Gib?"

Feeling smugly empowered by the diseased child's meekness, the doctor reached to hand her the treat. Without warning, Isabelle seized her wrist in a deathlike grip and yanked her into the bars. She dropped the treat as the suddenly snarling child attempted with both hands to pull her arm through. Clausberg, her face pinned into the bars, her gaze pinned on the gaping drooling mouth targeting her bare wrist, began screaming and tugging, terrified and irate at the same time.

Morris retrieved the cattle prod from the corner of the room and hurried back to the cage. He saw the other three children had zeroed in on Clausberg's predicament, and were already at the bars with Isabelle, grabbing at the doctor, pulling her hair, her arms, whatever they could reach. Clausberg screamed and fought back, fought to free herself from the unexpectedly strong predators. Morris poked the prod through the bars and shocked Isabelle, sending her flying backwards, releasing Clausberg. The others saw what happened to Isabelle and quickly released the doctor and retreated out of harm's way. Clausberg reeled back and stumbled to her feet. Enraged and trembling, she hotly spun to Morris. "Give me that!" Morris handed her the prod. In a fury, she commanded, "Take her to the post! *Now*, Morris!"

Morris pressed the intercom button on the wall, "Disciplinary! Retrieval Team! Stat!"

Four big men wearing padded gloves and padded uniforms rushed into the lab. One was carrying a long pole with an adjustable leather loop at the end of it. Morris pointed at Isabelle, "That one!"

One of the men unlocked the cage, and all four entered it. Hans, Rita and Ryan went for the men. Three of the men fought them off easily and sequestered them into a corner of the cage while the fourth threw the loop over Isabelle's head. The loop dropped around her neck, and the man tightened it with the push of a button on the handle of the pole. Isabelle began screeching as the man dragged her out of the cage. She fell to her knees on the floor. The man dragged her to the post in the corner where he detained her while the other men exited and locked the cage. Without a word, they assisted him with Isabelle. One wrapped a mouth guard across her lips and secured it around her head so she couldn't bite, while the other two gripped her hands and restrained her wrists with the handcuffs that hung off the pole by a chain. Once they had completely restrained her, the one in charge of the neck pole released the loop and removed it. The four men stood back to watch the show and await their next orders.

Isabelle screamed through the mouth guard and furiously tried to tug herself free.

Clausberg approached her. "You little Mexican shit!" She circled the post and glared into Isabelle's terrified eyes, "Don't you ever try to fuck with *me!*" The doctor delivered the first jolt into Isabelle's shoulder. Isabelle screamed and her body shuddered with the pain. Clausberg upped the voltage and rounded to Isabelle's back. "Don't ever fuck with me!" She delivered jolt after jolt to the child's back and legs, fueled further by her screams of terror and agony.

The children in the cage shrieked and screeched. They pounded and tugged the bars as they watched the brutal punishment of one of their own.

Crying and sobbing through the mouth guard, Isabelle begged,

"Peeze! Peeze! No! Peeze! Be good! Peeze!"

Clausberg only tortured her more with the prod. "You will learn, bitch!" She stopped only long enough to address the monster children in the cage, "*You* will *all* learn! Watch and *learn*!" She delivered six more jolts; with the third of those six jolts, Isabelle fainted.

Clausberg spun to the Retrieval Team, "Wake her up!"

"Renée!" Morris protested, "She's had enough!"

"She will *learn*!" Clausberg yelled back. To the team, she ordered, "Wake her up!"

On the video screen, *Sesame Street* continued.

CHAPTER 12

At first, Natalie thought she imagined the sound of the Harley in the driveway. After grabbing Bonnie, she hurried down to her bedroom on the second floor and peered out the window. He sat there on the bike in the driveway, awaiting her decision for him to go or stay. He lifted the face shield and met her eyes questioningly. She grinned and waved, and was down the stairs and into the garage in less than a minute. She unlocked and raised the big door and watched him pull in, her heart pounding.

Coltan shut off the engine and removed his mud-splattered helmet. Raindrops dripped down the soiled black leather jacket; his jeans and boots were saturated. His damp hair was matted and spiked every which way, while some remained pasted to his head. Mud covered his hair, face, hands, jeans and boots. He was a sight.

"Are you okay?" Natalie asked.

He nodded. His eyes searched hers, begging forgiveness. "Are you okay?"

"Now I am!" She didn't give him the opportunity to dismount the bike before she wrapped her arms around him and kissed his cheek. "I'm so sorry! I'm sorry. Oh... I'm so glad you're back. I've been praying all night!" She held onto him tightly.

She reeked of wine and cigarettes, and he could tell she was drunk. It was evidence enough to answer his question of how she had spent the night. Her condition dismayed him. If this was how she dealt with one night of loneliness and vulnerability, how would she deal with the terrible condition of the world outside? Brian had been more than right in his assessment of Natalie as being too young and emotionally fragile to get through this alone. Coltan felt responsible.

He hugged her, "I'm sorry, too." He swung his leg over the seat to leave the bike, and she stepped back and gave him room. As he stood there looking at her, and she looking at him, there was silence between them. Even rip-roaring drunk, she was still pretty, and her red-rimmed eyes were full of relief and happiness. He wanted to lift her into his arms and carry her up the stairs where they would both be safe.

She unstrapped the backpack from the rack and hoisted it over her shoulder. In the next second, she headed into the kitchen. "Close up the garage," she called back to him.

In the attic, she set the pack on the floor next to his mattress. She grabbed two spare sleeping bags and prepared his bed for him. She was spreading out the second sleeping bag to serve as his blanket when he entered the room. He watched her, grateful for her forgiveness and touched by her effort to welcome him home.

Natalie finished and turned to him. After a moment, she said, "You're soaked. Get out of those clothes before you die of pneumonia."

He rummaged through his backpack. The clothing inside was damp. He couldn't wear any of it yet. He took it all out and spread it on the floor in the north room to dry, the room Natalie's parents reserved. After a glance around, he spotted a chest of drawers in a corner and found a set of sweats Brian or Beverly had stashed there. They were a little big for him, but they would do.

From the main room, Natalie asked loudly, "What happened to you out there?"

Coltan returned there with the sweats. She was draping his jacket over the back of a chair. "I got rained on and snowed on," he replied.

"How'd you get all muddy?"

"I slipped."

"Oh..." She started to clean his jacket with a paper towel. "Did you see anyone?"

"Not a soul." He didn't see any point telling her about his ethereal visitors. It was all too fantastic for anyone to believe.

"Where did you go?"

"I started up the mountain. I changed my mind when it started to snow." He approached her, took the paper towel out of her hand and set it on the table. She looked up at him, puzzled. Coltan embraced her, "You got a little drunk, girl."

"Just a little." She knew she was more than a little drunk. The room had been spinning around her for the past two hours. She had thrown-up twice, and now assumed her stomach was finally empty. Still, it was too risky to lie down and rest while everything around her continued to spin.

"I love you so much," Coltan said. "I will never, ever, do anything to hurt you, ever again. I promise. It's all done. Last night was it. That was the end of it. I'm sorry I hurt you."

She wrapped her arms tightly around him and rested her face against his chest. She had heard his promises before. This time she was determined he would make good on his *"that was the end of it"* promise. For now, she wanted him to rest and recover. "We'll talk about it later. Go get a shower. Get out of those wet clothes. I'll make you some coffee."

He only held her closer, "I want to hold you."

"I missed you."

"I missed you, too." He took her face in his hands and kissed her lips. She tasted like wine. It reminded him of some of the street girls, the runaways, he had kissed; only they tasted like pot along with the booze. He hoped this was the last time Natalie would ever get drunk.

She responded passionately to his warm lips pressing so firmly upon hers. She didn't care about his muddy hands and face or that he was getting her all muddy as he held her and kissed her. It was okay. It was all okay. He was back in her arms, and that was all that mattered.

He wanted her to know she had not caused any of his pain; she had only almost become another casualty of it, and he wanted to protect her from that. It was the reason he walked away from her so easily.

Coltan found Natalie asleep in a sitting position on her mattress when he returned from the shower. He went to her and sat down on his knees beside her. Her hair fell forward and obscured her face. He gently lifted her head so he could see her. There was mud on her cheeks from when he had kissed her. He tried to wipe it off, and it made her stir to semi-consciousness.

"You can't sleep sitting up." He told her humorously.

"The room stopped," she mumbled.

"Promise you'll never get drunk again."

"Promise."

"You're gonna hate yourself when you wake up." He had plenty of memories of past hangovers, none of them pleasant.

She said nothing in return. He situated her body into a comfortable slumbering position and draped the sleeping bag over her. She began to snore. He hated the sound of it; there was almost nothing more disgusting to him than the sound of a drunk snoring. He turned her on her side, and she breathed quietly.

His ordeal of the past twenty or so hours exhausted him. It seemed like a dream at this moment, although he knew without a doubt it had all been real. He still marveled at the miraculous healing of his right leg; surely, it had been broken in the wreck. Now it was fine and didn't hurt a bit.

The pillow under his head was a comfort, as was the warmth of the two sleeping bags. There was something about finally feeling warm after freezing for so many hours that made one easily surrender all to the warmth. Maybe it stemmed from a distant memory of the safety of the womb. Whatever the psychology behind it, Coltan appreciated this safe place and its homey comforts. Above all, he appreciated the sound and presence of a fellow human being; something about that also helped to allay his anxieties. It had never mattered before. He had always preferred to be alone. He wondered if this is what *normal* felt like.

Coltan shifted onto his back and stared at the ceiling. A strong scent of roses filled the room. He noticed the scent immediately and felt the energy of another being near him. It seemed to be above him, so he watched and waited, hoped he would finally be able to see it. The aroma of roses seemed to settle above and upon him. He felt warmth descend to his chest. A translucent veil of white gradually manifested and hovered inches above him.

Unafraid, he whispered, "Who are you?"

Something warm and gentle caressed his face and forced his eyes to close.

"Shhh..."

He felt his body weaken and fall limp, and deep serenity filled him. Sleep overcame him, a deep, dreamless respite.

CHAPTER 13

D octor Clausberg stood at the end of the bed and observed Isabelle. The tiny girl was asleep, an IV bag feeding antibiotics, vitamins and sedatives through a tube in her right arm. A urinary catheter safely drained her virus-laden urine into a sealed bag for disposal in the hazardous waste incinerator. The child was no threat to anyone at this moment. Clausberg had ordered full restraints and a leather muzzle to prevent any more episodes like the last one.

Because Isabelle had somehow managed to retain her ability to speak, the doctor decided this one was worth keeping around for further study. And she was smart, too. Any child who could think, plan and deceive as Isabelle had done would be valuable in the team's research into the psychology of the mordants.

Near Isabelle's bed were five incubators that held infected babies. Until they grew teeth, the babies were also no threat. However, Clausberg and her team had discovered something interesting about the babies; they refused uninfected mother's milk. This necessitated isolating their mothers in restraints in another room, and using a breast pump to extract their milk for their babies. The only food the babies desired besides infected breast milk was warm uninfected human blood.

Clausberg considered this discovery exciting. To her it meant the mordants had metamorphosed into an entirely new species of human-like creature. This led her to consider all the possible uses for this new species. If they could be subdued and trained, if they developed a sense of loyalty to their *keepers*, they had the potential to become superior (and disposable) soldiers.

Back in the early days, when she and Carl Dunwalde first got wind of the existence of the virus, they had discussed this. It was too bad Dunwalde got stupid and invited Tyrone Flynn onboard. Clausberg had warned against it, knowing the UEF, United Earth Federation, was hot on his ass to retrieve the virus. Did Dunwalde listen? Hell, no! Dunwalde was thirsty for power, and Flynn held the beverage of choice in a triple-sealed test tube. With the capture and subsequent executions by the UEF of Dunwalde, Flynn and all the other higher-ups in their organization, Clausberg was the only officer remaining. The task of bringing down the UEF was now up to her.

Guffy entered the room and stood at attention. No matter how erect he stood, the early onset of arthritis and degenerative disk disease shortened his spinal column and caused his gut to protrude. Only thirty-two years old, Guffy had battled health problems all his life. Abandoned at the age of three, he bounced from one foster home to another until the System abandoned him at the age of eighteen. If it hadn't been for Clausberg taking pity on him, he would not have a job and would not have the tiny bit of freedom that job gave him; Clausberg would have ordered him carted off to the camps and exterminated with all the other *undesirables*.

He saluted her, "You wanted to see me, Doctor?"

"Good morning, Guffy." She didn't look at him, but kept her eyes on Isabelle. "How is your arthritis today?"

"Bearable, ma'am."

"Are you low on medication?"

"Yes, ma'am."

"Have any more babies been born?"

"Last night, ma'am." He was still saluting.

Clausberg finally turned to him and saw this. "For Christ's sake, Guffy! At ease!" She waited until he put his arm down. "How many?"

"One. But one of the males stole it from the mother and killed and ate it."

"Too bad." She thought about it for a second. It was common for primates in the wild to eat their young, something about eliminating the competition for mating. "So, they eat their own, do they?"

"Yes, they do." He added an afterthought he considered important, "The babies. The males eat the babies."

This didn't surprise her. "Are there any more pregnancies?"

"Not as far as I can tell."

"I've been looking over your reports. You don't seem to think the adults can be trained. Is that so?"

"Yes, ma'am. The teenagers are also untrainable. As a matter of fact, the teens are more vicious than the adults. If you ask me, I think the teens should be killed before they get out of hand."

"I didn't ask you."

"No, ma'am..."

"I understand the weather has been very hard on your health."

"Yes, ma'am."

"Would you like an inside job?"

"Very much." It could be shoveling shit, for all he cared, as long as it got him out of the cold and damp.

"How would you like to study one of our child subjects?"

"Study?"

"Observe and report. I have a special case in mind." She smiled at him. She knew he would jump at the chance, and she knew she could trust him.

"I'm interested."

The doctor gestured at Isabelle. "This one talks. She's also a conniving little bitch, and very dangerous."

Guffy approached the bed and took a long look at the child. He was surprised to see how clean she was, and he assumed someone had bathed her while she was under heavy sedation. Upon further observation, he noticed the IV set up and the urinary catheter bag.

The urine in the bag was brown. Guffy wasn't sure what to make of that. He surmised her urine contained a great deal of blood from all the warm human flesh she consumed. Another explanation he considered was the existence of the virus in her system; maybe it darkened the urine. Guffy wondered if anyone had tested her urine for the virus. Someone must have.

Her skin appeared pale within the frame of tangled long wavy black hair, and there was the hint of a peaceful smile on her lips. The innocence of her sleeping little face stirred his compassion for her. If Guffy had not known better, he would have taken her to be a normal child. "She's a pretty little thing."

"And very dangerous," Clausberg reiterated. "Her bite wounds have become infected. We've lost most of the children to gangrene. Dirty little creatures. Kids are wandering disease carriers, you know. I never particularly liked them—snotty, filthy little things—dirty hands and faces. They always smell like dirt to me. Do they smell that way to you?"

"Only the infected ones."

"Hmmm..." She shrugged, "Must be me."

NATALIE POURED A CUP of tea for Coltan and one for herself. She stood near the table for a few moments and observed him as he awakened. In all the time they spent together, she had come to recognize the subtle indications of him awakening; the rhythm of his breathing would change, he would turn over a couple of times, would wipe at his face, sigh, turn over on his back, and finally his eyes would open and he'd peer sleepily at the ceiling until his sleepiness faded away into wakefulness. He was now at the *peering at the ceiling* stage. In a couple of seconds, he would sit up and roll his head from side to side, stretching his neck muscles to relax out the cricks. Natalie waited for this. Here came the *uncricking* part. She approached him as he blinked and smiled warmly at her.

"You slept for over twelve hours," she told him as she sat down beside him. "No nightmares, either." She offered him his mug, "Thought you might like some tea."

He took it from her, "Thanks." She appeared pale and tired to him. "Hung over?" he asked.

"I'm better than when I first woke up." She grinned self-consciously.

"Gonna get drunk again?"

"Never!"

"You were scared being alone?"

"I didn't think I'd be, but I was." Her expression became serious, "You can't tell me you weren't, either. We've really come to depend on each other, haven't we?"

"Yeah." He sipped his tea and tried to recollect details of the previous night. He recalled being more angry, hopeless, and despondent than frightened. He didn't want to tell her, instead let her assume she was correct about the fear. As for their mutual dependence, he agreed with her.

She noticed something different about his face. It took her awhile to identify what had changed. The tension, the hardness of deep underlying rage, was gone. For the first time since she had known him, he was completely relaxed. There was something else, as well: he actually looked rested instead of worn. His eyes exhibited clarity and brightness formerly only present when he studied his Bible and prayed. All this gave him the appearance of someone younger than eighteen; there was an almost childlike innocence and openness to his entire demeanor.

"Something happened to you last night." She had to say it.

He thought she was talking about his display of temper, "Natalie... I'm sorry about that. I told you I'm sorry."

"I don't mean that," she said quickly, "You *look* different."

"What do you mean?"

"*You're* different..." She couldn't explain it. "What happened to you out there?"

It was too fantastic to reveal. He copped out, as usual. "Rain and snow."

Natalie was disappointed with him. "You don't want to tell me." She rose and went to her own mattress and sat. With a comfortable distance between them, she vented. "I'm so sick of this. You and your frickin' secrets. I'm sick of it. All we have left is each other, and you refuse to trust me!"

"Jeeze..." Coltan whined, "I just woke up." He spotted the cigarette pack on the floor between their mattresses, and he removed one and lit it. That felt better. "Lemme wake up." His attention returned to the pack of cigarettes. He counted the remainder. "Are we almost out of these?"

"We have two cases left."

"We'd better cut down."

"I wish you'd talk to me."

Why did women always want to talk? They wanted to discuss anything and everything. It was so different between men. With men, a grunt or an offhanded gesture was communication enough; at least, that was his experience with the men he had known. Except Brian. Brian was a *discusser.* Coltan realized this probably ran in their family. The Danburys were the vanishing model of the family unit that discussed their day and everything else around the supper table.

He sighed, feeling defeated. Her feelings were hurt, and it was his fault. Unsure how to explain the phenomenon on the mountain, he plunged ahead regardless. "God answered me last night."

Thank you, God. "What happened?"

"He made me confront myself, and I finally resolved things. It was painful, but I did it." He sat forward and looked at her intimately and honestly. "It's all done. It's all gone. That's what happened." The expression on her face told him she wanted the details. He took a deep breath and began. "You're gonna find it hard to believe exactly what happened, but I'm gonna tell you. I'm gonna tell you because I want you to understand how deeply it affected me. This is for keeps, Nat. I'm never going back to the way I was."

He gave her his account of what happened. She listened, and she believed him; the light in his eyes, in his face, the timbre of his voice—it all lent credibility to his story.

Coltan concluded with an affirmation, "God is real. He's real, Natalie. Never doubt."

"How can I ever doubt again?" Natalie responded, "His light shines from within you. I can see it."

This presented an opportunity for him to not only avow their belief in God, but also for Coltan to symbolically prove his love for her. "Stay right here," he told her as he arose. He had rediscovered the items a few days ago when he was rearranging his belongings for the long haul there. He took them from the front pocket of his Bible case and returned to her, the items concealed in his clutched hand.

"Remember that first night you and I talked? You mentioned something about your faith not being as strong as it used to be." She nodded, and he continued. "Well, I was thinking about that the next morning. So when we were out, and you were at the drug store, I made a side trip on the way to the lumber yard." She still said nothing, so he pushed on. "I know this lady, a street vender, who makes and sells her own stuff. Well, I knew she made something special for a select group of people. So, anyway... I got there just when she was closing up. She still had them."

"What is it?"

He opened his hand to reveal two leather necklaces, both identical. Tied to the leather cords were pewter crosses. Coltan commanded her attention to the detail on one, "See, the cross is made of two little nails, nails like they used back then. I thought it would remind you of his love for you."

"You got this for me?"

"Yeah. I got me one, too. I was gonna give it to you that day, but in all the confusion—you remember how it was—I forgot they were in my pocket. After that, I couldn't find the right opportunity, so..." He held it up for her, "Do you like it?"

"I love it." She reached for it.

"Let me put it on you." She ducked her head, and he placed the necklace on her. The leather chord was a bit too long. He leaned close to her, "Here. I'll adjust it so it fits better." He untied and retied the leather so the necklace fit securely. When he looked at her, he saw her eyes were bright with happiness at his thoughtfulness. He went to put his on, "I'll wear mine, too."

"Let me put it on you," she offered, "I want to." He handed it to her and she tenderly placed it over his head and draped it around his neck. It fit him perfectly. "There," she said.

"It's also my promise to you." Coltan placed his fingers under her chin and tilted her face up to see her eyes. "I promise we'll always stay together. I promise to always love you. As God is my witness."

The love in his eyes and in his voice washed over her and through her. It lingered within, and she felt it take root. Her words tumbled out breathlessly, "I love you so much." She slowly embraced him, her eyes never leaving his, "I love you forever, Colt. Forever."

He kissed her lips, kissed her face and her hands, kissed her face and her lips again. "Forever," he whispered, "My Natalie..."

CHAPTER 14

The snow was coming down heavily outside the refuge. Those who could work found plenty to do inside.

Carolyn handed another book up to Ian on the ladder. Thanks to her efforts, the library was now organized and inviting. Not only had she numbered all the books in her own version of the Dewy Decimal System, she had also organized the furniture into comfortable lounging areas, study areas and workstations. This project had given her a newfound sense of self-worth and purpose. For the first time in her short fifteen-year life, she was happy.

The current batch of books had to do with gardening and landscaping. It reminded her of Natalie, and she had been wondering about her all day. She had prayed for Natalie's safety. After she had prayed for Natalie, another person came to mind and she felt compelled to pray for him, too. She didn't know why she should pray for Harley Guy; he was probably dead. If he wasn't dead, maybe he had hit the road for parts unknown—a dangerous decision. As she thought more about him, she couldn't picture him surrendering to the authorities; he didn't seem the type of person who would submit quietly. After considering further, she pictured him kicked back on a beach somewhere, downing a six-pack, the Harley parked nearby, and him glad humanity was finally getting its due. Why God encouraged her to pray for him, she didn't understand. Still, she would obey God as best as she could. So, she prayed for Harley Guy, too. When she finished praying for him, she regretted she had never gotten the opportunity to jump his bones. Whether it was imagination or female instinct, she was certain he would have been worth the effort.

Ian descended the ladder, "Wake up, you!" He was teasing her out of her daydream. "Are you on break, lass?"

She loved it when he called her *lass*. "We could use a break. How about a coffee?"

"Yuck! You Yanks an' your coffee..." He wrinkled his nose.

She noticed he had grown a couple of inches over the winter and was now her height. His face had taken on the more mature appearance of a young man, and his body was beginning to develop muscle. She found herself often stealing glances at him. Sometimes, they made eye contact, and his blue-green eyes caused her to feel weak inside. Surely, he had noticed her blush. However, always the gentleman, he said nothing about it. Carolyn wished all boys could be as gentlemanly as Ian.

"We do have tea, you know." Just to tease him, she added, "Unless you and Trevor drank it all."

He grinned at her. He loved their bantering; she was a good sport. And pretty, too. She also had a good sense of humor. Humor was important to him.

However, this morning she seemed preoccupied, and he wondered if anything was wrong. He decided to ask in his own roundabout way, "You're missin' someone, ay?"

"Is it that obvious?"

"You've 'ad a far off look all mornin', lass."

"I've been wondering about my friend Natalie. Her folks, too. I hope they're alright. I told you about them. Remember?"

"That I do." He gazed at her sympathetically, "We'll keep 'em in our prayers. God willin', they'll turn up."

"Do you still think about your family, Ian?"

"They're in God's 'ands."

"Do you still think about them?"

"Every moment of every day."

"Why don't I think about *my* folks anymore?"

"Per'aps it 'urts." His own memories still made him ache for his family. Why wouldn't Carolyn's?

His insight impressed and touched her. "I think that's true. You're very wise, you know."

His face reddened slightly. No one had ever called him wise before. No one besides her had ever taken anything he said seriously. On impulse, he took her hand and kissed her cheek.

Carolyn wasn't sure how to react or what to do in return. He began to release her hand, and she didn't want him to. After a quick glance around to make sure no one was looking, she held onto his hand and briskly kissed his lips.

His face reddened more. "Oh, my..." he stammered, "Well there, lass..."

"Was that wrong?" She bit her bottom lip, her eyes begging pardon if she had misinterpreted and overstepped their boundaries.

"No..." He glanced away until he gathered his courage to meet her gaze. "It's quite well. Quite well, y'know."

For the first time in her life, she felt shy.

They strolled over to the commissary and sat down at a small table with their beverages. The lunch hour had ended over an hour ago, but the place was still a mess, and the crew was cleaning up.

Trevor entered and poured a cup of hot tea. He spotted the two teens. It seemed to him they had become an almost inseparable pair over the last two months, and he thought it was lovely. However, he had an image to uphold, so he approached them with his usual laid-back approach.

"Taking a ten, are we?" He winked at Ian to tell him he knew. Ian blushed.

"What's it to you?" Carolyn shrugged him off. She had never particularly liked Trevor. He came off as arrogant and condescending to her.

"Still sassy, there." He grinned, "You're quite the hard one, ay?"

Ian intervened before the inevitable tennis match of insults could start between them. "Say, Trev. Any more troops arrived today?"

He joined them without invitation. "Ten more. We lost fourteen along the way."

"The sickness?" Ian was certain.

"Some. The storm took others." Trevor sipped his tea and leaned back in his chair. "Will you be a soldier, Ian?"

"If God wants." He responded bravely.

Trevor eyed Carolyn, "And you, miss?"

"I'm the Librarian. That's good enough, isn't it?"

He smirked, "Carolyn the Librarian. Got a ring there."

She replied dryly, "Very funny. You're an ass, Trevor."

He looked at her seriously. "Some day this ass might save your ass."

"I doubt it," Carolyn challenged, "You'll probably run away screaming with your short little legs pumping away as fast as they can."

"Oy!" Ian exclaimed. "What venom!"

Trevor winked again and grinned at Ian, "She likes me."

"Excuse me while I puke..." Carolyn replied.

To Ian, he remarked, "She's a handful. More than a little spark. I could fall in love with her, y'know."

"Oh, barf!" Carolyn exclaimed.

"Thought you loved the doctor," Ian reminded him.

This shut him up. He thought no one knew about it. He and Suzanne had been careful to conceal their relationship.

Carolyn said, "Ian knows everything that goes on around here. Lucky for you, he's not one to talk about it."

Trevor leaned forward in his chair and said in a low voice, "Mum's the word."

Carolyn warned him, "Of course, *I* can be *careless*."

"Which means?"

"I heard they want to transfer me to Barracks Prep Committee." No way could Carolyn picture herself making beds and stocking cases and cases of toiletries and linens for the incoming troops. In the old days when life was normal, she had never kept up her own room at home. It was like housework. She hated housework. She was happy in the library and wanted to stay there. She leaned close to Trevor's face, "Get me out of it. I want to stay at the library. That's my job. Get me out of Barracks Prep, and I'll keep my mouth shut."

Trevor confidently assured her, "Consider it done." He admired her. He had never been able to intimidate her.

"Consider your secret safe." The corners of her lips turned up slightly in a satisfied smile.

"Ho...!" Ian whispered in a sigh. She was quite the bird, all right.

The chiming of the intercom system caught their attention and silenced them. A female voice came over:

"Joseph Davidson. Please report to Processing. Stat. Joseph Davidson. Please report to Processing. Stat."

Ian knew Joe was working in the infirmary today, as he did most days. The Processing Unit served new refugee arrivals and incoming Army of Christ troops where James's personnel welcomed, re-scanned and interviewed them. They provided tents and supplies to the refugees, also any needed medical care. The process for the military varied. Trevor told him they double-checked each soldier's identification documents, photographed them, gave them new dog tags and assigned them to barracks; those ill or injured went to the hospital. The only reason they would need Joe in the Processing Unit would be if someone turned up sick. Many had arrived ill, and it was not the mord virus, but something similar.

"Another sick one," Ian remarked worriedly.

"Not to worry," Trevor said, "Probably the Flu, or pneumonia.

No one with the mord virus gets past the edges of the compound. Not a one. Not to worry, Ian."

"Joe said they've been dyin'," Ian replied, "And, no one knows what they've got. It's somethin' new. Have you seen any of 'em, Trev?"

"What the hell are you goin' on about?"

"Some of the troops are showin' up sick. Not the Flu. It's somethin' else. Joe keeps his gob shut about it, on orders, y'know. But I over'eard 'im tell Darla it's bad. *Fatal*." Ian paused and looked from Trevor to Carolyn and back to Trevor, "So far, it 'asn't spread to the rest of us. They think it might be blood-borne or sexually transmitted—to the ones that don't got bites, I mean."

"Bites?" Carolyn gasped. "From people? Like the mord virus?"

"I don't know. I couldn't get all of what 'e said. 'e was whisperin' it, so the children wouldn't 'ear it." Again, he looked to each in turn, "We must keep this under wraps."

Trevor had not heard about this. He wondered if James knew. James had to know. Why hadn't he mentioned it? To Ian, he stated, "You keep on this, lad."

"I will." Again, he looked to each in turn, his eyes serious and a bit frightened, "Just the three of us, ay?"

Trevor and Carolyn said in unison, "Ay."

CHAPTER 15

"Isabelle? Would you like a peep fing?" Guffy sat down at the side of the bed and balanced the small plate on his lap. With tongs, he held up one of the two severed fingers.

Isabelle's arms and hands were still strapped to the bed railings, and she did not like it at all. Her back and her buttocks hurt from being in the same position for so long. Her mouth was sore, too, from the leather muzzle. She turned her head sideways and peered innocently at Guffy. Through the muzzle she managed, "Uh-huh, peeze."

Guffy set the plate on the nightstand and the tongs on the plate. He rose and leaned over the little girl. "In order for you to eat, I hafta remove your muzzle. If I do that, do you promise not to bite me?"

Isabelle nodded. This man was the only person in the whole place who treated her with kindness. She was used to his voice and the gentleness of his touch when he comfortingly patted her bound hand. His inquiry about the biting upon muzzle removal was part of the feeding routine, and she wished she could tell him he didn't need to remind her. As tasty as he smelled, she knew better than to bite her only friend.

Guffy leaned and began to unbuckle the straps to free her mouth from the muzzle. He maintained eye contact with her the whole time. "Remember, you promised. Don't bite Uncle Guffy, now. Don't bite me." He moved the muzzle away and drew his hands back quickly.

Isabelle licked her parched lips. "Peep fing? Peeze, Duff?"

"Guffy," He corrected her, "Uncle Guffy."

"Unka Duffy..." She said slowly. "Unka..."

"Close enough." He smiled warmly at her, and she returned his smile. For a moment, he forgot she was a dangerous monster and not a benign child.

"Unka, unka..." Isabelle said it with enthusiasm and a little bit of affection.

"Yeah. Unka Guffy."

"Unkaduffy..." It was now one word. She giggled at herself.

Guffy grinned and chuckled, "You little silly..."

Her eyes widened and brightened, "Peep fing?"

He took the plate and offered her one with the tongs, "Yeah. Peep fing." He placed the tongs close enough to her mouth so she could bend her head and use her teeth to take the people finger from its grip. She chewed, and the bones made crunching sounds in her mouth. That sound always made Guffy cringe inside.

"Mmmm!" she voiced her approval as she chewed, ground, and swallowed. "Good! More?" She ran her tongue over her upper front teeth to clean them. Her breath smelled like roadkill. "Peep fing, Unkaduff?"

"In a minute. Don't want you to throw up like last time." He patted her hand, "You eat too fast, girly. Gotta slow down. Enjoy your food."

"Taco!"

This surprised him. "You remember tacos?"

"Beefincheeze...!" All one word again. The memory was pleasant.

"Would you like to eat a taco?"

"No! Peep fing!"

That was bad news. He decided to change the subject and prompt her memory to see how much she recalled. "Do you remember your mama?"

"Mama...?" Her eyes became sad, "Bad hoot. No wake up."

"What about your daddy?"

"Dale. In dale."

Guffy had to think for a minute to realize *dale* meant *jail* in Isabellespeak. The kid must have had a hard life in her five short years. He felt sorry for her. "That's okay," he whispered to her, "You got Uncle Guffy now."

Isabelle began to sing softly, "Deezus uvs da iddle chill-den, aw da chill-den of da wood..."

"That's very, very good!"

Isabelle grinned, "Sing, unka!"

"I can't sing..."

She nodded each word of the lyric, "Deezus uvs da iddle chill-den..."

In a whisper, he joined her as she sang the next lyric, "All the children of the world."

She lifted her eyes to the ceiling and back to Guffy, "Deezus... Deezus see..."

His heart melted inside his chest, "Jesus. Yes. Jesus sees you." He said it softly, so Clausberg wouldn't pick it up on the monitor. She thought all religion was crap. He didn't want her to know he had accepted Jesus as his Savior years ago. It was his secret, and no one knew. Isabelle's comment made him think about Jesus. He wished Jesus would take the little girl out of this mess and out of her suffering. If he was truly watching her, how could he stand to see what has become of her? What possible reason could there be in keeping her alive to be tortured by Clausberg's experiments?

Guffy felt a strong impulse to smother the girl with the pillow and be done with it.

"Peep fing? Peeze? Peeze, unka?"

He offered it to her, "This is the last one for now."

She ate it, chewed it slowly this time. When she was done, she said, "Good food!"

"Good..." Guffy said. He didn't know what was good about it.

The child was eating a piece of a human body, for cryin' aloud.

"I hoot," She wiggled her torso under the sheet. "Butt hoot. Ow..."

"Would you like to lie on your side for a while?"

"Peeze?"

"Promise not to bite me?"

"Unkaduffy no food." She said it as if he should have known it all along.

"Are you saying you don't want to eat me?"

"No eat." She wiggled again and whined, "Duff, peeze hep. Peeze... hoot."

Over the intercom came Clausberg's voice, "Don't do it, Guffy!"

"She's in pain!" Guffy replied loudly.

"They don't feel pain! Not like us, anyway..."

He cussed under his breath. He looked apologetically at Isabelle, "I'm sorry, honey."

Clausberg's voice again, incredulous, "*Honey*?"

"Whaddaya expect? She's a little kid!"

"She's a monster. Don't ever forget it!"

Isabelle peered at Guffy conspiratorially, and whispered, "Mean... kew mean bit. Hoot me. Mean... mean...."

"Shhh," he cautioned her in a whisper.

"What'd she say?" Clausberg inquired.

"She says she hurts."

"She's lying. She's trying for your sympathy. Don't be an idiot."

To this, Isabelle had only one more whispered comment, "Hate 'er... *Ella es muerto*..."

NATALIE OPENED ALL the sliders to let the overcast daylight into the attic. The wind blew the rain against the south window, and the dampness loosened the scotch tape over the bullet holes. Coltan replaced the tape while Natalie napped.

With the exception of the evergreens, the trees outside were bare skeletons. There was not a hint of budding on any of them yet, which indicated spring was still far away. He watched the rain descend in a heavy downpour and wistfully recalled one day when he laid down in the mud and let the rain cover him. Coltan estimated he was maybe four or five at the time, and his mother had punished him for getting his clothing muddy. It had been worth it to him; the rain and mud served as instant therapy, a way of connecting with something that would not hurt him, a method by which he savored God's creation. Of course, he was unaware of it at the time; the knowledge would come years later during this introspective moment.

God's *berceuse*. How he loved the rain. He longed to go out and lie in the mud and let the rain wash through him once more. Only, this time, he wanted to do it without the clothing. He stole a glance at Natalie. Would she miss him for five or ten minutes? She had not stirred in an hour. Perhaps he could get away with it.

Natalie turned over and opened her eyes. Her gaze fell upon him at the window.

Perhaps not.

"Hey..." she said, "Still raining?"

"Yeah." He went over and sat down beside her, "You want me to make coffee?"

She sighed and sat up, "I don't know. I think I'd like a smoke."

Coltan took two from the pack and handed her one. He lit hers first and watched her as she inhaled that first satisfying drag. Her hair was tousled, and there was a crease line on her cheek from the pillow. Her cheeks had a pink hue, and her cheeks were always that color when she first awakened. Half-awake and half-with it, she was so cute and so sexy to him. She had no idea. It didn't help she was not wearing a bra, and the thin long-sleeved nightshirt she wore revealed more than she was aware. For a fleeting moment, Coltan pictured himself caressing her nipples.

Mister Dolce rose to attention and told him, *"Go for it, dude!"*

Coltan thought back to it, *"Naw... let her wake up, first."* So she wouldn't notice he casually draped one arm across his lower torso to conceal his arousal.

"I dreamed of the green lake again," Natalie said reflectively.

He had had a similar dream a few times. "That's a nice dream."

"I wish summer was here. I'd like to go swimming."

He found that peculiar. The world was vastly different than it had been since last summer. The summers she had known would never be again. Maybe she was still half-asleep and had forgotten.

In his dreams of the green lake, he swam without fear. His reality was different. "I never learned how to swim." He said.

"Never?"

"Nope."

"I'll teach you."

"If we find a safe place," he remarked hopefully.

Reality returned, and she pouted. "Forgot about that."

"That's okay." He caressed her hand with his fingertips. Her skin was smooth, warm and soft. She turned her hand over, wordlessly invited him to caress her palm. He did so, feeling as much pleasure as she. After a couple of minutes, he let his fingertips drift up to her wrist, then up her arm to just below the fold of her elbow. She breathed in slowly and deeply and closed her eyes.

Mister Dolce reminded him he was more than ready, willing and able.

Be patient...

She opened her eyes and took another drag off her smoke. He shifted his position and reclined against the wall beside her, propped the extra pillow behind him for padding. The rain seemed louder and more persistent. What else was there to do on a day such as this?

"I wish you hadn't stopped," she said.

He put his arm around her and encouraged her to lean against him. They shared the ashtray and listened to the rain. As an afterthought, he draped the sleeping bag over his legs and his lap.

She broke the silence. "I already saw it."

"Saw what?" He hoped she didn't mean Mister Dolce.

She patted his leg and smiled at him suggestively. He shifted uncomfortably. "Don't worry about it," she said. He stared across the room at the sky through the window. He was a little embarrassed. She put out her cigarette, nuzzled into his chest, and wrapped both her arms around his waist. After a moment, she caressed his tight abdomen through his sweatshirt, and the pleasure of it made him sigh.

He snuffed out his cigarette.

Natalie continued to caress his abdomen. She loved the feel of his tight muscles, even more the smooth skin beneath the sweatshirt. Her hand found its way underneath seemingly of its own volition. She wondered if he would protest, but he did not. He closed his eyes and enjoyed her touch. When he relaxed in surrender as her fingers lightly stroked his chest, she knew she had caught him at the right moment.

He embraced her tightly and kissed the back of her neck. She trembled slightly and sighed with a wavering breath. As he pressed the tip of his tongue lightly against her skin as he kissed her there again, she completely submitted to him. He caressed her shoulders and slowly brought his fingers to her upper chest and unbuttoned a few buttons; just enough so he could ease her nightshirt down to expose her shoulders and arms for his loving touch and his eager lips. Her skin smelled faintly of flowers, and the lotion was sweet on his tongue as he tasted and explored her neck, back and shoulders. Her barely perceptible moans encouraged him and excited him as she sank weakly on her belly over his lap. She began to remove her nightshirt as she lay there, and he did not want that yet.

"No," he breathed into her ear, "Let me do it. When it's time. Let me do everything." She murmured something. He stroked her hair and kissed her cheek, "Let me love you right. Let me do everything." She relaxed and sighed quietly. Ever so slowly, he continued to caress her skin with feather light fingertips as he whispered to her, "There's no hurry. Let me take you slowly, very slowly. Love you with everything in my soul." He whispered passionately, "*Mon belle ange! Mon belle ange...*" His lips brushed her cheek, and his breath skimmed her neck, "My beautiful angel..."

MITCHELL WAS BORED watching the surveillance cameras. "No new arrivals in over two weeks," he commented.

Glenda glanced at him, "Maybe they can't get through. This is the worst winter we've ever had up here."

Trevor watched the monitors over Mitchell's shoulder. "Hopefully, the rest will make it by spring."

"If we have a spring," Glenda said pessimistically.

"Don't give up hope, now..." he counseled.

"Any more come down sick?" Mitchell asked.

"No. Apparently, it's not airborne." Trevor scratched his chin, "The last one died two days ago."

"What the hell is it?" Mitchell again.

Trevor shrugged. "No one knows. The only thing most of them had in common was animal bites. One said he'd lost his whole team to a pack of wolves." He settled in Roger's chair. Roger's absence occurred to him after a few moments. "Where's the corn chip lad?"

"Oh... Roger?" Glenda yawned, "He's teaching a computer class today."

"Quite a wiz, is he?"

Glenda smiled, "Quite a wiz." Something on the screen caught her eye and she turned her full attention there. She sat up and stared. "Whoa... whoa!"

Mitchell and Trevor both shot up and checked Glenda's monitors.

"Hard to tell," Glenda said, "Looks like he's wearing two or three coats. Is that a hat on his head?"

"Looks like it," Mitch said.

The figure in the snow trudged slowly and carefully up the path about a mile east of the refuge. It was difficult to see the person through the snowfall, but they could make out the footprints behind the traveler.

"Male or female?" Glenda wondered aloud.

"Can't tell..." Mitch squinted at the screen. He looked closely at the footprints. They looked deep, which indicated a heavier weight than the average woman. "A guy, I think."

"He's wearing sunglasses," Trevor observed, "Right smart of 'im."

"A local, maybe?" Glenda glanced at each man in turn.

The stranger stumbled and fell on his face. They waited for him or her to get up, but the person stayed down. After a moment, the person moved and rolled over on his back and sat up.

Trevor stood. "I'll alert the team."

GUFFY WAITED UNTIL Clausberg went out on break to give Isabelle some relief from her restriction and subsequent pain. He unbuckled her left arm and hand from the railing, and then helped her turn over on her side.

"Okay?" he asked her.

"Tankoo, unka." The little girl was weaker than he expected.

He spoke to her as he secured her free hand to the right side railing, "I hate to do it, kid, but I have to. Safety, you know."

"Unka no food," Isabelle reminded him.

"Let me check your back. Okay? Your back hurts?"

"Butt, too." Isabelle grimaced, "Ow... Oh, Unkaduffy... hoot."

He went over to the left side of the bed where he could get a clear view of her back and buttocks. She had bedsores. Fetid brown liquid saturated the moisture retardant pad underneath her buttocks.

It reeked. She had suffered a bout of diarrhea, and no one had bothered to check or assist her. This made him angry.

"I'm gonna clean you up, sweetheart," he told her, "After I clean you, I'm gonna put some medicine on your back an' your butt. Okay?"

"Med-sin hoot?"

"No hurt. I promise."

He retrieved two pairs of gloves from the counter and put them on one over the other for extra precaution against the virus. After finding a hospital bedside tub, he filled it with hot water and antibacterial soap and dropped a washcloth in. Another search of the cabinets revealed a bottle of topical medicine for bedsores and chafing. He tucked that under his arm and returned to her bedside with it and the tub of hot water.

"I'm gonna clean ya, first."

Her voice was trusting and grateful. "Okay."

It was a filthy, disgusting job, but Guffy decided it was better than playing security guard out in the snow. Besides that, he was beginning to feel more and more sympathy for the child, even though he knew she could kill him in a minute if she had the chance and the inclination. He saw her as a semi-wild animal in captivity, and none of it was her fault.

He removed the soiled pad and replaced it with a fresh one after he cleaned her. He noticed the bite on her buttocks had healed completely; the only thing left of it was a deep imprinted scar of teeth marks. He checked the urinary catheter; it was okay.

The tub of water and the washcloth submerged were brown with her feces. He decided to dump the mess and change gloves before he applied the medicine. "I'll be right back," he told her gently.

"Okay..." She waited patiently, her mind occupied with a vague memory of her mother and a previous lifetime of normality. "Mama..." she whispered, "Deezus, hep. Peeze hep. Peeze. Bess Mama, Deezus. Bess, peeze."

Guffy could hear her whispered prayer. His eyes stung with tears he restrained. The child amazed him. Even through the effects of the virus, she had managed to salvage a little humanity, a little faith and belief in something good. Clausberg would dismiss it as another deceitful act on Isabelle's part, a ploy to get sympathy and a chance to win her freedom. Guffy told himself it was a good thing the old witch wasn't there to see it or hear it.

He returned to her with new gloves, antiseptic wipes, some gauze bandages and tape to cover her wounds. "I'm gonna clean your back and butt real good and then put the medicine on."

"Hoot?" she asked again.

"No. It won't hurt. It might feel a little cold, maybe." He wiped her clean and uncapped the tube of bedsore cream. "I'm gonna put the medicine on now."

"Okay..." Still, she braced herself for expected pain. There was no pain. The medicine was cool and soothing, and Guffy was very gentle as he applied it. "Fwend, Unkaduffy? Fwend to me?"

"Yeah. I'm your friend." He wondered something, and asked her, "Is your name really Isabelle?"

"Rosa Maria." She rolled her R's, and pronounced *Rosa* as *Rote-za*.

"That's your name?"

"Yeah."

"Do you want me to call you Rosa Maria?

"Eesabehwe pitty. Eesabehwe okay."

"Okay, then, Isabelle..." He pronounced it her way: *Ee*sabelle. "I'll go on callin' ya Isabelle."

"Fwend..."

"You're my friend?"

"Yeah. You nice. You nice, Unkaduffy. No food."

Guffy realized the more he conversed with Isabelle, the faster her language skills were returning. He started thinking if he could convince her it was wrong to eat other human beings, maybe he could get her back on a normal diet and slowly reintroduce her to living life as a normal human. She was certainly smart enough to reason, and she retained enough recall of her life before the virus to give her a foundation from which to learn. Maybe it was possible.

"Would you like to try some food other than people fingers?"

"No. Peep fing good. I like."

"What do you like about peep fing?"

"Mmmm.... Taste."

"There's other things that taste even better. How about ice cream?"

"No... No like thweet." She jumped suddenly. "Ow... dat hoot!"

It was a spot on her buttocks where she had been laying in her own liquefied stool. The area had developed a rash. He tenderly dabbed ointment on it as he stated, "I'm sorry, honey."

"Okay, Unkaduffy. Okay, now. Tanks."

"How about cheeseburgers? McDonald's?"

"Mmmm," She was thinking about it. She vaguely recalled the flavor of cheeseburgers and fries. "Like... maybe twy."

"It'd be better for you than peep fing."

"Mmmm... peep fing..." There was ecstasy in her voice.

That wasn't good. Guffy didn't know where to go from here, but thought it wise to get off the subject of food. They were both silent as he applied the bandages to her wounds.

"Feel better now?" he asked.

"Bettew." Her eyes met his as he reached the right side of the bed where she could see him. "Tankoo, Unka. Aw bettew." An expression of consternation came to her face, and she sniffed the air. "Oh, no," she whispered to Guffy, "Dockitew Mean hehw. Hide. No see me. Peeze."

He assured her, "I won't let her hurt you anymore."

Isabelle shook her head. "Mean. Hoot me. *Ella es muerto!*"

Guffy didn't speak or understand a word of Spanish. This *muerto* she had said twice, already, and he wanted to ask her the meaning. On second thought, the word seemed to have a negative connotation, and he decided he didn't want to know.

JAMES, TREVOR AND SUZANNE escorted the shivering and exhausted stranger into the processing room. They had already performed the chip scan, and it came back negative. They asked questions, but only learned by an affirmative nod the stranger was male. He was shivering and chattering his teeth too much to be able to speak.

As a precaution, Trevor kept his rifle ready.

"Have you been bitten?" James asked the stranger.

He shook his head no. The wool scarves he had wrapped around himself to protect his skin from frostbite hid his face, and the many layers of wet and soiled clothing hid the rest of him.

"We gotta get your clothes off," James said. "Is that okay with you?"

He nodded, but cast a worried glance at Suzanne.

"I'll find you a blanket," she told him.

After she left the room, the two men began the task of removing the layers, starting with the hat and face scarves. They uncovered a blond boy just over five feet tall, with light brown eyes and pale bluish skin scarred with the remains of a few adolescent pimples. He was still shivering too violently to do anything on his own. James and Trevor continued to remove the layers of clothing, all the while comforting the boy and reassuring him he was safe.

The door opened, and Suzanne's arm appeared through the opening and tossed a blanket onto the exam table. She closed the door and inquired from behind it, "Okay, so far?"

"Okay." James said. He examined the boy's upper body. There was no sign of bites. However, the boy's skin was bluish and he was bony and obviously malnourished.

Trevor set his rifle aside and wrapped the blanket around him. "Is that better, lad?"

The boy nodded, his teeth still chattering. His eyes were full of shock, something Trevor had seen too often in the survivors who had reached the refuge.

The men removed the rest of his clothing and examined him. He was free of bites. They noted some bruises on his limbs and blisters on his feet. Otherwise, he was in relatively good shape, except for the starvation and hypothermia.

"A few good meals and you'll be fine," James said as he covered him fully with the blanket.

"Can I come in yet?" Suzanne asked from behind the door.

"Come in," Trevor said. When she entered, he told the boy, "That's Suzanne, that big guy is James, and I'm Trevor. What's your name?"

Through his chattering teeth, he said softly, "D-d-d-d... Dillon."

Suzanne asked him, "How old are you, Dillon?"

"F-f-f-f-...fif... t-t-teen."

"We need to get a temp and a blood work-up," Suzanne told James. She glanced around the room. "Don't we have an electric blanket or a heating pad around here?"

"Not in here," James said. "The infirmary."

"We need to get Joe in here." She reached for the phone, "I'll have him paged." She told Dillon, "You're gonna be fine. Don't be scared. Lie down and relax. Would you like some water?"

He blinked twice and lay down on his side, shivering under the blanket. She noticed the shock in his eyes. He was too exhausted to be frightened or even to speak anymore. He closed his eyes and drew the blanket close around his body.

Trevor searched the room for anything else he could substitute as an additional blanket. There was nothing. He removed his brown leather jacket and placed it over the boy. James took a cue from Trevor and placed his jacket over the boy's legs.

Suzanne put the call through to request an electric blanket and to page Joe. After, she brought the boy a glass of water and encouraged him to drink. He couldn't sit up. He had managed to open his eyes, but he stared vacantly up at the ceiling. She could see he was breathing, and he was still shivering. She tried again to get him to drink. He did not respond.

Whatever had happened to him, it had been more than he could endure.

CHAPTER 16

Suzanne followed Joe as he wheeled the gurney into the ward and transferred Dillon to a bed. A warm IV solution fed nourishment and heat into the boy's system. Suzanne had ordered a sedative for him and it had already taken effect.

Joe drew the blankets over the boy. "Did he say where he's from?"

"No." She tucked the blanket under the mattress on her side. "By the blisters on his feet, he walked a long way. There's some mild frostbite on his toes, but I think he got here in time. At least he had the good sense to line his shoes with plastic and wear extra socks."

"Was he carrying any weapons?"

"Nothing."

Joe shook his head. "This is a miracle..."

It was, indeed. She turned toward the doorway. "Let me know when he wakes up."

TREVOR DROPPED BY THE surveillance room to update Mitchell and Glenda. "Nice catch," he told them upon entering.

"Infected?" Glenda asked.

"No. Starved and freezin', poor lad."

Glenda's eyebrows rose. "You mean that was a kid?"

"All of fifteen."

Mitchell pivoted his chair to one side and stretched his legs. "What's his story?"

"Don't know yet. He's too weak to talk. We'll give 'im a day or two." He took Roger's chair and made himself comfortable. "Any more chatter on the lines?"

"Picked up somethin' from Baker Creek, but it was spotty. Couldn't make it out." Mitchell's brow folded with contemplation. He popped open a can of soda and drank while he mulled over a memory that he finally shared with them. "When I was makin' my way up the mountain when the shit broke loose, I saw choppers out that way."

"Military, ay?"

"Looked like it." He swung the chair around to face Trevor. "It doesn't make sense. A dumpy little burg like that between the hills is no place for a base. Can't hardly get radio signals out there." Mitchell shrugged and nodded his head from side to side. "Doesn't make any sense..."

Trevor thought about it. "We should send undercover ops in there."

"Not in this weather," Glenda said. "They wouldn't make it."

Trevor persisted, "When'll the storm break?"

She looked at him doubtfully. "According to the satellite photos, not anytime soon."

ONLY TEN OF THE MORDS in the outdoor cage survived the cold and their injuries. On Clausberg's orders, Smith had a team burn the bodies in a massive bonfire in the field between the bar and the old Oddfellows Hall. It was during this task of overseeing the team when he noticed the small-framed man wearing a uniform obviously too big for him. Smith knew this guy wasn't one of their own.

He casually pulled the man aside. "Haven't seen you before. What's your name?"

The little man stared at the ground and twisted the toe of his boot into the snow as he spoke. "My name is Richard. And, who are you? Are you a big wheel?"

Smith detected the trace of an accent, a peculiar mix of Deep South and French. "Richard what?"

"LeBreu." Richard finally looked up at his face to see the man's response.

"Where'd you get the uniform?"

"It was assigned to me."

"By who?"

"The Brass."

"It doesn't fit you."

"They don't make many in my size." He laughed nervously and adjusted the coat over his shoulders. "I am only a little soldier in a big uniform. Yes?"

"Don't bullshit me," Smith said. When the man laughed, Smith noticed the missing, damaged, discolored and rotting teeth. He could tell a meth-head a mile away. "Who are you? Where are you from?"

Richard sighed resignedly. "They captured me. They tried to take me to the camp. I stole the uniform from a dead man and escaped. Enough for you, Big Wheel?"

"Which camp?"

"Reyton."

"How'd you make it up here?"

"My feet."

"When?"

"Last month."

Smith knew there was no way this guy could have walked it, not in the weather they'd been having. Also, if he had been living in the camp for a month, why hadn't he noticed him before this? Had he been hiding in the woods all this time, only to come out at mealtime to join the chow line? The little man's story didn't add up.

Smith unhooked his cuffs from his belt and quickly twisted Richard's arm and brought it behind him. He slapped the cuff around his wrist. "You're under arrest."

Richard attempted to wrestle away, but Smith was much stronger. Smith gripped his hand fiercely and bent his thumb, putting painful pressure on the joint. "I've done nothing wrong!" Richard protested.

"Then you got nothin' to worry about," Smith stated. He put more pressure on Richard's thumb. "Now... are you gonna be a good boy, or do I hafta beat the shit outa you?"

Richard offered his free arm to him. "You will see. I am a survivor like you."

Smith roughly escorted him to the holding cell in the town's miniscule jail. Once he threw the prisoner in lockup, he called for the Interrogation Team and contacted Clausberg.

IN THE RESEARCH FACILITY, Guffy wrote his report at the table across from Isabelle's bed. He noted the little girl had become more talkative, now that he'd won her trust. Her wounds had healed, but she was weak with malnutrition. He put in a request for a cooked hamburger patty to offer her in hopes he could wean her off human flesh.

Clausberg's voice over the intercom made him put down his pen. "Is she still asleep?"

"Yeah."

A loud boom and scratching sound came over the system. Clausberg entered the room. "I want to transfer her back to the cage."

He wouldn't consider it. It would be cruel to cage Isabelle after more than a month of relative safety and comfort in the infirmary.

He stood and faced the doctor. "Let her stay here."

"She'll be more useful in the lab."

"No!" Guffy spat. "If you do that, you'll destroy every bit of progress we've made! Let her stay in here. She trusts me."

"So I hear, *Unkaduffy*." She smirked cruelly. "Do you really believe that creature won't have you for dinner the minute your back is turned? Do you really believe that?"

"She don't see me as food!"

"Boy! Has she got you fooled!"

"Did you even look at the disks? Did you, Renée? Ma'am?" He lifted the stack of papers on the table and shook them in her face. "Have you read my reports?" She placed her hands on her hips and said nothing. That verified Guffy's assumption. "No, you didn't. You ain't got a clue what's goin' on here."

"I watched the disks," she replied. "I've read your reports. Frankly, you're beginning to worry me, Guff. She isn't your child, you know. Yet, you seem to have adopted her. What kind of sick fuck adopts a menace like her? You think she can be normal. She can never be normal. She's a disease infested and very dangerous *cannibal*, and that's all she will ever be."

Guffy placed his hands flat on the table and leaned into her. "There was a time when you believed they were trainable. My work with her has proven you're right. *You're right!* You know somethin'? Last night I let her out of bed and took her to the bathroom. She remembers how to use the toilet, and even remembered to wash her hands afterwards. Later on, I re-taught her how to brush her teeth and comb her hair. She recognized herself in the mirror. She recognized me in the mirror. And, never once in all that time did she try anything with me. She behaved herself. My God, Renée! She laughs, she sings, she plays! She even remembers things from her past before all this happened to her. You oughta hear her talk! She understands everything I tell her, and she talks with me. I'm tellin' ya, Renée, she *can be* trained. She's proven it to me."

The doctor's walkie-talkie squawked, and she released it from her belt and answered the caller impatiently, "This better be good, Smitty."

Smith's voice crackled over, "I got a suspected spy in custody and the Interrogation Team is here. You wanna come supervise?"

"They don't need me. You tell Interrogation I said to do whatever it takes to get the truth out of this suspect. You hear me?"

"I hear you."

"Keep me informed."

"Will do."

Clausberg shut off the squawker and replaced it on her belt. She returned her attention to Guffy. "Now, where were we?"

"Let her stay in here. Give me more time with her." He was a step away from begging.

She thought it over. If Guffy was correct that he could tame and retrain Isabelle, she could be instrumental in converting her fellow mordants. In time, Clausberg might have her army, after all. She turned to leave, and the empty bassinets caught her eye. She looked disappointedly into one and remarked, "All the babies have died. Isabelle's the only child left."

"What'd you do with their mothers?"

"We killed them. They were all dying, anyway. We've lost most of the mordants outside, as well. Most of the ones that have survived are the younger ones, the teenagers. We'll have to try them next."

"I warned you about them," he reminded her. "I'm tellin' you they're dangerous. It'd be a big mistake."

"We'll see." She went over to the bed and glanced at Isabelle who was still asleep. "You'd better be right about her. You got one month."

"For what?"

"To make her human again."

That was a mighty heavy order. "And, then what?"

"She has insight into how the mordants think. She could teach them, as you're teaching her. If so, we'll have our army. We can bring down the UEF. That's what we all want, isn't it?"

"Yeah." Actually, he couldn't care less anymore about the UEF. If he had his way about it, he'd abandon Clausberg's program and retire on a ranch somewhere. Of course, his fantasy contained a gaping hole. What would he do about Isabelle? She was too sweet and vulnerable to leave behind, and too dangerous to take along. As much as he'd grown attached to the girl, he had to follow his head and not his heart. It also begged the question, what if the experiment failed and he couldn't tame her? He already knew the answer, but he found himself asking, despite it. "What if she can never return to being completely human?"

"We'll exterminate her." On her way to the door, she said to him, "By the way, Guff... good work!"

Even though it was what he expected to hear, his heart felt heavy with grief for the poor little girl. He looked away from Clausberg and offered no further comment. It crossed his mind again to smother Isabelle with her pillow and leave the compound behind. However, there was still plenty of time to work toward a miracle in his work with the child. As Guffy morosely watched Clausberg leave the room, he returned to the table and resumed writing his report.

Only a minute had passed when he heard Isabelle's voice.

"Unkaduffy?"

He rose and went to her bedside. She was no longer strapped down. The IV setup and catheter were gone, too. He leaned against the bed railing and rubbed her arm, "Sweetie?"

"Dockitew gone?" Her eyes revealed fear.

"Yeah. She's gone." He sat in the chair next to the bed and whispered to her, "Were you pretending to be asleep while she was here?"

"Yeah. Okay? Okay, Unka?"

He wondered how much of their conversation she had heard and understood. Instead of asking about that, he went for the obvious. "She scares you, huh?"

"Mean. Mean bit." Her eyes narrowed, "Mean bit. Hoot Isa. *Ella es muerto.*"

"What does *ella es muerto* mean?" He was still whispering.

Isabelle touched her chest and made a circle with her index finger over her heart, "She dead. No heart. Dead heart."

"Oh…" he nodded slowly. It was an accurate impression of the doctor, all right.

"Stay wiff you, Unkaduff?"

"Yeah. You get to stay here."

"No cage?"

"No cage. I protected you."

"Hug, Duff? Hug?" She reached out her arms. He stood and lifted her and gave her a good long hug. He wasn't afraid of her anymore. She hugged him around his neck. "You good, Duff. You good." She noticed the slight bend of his spine between his shoulder blades, and she patted it and rubbed it. "Is dat hoot, Duff?" She leaned back in his arms and looked into his face. "Is dat hoot?"

"Sometimes."

Isabelle regarded him sympathetically, "Po' Unkaduff. Pay Deezus, Duff. Pay bettew. Deezus hep Duff." She looked up at the ceiling and folded her arms to her chest and clasped her hands. "Deezus, peeze hep Unkaduff. Amen, Deezus. Amen."

He kissed her cheek. "Thank you for praying for me."

She grinned at him. In the next moment, she became serious and her eyes scanned the room. She looked again at Guffy and put her index finger to her lips.

"What?" he whispered.

"Dockitew listen. Dockitew see."

"Oh," he said into her ear. "Let's show her what a good girl you are."

"Comb haihw?"

"That's a good idea. Would you like to go to the mirror and comb your hair?"

"Yeah, peeze."

He carried her over there. The mirror was a two-way, and he knew Clausberg was watching them. He stood Isabelle on the stool so she could see her reflection. She was wearing a second-hand pink nightgown Guff had found for her, and she looked adorable. He hoped Clausberg would take note of it. Isabelle took the brush and began to brush her hair. She smiled at herself in the mirror.

."Pitty haihw, Unkaduff?"

"Very pretty hair."

She offered him the brush. "Comb Unka haihw?"

He swiped his hand over the sparse strands on his head. "Naw... You go ahead and comb yours."

Isabelle studied her reflection in the mirror and resumed brushing her hair. She could plainly see Clausberg on the opposite side of the glass. The little girl continued with the innocent performance, and she kept a smile on her lips, and in her eyes, too. *Muerto*, Isabelle told the doctor silently, *Die, bit. You die.*

FOUR HOURS LATER, CLAUSBERG was just falling asleep when the walkie-talkie beeped an incoming signal. She sighed tiredly and answered.

"What is it, Smitty?"

"The Interrogation Team's done with the prisoner. He's clear of the spy charges."

"Is he chipped?"

"No. Seems he was telling the truth."

"Why couldn't this wait until morning?"

"There's another allegation..." Smith paused uncomfortably.

Clausberg was impatient, "What?"

"One of the interrogators thinks this is the guy who tried to molest his son."

Clausberg almost laughed. "No shit?"

"The kid's on his way in to identify him. Thought you'd like to be here."

She was looking forward to the show. "I'll be there."

When she reached the jailhouse, the boy was waiting for her in the office with his father. "Did you get a look at him yet?" she asked the boy.

"We're waiting for you. They said you gotta witness it." The boy seemed uncomfortable.

He was small, and Clausberg couldn't estimate his age. Kids were just kids to her. "How old are you?"

"I turned nine last month."

She turned to the man beside him, "Are you his father?"

"Yes, ma'am."

"Is there a written report of this incident?"

He produced a piece of paper and handed it to her. "It happened two weeks ago. The date's stamped on the report." The man tousled his son's hair, "The little guy didn't wanna tell me at first. Glad he did. Read the description he gave. It fits."

Clausberg speed-read the document. "Let's go take a look."

The three of them entered the cellblock. Smith stood guard near the end of the hallway at the only occupied cell. They stopped there and looked through the bars. The Interrogation Team had thoroughly battered the suspect, stripped him of his stolen uniform, and confined him in the cell in nothing but his boxer shorts soiled with both dried and freshly leaked urine.

The boy took a long look at Richard. His face flushed red with anger.

"That's him. That's him, alright." He turned to Clausberg and whispered to her, "He's got an accent. Ask him to say something."

Clausberg ordered Richard, "Repeat after me. *Rain, rain, go away. Come again some other day. Shine my shoes for a quarter.*"

Richard glared from one to another in turn. "Fuck you!"

The doctor looked around. "Is there a cattle prod handy?"

The boy's father went to a corner of the hallway where it hung on the wall for emergency use, which was often. Any excuse was an emergency, even boredom. He brought it to Clausberg and put it in her hands.

"Get the guards in here. Cuff the bastard. Hog style!" When Smith lingered a second too long, she spun on him. "Now, Smitty!" To the boy's father, she said, "You don't have to be here for this."

"Thank you, ma'am." He put his hand on his son's shoulder and they started down the hallway.

"No!" Clausberg demanded loudly, "The boy stays."

The man disdained the idea. "Why?"

She glared at him through narrowed eyes. "Do you dare to question me?"

He'd heard rumors about the fate of those who dared to disobey. Knowing he had no choice and knowing he would lose his son's respect, the man backed down. "I'll wait in the office, ma'am."

As the man exited the cellblock hallway, Smith returned with four guards. They stopped in front of the cell and peered at Richard. Smith twirled the keyring around his index finger. The keys banged together and created an awful music.

"Repeat the phrases!" Clausberg ordered Richard.

"Fuck you!" Richard repeated.

She told the guards, "Subdue the little piggy."

Smith unlocked the cell, and the guards wasted no time hog-shackling Richard. Clausberg readied the prod and entered the cell.

She pointed the weapon at Richards's ear, "Shine my shoes for a quarter. Repeat!"

"Fuck you, bitch!"

She shocked his ear. He screamed in pain and tried to roll onto his back; with his arms and legs shackled together behind his back, this was impossible. She shocked his elbow, and he screamed again. She commanded him, "Shine my shoes for a quarter!"

He finally delivered. "Shine my shoes for a quarter! Shine my shoes for a quarter!"

The odd accent was clear to all.

She said to the boy, "Is that the accent you heard?"

He nodded. "Yeah!"

Clausberg ordered Smith and the four guards, "Wait outside the door. Go now." She and the boy watched until the men disappeared and the door closed behind them. Clausberg motioned the boy to enter the cell. He did so, and the doctor said to him, "Do you think he should be punished for what he did to you?"

The boy peered at Richard with hate in his eyes. "Yes, ma'am."

"Would you like to punish him?"

His gaze drifted uneasily to her, "Ma'am?"

"Did he put it inside you?"

"No, ma'am. He tried to. I hit him and got away."

She eyed him encouragingly. "He should be punished for that. You should punish him. He would've hurt you badly. He would've hurt others, too. You should punish him." She offered him the prod. "Push this button and set it on *high*."

He took it apprehensively and looked at Richard. He raised the prod and pushed the power button, glanced ambivalently at Clausberg.

She nodded approval, "Go ahead. Do it. He's evil."

His first administration of the shock was quick and timid.

Richard shouted out in pain.

"Again!" Clausberg encouraged him, "Hold it there longer. Again and again. Do it."

He was bolder the second time and even bolder the third time. A feeling of power overcame him with each scream from his victim. By the fifth shock, the boy was grinning, enjoying it. On the sixth, he spit at Richard, "Mother fucker baby raper! Repeat *that*!" He shocked him once more, "Repeat it! *I'm a mother fucker baby raper!*"

Clausberg laughed aloud, "That's the way! Let him have it!"

Another shock. He pressed the prod to Richard's quivering bare skin. "Repeat it!"

Richard screamed, "I'm a mother fucker baby raper!"

"We have a confession!" Clausberg clapped her hands together. To the boy, she suggested, "One more for the hell of it!"

The boy grinned at her, "Yes, ma'am!" He aimed it at Richard's privates. "Remember this next time you piss!"

The tortured man's screams echoed throughout the building.

Clausberg had plans for the *Motherfuckerbabyraper*. She had plans.

CHAPTER 17

LILACS KNOW IT

Natalie awakened a half hour before Coltan. It was still too chilly beyond the warmth of the sleeping bag to get out of bed, so she sat in a half-reclined posture against the wall, lit a smoke and watched Coltan sleep. He was on his side, facing her, curled up in a fetal position. She noticed his sleeping bag was off his shoulders, and she pulled it over him to keep him warm. They had slept with their mattresses pushed together every night for the warmth and security of each body touching the other. She had lost count of the many times he made love to her over the past two months, the many nights and days they drifted to sleep exhausted and satisfied in each others' arms. It was therapeutic for both of them; neither had experienced nightmares in a long time and their sleep was restful.

As daylight gradually arrived earlier and the first birds of spring sang their morning songs, they returned to their original dawn waking schedules with the birdsongs as their pleasant alarm clocks.

Natalie slid open the plywood window panel above her head to let in the morning light. She cracked the window open for fresh air. The air outside was warmer than the air in the attic. She pushed the window open a little more. The intoxicating aroma of lilacs drifted in. She breathed it in deeply and smiled contentedly. It rekindled her memories of helping Mom cut a couple of new branches to bring in and set in a vase, and the whole main floor would smell like lilacs for a couple of weeks. She longed to go out now and cut a branch to bring up to the attic, but there was still mud on the ground and she would leave tracks that would give them away. She hoped the ground would dry enough soon, so she could go out without leaving footprints. Till then, the aroma of the lilacs drifting up with the morning air would have to do.

Coltan coughed and turned over on his back. She looked down into his sleeping face and studied him. He seemed happier these days, and it showed in his features. The former haggardness of anger, fear and internal turmoil was completely gone. With the exception of the scars on the left side, his skin was smooth, and the lines of worry and discontent had softened to where they almost disappeared. She noticed he had finally begun to grow whiskers and a faint, soft mustache. Soon enough, he would have to start shaving, and it made her realize how much time had passed since the first day she had seen him close up. He impressed her as handsome then, in a rugged and rough sort of way; but now he was handsome to her in a strange combination little boy-mature man sort of way. She thought it was like him to express that duality in his looks, for his personality impressed her the same. One moment he was on the floor giggling and teasing her, and the next moment he was holding her in his arms, protecting her and pledging his undying love for her. She loved his duality and hoped he would remain like that for the rest of his life.

He turned over again on his side and mumbled something, perhaps a snippet of dream conversation. She wondered whom he was talking to and what it was about. There came a faint smile to his lips, and he chuckled shortly and sighed. She slid down next to him and kissed his forehead. He responded by scratching the spot and turning over on his back again. If all went according to his normal waking pattern, the next thing he would do was rub at his face with both hands, sigh loudly, open his eyes and stare at the ceiling. Natalie waited. Sure enough, his hands went to his face and the rest of the waking ritual began. Once the ceiling came into sharp focus, he sat up and uncricked his neck, closed his eyes once more, opened them again and looked at her and smiled.

"How's my baby?" he whispered sleepily to her.

"Glad to be with you," she replied in a soft voice.

He shifted and placed his arm around her and tugged her against him. After a sound that qualified as both a contented moan and an invitation, he began to kiss her face and neck.

IN BAKER CREEK, ISABELLE was already wide-awake waiting for Unkaduffy. She had set her plate, spoon and water cup on the table and sat there to wait. The napkins were in a holder in the middle of the little table, and she took one out and set it carefully under her spoon. She could already smell the food, even though Guffy had only reached the foyer at this moment. She listened for the sound of the door in the next room opening and closing; she knew after that the door to her room would open and he would appear. The door in the next room opened and closed. She watched her door expectantly. The knob turned, the door opened, and Guffy poked his head in and grinned at her. As he entered, she pinned her sight on the tray of food, and her mouth watered.

Guffy set the tray on the table and removed the plastic lid from the main dish. "Hamburger with cheese on it this time."

"Mmmm!" She clapped. Hamburger was good, even though they cooked it more than she preferred. They had cooked all the tasty blood out of it. "Tankoo, Unkaduffy!"

He handed her a spatula, "Here. Now, you use this to put it on your plate like I taught ya."

She took the spatula and deftly lifted the burger patty and transferred it to her plate. "Aw done!" She grinned and regarded Unkaduffy for the next revelation.

He directed her attention to a small bowl of lightly fried white stuff with a large spoon in it, "This is hash browns. Potatoes. Cooked up in little pieces. I put butter on 'em. Put some on your plate with the big spoon."

She followed his instructions and waited expectantly.

Guffy set a small bowl of fruit within her reach. It also had its own spoon. "This is canned apricots," he told her, "You try them."

Isabelle shook her head from side to side, "No, Unka. No fwoot. Make tummy hoot. No fwoot."

"Well, okay," Guffy replied, "I'll eat 'em." He drew her attention to a large glass of milk, "How about some milk? This is the new powdered kind with water. It's good for you."

"No... no milk, Unka. No like. Watoo okay." She smiled at him with her big brown eyes, "Okay, Unka?"

"Okay."

She offered brightly, "You dink it."

He laughed, "Okay. I'll *dink* it."

"Eat wiff me, Unka. Okay?"

"Okay. You start, honey."

She paused to say grace, "Deezus, tankoo fow dis food. Tankoo. Peeze bess food an' Unkaduff. Amen, Deezus, amen."

Clausberg's voice came over the intercom, "What a load of shit!"

Guffy sighed crossly.

"Mean bit..." Isabelle whispered angrily.

Guffy pointed to her plate, "Eat your food, honey."

She started in on the hamburger covered in melted cheese, using the spoon to cut the patty. After two mouthfuls, she murmured, "Mmmm! Good!"

"Better than peep fing, huh?" Guffy remarked.

"No..." she considered, "Awmose..."

That wasn't what he wanted to hear, and it certainly wasn't what he wanted Clausberg to hear.

Isabelle understood. She said loud enough so Clausberg could hear it clearly, "Hambooga good, doe. I like it. It's good, Unkaduff.

Good. I eat. Happy. Isabelle happy wiff hambooga."

"I'm glad," Guffy told her. "Try the hash browns."

She took a taste. At first, she made a face. She was not certain if she liked it or not. After she chewed and swallowed, she took a second sample and considered it while she chewed. "Okay," came the ultimate judgment, "Like okay." Her eyes met Guffy's and she pointed at the bowl of hash browns, "You eat bowns, too, Unka."

He spooned some onto his plate next to the apricots.

Isabelle paused and reached for her water cup. Finding it empty, she filled it at the sink and returned to the table with it. "Want watoo, Unka?"

"I have milk. Thank you, Isa." After she sat, he said, "You're a very good girl."

She glanced out the corner of her eye to determine if Clausberg could see them. It seemed safe to her. Slowly, she reached her hand to Guffy's and patted it affectionately, whispered, "Uv Unkaduff. Uv you."

He patted her hand in return.

"What did she say?" Clausberg's voice.

Isabelle stood and faced the direction of the voice, "Come eat wiff us, Dockitew!"

Clausberg couldn't believe her ears. After a long hesitation, she answered, "I already ate. You sit down and have your breakfast."

Isabelle sat. She made eye contact with Guffy and smirked at him. He smirked back, amused by her private joke.

SUZANNE TOOK DILLON outside in a wheelchair to enjoy the warmth of the midday sun. The snow had mostly melted and the fruit trees in the garden were setting off their first blossoms. It was still cold, though, but the days were longer and the sunlight helped to warm the air by afternoon. They were in the smoking area under the trees near the garden. She offered Dillon one of her cigarettes.

He lit it with Suzanne's lighter. "I guess they told you about the leukemia. Smoking don't matter anymore, or you wouldn't be giving me one."

"I was sorry to hear about it, Dillon."

He shrugged. "I knew the remission wouldn't last long."

"There's so much equipment and medicine we need. If we only had access to the hospital in Bonito Valle, we could treat it."

"I don't want it." Dillon regarded her sincerely. "I'm sick of the meds and all that. I just want it to be done with."

"That's a hell of an attitude!" She lit her cigarette and wished Trevor was there. Trevor had developed a rapport with Dillon no one else in the refuge could. Trevor would be able to convince him not to give up hope. Unfortunately, Trevor was on duty, and Dillon was her patient.

She had tried for two months to get him to talk about what happened to him, and he steadfastly refused. His story was still a mystery to everyone, and he seemed to prefer it that way.

"I'm just bein' realistic, man." He tucked the blanket around his lap and rubbed his legs. The weakness and pain had set in four days ago, and he could only walk from his bed to the bathroom before collapsing. His body had developed bruises, a telltale symptom one of the doctors spotted right away. Dillon could have come out and told him, but he let the man draw and test his blood in order to know for sure.

"How long have you had it?"

"Since I was little."

"Were you treated in Bonito Valle?" She was fishing for clues, trying to discover where he came from.

"Yeah. Where else?"

"So, you're from around here."

He coughed and waited for the spasm to pass. "I lived with my dad in Baker Creek."

"What kind of work does your dad do?"

"He ran the sport and bait shop."

"Your mother?"

"Dead. Cancer." He didn't try to hide his irritation with her, "How many more questions you got for me, lady?"

"Where's your dad now?"

"In the shit hole of one of those diseased fucks they got caged down there." His eyes glinted with rage when he looked at her. His rage subsided a little when he saw the shocked expression on her face.

"They've got the mords in cages?"

"Yeah!" His chin trembled, and he looked away from her.

Suzanne determined to hear the rest of it. She knew she had to tread lightly, but it was difficult.

"Who has them caged?"

He regarded her incredulously, "You don't know?"

She shook her head. "What's going on there?"

Dillon stared down at the gravel and smoked. He couldn't talk about it. He didn't want to remember it or even acknowledge the reality of it. Like his life, he wanted it to fade to black.

Suzanne leaned forward and tried to look into his face, "Dillon?" There was no response from him. She rubbed his shoulder. "Dillon?" Still nothing. "This is very important. Our survival may depend on what you know." Nothing. Either he was stubborn, or he had chosen to shut down as he did previously. She rubbed his shoulder again. "Dillon, please..."

He shrugged her hand away. That was his answer.

Something rustled and stepped in the brush. Suzanne shot up and, in the same move, freed her revolver from the holster and pointed it toward the sound. Something reeled against a bush, and she saw it was only a deer. The animal fled when it saw her. She relaxed and replaced the gun in the holster.

Dillon eyed the revolver and considered it for another day.

COLTAN OPENED HIS BIBLE. He was starting a new lesson in the series, this one on Sin and Redemption. It would have a lot of meaning for him, and he knew his notebook and journal would fill up with his thoughts and questions.

Natalie opened all the windows. The scent of lilacs drifted in.

Coltan detected it. "What's that smell?"

At the south window, she breathed it in, "Lilacs. Spring is finally here."

It brought to his mind the fact they planned to leave for the refuge by early summer. He watched Natalie at the window and wondered how she would react when the time came. This was the only home she had ever known.

"Mom and I always cut a branch or two to bring inside," she said, turning to face him. "The whole downstairs smelled like lilacs. I don't think Dad liked it so much. Not like us. I think he put up with it because he knew it made us happy."

"They're kinda strong smelling."

"That's because they know their time is short," Natalie mused. Coltan found her comment puzzling. She elaborated, "Most lilac bushes only flower for three weeks at the most, and then they're all gone. So, they put out all their blooms as fast as they can, and that's why their aroma is so strong. They want to make sure they're noticed, that they make an impression in the little amount of time they've got." She smiled, understanding her explanation was probably foolish to him. "When I was little I used to talk to the lilac bush every spring. I used to beg it to try and flower for the whole summer up into autumn. It couldn't of course."

Coltan laughed as he said, "I don't think it could hear you, Nat."

His reaction didn't embarrass her. She expected it. Yet, in her memories and in her experience, she was convinced the lilac bush could hear her and understand her. One time she could have sworn it thought back to her telepathically; it told her it was trying, trying very hard, but its time was still too short. Stubbornly, she insisted to Coltan, "It could hear me. I know it could. It understood me, too. I know it did." As if revealing a long-kept secret, she told him, "I still talk to it every year. Laugh at me if you want. I don't mind. I only know what I feel, and I feel it hearing me. I really do."

Coltan considered it a child's fantasy. However, he thought it was harmless enough to let her go on believing it if it gave her comfort. "Maybe we can bring a branch up here," he offered.

"When the ground dries up." She approached him at the table. "Footprints, you know. Dead giveaway. You want some coffee?"

"Sounds good." He watched her as she fired up the propane stove to boil the water. It occurred to him she had hardly looked at her Bible since they had come to live up there. He didn't want her to stray from God's Word. "Say, Nat, why don't you join in this study?"

"What's the topic?"

"Sin and Redemption."

"Do you think God's mad at us for having premarital sex?"

"I don't think He's mad at us. A little disappointed, maybe." He considered it further, "I think He understands."

"I hope so." She went to him and kissed the top of his head, "I don't regret a single moment."

He blushed slightly. "Go get your Bible."

She said as she retrieved it and brought it to the table, "Bossy, bossy... You're so serious when it comes to this."

"It's a serious subject." He tapped his Bible, "This saved my life. This *is* life. I want you to walk the path with me."

She saw the light in his eyes. There was a time when she possessed that same light. Over the past two years, her eyes in the mirror stared back at her lifeless and dark. She couldn't remember when or why she had abandoned the Word of God. Now, seeing Coltan's light, she wanted to have it, too.

She sat down and opened her Bible. It fell open where she had tucked her photo of Coltan.

He caught it right away. "Is that me?"

"Yeah."

"When did you take it?"

"The second day you were here. Wanna see it?" He nodded, and she handed it to him. "You were studying, and you stopped to think about something."

He examined the photo and saw in it what Natalie had seen at that moment. The day she took the photo, he would not have been comfortable with the revelation. As a matter of fact, if he had known at that moment she had planned to photograph him he would have protested angrily and taken the camera from her.

"I never saw you with a camera," he said. "How'd you get away with it?"

"I waited where you couldn't see me." She paused for his response, hoping he wouldn't be angry with her. There were a myriad of emotions in his face as he sorted through his feelings about it. Defensively, she attempted to justify herself, "You looked so peaceful when you were studying, so... beautiful. You have such beauty within, and I saw it then. I wanted to capture it. I guess I invaded your privacy. I shouldn't have done that. I'm sorry, Colt."

"I'm not mad at you." He handed her the photo. "I never had a photo taken before."

"Not even at school?"

He grinned. "I always ditched that day." The water began to simmer. She tended to it and prepared a cup of instant coffee for herself and him. After she brought it to the table, Coltan said, "I didn't know you were interested in photography."

"It was a hobby for a while."

"Do you have other photos you took?"

"Yeah. My album's over there." She pointed to the stack of mattresses and assorted bedding now a catchall for things with no specific place.

"Let me see."

She retrieved it and brought it to the table, placed it over his Bible and opened the album to the first page. As he observed the photos, she explained.

"This one was at the train station in Reyton. Me and Carolyn used to bike over there. There were always lots of good subjects at the station." She pointed, "This couple here, they were saying goodbye. I like candid shots. They never knew I took it. See this lady here? She's homeless. Always hung out there. I thought she was interesting because she had stuffed all her stuff into that old Sak's Fifth Avenue bag. Kind of a contrast, don't you think?" Coltan nodded and she continued, "This was taken over at the Dairy Delight."

Coltan tilted his head to one side, studying the image. "That's Carolyn, isn't it?"

"Yeah. Before she gained all that weight."

"She's got a look on her face like she's watching something that... hmmm... she looks like she wants something... she's looking at something she wants. Am I right?"

"Yeah."

"What was she looking at?"

Natalie smiled subtly and met Coltan's inquiring eyes. "A boy she liked."

"Oh. That explains it." The inquiring expression had not left him. "You haven't talked much about Carolyn. You must miss her."

She didn't want to think about it. "Yeah."

"What do you think happened to her?"

Natalie gazed at the floor. "I think she's dead."

"Why?"

"She couldn't have handled this. No way. Her folks, either. They're all dead."

"Maybe not."

"Or, in the camps." Natalie settled in the other chair as sadness welled up within her. "I hope they're dead. Dead is better. Don't you think so?"

He considered it. He knew if it were himself, he would have preferred death. "I guess."

She closed the album.

"You haven't grieved for her."

"I don't want to." She leaned to take the album from him.

He put his hand over it. "I want to look at the rest. You're a good photographer."

"It was a hobby. I'm not interested in it anymore."

"It might come in handy, Nat. You could document everything that's happened. Did you ever think of that?"

"No."

"Let me look at the rest." He opened the album and looked closely at the pictures. It reminded him how things used to be. Perhaps that was why she discarded the album to the miscellanea pile on the extra mattresses. He came across one of Brian and Beverly in the garden. Beverly was spraying Brian with the hose; they were laughing. His heart became heavy. His eyes lingered at their image.

She regretted showing him the album and her memories there. It was unlikely life in America would ever be the same. The acknowledgement of that fact only gave her something else to mourn, and she was sick of mourning the many losses.

"Please," Natalie said. "Let's get to the study." It was a plea.

Coltan closed the album and set it aside. "I'd like to hang on to it and look at it later. Is that okay?"

She sighed sadly. "Yeah. I suppose..."

MORRIS ENTERED THE nursery cautiously with a small plastic toolbox containing rubbing alcohol, cotton balls, bandages, syringes and blood collection tubes. Isabelle was sitting on the bed, and Guffy was reading a children's book to her. When Morris entered, Guffy stopped reading, and he and Isabelle regarded him curiously. He stopped at the end of the bed and kept his distance. Although he had viewed the disks with Clausberg, he still didn't trust Isabelle, and thought Guffy was a fool for trusting her.

"What's up?" Guffy asked him.

"Clausberg wants me to check her blood, do some tests."

Guffy had anticipated this due to Isabelle's physical as well as psychological change over the past two months. Because of these changes in Isabelle's condition, Clausberg agreed to extend Guffy's time with her by three months. The child was becoming close to normal—more human—and the doctor mentioned wanting to test the virus levels in her blood to see if Isabelle was still at overload level.

Isabelle shrunk against Guffy for protection and emitted a low growl at Morris.

"It's okay." Guffy soothed her. "This is Morris. He won't hurt you."

"He cawa me." Her eyes never left Morris.

Guffy cuddled her. "We need to check your blood, Isa. It won't hurt." He glanced at Morris for confirmation. "Will it, Morris?"

"No one's ever complained," Morris stated assuredly.

"You do it, Unka."

"I don't know how," he told her. "Morris is a good guy. He knows how to do these things."

All Isabelle recalled of Morris was the fact he had ordered the mean men to shackle her to the post so Clausberg could torture her with the burning thing that made a hissing noise. As far as she was concerned, Morris was not a good guy.

Morris set the toolbox on the bed and removed the rubber tourniquet first, then the rest of the supplies he would require. To Isabelle, he said, "I promise it won't hurt."

She gaped in terror at the syringe and nestled her face into Guffy's chest. "No, Unka! Needew hoot! Peeze, Unka! No shot! No! No, peeze!"

Morris rounded the left side of the bed slowly and stood there nervously. "Is it safe to—is she safe to—Guffy, is she gonna bite me?"

"She won't bite you." He glanced down at Isabelle with a subtle smile. "Will ya, sweetheart? You're a good girl, huh?"

"If he hoot me, I bite!" She eyed Morris with this warning.

Morris cussed under his breath.

Guffy grinned at her and placed his fingers under her chin. He gently tilted her head up to see her face. "You will not. You're a good girl. You don't bite no one no more."

She insisted, "If he hoot me..."

Morris offered her a green lollipop from the toolbox. "This is for you, Isa."

She scrunched her face in consternation. "No like sweet!"

"I forgot..." He soaked a cotton ball with alcohol and showed it to her. "This has special medicine to help it feel better." He gently straightened her left arm while he told her in his gentlest voice, "I'm gonna dab it on your arm right there, and it's only gonna feel cold. Okay?"

She pleaded to Guffy, "Unkaduff?"

"Why don't we sing while he does that?" Guffy offered. He began to sing softly, "Jesus loves me, yes, I know..."

She joined him, "For da Bibew tews me so..." Morris dabbed the alcohol on her skin. It felt cold and good. Neither she nor Guffy remembered the next line, so they improvised, "Naw, naw, naw, naw, naw, naw, naw... Naw, naw, naw, naw, naw, naw naw...."

"Look at me, Isa," Guffy suggested. She looked at him, and he encouraged her to keep singing with him while Morris tied the tourniquet around her arm and uncapped the needle. His hands were shaking, and he took a deep breath to stop the trembling.

Guffy and Isabelle sang together, "Yes, Jesus loves me! Yes, Jesus loves me. Yes, Jesus loves me..."

Morris inserted the needle gently and carefully. He quickly looked at Isabelle, expecting her to react and strike out at him. She did not feel the needle at all. Very diligently, he connected the blood receiving tube to the feeding end of the needle. The mating of the two items produced a barely discernible *pop* sound. Morris stole another glance at the girl out the corner of his eye. She did not react to the second step in the procedure. Her blood oozed unhurriedly into the tube. He inhaled a slow breath of relief, felt his racing heartbeat decelerate.

Her singing continued, "Da Bibew tews me so..."

Guffy began again, "Jesus loves me..."

"Dis I know. For da Bibew tews me so... Naw, naw, naw, naw, naw, naw, naw..."

"Each is precious in his sight..." Guffy recalled, sort of.

"Yes, Deezus uvs me.... Yes, Deezus uvs me..."

Morris removed the first tube and connected the second. Tube number two began to fill, and he released the tourniquet. He softly began to sing along, "The Bible tells me so..."

"Deezus uvs me, dis I know. For da Bibew tews me so..." She gazed at Morris. "Sing, too, Bowis... Deezus uvs me, dis I know..."

Morris's fear of the child subsided. He smiled at her and sang with her, "For the Bible tells me so..."

Guffy held her a little tighter, cuddled her even more.

She looked down at the tube filling with her blood and studied the process with great interest. "Dat my bud?"

Morris caught her gaze. "That's your blood."

"Don't hoot..." She said it admiringly. "You do good, Bowis... Good. No hoot."

He withdrew the needle and swiftly covered the little hole in her vein with cotton and a bandage. "All done."

She pointed at the blood at the tip of the needle. "Taste?"

It bothered him she wanted that. "Why?"

"Taste like peep fing?"

He silently questioned Guffy. Guffy shrugged and nodded.

"Put out your finger," Morris said, "And I'll put some there."

She extended her index finger, "Okay..." He dripped it off the needle without touching her skin. She examined the blood drop and sniffed it before tasting it. Her eyebrows moved toward each other as she thought about it. "No peep fing taste. Some... yeah... some peep fing taste... Hmmm..."

Morris remarked to Guffy, "That might be a good sign."

Guffy cuddled the little girl and kissed her forehead. "Why? What's it mean?"

"If she was still overloaded with the virus, it wouldn't taste like people... uh... peep fing... to her."

Guffy grinned and looked down at Isabelle, "Say... you're gettin' better, little girl. Better. How 'bout that?"

"No mow biting sick?" Her eyes held a strange combination of relief and trepidation.

"Maybe."

"Deezus hep?"

"Probably!"

Morris shook his head doubtfully and began to repack the toolbox. He whispered to Guffy, "Don't let Clausberg hear that."

"What's she gonna do? Feed me to the mords?"

"They only got one prisoner left. Who do you think's been

keeping her and the others alive?" He closed and latched the lid and continued in a hushed voice, "There's six mords left, counting her."

"What's killing them?"

"We lost a lot to gangrene and staph. We lost even more to the weather. Froze to death out there in the cage. She had them set up a heater for them and tossed in a bunch of blankets so they wouldn't die off so fast." His eyes darted off to the side, and he asked Isabelle in a whisper, "Is she watching and listening to us?"

"No," Isabelle whispered back. "She outside. She moke." Isabelle pretended to smoke a cigarette. "She moke."

Her ability to sense Clausberg's whereabouts still amazed him. Clausberg, herself, found it disturbing and had tried to fool the girl to no avail. As a defense, the woman listened in more often in an attempt to discover clues to the girl's ability.

In case they were being recorded, Morris returned to the subject of the mordants and continued in a hushed voice. "Most of them got rid of their clothes so they could shit. The rest just got rid of their pants. The cage is full of piss and shit, not to mention all the soiled blankets. No one wants to clean it. The mords won't let any of them near, anyway. They're walking and sleeping in their shit. It's disgusting."

Guffy adopted a hushed tone of voice per Morris's example. "I overheard you and her talkin' about deserters. Is that true?"

"Yeah. Soon as the weather warmed up, a lot of them split. Now that the food's almost gone, for both normal people and the mords, the staff and the soldiers are afraid they'll become food."

"You said one prisoner's been food for the mords. How so? Did they cut him up and freeze his parts, like he was a deer or somethin'?"

"This is where it gets crazy. Clausberg's got some French guy, a child molester, in the isolation room at the jail. She's been keeping him alive. Got him strapped down to the bed. Feeding him IV fluids and force-feeding him food. At first, she had some of the guys cut off a few pieces of him to feed the mords. No painkillers, nothing. Those guys couldn't handle it, man. Seriously messed with their heads, you know. After they split, no one would replace them. They know what's going on. So now, Clausberg's' taking it upon herself to slowly carve up the guy. She don't give a shit. She likes it. I think she's losing it."

"Are you gonna split, too?"

"Thinking about it. You oughta, too."

Guffy cuddled Isabelle on his lap. "I can't leave the kid behind."

"Are we goin', Unkaduffy?" Isabelle liked that idea.

"Shhh, shhh..." Guffy told her, "Don't you say nothin' about this, Isa. Don't say nothin'. Promise!"

"Seeket..." Isabelle assured them both.

He asked Morris, "When you gonna check her blood?"

"Right away." Morris didn't indicate it, but he felt certain releasing Isabelle into the world was a bad idea. He didn't want to tell Guffy in front of the girl.

"She might check out okay," Guffy said hopefully.

Morris picked up the toolbox, "You never know."

"Dockitew back!" Isabelle whispered.

"I gotta go." Morris said. To Isabelle, he said in a whisper, "Don't talk about this!"

She whispered conspiringly, "Seeket."

*T*revor worked late into the night at his various duties. Suzanne informed him early that evening regarding Dillon's degenerating condition. She felt guilty about ignorantly letting Dillon smoke, for it exacerbated his breathing difficulty and necessitated the administration of oxygen. Only Trevor knew about the smoking issue, and he didn't hold it against her.

Dillon was half-asleep and receiving oxygen. The nurses had left him in a reclined position in the bed, more sitting up than reclined. His eyes opened at the sound of footsteps approaching.

Trevor stood there looking over him. "You've 'ad a rough day, lad."

"No shit," he replied weakly through the oxygen mask.

Trevor pulled up the chair and sat down. He held Dillon's hand.

"You know about me..." Dillon glanced at Trevor's hand holding his.

"I know about the leukemia."

"You know about the other. What I am."

Trevor squeezed his hand gently. "Shall I be frightened, lad?"

"If I was healthy..." Dillon tried to smile through the mask.

"Not a chance." Trevor smiled sympathetically.

His voice came weakly. "So, why hold my hand?"

"Because you're frightened."

Dillon's eyes slowly closed. He forced himself to open them again. He was glad Trevor had come to his bedside, and he wanted to enjoy the time with him.

Trevor felt his forehead. "You're still feverish." It saddened him and he knew Dillon had little precious time remaining. He felt powerless to help him; he hated feeling powerless. "What can I get you, lad?"

It was a struggle to get the words out in between labored breaths, and this told him his condition had worsened over the last minute or so. His bones ached steadily with increasing pain. "More morphine."

Trevor pressed the code numbers for the nurses' station on his radio. A nurse answered and he spoke. "Dillon in room two needs morphine."

The nurse came back, "He had his latest dose less than thirty minutes ago."

"Well, he needs more." Trevor looked encouragingly at Dillon. He rubbed Dillon's hand, being mindful not to disturb the IV line some genius had inserted just above the fold of his wrist.

The nurse stated, "Not without doctor's approval."

Trevor became impatient. "Who's on tonight?"

"Quimby."

"Get him in here. *Now*."

"Will do, sir."

Trevor shut off the radio and replaced it on his belt. He reassured Dillon, "Soon, lad." Dillon nodded tiredly. Blood oozed and pooled inside the oxygen mask. Alarmed, Trevor lifted the mask and saw Dillon's nose was bleeding. He removed the mask completely and set it on Dillon's bruised chest. He reached for a tissue and began to gently mop up the blood dripping from his nose. Under his breath he said, "God help us."

Dillon murmured, "He fucked me over. Don't ask no favors."

"Now... lad." Trevor said, "We're takin' care of you." He held a fresh tissue to Dillon's nostrils and applied a small amount of pressure to stem the bleeding. Dillon tried to take over the task, but Trevor moved his hand away.

"Even my fingers hurt," Dillon whispered.

"I know, lad."

"How do ya know, Trev? Huh?"

"My sister died from it."

"Oh. Sorry, man. That sucks..." He gasped for a breath and reached for the oxygen mask. Trevor wiped it clean and helped him place it in front of his nose and mouth so he could take a breath of it. It seemed to help.

"Shall I lower the head so you can lean back?"

"No. I can't breathe. Leave it up." Dillon winced. The pain was worsening. He wished the doctor would hurry up.

Trevor almost couldn't stand it. If there was only something... some comfort he could offer. When Dillon pushed the covers further down off his chest to cool off, it told Trevor what would help. He went to the sink where he soaked a washcloth under cold water and wrung it out. As soon as he reached Dillon, he folded the cloth, laid it on his forehead and held it there with his palm.

Dillon closed his eyes. "That's good."

"My sis... she found comfort with it." He took Dillon's hand again. "It helps, ay?"

He labored for another breath under the oxygen mask. "Yeah."

It was taking too long. Trevor reached for his radio to nag the desk.

At the same time, Doctor Quimby arrived and rounded the other side of the bed. Quimby was bald, and the dim light behind the bed made the skin at the top of his head shine. If Dillon had been feeling well, he would have teased the old fossil, *shine your head for a nickel!*

The doctor inquired with concern and sympathy, "You're still in pain?"

Dillon removed the oxygen mask and whined sarcastically, "Like you fuckin' care..."

Trevor scolded him. "Be nice, now."

Quimby addressed Trevor, "Irritability is part of it. We don't take it personally." He returned his attention to Dillon, "I've okayed an increase in dosage, Dillon. Let them know if it's still not enough." He replaced the oxygen mask over the boy's nose and mouth. "This won't help you if you don't wear it."

At this point, a nurse entered and injected morphine into the IV Dillon's eyes closed, and his fingers flexed and relaxed. His skin flushed red for a second and returned slowly to pale.

"What else are you givin' 'im?" Trevor asked.

"Prednisone and antibiotics." The doctor shook his head, frustrated. "That's all we've got."

"We can send a team to Bonito Valle." Trevor offered.

"The army took over the hospital," Dillon slurred, "You can't get in. They got it."

"We can send James back in. He knows the place."

"They got the whole town sewed up..." Dillon opened his eyes and looked sadly at Trevor. "There's no way. No chip, no food, no service..." The additional morphine was just enough to send him flying a little.

Trevor felt Dillon's hand slowly fall limp in his grasp. Dillon's eyes closed once more. Trevor let go of him and motioned the doctor into the hallway.

"What's the prognosis?"

"Not long. I'm sorry."

"What if we get the medicines?"

"It would only buy him time." He shifted wearily on his feet, "Even if we could buy him some time, it would be very little. The boy's dying. He knows it."

"I can't accept that," Trevor stated. "God brought him here for a reason."

"I also believe that," Quimby replied. "The reason—I couldn't tell you."

Trevor resisted despair. "What have we got left? What? Say?"

"Prayer. Keep praying for him."

All his hours of prayer did not save Julina. Why would God spare Dillon? "I've been prayin'."

Quimby patted his arm in a fatherly manner. "Don't stop. I've seen miracles, Trevor."

Trevor returned to the room and pulled a second chair in front of the one he sat on. He slipped off his shoes, propped his legs across the second chair and slouched down for a nap. He intended to watch over Dillon all night.

CHAPTER 18

C oltan finished his cigarette on the back porch. The morning was warm enough he didn't need his jacket. As he planned to be outside for just a few minutes, he sat there in only his sleeveless undershirt and jeans, his feet bare. He enjoyed not needing bulky winter clothing this morning, and he couldn't wait for the warmer weather to set in. He stood and took one final drag off his smoke before snuffing it out.

It had been a long time since he'd been out here, and he saw the winter storms had added to the damage created by the mords and the military. A tree limb had broken over on the west side and had smashed the railing and part of the wood decking. Debris, brittle dead leaves and dirt littered other areas on the deck. The plywood slider across the dining room window suffered water damage and had warped and cracked in its frame. It was no longer useful as a security measure, and Coltan tried to remember if any plywood remained in the basement. He made a mental note to check after he returned inside.

The soil along the gravel path was finally dry enough to walk on without leaving footprints. He knew he could easily cut a small branch from the lilac tree without tracking any mud onto the porch. Looking around, he found no tools on the porch, and decided to raid the metal tool shed at the side of the house for a pair of clippers. As he neared the shed, he was pleased to find the padlock missing and immediately recalled he had forgotten to replace it during the height of the crises.

Just when he reached for the door, he heard whimpering behind the shed. Cautiously, he rounded the side of the shed and found a familiar white mutt shivering in the shade there.

Coltan squatted and eagerly reached out his hands. "Muffy!"

Muffy stood and took a couple of timid steps toward Coltan. The dog's fur had grown and was filthy and matted. Coltan barely detected the pink collar with the heart shaped tag that read *My name is Muffy. Please call...* Mud-encrusted fur obscured the rest. Her feet were wet and muddy, and there was a brown discharge coming out of her eyes and her little nose. Coltan smelled an earthy and rotten odor of puss-weeping flesh as she inched closer to him. She hardly resembled the groomed and pedicured little princess the Spencers had pampered since she was a pup.

Coltan felt sad for her but at the same time was relieved she had survived the winter on her own. He squatted and reached out again to her. "My pretty girl. Come here, Muffy. It's Uncle Coltan. Remember me? I remember you."

Muffy hesitated and growled at him.

Upstairs, Natalie awakened to the sound of Coltan's voice under the window above their mattresses. She took her sweatshirt from the end of her bed and put it on over her nightshirt to ward off the chill. Slowly coming awake, she wondered what Coltan was doing outside so early in the morning. Her next thought was also a question: Did he remember to carry Clyde? She looked for it on the floor on his side of the mattress. It was gone. It made her less worried to know he had remembered it.

She looked out the window and saw him crouched at the side of the metal shed. At first, she couldn't tell what he was doing; he seemed to be reaching for something and talking to someone. She understood when Coltan stood slowly with a small dirty white dog in his arms. He talked to the dog in soothing tones as he cuddled her to his chest. Natalie realized the dog was little Muffy. Coltan had been so worried for her over the winter. Now he knew she was okay, and that made Natalie happy for him.

Natalie expected he would want to bring the dog inside and up into the attic with him. Muffy's inevitable barking would draw attention to their hideout. Coltan had not considered the ramifications.

She opened the window the rest of the way and leaned out. "Colt! Is that Muffy?"

He looked up, grinning, "Yeah! She's a filthy mess, but she's okay!"

"You can't bring her up here."

"Why not?"

"She's loaded with fleas. Besides that, her barking will give us away!"

"Do we have any of her dog food left?"

"You can't feed her!"

He implored petulantly, "Why not?"

"Number one, the food dish is a dead giveaway and, number two: she'll hang around here barking and scratching to get in. We can't have that!"

He hugged Muffy to his chest and petted her. "Aw, Natalie. Stop being such a tuff-ass. I'm gonna feed her. It's the least I can do."

She leaned out a little farther, "No, Colt. Think about it."

Muffy growled and bit his hand. "Ow!" He protested as Muffy scrambled out of his arms and landed on her side in the dirt. "Whad'ja do that for?" The wound around the base and mount of his thumb spurted blood. He sucked at the blood without thinking about it.

Muffy foamed at the mouth, not white foam, but brown foam. It looked hideous.

"Did she just bite you?"

He looked from Muffy to Natalie. "She's just scared." He squatted again and attempted to re-establish trust. "C'mere, girl. I know you didn't mean it. C'mere." The blood began to stream down his hand and pool in the dirt.

Natalie heard faint growls and panting from the north corner. Just as she looked, an estimated dozen dogs of different breeds and sizes rounded the edge of the house and spotted Coltan with his back to them. Before Natalie could shout a warning, the dogs galloped and pounced on him in what seemed to be a group decision. The weight of them knocked Coltan onto his belly in the dirt. They began scratching at him and biting. Natalie could see Coltan's hand reach for Clyde tucked in the rear waistband of his jeans. Two of the dogs bit his hand and his arm hard, drawing blood. Coltan began to scream and tried to fight them off.

Natalie dashed across the room and grabbed a rifle from the wall rack. As she raced down the folding staircase barefooted, she was aware she had missed a couple of steps and was almost flying down in her haste to reach the back porch. She landed on her back on the floor and banged her head on the bottom step. Mildly aware of the injury, she quickly scrambled up and dove through the hidden access door. In less than a minute, she was down the main staircase and out onto the porch.

She could hear the growls and whimpering of the animals before they came into view, and beneath those sounds was Coltan's angry and terrified yelling.

She ran to Coltan, screaming profanities at the wild dogs as they continued to assault him. Under the mass of fur, she could see Coltan's arms swiping at and punching some of the dogs. He managed to crawl out from under them, roll over on his rear and lean half-sitting against a tree. Kicking at them, he reached his arm behind him to free Clyde. At that moment, three dogs jumped on him, biting at his face, neck, chest and arms.

Natalie took every clear shot she could get and killed four of them. The others were upon Coltan, and she feared if she tried to shoot them, the bullets would go through them and hit him.

"Try to push 'em off!" She yelled, "Push 'em off so I can shoot 'em!"

With one hand, he pushed at two of them and, with the other that held Clyde, he aimed and fired and killed one, a German shepherd. A pit bull mix latched stubbornly onto his right wrist; this was Coltan's gun hand, and the painful pressure of the sharp teeth around his wrist caused him to drop the gun.

He screamed at Natalie, "Shoot 'em! Shoot, 'em, Nat! Shoot'em!" A little black mutt pounced and latched its teeth into his left shoulder. "Ow...!" he bent his arm, got the bitch by the neck, and threw her across to the gravel path. "Shoot 'em!"

By this time, Natalie had moved closer and was not only shooting, but was striking the dogs with the butt of her rifle to distract them. It didn't work. They clung persistently to Coltan, and it appeared to her they were trying to bring him down like prey and eat him. She managed to grab one and pull it off by the scruff of its neck. Once it hit the dirt, she shot it in the head and turned to grab another. Coltan screamed and cussed. With the pit bull still latched onto his right wrist, he retrieved his gun with his left hand and shot one that had fallen and was going for a second try at him. Even at point blank range, he missed; he was shaking uncontrollably and the blood flowing over his hand made his grip on the weapon slippery. It fell to the dirt, leaving him helpless. He could no longer feel the pain of the pit bull's death-grip around his right wrist. The blood dripping from his head wounds fell into his eyes, and he battled to see his attackers. With strength that came only through desperation, Coltan kicked two more dogs away, and Natalie shot them. As one more dived at Coltan, Natalie pulled it away by its neck, flung it onto the gravel walk and sent a bullet into its brain.

Only two of the dogs remained; the pit bull that had maintained its grip on Coltan's wrist, and Muffy who was attempting to go for his throat. Coltan managed to fasten his left hand around Muffy's neck. He hoisted her at arm's length away from him and mournfully ordered Natalie, "Do it, Nat!"

Natalie shot the bullet between her eyes. Without looking at Muffy, Coltan dropped the limp little dog to the dirt.

The pit bull clung stubbornly to Coltan's wrist, growling and foaming brown gunk around the bleeding bite wound. Coltan couldn't reach his gun.

"Hold your arm out!" Natalie ordered.

He extended his arm sideways with the dog still attached. She shot it in the lower spine. The pit bull cried out in pain as its legs went limp, but it hung on by its jaws. Coltan sat up and began to swing his arm and pound the shrieking animal against the ground. It would not let go. He screamed and wailed words no human could understand. His eyes were wild with panic under the curtain of streaming blood. Yet a spark of lucidity snapped on in his brain and, with it, a simple idea. He extended his arm sideways again and used his left hand to pull the dog's head sideways by the back of its neck.

"Kill it! Kill it!"

Natalie set her rifle down and scurried to Coltan where she retrieved his handgun—Clyde—that he had dropped. After she confirmed it was loaded, she ducked under Coltan's arm and leaned in against his chest where she could see the position of the animal's head in order to ascertain the precise trajectory of her intended shot without further injuring Coltan in the process.

She told him in a whisper, "Try to turn and hold his head so his teeth are flush with your wrist and his head is away from your arm."

Without questioning her logic, he adjusted the position of the dog's massive head. In response, it dug its teeth further into his wrist and emitted a frothy rolling snarl. Coltan growled with the pain.

Natalie hesitated only long enough to wrap her other hand around the grip to subdue her trembling. With a sharp intake of breath, she pulled the cock, squeezed the trigger and shot the beast through its temple. Coltan yelped and recoiled at the pain in his ears from the volume of the blast. He followed that with an irate screech as the dog's body went limp with its teeth still imbedded in his wrist. Natalie set the gun aside and pried the beast off.

Coltan drew his wrist to his chest and held it there. His blood spurted from the wounds onto his neck and chin. Blood saturated his clothing. He sat there panting, trembling, and sweating. His eyes were wild with residual panic.

"Aw... God!" he gasped. "God...!"

Natalie used her leather necklace as a tourniquet to stem the bleeding.

"Keep your wrist up against your chest. Got it?" As he nodded, she reached for her rifle. "We gotta get you inside!"

He gazed at her, terror-stricken and incredulous. "I pissed my pants!"

IAN DROPPED THE STACK of books, and his legs crumbled beneath him. He hit the floor of the library on his knees and, for a minute, everything before his eyes seemed bathed in a crimson veil. Not understanding the pain in his legs and everywhere else on his body, he stayed there on his knees for a few more minutes until it all subsided. The veil lifted, and the world looked normal again. His heart pounded in his chest and he couldn't catch his breath.

Carolyn happened upon him in the aisle as he was still waiting for it all to pass. She had heard the books hit the floor, but thought nothing of it; they were always dropping books. When she saw him, his confused expression and wide, terrified eyes told her something was terribly wrong.

She knelt next to him and put her arm over his shoulders, "Ian!

What happened? Are you okay?"

He caught his breath and wiped his eyes. "Okay, mum." The words came out softly and hesitantly. He glanced around to be certain no one else had seen.

"What happened?"

"I tripped an' dropped me books..."

That didn't explain the terror in his eyes.

"Can you stand up?"

"I'd rather set about 'ere presently."

"Did you get dizzy?"

"I tripped, lass. Let me 'ave some air." He began to gather the books together as he irritably mumbled, "Growin' outa me own feet, I am..."

"Something's wrong, Ian!" She faced him squarely and forced him to return the favor, "Are you in pain?"

The pain had vanished as abruptly and mysteriously as it had appeared. "No, lass. I'm fine."

"I'm gonna go get Joe."

"No, you won't!" He gripped her arm. "'twas nothin'. I tripped an' fell. Clumsy is all. I'm growin', y'know. Boys are clumsy when they're growin'. Don'cha, know it, lass?" He forced a smile. "Just a clumsy boy growin' too fast for 'is feet, is all. Nothin' to fret." Slowly, he stood up on his feet, "Caught me by surprise, is all. Leave Joe to 'is patients who need 'im. There, lass. Good as new. See?"

GUFFY ROCKED IN THE solid oak rocking chair with Isabelle on his lap and a children's book open before them. She was more interested in the illustrations and pointed to one that was exceptionally colorful.

"Is dat a pincess?"

"Yeah. That's the princess. And over here is her castle."

"What's castle?"

"Big house. Big, big house. For a princess."

"Doze windows?"

"Those are windows."

"Who dat?"

"That's the guard."

"What he do?"

"He keeps the princess safe."

"Fum who?"

"The evil queen."

"Dockitew Mean..." she giggled at her own pun.

He giggled, too.

"Unkaduffy guawd Isa?"

"You bet."

She paused and sniffed the air. "Unkabowis come see us."

Morris entered the room before Guffy could respond. Morris grinned at the sight of Guffy with the child on his lap for story time. It reminded him of something out of a Norman Rockwell painting.

He teased Guffy, "Ain't this cute...!"

"We expected you," Guffy said. He looked down at Isabelle, "Didn't we, sweetie?"

Isabelle informed Morris, "I melled you, Bowis."

He replied to her in a playful manner, "You *melled* me, huh?"

The little girl nodded and smiled with her lips pressed close together. She was proud of herself. "Yep." She noticed the little brown teddy bear he carried, "What dat?"

"This is for you. A teddy bear." He set it into her reaching arms.

Her eyes lit up and she grinned from ear to ear. "Oh! Pitty! Tankoo, Bowis. Tankoo!"

"It's from the doctor." Morris said this with his eyes on Guffy's. He sneaked a note into Guffy's hand.

Guffy set the note against the open book on his lap in front of Isabelle and read it quickly:

Bear bugged. Virus load minimal & dying. Eat this.

Isabelle hugged the bear to her breast. "Deezus, peeze bess Teddy. Bess, peeze. Amen." She caressed it with her cheek and said to Morris, "Soft. I like! Tankoo! Oh... pitty." Her nose caught the doctor's scent, and she frowned, "Teddy mell like—"

Guffy interrupted quickly, "Can I hold him, too?"

"Okay, Unka." She set the bear in his arms.

He hugged it to him and felt for the bug. It was at the base of the tummy. Isabelle turned her attention to Morris and gabbed on about how much she loved Teddy and how much she missed her dolls. Morris interacted with her in order to distract her. Without Isabelle noticing, Guffy began to pick at the seam with his fingernail until the threads broke loose. He dug his finger into the hole and brought the tiny microphone out under his fingernail. "This is a very pretty bear!" He told Isabelle. "Here, sweetheart. He wants *you* to hold him."

She took him back in her arms. "Teddy... Isa Teddy..."

"Say, Isa," Guffy said. "I'm gonna get a cup of coffee. How about you sit here and wait for me?"

"Okay." She hopped off his lap and let him get up. She waited until he reached the coffee maker on the counter before she sat in the chair. It was warm from them sitting in it, and she liked the warmth. She rocked back and forth, cradling Teddy in her arms like a baby, humming to it. She paused and looked up at Morris, "You like wock chaweh, Bowis?"

"Yes. All people do."

"Mama wead you?"

"When I was your age."

Morris kept Isabelle occupied with small talk while Guffy poured each man a cup of coffee. Guffy dropped the bug into the coffee in his cup. He had expected her to try something like that, and she did not disappoint him. *The Evil Queen Dockitew Mean...*

When Guffy returned to the chair, Isabelle was busy showing Unkabowis her storybook and describing all the illustrations. Guffy stayed quiet and moved over to the table, observed her conversing and behaving like a normal five year-old. The knowledge her virus load had gone down to minimal suggested she was fighting off the virus, a not so small miracle. Silently, Guffy thanked God. *Tankoo, God. Tankoo, Deezus for hepping Isa. Amen.*

Morris glanced at Guffy over the storybook while Isabelle rambled on in her unique Isabellespeak accent. He grinned and winked at Guffy to tell him it was okay.

Isabelle stopped gabbing long enough to yawn. She swung her little legs back and forth over the front of the chair. She yawned a second time and hugged Teddy close.

"Are you sleepy headed?" Guffy asked her.

"Oh..." she said, "Teddy seepy. Isa seep wiff Teddy so he no cawood. Okay, Unka?"

"Okay." He pointed to her bed. "You go get into your nightie, hon."

"Teddy need nightie, too."

"Give him the extra pillowcase for a nightie."

"Oh! Dat wook good!" She grinned and ran to her bed.

Morris joined him at the table where Guffy had set his cup. He noticed Guffy chose one of the two chairs that faced at a half-angle away from Clausberg's video recording camera. Morris also noticed the tightly wadded note floating in Guffy's coffee. Morris presumed the man had dropped Clausberg's bug in there too.

Guffy swallowed the wadded scrap of paper with his next gulp of coffee. The bug had sunk to the bottom of the cup, and he hoped the acid in the coffee had killed its reception.

"You've done wonders with her," Morris said in a low volume

voice, almost a whisper.

Guffy followed his lead with respect to the volume, "She's a great kid. I don't know what's gonna happen to her. Do you know anything?"

Morris ducked his chin and sighed tiredly and sorrowfully.

It was answer enough for Guffy. He whispered, "Is she listening? Watching?"

"She's taking a nap."

"For how long?"

"Hours, I hope." He smiled wryly. "I put some meds in her coffee. She's still recording. Talk in a whisper."

Guffy laughed silently. After a minute, he got serious again, "Does she know about the viral load?"

Morris continued in a whisper, partially so Guffy wouldn't forget. "Yeah. She plans to tell you it's through the roof."

He set his jaw angrily. "Damned bitch!" It didn't make any sense. "Why?"

"She wants you out of here. You've gotten too attached to the kid. She doesn't like that, Guff." He stretched out his legs under the table and leaned back in his chair to look casual so their conversation would not appear conspiratorial on the videodisk.

"What's she gonna do with Isa?" Guffy remembered to whisper.

"Raise her as her own. Breed her when she's old enough."

"What?"

"She thinks she's gonna breed a new race of super soldiers."

"You gotta be kidding!"

"Keep your voice down." He leaned forward on the pretense of reaching for his coffee. "Don't let her know you know."

"I'm taking her out of here."

Isabelle approached them with Teddy in her arms. She had changed into her pink nightgown and had wrapped Teddy in the spare pillowcase. "G'night, Unkaduffy." She kissed his cheek, turned to Morris and kissed his cheek. "G'night, Unkabowis. Tankoo fow Teddy."

"You're welcome," Morris told her with a smile.

Guffy reminded her, "Say your prayers, sweetie."

As she went to the bed, she said over her shoulder, "I pay evwy night, Unka. Pay for you, too." She turned and grinned at Morris, "An' you, too, Unkabowis. Night..."

They watched her climb into bed and tuck Teddy next to her under the covers. In the next minute, she clasped her hands over her chest and mouthed a whispered prayer with her eyes closed. After her prayer, she turned over on her side, kissed Teddy, and drifted off to sleep. She was the picture of normality.

Guffy whispered his question to Morris. "When you leavin'?"

"I had planned on tonight." He glanced sadly at Isabelle. "But that would leave you in a hell of mess."

"How so?"

"Almost all the staff is gone. Outside, there's a few die-hard soldier boys watching the mords. Actually, they're not really watching them; they're harassing them. I keep telling them it's dangerous. They think it's hilarious." Morris soberly shook his head. "Idiots..."

"This was supposed to be a research facility," Guffy replied. "Looks like there's only three of us doin' research, and one of the three is a frickin' lunatic. Say... what happened to Doctor Brandewynn?"

"One of the mords got him early on. Clausberg had him killed." He sat up and reached for his coffee again as a pretense. "To tell you the truth, I think she set him up. She got total control now. So she thinks."

"You still goin' tonight?"

"Naw... I'll wait until you and the kid can get out." He gulped down his coffee and said softly as he set the cup down, "I'll spike her coffee with something stronger when the time comes. The three of us can get out together then at the same time."

"Sounds like a plan." Guffy felt only a little relieved. He knew the time had to be soon. As far as where they would go, he would think about it later. The priority was to get the hell out of there before Clausberg flipped her nut and did something they would all regret.

IT HAD TAKEN NATALIE almost three hours to clean, treat, stitch and bandage the numerous bites all over his body. Coltan had lost a lot of blood and had spent most of the ordeal of painful medical treatment in and out of consciousness.

During the entire time, Natalie silently thanked her mother for the many small surgical lessons given during meal prep. All those chickens, turkeys, and sides of beef came in handy for a lot of things before they became food. While recollecting as she stitched another of the bites, she remembered one Thanksgiving when Dad bit into one of her impromptu stitch jobs on a drumstick. It was funny, and she almost laughed at the recollection had she not been so distraught over Coltan's condition.

He began to awaken after she cleaned the blood off his body and transferred him to a clean mattress. He grimaced and tried to sit up. She put her hands on his shoulders and eased him back down. "You be still," she told him.

"How bad is it?" His voice came weakly; she could barely hear him.

It's real bad. That was the truth. However, she opted wisely for a fib. "You're gonna be fine, Colt. It looks worse than it is."

He knew better. The pain was everywhere. He was cold and dizzy. Even lying down, the vertigo gripped him and made his stomach protest.

He turned on his side. "I gotta puke!"

She set the small bucket full of soiled gauze and cotton balls under his face and braced him. "Go for it."

He vomited, and some of it was blood. Natalie hoped the blood he vomited was only blood he had swallowed, and not from internal injuries. If he had suffered internal injuries, he was as good as dead. He gripped his stomach as he emptied it into the bucket.

"Is your stomach painful?" she asked.

He purged one more stream of watery waste into the bucket before he answered. "It hurts a little."

She had stitched up three deep bites on his abdomen. The remainder of his injuries there were deep scratches from the dog's claws, only one of which was deep enough to require stitches. She worried she might have screwed something up.

Coltan collapsed exhausted on his side and weakly pushed the bucket away. There was still dried blood, brown dog slobber and dirt over and around his eyes, nose and mouth. The splash back of vomit only added to the color palate. He was unaware of it. He grimaced again; his body shuddered through another wave of pain from every extremity, and places he had not known existed. A pitiful groan escaped him, despite his efforts to suppress it.

The daylight faded outside the windows, and it was time to switch on the lanterns. Natalie closed all the sliders and brought an illuminated lantern to the bed where she switched on the other lanterns close by. In the warm yellow light, she brought clean towels and a small bucket of fresh water to wash his face.

Coltan whimpered like a child. He began to drift off again and had made the sound unknowingly.

"You'll be alright," Natalie said.

"Why'd they do it?" Coltan whispered pathetically.

"I don't know."

"I never hurt an animal. Never."

"I know."

"God..." his voice weakened further.

"Hush. You'll be alright. Try to sleep."

"I didn't do nothin'..."

"Of course not." She filled the glass with water and took two antibiotics and two painkillers out of her pocket. She gently lifted his head, set the pills into his mouth and offered him the water. "For the pain. Drink. Careful now. I got you. Let me help."

His strength was rapidly diminishing. He allowed her to guide him through the pill-taking process. He choked on the water and coughed some of it out. She pulled back slightly as he showered her with it. She waited a bit before she gave him more.

"Sorry..." he whispered.

"It's okay." She poured antibacterial soap into the bucket and stirred it with a washcloth. She tenderly went about cleaning his face.

"Cold..." he said.

"It cleans the blood off better."

"What'd I do...?"

"Be quiet. It's over. It's all over. You're okay."

"What'd I do...?"

"Shhh..."

He slept for six hours, at which point she had to awaken him to give him another dose of antibiotics and one more painkiller. She took a painkiller for herself, as her back was hurting from all the hours sitting with him between the tasks of washing out the towels and cloths and medical instruments in a bleach solution. Now she realized why Mom had insisted on so many gallons of bleach; it was for times such as this. She only wished Mom had gotten hold of more pain meds.

In the next six hours before dawn, Coltan fought off the dogs in his dreams.

He slept through the bulk of the next day, only to awaken with a raging fever at sunset. Natalie forced him to drink water. The water came back up minutes later, along with a fourth round of antibiotics and pain medication. She laid towels soaked in water and rubbing alcohol over him to drop his fever. The results were temporary, and their battle continued into the night. He became weaker and his dreams were silent.

When dawn broke the second morning and she awoke from an hour's nap to tend to him, she discovered his face had paled to a sickly white. He did not respond to her voice or touch. Finding his pulse was difficult, and she finally detected it under his jaw. It was racing. His heartbeat was rapid and weak. She checked his blood pressure and found it to be low. The fever had risen still higher. All together, it was bad news. Before noon, he went into convulsions.

She cried and held him and prayed. She began another treatment with the water and alcohol soaked towels. After three hours of this, his temperature dropped to a low-grade fever. He gradually awakened, and she gave him a triple dose of two different antibiotics with a slow dosing of water. This time, he kept it down. In the early evening, she gave him vitamins and a painkiller, and another slow dosing of water. It stayed down, and she hoped for the best.

He had not been able to speak during the crises hours of that day, although he wanted to. He wanted to thank her for saving his life.

CHAPTER 19

Once again, James donned the stolen UEF Armed Forces uniform. Trevor and Franks intercepted him on his way to the jeep in the bowels of the refuge compound. The men were dressed in fatigues and fully armed.

"This is my idea," Trevor told James. "I'm goin' along."

James continued walking quickly down the corridor. "It's easier if I go alone."

"You'll need backup," Franks said.

"Look, you two. I took on that hospital by myself; I can handle this." He stopped and faced the men. "Y'all are needed here." He patted Trevor's shoulder. "You're in charge while I'm gone."

Trevor protested, "Bloody hell, James!"

"At least let *me* go with you!" Franks offered.

"This is an easy one. Mitch told me there's a mom an' pop drugstore right at the eastern edge of Bonito Valle. All I gotta do is spot the Dairy Delight, and it's right there on the street behind it. It's a slam dunk." He continued on his way, "I need you two here!"

"But, James! I can go—" Franks persisted.

James cut him off, "I need you to train those troops! Quit arguin', Franks!" To Trevor, he said, "You tell that boy we're gettin' him those meds. Tell the doctors the rest of the supplies will be here soon—whatever that store's got, anyway." He patted the radio on his belt, "I'll check in with y'all. Now, get your butts upstairs!" He reached the jeep and hopped in, set his duffle bag and rifle on the passenger seat, and double-checked his holster for his handgun. "I should be back around fourteen-hundred hours."

Franks backed out of his way. "We'll pray for you!"

James fired up the vehicle and started forward. "I could use it!"

James had barely cleared the camouflaged doorway of the underground compound in his jeep when Mitchell Fenny hopped into the passenger seat. As he hopped in, he swept James's duffle bag onto the floor and grabbed the rifle.

James hollered, "What do you think you're doin'?"

Mitchell settled into the seat and placed his own duffle bag with James's on the floor at his feet. "I'm goin' with ya!"

James slammed on the brakes. "No, you're not!"

Dressed in fatigues and fully armed, Mitchell determined to go whether James liked it or not. This was his opportunity to discover what happened to the Danburys. If they were still bunkered down in their house, he and James could transport them safely back to the refuge. "I got people there I gotta check on!" Mitchell stated.

"I'll check on 'em!" James glared at him. "Get out!"

"They don't know you!" Mitchell argued, "Besides that, you ain't goin' alone. You gotta have backup, and I know the area." He bent and reached into his duffle bag and retrieved a lock cutter. "Bet you didn't think of *this*, did ya?"

"Hell... I can just bust in a window."

"Not at Swain's you can't. They got the windows and doors protected by bars. Been that way for years." He rapped his knuckles upon the dashboard. "Move this thing! We're wastin' time! The sun's comin' up."

James gritted his teeth, shifted the jeep and stepped on the gas.

SMITH WAS ONE OF A handful of soldiers remaining at the Baker Creek research facility. He was not looking forward to another shift babysitting the five cannibalistic teenagers in the cage.

Teenagers were a pain-in-the-ass enough as normal people; as mords, they were even more rebellious, violent and downright dangerous. After he relieved the poor bastard stuck on graveyard shift, Smith stood back and observed his charges, four young men and one girl. The girl sported a number of bite wounds on her back, which were visible through her stained and ripped blouse. Lately her pregnancy showed, and he couldn't guess how far along she was. The young men were a mix. The youngest looked to be about thirteen, judging by his immature body and face full of acne; the Asian with half his face chewed carried around a broken pair of eyeglasses he refused to surrender; the tall, obese Black guy covered in gang tattoos sported a nice sprinkling of human bites plus old scars all over his body—most of them remnants of gunshot wounds; the Hispanic guy, tall, lean and muscular wore only the shredded remnant of a white shirt and Bujjet Mart vest, complete with a yellow smiley-face button and a nametag that read, *I'm Mario. How may I help you today?* Mario had bites on his neck, arms and legs. All the teens had shed their shoes, socks and pants. Drip trails of urine, blood and loose feces stained their legs and feet.

They smelled as inviting as they appeared. Smith kept his distance and made it a point not to stand downwind of their stench.

He watched as the little acne-faced boy picked up a soiled wool blanket and wrapped it around himself. That one was always cold. He was also the one at the bottom of their group hierarchy and the one that took most of the beatings at mealtime. Little Acne Boy was slowly starving to death. When he turned his back to Smith, Smith saw through the gap in the blanket the gaping wound on his butt cheek where some monster had tried to have him for breakfast. Smith figured a mord chased the kid and overcame him. It was a mystery how the boy escaped being devoured alive.

The Asian kid compulsively traced the cracks in the concrete floor of the cage, while the gang-banger guy bobbed his head and grunted to himself in four-four time. Mario polished his nametag with a shredded strip of his white shirt. Smith thought this kid probably spent a lot of time primping in the mirror before the mords claimed him; he was still a good-looking specimen, in spite of the virus. A week ago, Mario's mature-boy beard and mustache made its presence known to the world, and the hair was growing fast and thick.

The pregnant girl sat down against the back wall, and extended her filthy, wiry legs straight and far apart on the cement. Smith could plainly see everything he did not want to see. She urinated right there, and didn't bother to get up. The girl was a genetic racial mixture with dark curly hair. He thought she might have been pretty before the disease whittled away whatever beauty she once possessed. She moaned to herself while she twirled her long hair in her fingers and stared at handsome Mario the Prince of Bujjet Mart.

Bored and looking for something to cover the stench in the air, Smith lit a cigarette. He stood there and smoked, and glanced around the compound. The tiny medical clinic up the street had been bustling with personnel and activity up until the warm weather kicked in and the staff gradually went AWOL; it now had all the appearance of being deserted and was ominously quiet. The wet green grass overtook the sidewalk and concrete entry path up the wheelchair ramp. He knew Clausberg, Morris, Guffy and that little infected Mexican kid were somewhere inside. He had not talked with Guffy in weeks, so he had no idea what was going on there, and he didn't want to know.

Across the way and down a side street, the sheriff's station and miniscule jail, a temporary holding facility, was finally quiet for a while. Smith had heard the screams from inside and had done his best to ignore it. He knew what the screams were about—everyone knew. They had all seen Clausberg march over there every morning like clockwork, carrying a fresh IV bag and a bucket, and the screaming would start anew, only to cease a couple hours later. Clausberg spent about ten minutes or so inside, and she would always come out with the bucket full of something awash in fresh blood. He knew what it was. The mords still got their meals once a day. Now, listening to the quiet, Smith hoped the wretched child molester had finally died, even though he felt the bastard had gotten what he deserved.

The boy he had attempted to molest had disappeared along with his father a week ago. They were only two of the multitude that had fled for Anywhere But Here. The fates of those who fled were anybody's guess.

With the exception of those taken over by the soldiers all but a few of the nearby houses were empty. It seemed what remained of the Research Team: Clausberg, Morris and Guffy, lived inside the clinic.

When the researchers first arrived, supposedly under Presidential orders with their phony military protection, they convinced the denizens of Baker Creek they would protect them from the mordants. They promised the people food, supplies and medical assistance, as well as guaranteed gas and electricity to see everybody through the winter. Doctor Clausberg and another doctor named Brandewyn waved some impressive-looking psuedo-government papers (on official White House stationary, no less) at the owners of the town's medical clinic and took it over easily. Once established, they insidiously claimed the rest of the town as their own.

UEF soldiers arrived one week after the Research team. They surreptitiously imprisoned, bound, gagged and shackled in the little jail the residents of this tiny community in small groups. Those whisked behind bars never spent more than five minutes of their imprisonment fully conscious, for the scientists heavily sedated all almost immediately to keep them quiet and manageable until the Prep Team came in to kill the victims and transport their bodies to an old railroad cargo container where they were cut up into meal size portions for the mords. The initial assumption was the missing had simply either fallen prey to the wandering mords, or had taken advantage of the many (fake) military transports to the rescue center outside Reyton. In the beginning, it had been easy to fool the populace; the vast majority was hard drinking, hard drugging country white trash that lived in blissful ignorance of the world outside Baker Creek.

The clandestine round-ups went on for two weeks before someone finally got suspicious when a crew in an unmarked semi-truck deposited their cargo of fourteen lethargic mords into the empty bear cage at the wildlife refuge at the end of town. Some big mouth community activist protested the researchers brought the dangerous mordants into his town without public notification. *And wasn't that just like the Yoo-Ess Government to ignore the rights and safety of the people to push through another one of their insane, costly and ultimately useless research programs?* The whole scenario reeked of *eminent domain* abuse. Many noticed the captured mords were eating more often than the remaining *normal* populace. That's when the shit hit the fan, and Doctor Clausberg ordered Smith and his underlings to massacre the remaining residents.

Someone told Smith Clausberg ordered the bodies butchered and frozen to keep the mords alive through the winter. The way the Research Team looked at it, the mordants were vastly more valuable than a hundred or so ignorant white trash hillbillies out in the sticks.

As far as Smith was concerned the townspeople were disposable collateral in this most unique of wars. He felt nothing for them. He felt no regret over his willing cooperation with this twisted group, either. All that mattered to him was his safety and survival in this demented world, and Clausberg's fragmented remains of an organization provided him just that. Their only requirement of him was he shut up and did what they told him to do. That suited him just fine.

Smith observed the remaining mords and they observed him. Mario charged the bars, thrust his hands through and growled. Smith backed away. Unlike the rest of the soldiers who babysat these monsters, Smith knew better than to antagonize them.

All his comrades were getting shit-faced across the street at the only bar in town, as they did every day. It seemed to be the only other thing to do around here. He wished he could join them.

A loud grunt and a knocking sound on the bars of the cage drew his attention back to his subjects. The big gang-banger eyed him and nodded his head invitingly. To Smith's amazement, the cannibal formed his fingers and brought them to his lips, pantomiming smoking.

Smith stepped closer to the cage. "You want a smoke, Jimbo?"

He grunted and nodded his head.

"What the fuck..." Smith tossed what was left of his cigarette near the big man's feet. He watched amusedly as the creature picked it up and began smoking.

Smith scratched his head and looked around for witnesses. The street was empty. He decided he'd go across and have a beer.

NATALIE ZIPPED UP THE sleeping bag around Coltan. His temperature had dropped below normal and he was shivering. He had been shivering for the past hour. She lifted his head to give him more antibiotics and painkillers. Coltan turned his face away from her and whimpered as another wave of pain traveled through his body. The accompanying constant pain in his stomach was more than he could tolerate, and the painkillers were only making it worse. He curled up inside the sleeping bag and wrapped his arms around his middle.

Natalie tried to hold him still. "Colt, you have to take these!"

He painfully turned over on his side, his back to her. All he wanted was warmth and sleep, and his voice would not come so he could tell her.

She set down the water glass, and forced him onto his back and held him there. "Colt, please!"

He turned over on his side again and curled up, this time facing her. He managed to mouth the word, "Pain!" but his voice was too weak to create a clear sound.

"What?" She bent her face close to his.

"Pain!" He struggled to make the sound of the word.

She understood. "Where?"

Coltan tried to explain in words. Nothing came out but a whimper. He curled up into a ball, shivering.

She observed his position; saw his knees drawn up to his chest under the sleeping bag. She finally got a clue. "Your stomach?"

He nodded weakly, and took quick, shallow breaths. His eyes closed slowly only to spring open again, begging her to understand.

"It's the painkillers doing that." Natalie hoped that was all it was. She brought her fingers to her forehead and thought about it. He required intravenous pain control, and Mom had not obtained any intravenous medications. She pondered for a long while, wondering what place was close enough that would have those items. She recalled Swain's Drugs behind the Dairy Delight. It was a tiny store, but they had a decent pharmacy.

Coltan groaned and tried to sit up on his side. His stomach was rejecting its contents again. He punched the word out high-pitched and hoarse, "Bucket!"

She grabbed it and helped him sit up, and she placed the bucket under his chin. He barfed up some black liquid containing traces of fresh dark pink blood. His body shuddered, and tears ran down his face as he expelled a second round into the bucket. When he was certain it was over, he groaned once more and sank onto his side, panting to catch his breath.

Natalie adjusted the pillow under his head and wiped his hair off his sweaty brow. He shivered again and closed his eyes, a crumpled-up ball of misery inside the sleeping bag.

"I'm going over to Swain's," she told him. "I'm gonna get you some morphine."

He opened his eyes and mouthed the word *no*, desperation in his face.

"It's close enough to get there safely," she assured him. "I'll take the storm drain across so no one will see me. Carolyn and I used to do it all the time when we were little. There's an inlet right across from the store, and I can still fit through it."

He mouthed the word *no* again.

"I have to," she said sternly. "You need more antibiotics, too. You gotta trust me, Colt."

There was no reply this time, only a sad and fearful expression in his eyes.

"It won't take long. I'll be careful. I promise you I'll be back in a half-hour or so."

"Dogs…" he whispered.

"I'll take Bonnie along."

He closed his eyes tightly, and more tears fell. The possibility of something happening to her terrified him; alone he would die a slow, agonizing death.

She kissed his cheek and his forehead. "I promise we'll be okay."

Coltan grudgingly accepted he could not change her mind, and he nodded feebly.

She put on her shoes and leather jacket. After checking and adding some ammo, she tucked Bonnie into her pocket with an extra two dozen loose bullets. She grabbed an empty backpack and dropped in a flashlight and binoculars. "See you soon, hon."

He prayed silently.

The rear of the house provided the most direct route to the storm drain, which took her through the kitchen first. She did her best to ignore the blood drops, smears and stains on the kitchen floor and the two exterior doors. The mess gave silent testimony of the brutal attack and Coltan's battle to stay alive. She didn't need a reminder; it was all she thought about.

Natalie closed the back door and locked the security door. She covered her nose and mouth when the rank odor of the rotting dog corpses drifted her way on the breeze. The buzzing of flies hummed. She knew the flies were feasting and nesting inside the dead dogs. The thought of it made her want to puke.

The dogs had obviously been sick with something and, whatever it was, she was sure they gave it to Coltan. From what she could ascertain by Coltan's symptoms, the human effects of the canine disease did not resemble the mord virus, although the dogs themselves seemed to be canine versions of the mords. So far, Coltan had not presented any of the symptoms of the mord virus. If anything, he seemed to be suffering from a combination of blood loss and blood poisoning. But, what if that was only the beginning? What if he did have the virus and it had manifested differently in him because the host who infected him was a dog and not a human? Would the virus act differently because of it? Would the onset of the rest of the symptoms—the stroke, the sudden and brief recovery, followed by insanity and cannibalistic tendencies—only come on more slowly because the dogs transmitted it? If that was the case, she feared he would go insane from it just like they did, and he would pose a threat to her. If that turned out to be the case, what could she do? She doubted she would find it easy to put a gun to his head, no matter how dire the circumstance. If it came to that, she decided she would have to kill herself as well, because she did not want to live without him.

The air was warmer now with the sun high in the southeast. She unzipped her jacket to prevent overheating. The last thing she needed was to come down sick; there was no one to take care of them both. Natalie tried not to think about it. Instead, she focused on enjoying the welcome promise of spring as she continued on her way in the late-morning sunlight on her quest to save Coltan's life.

She hurried down the steps and onto the garden path. From there, she crouched as she ran to the edge of the gully. The storm drainpipe was down there, and all she had to do was slide down on her butt until she reached the spot where the pipe protruded out of the dirt in the side of the hill along the gully.

The gully was full of water from the heavy winter and spring rains. The rotting corpse of a woman floated and swirled in the moving water. Natalie wondered if the presence of the corpses not only in the gully, but also all over town, had compromised the quality of the well water she and Coltan depended upon. It was another worry she didn't need.

The thump-thump-thump of a helicopter off in the distance over Reyton caught her attention. She spotted it and scrambled into the drainpipe to avoid detection. For all she knew, they were scouring the area with binoculars. Getting caught would be the worst thing. She crouched inside the entrance to the drainpipe and used her own binoculars for a better look. The whirlybird started to veer in her direction, but dipped and began to waver erratically. It swung violently in the opposite direction, picked up speed, then slowed and dropped. It crashed on the west side of the freeway on the outskirts of Reyton, just in front of the foothills. She saw the craft disintegrate and explode on impact. Even though she felt relieved to be free of the danger, she felt sorry for whoever had died in the crash. Her next thought was a question as to what had caused the crash.

There was plenty of time later to ponder it. In the meantime, Coltan was suffering, possibly dying, and she had to get the medications he needed.

She followed the pipe and took a left at the junction where it led to Swain's. The sunlight hurt her eyes as she climbed the ladder into the storm drain entrance. It was a tight squeeze, but she got through. As she popped her head up to see the street there, she scanned the area for mords, soldiers, and any other surprises. There was no one. She listened for dogs. No dogs. Swain's front door was directly ahead across the road. She climbed out the storm drain entrance in the curb and sped across, crouching and glancing in all directions.

An iron security gate protected the front door, and bars protected the windows. She had forgotten about that. In the cover of the bushes at the side of the store, she sat and reconsidered her plan of action and tried to remember the little details about the place she and Carolyn had discovered as children. The place had an attic with a tiny window in the back of the building. A tree sat front of the window. Back in the day, old man Swain caught them climbing the tree and called their parents. If the tree was still there, she could climb it again and reach the window that way. After taking a minute to catch her breath and survey her surroundings, she rounded the corner to the rear of the building. The tree was still there. Natalie wasted no time climbing it and reached the window quickly. The window was single-pane and already cracked from years of weather abuse and one minor earthquake. She encountered one problem. She had nothing with her to break the window. She draped herself over the tree limb and considered what she had on hand: Bonnie and the binoculars. Bonnie had less chance of being damaged breaking the window. Her decision made, she used the butt of the gun to shatter the glass. It broke easily, but it made a good deal of noise.

After popping out the jagged remnants of the pane, Natalie slid on her belly from the tree limb and over through the window frame. The space was only big enough for an older and larger child to get through, and it presented one of those rare moments when Natalie was happy to be small in stature. She alighted softly onto the dusty wood floor and squatted under the window until her eyes adjusted to the dim light inside. Boxes covered in dust and spider webs slowly came into focus. She assumed the boxes held old pharmaceutical records from eons ago. Once she could see clearly, she made her way to the flip-up panel in the floor that led to the store downstairs. She pulled it up and peered down. There was no staircase or ladder. She would have to drop eight feet onto the floor below. Natalie lowered herself and hung by her fingertips from the frame of the panel above. She said a quick prayer, took a deep breath, and dropped.

Her feet and her ankles met the concrete under the cheap and worn 1970's linoleum floor covering with a stinging, bone-rattling pain as she landed. Her legs buckled and she stumbled and fell on her buttocks. She sat on the floor, watched and listened while she recovered from the landing. The place was dark and silent.

She could see the shelves of medicines and supplies by the sparse sunlight beaming through the barred windows. Beyond, a section of wall and a counter separated the customer area of the store from the pharmaceutical stock. She noticed the cash register was open. Someone had taken the money. A quick visual check revealed no open doors or windows anywhere in the store. Whoever had taken the money had obviously been an employee, or maybe old man Swain, himself. She flipped the light switch on the wall. It was dead. That was a good thing. No electricity meant the alarm was also dead. She could leave through the back door.

In the dim light, she searched the shelves for the little glass bottles of morphine. There were lots of large plastic bottles filled with different drugs, but nothing resembled what she sought. She stuffed a box of diabetic syringes it into her backpack. Again, Natalie searched the shelves for morphine and still couldn't find it. Where would they put it? As she scanned the space, she spotted a partially open door marked "OFFICE." Inside she found the safe on the floor in a recessed niche behind the door. It occurred to her all pharmacies stored high-demand drugs like morphine, methadone, certain antihistamines and steroids in safes during off-hours to keep them out of the hands of criminals.

Damn...

How to open the safe?

She squatted in front of it and took a close look. Someone had forgotten to latch it. Not believing her luck, and expecting it to be empty, she opened the door and peered in. Someone had already picked through the toppled contents. More than likely, all the good stuff was gone. She prayed as she examined the assortment: codeine, pseudoephedrine, arsenic, assorted steroids and some other things she did not recognize and couldn't pronounce. Under her breath, she cussed in frustration and disappointment.

The next nearest pharmacy was all the way down the hill on the other side of the freeway at the west side junction. She presumed scavengers and criminals, and maybe even the soldiers had already picked the store clean. Additionally, that store stood alone amidst a huge treeless parking lot.

Coltan was worth the effort and the risk. She vacillated between fear and determination. If she risked it and the soldiers apprehended her...

Natalie didn't know what to do.

She felt compelled to re-check the safe. In the rear, under some small overturned boxes, she spotted some smaller boxes, white, the size of the morphine vials she had seen at the hospital. The image in her mind was only of the little glass vials, and that was what she had been looking for. Of course, the vials would be in a box when they were new. She took one out and read the print on the box: *Morphine Sulfate.*

Thank you, Jesus!

There were eight boxes. At first, she grabbed all eight to put into her pack. However, something stopped her, caused her to consider the remote possibility someone else would visit here soon for the same reason. The compulsion to leave some behind was strong, so she trusted what she believed was God's prodding and took only three of the boxes.

She found assorted antibiotics in large plastic bottles on the shelves. She chose three kinds and put one bottle of each in her pack, leaving the rest for whoever was on their way for them. On another shelf, she found some stomach remedies and took a small assortment, and then grabbed a large box of syringes from another shelf under the counter.

From the customer shopping area she found more rubbing alcohol, alcohol prep pads, hydrogen peroxide, sanitary wipes, and an assortment of bandages; she took some of each and stowed it in her pack. Another section offered towels, washcloths, electric blankets, sheet protectors and heating pads. She grabbed some of the towels, washcloths and sheet protectors and added them to her pack.

The pack now full and heavy, she decided she had gotten enough for Coltan's immediate needs. It was time to go.

She unlocked the rear door and the iron security door and stepped out into the sunlight. A thorough look around revealed no other people and no dogs. After quietly closing both doors, but leaving them unlocked, she dashed around to the front of the building and across the street to the storm drain in the curb.

JAMES PARKED THE JEEP under a grove of pine trees in the backyard of one of the houses. He did not plan to spend much time on Mitchell's endeavor to check the Danbury house as he fully expected the house would be empty. Once Mitchell got in and verified it, they could go on to the pharmacy and complete their main mission.

They approached the house on foot from the rear. The charred shell of Beverly's car was the first thing they noticed. The vehicle was too burned up, even the license plates, for Mitchell to identify it as belonging to the Danburys. They looked it over and were relieved there were no human remains inside. For the moment, it was just one of many burned-up vehicles they had seen on this street. It could have belonged to anyone. Mitchell pointed out the garden, which was now a dilapidated shell of its former self. Off the garden path, on its side under a tree was Brian's old truck. It looked like a bulldozer had pounded it. They found the interior empty.

The putrid odor of rotting flesh directed their attention to the area near the tool shed. The men discovered the many dead dogs scattered in the immediate vicinity. James had the stronger stomach, so he bent and took a close look at the carcasses.

"They've been shot." He remained squatting next to a stiff bloated pit bull for a few extra moments, "Maybe two or three days ago at the most."

Mitchell noticed the blood in the soil a second after James saw it. A revolting scenario played out in his mind and he used all his effort to push it away. *Maybe it had not been one of them. Maybe they're okay.*

James stood. "Whoever it was—it looks like they put up one hell of a fight!"

They followed a trail of large blood drops and large smeared blood drops to the bottom of the rear porch steps. The trail continued up. When they stepped up on the back porch, Mitchell saw the exterior of the once beautiful house was now sorely battered, but he knew Brian and Beverly would have had enough sense to let it go to avoid detection. As he and James neared the rear entrance to the house, they saw plainly the smears and spatters of blood on the exterior security door that protected the door to the kitchen.

The doormat was saturated, and the dried blood had hardened and mixed with the dirt there; it created a crust upon the thick rubber under-pad that cracked under Mitchell's weight.

As the two men circled the exterior of the house on the three-quarter wraparound porch, James recognized the plywood sliders on the windows and vaguely recalled performing a house search there. He mentioned it to Mitchell as they rounded the front to find a loose or damaged window panel. They were at the front when James recalled he had entered the house through the living room window. He tried the panel and found someone had reinforced it from the interior.

"Someone's gotta be in there," he whispered to Mitchell.

James wondered privately what they would discover inside, and what they would do about it if the residents were alive and well. Could they fit everyone in the jeep? He also considered the alternate scenario. What if the survivors were infected? Could Mitchell handle it, knowing they would have to kill them?

Mitchell found the front door locked securely, which he expected. He eyed the den window and tried it. Secure.

"We might as well try 'em all," he told James.

At the rear of the house where they had begun, James discovered the weather-compromised slider at the shattered dining room window. He also noticed more droplets of blood on the decking. The droplets led back to the rear security door. He decided not to mention the blood, and drew Mitchell's attention to the damaged slider.

"This one!" he whispered.

He and Mitchell gently worked it loose. They climbed through and stood in the darkness for a moment, listening. It was quiet. Mitchell clicked on his flashlight, James his headlamp. James readied his weapon and they searched the bottom floor together.

Mitchell thought he remembered a door in the kitchen that led to the basement. He searched for the door, but could not locate it. Things seemed different than he recalled, but he had not spent a lot of time inside the Danbury's home over the last few years; their get-togethers had largely taken place out in the back around the barbeque grill. They had been good days. Mitchell considered the possibility the kitchen to basement door actually existed in some other friend's house. His memory was not accurate anymore, a casualty of the brain injury sustained during his last tour of duty.

His flashlight exposed large drops of dried blood on the kitchen floor, and large smears of blood on the interior lock and doorknob of the door to the rear porch. He told James, "Check this out!"

They followed the drops to the bottom of the staircase where a large pool of blood stained the carpet. Bloodied handprints on the first two steps indicated someone had fallen. Small bloody footprints and some large footprints circled and smeared through the pooled stain. The prints belonged to two people, both barefooted at the time. Mitchell shined his light on the steps and saw the bloody footprints continued to the second floor. Mitchell thought the small footprints might be Natalie's, and his gut twisted sickeningly.

James paused with him at the foot of the stairs. It slowly came back to him this was the home of the woman surgeon he had met at the hospital, the Christian doctor who prayed in all circumstances, the doctor he had supplied with the coordinates of the refuge. If his memory served him accurately, there was a room upstairs, a closed door bolted shut from the inside. He had slipped a card under that door.

He cautiously took the stairs up as Mitchell shined light ahead of them to guide their way. At the top of the staircase, the blood trail led directly to a room with a wide open door.

Mitchell paused and stared at the open doorway. Sunlight spilled into the room through the window. Mitchell welcomed the natural light.

As a precaution, he shined his light around the hallway and glimpsed the other rooms through their open doorways. He could not detect any movement, and he could hear no breathing or other sounds indicating the presence of another living person.

James stepped over to the sunlit room and peeked in. The trail of blood led to a blood-soiled full size bed near the wall; the bunk beds against the other wall were clean and appeared undisturbed.

"They must've collapsed on this bed," James said it softly when Mitchell caught up to him. "I don't see anything else, though. No, wait..." He noticed a large smear of blood on the wall paneling opposite, and another pool of blood on the carpet there. "Looks like they fell against that wall." James bent and examined the carpeting, "There're more footprints, too, but they're smeared. Can't tell much. There's footprints over footprints and it's all smeared up. Shine that light again down the hall. Let's see if there's blood down that way."

Mitchell pointed the light to the carpeting and followed it down the hall and back again. There were no prints leading to any of the other rooms. Sadly, Mitchell slunk down against the wall and bowed his head. A number of possible scenarios came to mind, none of them comforting.

James understood the Danburys were good friends of Mitchell's, and he could see the grief in Mitchell's posture. "I don't know what to tell you, man..."

Mitchell stood and desperately called, "Brian! Bev! Natalie! It's Mitchell! Are you here?" He paused and listened while James stood hopeless.

Up in the attic, Coltan was unconscious inside the warm sleeping bag. He was not aware of anything, not even the fact he was still alive.

"Let's search all the bedrooms thoroughly," James suggested. "Maybe they're out of it and can't talk."

"Brian...?" Mitchell called once more.

James let the silence answer before he spoke again, "Let's check it out. C'mon, Mitch. Let's do it and get the hell outa here." James repositioned his headlamp for a broader sweep of light. With his rifle pointed and ready, he started in the girl's room at the other end of the hallway.

Mitchell lifted his weapon and followed James's lead. They searched every room, every closet, every corner and under every bed. There was no one. A second, more thorough, search of the downstairs also revealed nothing. They returned to the dining room and paused at the window.

"They must've got out," James said, "They must've."

Mitchell scanned the room, shook his head sadly, "Shit..."

"You say the whole family was here?" James asked.

"Yeah. Brian, Bev, and the girl—Natalie." After a breath, he remembered, "And their other kid, sorta, a teenage boy. What was his name? Colt? Yeah... Coltan. The four of 'em."

"Is there any other place they coulda gone?"

He couldn't remember. "I don't know." However, the idea of *going* somewhere made him think of vehicles. He hurried through the kitchen and swung open the door to the garage. The only vehicle there was Coltan's Harley. As James came up beside him in the doorway, Mitchell said, "That's the kid's bike. Brian mentioned it a lot. He worried about the kid crashin' it like his brother did. What the hell... it's still here."

"They probably took off in the parents' car."

"They had two cars and a truck."

"We already saw the truck and that one car out back," James said, "So that leaves one vehicle missing. My guess is they split in it. Maybe whoever got hurt, all that blood upstairs, wasn't even one of them. It was probably someone who broke in for shelter."

"The doors are all locked," Mitchell reminded him. "They woulda needed a key. There's no blood around the windows. That means they got in usin' a key. I don't know anybody outside their family who'd have a key."

"Well... They might've left it unlocked in their hurry to go." James replied, "There's no one here. They must've got out." He turned to go out the window, "We gotta go, too. Let's move it, Mitch."

"Why are we goin' out the window?"

"To keep the place secure for them in case they come back."

Mitchell could not see the sense in James's intention, but he let the man have his way. He knew James sometimes looked at things differently than other people, considered things most people would not think of. There was no harm in it.

They replaced the slider in the window just as they found it and headed back to the jeep to complete their original mission.

AS NATALIE REACHED the mouth of the drainpipe, she heard the sound of a vehicle's engine get louder as it neared her house. She waited inside the pipe to hear if the vehicle would stop or continue on its way. It passed her house and continued down the hill toward the Dairy Delight. She popped her head out the end of the pipe just in time to catch a glimpse of the rear of the jeep as it rounded the curve and sped away from her. Natalie waited a few extra minutes to be certain it would not return. It was the first jeep she had seen since that day when—

She pushed the memory away.

She hadn't seen the driver or passengers. Still, she assumed it was at least two soldiers, probably four. Perhaps they were scouting the area for survivors. Maybe they were looking for her. It was possible one of the soldiers had spotted her, even though she had been careful. Could they have traced her back to this neighborhood? Had they followed her trail using thermal imaging? Anything was possible. The thought made her uneasy.

She explored the area through her binoculars. If anyone was out there, they concealed themselves well. She considered staying in the pipe until sunset. That idea died quickly when she thought about Coltan. There was no time to waste. She had to take the risk and make it back to the house.

As soon as she entered the kitchen, she spun and locked both doors. When she turned to walk into the living room, something felt different. She remained in the darkness for a few moments, studying the energy in the house before she finally switched on the flashlight. Although everything appeared the same, the house contained that strange energy that fills every home when guests have left—that odd phenomena that gives one a vision of the guests dumping their residual energy onto the floor before they leave.

She readied Bonnie and continued along slowly and cautiously, her senses cranked up to high radar.

Some of the light from the window in the open bedroom upstairs spilled into the living room and made it easier for her to see. She didn't recall leaving that door open so far. However, she had been in a hurry, and they had decided weeks ago to leave that room open to allay any suspicion of a hideaway beyond its walls. On further consideration, she thought she should have left it completely open to give the appearance it had always been open. She decided not to over-think it. Stuff like that could drive a person crazy.

On feather-light steps, she checked all the rooms on the main floor, including all the closets. Everything was fine. Nothing was out of place or missing, and nothing smelled different. She wondered if she was imagining it all. The journey outside had been stressful. It was too easy to be paranoid over every little thing.

Another glance up the stairs reminded her Coltan was up there. He was probably worried and maybe even frightened. Certainly, he was still in pain.

She hurried up the stairs and into the attic access room. Once inside, she barricaded the hidden door and hurried up the retractable stairs into the attic.

The sunlight brought welcome illumination into the space. She could see Coltan's form curled up in the sleeping bag on his mattress. She could hear his faint breathing. As she neared him, he did not move.

"Colt?"

No answer.

She knelt at his side and gently dropped the backpack onto the floor. He failed to stir at the sound and vibration as if unaware of everything around him. She leaned over him and tenderly shifted him onto his back. His face was white, except for the dark circles under his eyes. She felt his skin. It was dry and cold. For a moment, she thought he was dead.

She shook him. "Colt!"

The sound came weakly and slowly from him, in a raspy breath, "Huh...?"

Thank God!

"Please, wake up..." She held his face in her hands and stroked his cheeks with her thumbs. "Wake up, hon. Please..."

His eyes opened slowly, unfocused, but still a sign of life, a sign of returning consciousness. He attempted to speak, but his voice would not come.

"I got the morphine," she told him, "And some stuff for your stomach."

He closed his eyes for a few moments, opened them again and tried hard to focus his sight on her. He was so glad, so relieved she had returned. He longed to tell her, to hold her in his arms and never let her go. Yet, all his ailing body could deliver was a soft groan and the slightest hint of a grateful smile.

"Is the pain any worse?"

He blinked once.

What did that mean? "Blink once for no and twice for yes."

He blinked twice.

"Oh, my god...," she whispered. "I got the morphine right here. But I gotta check the PDR first to make sure of the dosage, okay?"

He blinked twice.

Natalie rose quickly, grabbed the heavy drug reference book, and brought it back to his bedside. She hastily found the page and read the indications and dosage information. She read it through a second time for certainty.

Coltan watched her remove the medicine, syringe and alcohol prep pads from her backpack. He admired her calm and determination under such dire conditions as she carefully performed each step. He thought she had no idea how much she resembled her mother as she filled the syringe with the morphine; the expression on her face, the concentration and confidence there, the compassion in her eyes when she looked from the syringe to him, it was all Beverly. He decided at that moment, Natalie should be a doctor. He wanted to tell her.

She recapped the needle, propped the capped end of the syringe between her front teeth, and helped him bring his arm out from inside the sleeping bag. She laid his arm flat, palm side up, tore open and applied the alcohol pad to the intended vein site. Just like Beverly, she squinted as she searched and identified a good vein. She peered at him comfortingly and said as she uncapped the needle, "A little stick, that's all. You'll feel better soon." Diligently, gently, she inserted the needle and pulled the pump back a little to suck up a tiny bit of blood that indicated a good vein and no air in the needle. The blood backed up without an air bubble ahead of it. Natalie knew she got it right. She fed the morphine into his vein slowly to prevent the hot rush some people experienced with rapid injection.

He felt the warmth of the drug spread lazily through his body, and it felt wonderful. His pain immediately began to lessen. He closed his eyes and moaned the release from all the days of increasing misery.

"Good?" she asked.

"Uh-huh." It was more a breathy contented sigh than anything else.

His muscles relaxed completely and he sank once more into the sanctuary of sleep.

CHAPTER 20

FLIGHT

Dillon's condition had changed only a little since the previous night when the doctor last visited. The boy was deathly pale, and fresh bruising had appeared near his collarbones and on his arms. The lymph nodes in his neck were noticeably swollen. Dr. Quimby ordered a second round of intravenous antibiotics for him, although the drugs had reached their expiration date. Dillon still required steroids and oxygen to assist his breathing. It seemed the weak antibiotics, the oxygen and the vitamin enriched intravenous fluid helped, for Dillon was alert and seemed to have a little more energy than the previous day.

Dr. Quimby found Dillon sitting up in bed reading a book. By the cover, the book appeared to be some kind of Science Fiction paperback in almost new condition. He noticed Dillon was already halfway through the novel, and he considered this a promising sign.

The doctor hesitated at the foot of the bed, "Is that a good book, Dillon?"

He paused in his reading and glanced up at him, "It's okay. Not enough sex. I woulda added more sex and made the Plachetas dual-gendered. It would be more interesting that way. They could fuck themselves and reproduce like rabbits. Then they could wipe out all the stupid humans, who don't deserve to live, anyway."

"Aren't the Plachetas the bad guys?"

"Supposedly. They have more guts than the weenie humans, though. I like that."

Quimby decided not to pursue the subject further. Dillon had a unique and sometimes disturbing viewpoint when it came to his fellow humans. The boy did not particularly like people and he considered them as nothing more than mirror images of the cannibalistic mords. In his opinion, people fed on each other just as greedily, only they devoured each other's souls instead of their flesh. The doctor considered Dillon's observation revealed a sorry truth about the current state of the human race, and he found himself privately agreeing. However, unlike Dillon, the man still clung to hope for the people of the world.

Getting back to business, Quimby approached with a full hypodermic. "Today you get a triple cocktail."

Dillon laid the paperback flat on his belly. "You mean they got back, already?"

"A few minutes ago." He inserted the needle into the meds administration port on the IV set-up and injected the triple drug recipe there. "The nurses tell me you've been nicer to them."

"I gotta be," Dillon grunted.

"Why's that?"

"I'm at their mercy." He made a crude attempt at humor, "Better to get it with grease than without."

The doctor knew all about Dillon and knew what the pun referred to. He did not find it humorous. "That's offensive, son."

"You shouldn't judge me." He cast the old guy a flirtatious smirk, just for the hell of it. He missed the good old days when a little bit of flirting at the right tourist ensured a fun weekend and a little cash in his pocket.

Dr. Quimby ignored the boy's unflattering flirtatiousness. Keeping his cool, he told Dillon, "I've never judged you. What ever gave you that idea?"

"You don't like me. I can tell."

"I hardly know you, Dillon." He pulled up a chair next to the bed and sat. "Your attitude makes it difficult for anyone to know you."

"I like a mystery. Don't you?"

"Not when it's contrived."

"What's that mean?"

"It means you're trying to create mystery where none exists."

Dillon laughed weakly. "You think you know everything."

"I know a child who's crying out for attention and acceptance."

He tilted his head to one side, smirked, and narrowed his eyes at the doctor. "Believe me, I got lots of attention."

"Perhaps the wrong kind?"

"What would be the wrong kind?"

"You know what I'm talking about." He opened the chart on his lap and wrote a notation in the medication record.

Dillon became suspicious. "What are you writing?"

"I'm updating your medication list." He set the open chart on Dillon's lap. "Read it for yourself."

Dillon read it. "You got me back on all that shit I didn't want. I told you I didn't want it." He closed the chart and brusquely tossed it to the doctor. "Fuck you..."

Quimby did not attempt to conceal his irritation. "Those men risked their lives to go out and get this medicine to save your life. The least you can say is *thank you*!"

"I didn't ask them to!"

"If you want so much to die, why did you fight so hard out there to stay alive?"

Dillon could not readily find an answer. He sunk back against the pillow, his eyes scornful and full of confusion. He thought back to his days trekking through the snowstorm and tried to remember what had spurred him on. It came to him the leukemia had not returned yet, and he had believed he had finally beaten it. That belief was what made life worth pursuing. He offered his explanation to Quimby, "I wasn't sick then."

At that moment, Trevor entered the room and neared the other side of the bed. "How are you feeling, Dillon?"

He snapped at Trevor, "Quit tryin' to save me!"

Trevor grinned. "Ah...! Still full of piss and vinegar, I see. Status quo."

"Fuck you, Trev. Fuckin' Limey."

Trevor kept it light and retorted humorously, "Fuck you, too. Impertinent little snot." To Quimby, he inquired, "Have you given him the meds already?"

"Yes, I did." The doctor stood. "The rest is up to the brat." He looked down at Dillon and addressed him sternly, "Of course that means *you*."

"*That means you!*" Dillon mimicked in a squeaky, sarcastic voice. "Go save some dumb fuck who thinks this is worth it."

Quimby sighed, a bit frustrated. He said to Trevor, "He's all yours."

"That would be nice..." Dillon mumbled loud enough for them to hear.

Trevor eyed the kid and gently slapped his cheek with his fingertips. "You will apologize."

"Fuck you..."

With no intention to hurt him, but only to command respect, Trevor delivered a second gentle slap. "Apologize."

Dillon challenged him, "I ain't sorry. You assholes are giving me shit I told you not to. You should apologize to *me*."

"We're tryin' to save your life, lad!"

"I told you I don't want it. Let me fuckin' die in peace. *That's* all I want."

Quimby walked slowly to the doorway. "I'll have Suzanne come talk to him."

"That hippie cunt?" Dillon sneered. "Fuck that. I ain't talkin' to her."

It took everything for Trevor to hold back his temper. He could tolerate jabs directed at his own self, but he could not and would not tolerate any abuse of Suzanne. He took a deep breath and silently counted to five before he said to the doctor, "That won't be necessary."

Doctor Quimby shrugged. "The little beast is all yours, Trev."

Trevor waited until the doctor was down the hall before he rose, closed the door and returned seething to Dillon's bedside. Without warning, he seized Dillon by his blond hair and forced the boy to look at him. "You worthless piece of shit..."

Dillon struck at Trevor's hands, and Trevor only pulled harder at his hair. "Ow, ow, ow, ow!"

"Is that what you want to hear?" Trevor asked. "Is this what you want?"

"Ow...! Ow...!"

"You will never, ever, talk about Suzanne that way. Am I clear?"

"Ow...! Let go!"

"Am I clear?"

"Yeah!"

"And, you will never, ever, treat the doctor with disrespect. Am I clear?"

"Leggo of me, Trev!"

"Answer me."

"Okay, okay!"

"That reeks of insincerity, lad."

"I promise! I'm sorry! Let go!"

Trevor released him and shoved him back against the pillow. "You will behave yourself from now on."

"Man! I'm gonna tell the AMA about this. You can't treat sick people like this."

"There is no AMA, Dillon. The world you remember no longer exists." He settled in the chair, and his tone of voice seemed to lower with his body, "The sooner you accept it, the easier 'twill be."

"You think I don't know? Whadaya think I ran from?" He looked away from Trevor, and saw his book had fallen to the side of the bed and had closed. He recovered the book and held it in his hand. "Shit, Trev! You made me lose my place."

Trevor reached his limit with Dillon's attitude. He considered Dillon's major issue his phony display of emotional coldness regarding the loss of his family and his refusal to reveal the details of it. With Dillon their only eyewitness to the goings-on in the mountains outside the refuge, James and the rest of the team urged Trevor to get the truth out of the boy. Trevor wanted the details, who, what, where and why. He would not give up on this quest, and began this third round of investigation with the most sensitive of Dillon's emotional buttons. "Who killed your father?"

Dillon rolled his eyes, tired of the endless prying. He decided to play along in hopes to satisfy Trevor enough to cease the interrogations. He figured that was the real reason they wanted to keep him alive.

Dillon answered in an exasperated tone. "The fuckin' scientists and their goons."

"What scientists?"

"Some government assholes. Supposedly. That's all I know." He opened his book and flipped the pages in search of where he left off. "I need a bookmark..."

Trevor snatched the book away. "This is very important."

"If I tell you, will you let me die?"

"No."

He bargained for second best. "Will you let me finish my book?"

"Yes."

Dillon took his time remembering it all, and even more time on a few extra hits of oxygen, a passive-aggressive display to remind Trevor who was in charge for the moment. Familiar with that game, Trevor waited patiently. That irked Dillon. Finally, the boy started.

"They took over the clinic in Baker Creek. Then, people started to disappear. Some bailed in their cars—I know that—I saw it. Others... fuck, I don't know. Vanished. Just vanished." He stopped and began to pick at a bandage on his arm that covered a dead IV site. The spot was swollen, bruised and sore, and the adhesive medical tape itched relentlessly. He removed the tape and the cotton ball. "I don't know nothin' else."

Trevor did not believe it. "What else did you see?"

"Nothin'."

"What else?"

Dillon became quiet. He tossed the tape and cotton on the nightstand, sunk against the pillow and closed his eyes. He faked sudden fatigue in order to avoid the issue.

Trevor knew it was an act. "What else did you see? I know you saw somethin', lad."

"Nothin'. Lemme sleep. I need some pain meds."

"Tell me."

"I'm tired." Dillon anticipated Trevor would persistently bat it back at him. Instead, Trevor only stared at him, waiting patiently. Actually, Dillon was beginning to tire, and he felt not only his physical strength ebbing, but the sedating effects of the medications as well. He scooted over towards Trevor and persuasively pressed his hand over the man's wrist. "I really am tired, Trev."

Trevor chided him. "All your runnin' of the mouth did it." He moved his arm from under Dillon's hand. "Tell me what you saw, lad. Tell me what you saw, and I'll leave you to sleep. That's all I ask."

"I can't remember."

Trevor stood to leave him, hoping the threat of abandonment would sway the boy. "Very well." He tossed the book onto his lap. "Enjoy your readin'."

Dillon seized his arm. "Don't leave."

"I've got better ways to spend my time." Trevor mistook Dillon's plea as a come-on, another one of his amateurish attempts at emotional and sexual manipulation. He removed Dillon's hand and walked away.

"Don't leave!" Dillon pleaded.

"Why should I not?" Trevor reached for the doorknob.

"I got no one left." Too late, Dillon realized he had revealed his one need Trevor could use as advantage. He wanted to slap himself for being so careless and desperate.

"That's not my problem." Trevor opened the door.

"I got no one left 'cause they fed 'em all to the Puss-heads!"

"The *Puss-heads*?"

"The scientists had 'em all caged. They fed my family, my neighbors, everybody, to those fuckin' things. I hid and followed 'em. I saw it." He gazed at Trevor, reliving the horror. "I ain't lyin', man. That's how it went down."

"Whom do the scientists work for?"

"I don't know. I swear." Dillon sat up painfully, "Don't leave me alone, man."

Trevor remained at the doorway. "How many scientists are there?"

"I don't know."

"How many did you see?"

"Two. Some older woman with long gray hair. A guy—hardly no hair. Wears glasses. The woman's the boss. One mean-ass bitch, if you ask me." He hoped Trevor would return to his bedside. When it was apparent Trevor would not, he said, "I'm tellin' the truth."

Trevor stepped to his bedside and paused there. "What about the woman? What tells you she's mean?"

"She stole all the babies outa the cage. Had the moms rounded up. I snuck into the back of the clinic and saw the room where they kept the mothers gagged and strapped down to beds and chairs and stuff. I saw her order some guys to use these... things—I don't know what they're called—to get the milk outa the women. And, I saw..." Dillon stopped and looked away from Trevor. He was becoming agitated as he recollected the scene. He became short of breath and had to pause long enough to suck in a long inhalation of oxygen and try to calm his nerves before he could continue.

Trevor saw the distress on his face. He sat and watched him. "It'll pass, lad."

"I saw the place where they cut up the bodies to feed the Puss-heads. I saw them cut up my dad and my two sisters."

Trevor rubbed his forehead, something he did when he felt nauseated.

"They hung 'em up and cut 'em up like the butcher carves up a steer." Dillon began to tremble with the horror of it. "That's when I ran."

"How many mords do they have there?"

"About twenty. That's the ones in cages. There might've been more, but I didn't see. It was hard to see what they were doin' without gettin' caught." Dillon's trembling increased. He slunk against the pillow, a feral-like terror in his eyes when he looked once more at Trevor, "They got their own fuckin' army runnin' everything. I only got half a mile away before one of 'em caught me. Thought the fucker was gonna drag me back there. Y'know. Thought they were gonna cut me up, too."

"How'd you get away?"

"I made a deal with him. I gave him somethin' he hadn't had in a long time." Dillon paused when it occurred to him he was ashamed of this. He felt a need to justify his action. "It was all I had."

Aghast, Trevor blurted, "Bloody hell! You mean you—"

"I had nothin' else to offer him." Dillon gazed at Trevor, begging him to understand. "It worked. I got out. He let me go. He didn't give a shit once I gave him what he wanted. There was nothin' else I could do!"

"A soldier?"

"Yeah. A fake one. His uniform was too big for him, and he wasn't even American. I think all the soldiers were fake. Most of 'em didn't act like real military. No discipline. Y'know what I mean? But they could all shoot. Don't know where they got the weapons. I once saw 'em hang up one of the dead Puss-heads and use him for target practice. Fuckin' twisted, if you ask me." Dillon felt his fatigue and the medications kick-in full force. His eyes began to weigh heavily and show the effects of the meds. "I gotta sleep, man. I'm really tired. I ain't kiddin'. No bullshit, Trev."

Trevor could tell it was not an act. Dillon had finally revealed most of the information he needed. Trevor wanted to move on to the task of securing the boy's trust, a goal of which he was most capable. He had counseled many Dillon's in his time. Unbeknown to the boy, Trevor felt much compassion for him. "I'll drop by and see you tonight, lad."

"Can you stay for a few minutes more? Just for a while?"

"I could." It puzzled him as to why Dillon was so frightened of everyone. "No one will hurt you here. Do you realize that?"

His speech began to slur a little from the medications. "Dude, I've taken my share of beatings from the so-called *moral* citizens. And this place is full of 'em."

Trevor knew that would not happen here. "Has anyone here ever threatened you?"

"No. Not so far."

"It won't happen, Dillon. We all want to survive. We all want you to survive with us." He drew the covers over Dillon's chest. "You keep pushin' us away. You must trust us."

"I can't change what I am. I tried."

"That's between you and God."

Dillon wearily gestured at the IV "This is God's answer."

CLAUSBERG INSISTED on serving raw human flesh to Isabelle. Guffy balked at the idea of presenting it as dinner, even though the appalling offering had the innocent appearance of a small raw beefsteak. He had weaned the child off this diet and restored her desire for acceptable food. Now, Clausberg's spontaneous little food experiment only posed the risk of renewing Isabelle's desire for the taboo.

Clausberg set the plate in his hands. "I'm watching you."

He accepted it remorsefully, hating the fact she still intimidated him. Without a word, he brought it into the treatment room where Isabelle resided as a protected but still threatened lab animal.

"Dat my dinnew, Unka?" She was waiting at the little table, her place set neatly and her paper napkin on her lap. She wore a frilly blue dress, white ankle socks and a pair of used slightly oversize sneakers. The pink ribbon he tied around her curly black hair that morning was lopsided on the crown of her head yet added a sense of innocent abandon to her appearance.

Guffy felt he was betraying her by serving her this atrocity. "The doctor wants you to try this." Regretfully, he gently set Clausberg's *experiment* on the table.

She scrunched up her face. "Dis not cooked."

He sat down with her at the table. "I know."

She bent her head and sniffed it, crinkled her face in disgust as she looked up at Guffy. "No good. No want." She pushed the plate away. "Peeze, Unka. No eat."

Guffy turned his head in the direction of the two-way mirror and told Clausberg, "She don't want it."

Her voice came authoritatively over the speaker. "Take a taste of it, Isa."

Isabelle stood and faced the mirror, "No! No like. *You* eat!"

"I'll give you a spanking, missy!"

Guffy refused to allow even the threat of it. "Renée! Don't! You don't need to do that!"

Isabelle flung the plate across the room toward the mirror in a fit of rebellion. It hit the floor and shattered, and the meat skidded to a halt. "*You* eat it, Dockitew Mean!"

The door immediately burst open and slammed loudly against the wall. Clausberg stormed in, her face crimson with anger. "You will do as you're told!"

Guffy intercepted her and stopped her with his hands against her shoulders. "She don't want it! She wants regular food!"

She glared at Isabelle and pointed at the meat on the floor and the broken plate. "Pick this up!"

Isabelle stayed at the table, her own face red with anger. "No!"

Guffy remained between them. He held Clausberg back and tried to reason with her. "This is a good sign. Don't you see? She don't want it. No taste for it. She's not dangerous anymore. Isn't that what you wanted?"

"She's still loaded with the virus!" Clausberg lied. "She wants it. She's putting on an act for you! All this innocent bullshit! She's got you fooled, Guffy! Maybe if we starved her, she'd reveal the truth!"

Guffy stated with uncharacteristic challenge in his voice, "You ain't gonna starve her."

"You think you're going to stop me?"

Isabelle screamed at her, "You *muerto*!"

To Isabelle, she inquired, "What did you just call me?"

"*Muerto*!" The child repeated. "*Muerto*! You *muerto*!"

Clausberg glared at her over Guffy's shoulder. "What does that mean?" When Isabelle refused to answer, she directed the question to Guffy, "What does she mean?"

"I don't know," Guffy sputtered. "I don't know Spanish." He kept his grip on Clausberg to prevent her from attacking the little girl. To

Isabelle, he ordered gently, "Sit down, Isa. It's okay. Sit down and be a good girl."

"She hoot me!" Isabelle yelled.

"I know," Guffy replied. "And I promised you I wouldn't let her do it again, didn't I? You have to trust me, Isa."

To Clausberg, Isabelle implored, "Food no good. Peeze, Dockitew. No hoot Duffy. No hoot. Peeze." She patted her chest in an effort to sway the doctor's opinion of her, "No mow biting sick. Isa bettew. No want peep fing. No mow peep fing. Want good food. Peeze! No bite no mow. Peeze, Dockitew. Peeze."

Clausberg relaxed slightly. She had not anticipated a direct plea from the child, and she was impressed with her courage. She pointed at the mess on the floor. "You come pick this up."

"No hoot?" Isabelle asked.

She met Guffy's distrusting eyes before she answered Isabelle in a compromising voice, "I won't hurt you."

"No hoot Duffy?"

"I won't hurt him, either."

"Pommis?"

"I promise." She glanced impatiently at Guffy. "Let go of me."

Guffy ordered in a soft voice. "Promise *me*."

"Alright, alright!" She stepped back when Guffy released her and gruffly told Isabelle, "Clean this up. *Now.*"

Isabelle cautiously approached the mess, which was too close to the doctor for comfort. She went on her knees and began to gather the broken pieces of the plate. Out of the corner of her eye, she maintained an uneasy watch in case Clausberg changed her mind.

Clausberg squatted in front of her and offered the child her wrist. "Would you like to bite me?"

Isabelle recoiled, expecting the doctor would hit her. "No."

"Can you smell my blood?"

She could, but she would not tell her. "No."

The doctor pointed at the meat. "Pick that up, too."

Guffy bent. "I'll do that."

"No!" Clausberg snapped. "I want her to do it."

Disgusted, Isabelle retrieved it in two fingers and laid it on the gathered pieces of broken ceramic. She offered the whole thing to Clausberg. "Bettew?"

"I want you to meet someone." Clausberg said brightly.

Isabelle looked at Guffy to see if he knew what the doctor was talking about. Guffy appeared surprised, curious and dubious all at the same time. Her question answered by his reaction, she returned her gaze to the doctor. "Who?"

"A young man. He's waiting in the lab."

She remembered the lab as the scary place where she had been caged and brutally punished. "Isa 'tay hew."

Guffy took Isabelle's hand and guided her up on her feet. Once she stood, he hugged her to him with one protective arm. "What are you up to, Doc?"

Clausberg held the broken plate with the human steak draped over it. "He'll eat this." She eyed Isabelle. "Come meet him. I would like you to talk to him."

Isabelle stared at the plate. "He biting sick, huh?"

"Yes. I want you to tell him how you got well."

"No way!" Guffy protested, "You ain't exposin' her to that! No way!"

"I want to see if they still regard her as one of them." She stood up and faced Guffy sincerely. "She'll be safe. He's caged." To Isabelle, she said, "I even know his name. He has his name written on him."

This piqued the child's curiosity. "What name?"

"Mario."

Her eyes brightened and widened. "Fum Bujja-Mot?"

Clausberg smiled, "You know him."

Tears filled Isabelle's eyes. "My buddew... Day bittim. Day bittim hod. He cawy me. He hoot bad. We hide in 'tore long time. We hide in waw. Got biting sick wiff me. Oh... Mawio!"

"Sonofabitch...!" Clausberg marveled. "So, he's your brother! Would you like to see him, Isa? Would you like to help him get well?"

"He 'tiw biting sick?"

"Yes."

"You hootim?"

"No."

Guffy held Isabelle closer. "Don't make her do this."

"I won't make her stay with him. I just want to see his reaction to her. That's all." She reached for the girl's hand. "Come see him. I know he wants to see you."

"Don't...!" Guffy begged.

Isabelle reached her hand to Clausberg. The doctor grasped her hand and began to lead her out of the room. "Come see him, Isa."

Guffy gripped the girl's arm and tugged her to him as he begged the woman, "Please...!"

"You can come, too." Clausberg replied casually.

Guffy and the child were not prepared when Mario tugged violently at the bars as they entered the lab with the doctor. The crazed boy was infuriated and starving.

Isabelle peeked at him from behind Clausberg. The horrible odor and his partial nakedness shocked her. She tightly shut her eyes and turned her head away. "Where his pants?"

As the doctor neared the cage, he screeched at her and attempted to grab her. Clausberg was too far out of his reach. She shrugged as she answered Isa, "He lost them." She wordlessly urged the girl to stand beside her, but the girl turned to Guffy and clung to his fat waist with her eyelids squeezed shut. Undaunted, Clausberg cooed sweetly to Mario, "Mario! Do you remember Isabelle?"

"Rosa!" Isabelle corrected her, rolling the first consonant.

Mario screeched and gnashed his teeth.

Isabelle opened her eyes at the horrible sounds. She stared aghast at Mario's emaciated and ravaged condition. She avoided the sight of his exposed genitalia; her brother, her dear Mario would have been mortified for her to see it. A film of putrid bowel residue and rancid blood veiled his beautiful smooth bronze skin. Patchy, matted facial hair hardened the once boyishly handsome face. A bestial snarl exposed brown, shattered teeth where a perfect smile of straight, white teeth had once greeted all. Even his eyes were different. The eyes she remembered regarded her with love and tenderness. The eyes regarding her now were ravenous and dangerous. Yet, she perceived a bitter sorrow there. This tragic caged monster was not the person she remembered, and she was afraid of him.

"Talk to him," Clausberg suggested.

Guffy demanded, "Stop!"

At the same time, Isabelle took one hesitant step forward and established eye contact. "Mawio? Mawio, it's *Rosa*." She rolled the "R" again, the only "R" she could pronounce. "Weemembew me?"

Mario screeched and lunged for her. There was no recognition in his eyes.

Isabelle screamed and jumped back, almost landing on the doctor's foot. "No, Mawio! No! No hoot!"

He sniffed the air, and his sight rested on the human steak the doctor carried. He tried to reach for it.

Clausberg handed Isabelle the steak. "Feed him."

"No!" Guffy yelled.

"Shut up!" Clausberg ordered.

Isabelle soothed him. "It okay, Unkaduffy. I can do dis." She bravely took two steps forward and timidly tossed the steak to Mario. "Peep fing, Mawio. You eat. Get bettew."

It landed on the floor of the cage. Mario retrieved it and stuffed it into his mouth. He chewed it ravenously and demanded more.

"Aw gone." The girl said apologetically. "Weemembew me,

Mawio?"

He cocked his head sideways, stared at her with no recognition. If anything, she represented food. He screeched again and reached hungrily through the bars for her.

"No!" She scolded him, "No food, Mawio! Wook at me! I'm *Rosa*! *Rosa*!

Mario snarled, persistently lunged at her.

Isabelle shook her head from side to side and peered at the doctor sadly, "He no membew me..." She dissolved into tears and sobbed, "Mawio! Get bettew, Mawio!" To Clausberg, she pleaded, "Peeze, make bettew." To Guffy, she asked, "Unka, peeze hep Mawio. You hep me. Hep Mawio."

"I can't help him," Guffy replied hopelessly.

"But, *you* can!" Clausberg told her.

"No..." Isabelle said with equal hopelessness, "Isa no Dockitew. Mawio too sick. He awmose *muerto*. Maybe Deezus hep. Peeze, Dockitew... pay wiff us Mawio get bettew? Peeze pay. Peeze?"

She found this amusing. "You want me to pray?"

Isabelle reiterated with unwavering faith, "Pay Deezus!" She wiped tears, "Deezus hep. He hep Isa." She turned to her brother, "Mawio, pay Deezus."

Mario responded with another screech, a growl and another lunge against the bars.

Tears raced down her cheeks. She sniffled and backed away.

Guffy protectively pulled the child to him as he bitterly told Clausberg, "You got your answer!"

Mario wailed and beat his ears violently. His body shuddered. He collapsed and went into a convulsion.

"Go wiff Deezus, Mawio!" Isabelle cried out, "Go now! Go! Deezus, peeze take now! Take Mawio. Go wiff Deezus, Mawio!"

His screeching abruptly ceased, as did the convulsion. Mario's body fell limply flat on the floor of the cage, his life mercifully lifted out of the diseased shell. Serenity replaced his maniacal expression.

Isabelle kissed the palm of her hand and blew the kiss to her brother's corpse. "Be bessed, Mawio. Deezus hode you now. Aw bettew." She turned away and rushed into Guffy's arms, sobbing.

Guffy lifted her and turned to leave the lab. Over his shoulder, he said to Clausberg, "Are you happy?"

Clausberg gaped at Mario. The disease must have killed him. If so, it would be the first time she had ever witnessed an actual death caused by the virus and not some other mitigating condition. If that was indeed the case, it meant the virus was fatal.

If the virus by itself was fatal, that meant her plans for an army required some serious further tweaking. The child was her answer.

She needed to eliminate Guffy, and she needed to do it soon.

CHAPTER 21

Natalie heard the intermittent hum of traffic from the interstate through the open window above her bed. She spied the area through her binoculars, saw military vehicles, mostly jeeps and large camouflage canvas covered trucks headed downtown. She took the opportunity to get a look at the hospital and observed armed troops on the roofs and an Army helicopter on the helipad. Their sudden activity in the heart of her hometown after all these months of stagnation alarmed her.

Coltan weakly and painfully pulled himself up to the window. He reached for the binoculars. "Let me see."

She gave them to him, and she noticed his face was still pale. His arms trembled as he rested his elbows on the windowsill to balance the binoculars. One of the bites she had stitched on his left shoulder had broken open and the wound was now bleeding.

"I have to clean that," she told him.

He was preoccupied with the scene in the valley. "Clean what?"

"Your stitches broke on your shoulder."

"That's okay."

"It's bleeding."

"In a minute." He tried to interpret the sudden invasion downtown. "What the hell? What are they doing?"

"They got the hospital. They took it over."

"What's with all the troops?" He lowered the binoculars and rested. His rest was brief, for something curious caught his attention. He brought up the binoculars again. "Those are civilians in the back of those trucks!"

She reached for the specs. "Let me see!"

He held on to them. "We have two. Where's the other one?"

"Dang it, Colt..." Irritated, Natalie retrieved the second binoculars from the storage room. She figured by the time she returned to the window, whatever Coltan had seen would be gone. She hurried back and focused the lenses as she sighted the valley.

Troops were supervising civilians carrying and utilizing tools of all kinds. It seemed to be a clean-up and restoration operation.

"Looks like they're rebuilding the town," she remarked.

"They'll be up here soon," Coltan said forebodingly.

He felt dizzy and pulled away from the window. An unexpected wave of cold sweat burst from every pore in his body. He curled up on his knees and waited for it to pass.

Natalie heard him groan softly. She set down the binoculars and went to him. "Hey! What's going on?"

His voice came in a frustrated sigh, "Sick again!"

"Sweats?"

He pursed his lips and blew out a lung full of air. "Dammit!"

This wasn't his first spell of cold sweats over the last two days. Natalie took the towel she kept handy for this and began to pat him down. She patted around the area where his shoulder dripped blood. His skin was ice-cold, and he was trembling with exhaustion. He needed another round of care, nourishment and rest. She opened the medical kit and removed tweezers, scissors, topical meds and bandages.

She ordered him gently, "Lay down on your side."

He groaned again and rolled over on his side, facing her. She cut the stitches on his shoulder and removed them. The wound split open, a shallow cavity where canine teeth tore away the flesh. He remained passive, compliant, and uncomplaining as she cleaned the wound and applied triple-antibiotic ointment. Re-stitching the injury would likely cause it to become infected. The only thing she could do now was bandage it and hope for the best.

"Okay, hon, what do you want me to wash first—the back or the front?"

"The back, I guess." He rolled over on his stomach while she reached for the bowl containing a solution of rubbing alcohol and warm water. Coltan felt a tad humiliated at his condition. He thought he should be taking care of her, not the other way around. Instead, he was lying there weak and naked for her to bathe him as if he was an infant. As she laid the first of many washcloths over him, he asked, "Are the bites healing all right?"

"So far, so good." She paused long enough to comfortingly pet his hair, "How's your pain?"

"Not as bad today."

"Do you want some more morphine?"

"I'd like to wait."

"The longer you wait, the worse the pain. It's better to treat it before it gets worse."

"I'll wait. It might not get worse."

"You want to be a tough guy." Her tone lightened humorously, "Huh, Colt?"

"Yeah, that's me... Tough guy."

She kissed his cheek. "You are tough!"

He couldn't resist smiling at her. She was one in a million, an angel of mercy, *his* angel of mercy. He had lost track of the hours she spent patiently and tirelessly tending to his every need. She emptied for him countless buckets of vomit and who knows how many bottles of brown urine. She tenderly bathed him in the middle of the night when he barfed all over himself. When his temperature spiked, fell rapidly and spiked again, she knew exactly what to do. When his ailing body decided to spontaneously puke all its fluids through every pore, she readily and willingly cleaned him and consoled him. She kept track of his medication schedule and double-checked the dosage. When his body chilled, she warmed him. She prepared broth for him and held him in her arms as she fed it to him from a coffee mug. Without her help through it all, he would have died.

"Turn over." She reached for him and assisted him to turn over so he wouldn't hurt.

Coltan observed her face as she swept his hair off his forehead. She seemed so tired, yet she appeared serene as she tended him. He reached up weakly and stroked her cheek. She took his hand from her face and kissed his fingers.

"I love you," he whispered.

"I love you, too." She placed his hand over his chest. "You're gonna be just fine, Colt. Don't worry." She pulled the sleeping bag over his privates. "You're probably cold. At least, we can keep Mister Dolce warm. Why do you call it that, anyway?"

He chuckled. "It's a musical term. Italian. It means *'sweetly and gently.'*"

"Well," she laughed, "That's your style, alright!" She towel-dried his damp hair. "Would you like to listen to some of your music? You haven't listened in a long time."

"I'd like that."

She checked the disk in the player. He had written on it, *'Relaxing'*. "Is this the one you'd like to hear?" He nodded and she asked, "Which one do you want to hear first?"

"Number one," he answered. "*'In Trutina'*. You can just let them all play in order."

"Okay." She started the player and listened with him as she bathed him. The music was not the screechy type of opera she hated, but a gentle and moving sound of beauty and emotional depth. It surprised her she liked it. "That's beautiful!"

Coltan grinned, "All you have to do is give it a chance." He closed his eyes and tried to relax. It was difficult for him to let someone else be in charge, and this illness had taught him a lot about trust and submissiveness. The combination of the music and the weakness of his body helped him relax. Only a few minutes passed before he drifted into a light snooze. The beautiful *In Trutina* danced delicately in his brain like a feather carried on a slow gentle breeze.

The strong scent of roses mixed with the scent of lilacs from outside the open window. He sensed the presence of the invisible and loving entity that had visited with increased frequency over the past five days. It seemed Natalie was unaware of its presence every time, and Coltan knew she was ignorant of it now. This time, the entity communicated a feeling of urgency to him. An image formed in Coltan's mind of the first rays of the sun and riding his motorcycle toward the mountain. Natalie was with him, her arms wrapped around his chest.

He settled back into a light sleep as he silently acknowledged the message.

Natalie removed the wet cloths and covered him fully with the sleeping bag. The sudden bouts of sweating were a sign his body was conquering the infection. However, the illness had ravaged his system and it would take perhaps months before he returned to top form.

She doubted they had that much time. The military would find them eventually. They would have to leave for the refuge sooner than planned. How much sooner depended upon Colt's recovery and his ability to travel.

The second song, a classical instrumental number as beautiful as *In Trutina* calmed her. She listened attentively as she tenderly pressed a washcloth to his face. His pale skin reminded her how much blood he had lost. He breathed in deeply and whispered, "Thank you." She was not sure if he was asleep or not. The music of the third song, a longing violin solo, settled into her and sent a chill up her spine as she removed the cloth from his face and dabbed his skin dry with the towel. Afterward, she folded the towel and then wrung out the washcloths. She gazed at his slumbering face. He was so beautiful in her eyes, so profoundly splendid in every way.

Coltan slowly turned over on his side and opened his eyes. She watched and smiled warmly at him. He gazed at her, appreciating her love for him.

The angel's message repeated in his memory. He wondered how to bring it up without frightening her.

"What is it?" she asked softly.

"We have to leave soon."

"I know. The military..."

"They'll be here."

"How soon should we leave?"

"Tomorrow. As close to first light as possible."

"You're not well enough." She bent and caressed his face. "Let's give it a few more days. See how you're doing."

"We don't have a few days." He took her hand and squeezed it. "I'll sleep and rest today. Tonight, we'll pack up. It has to be this way."

"How about one more day?"

"Trust me, Nat. Trust me like I've been trusting you." His expression was sad yet loving. "Lie with me. I miss holding you."

JIMBO THE GANG-BANGER Guy grunted and begged another cigarette from Smith. Smith wisely kept some distance. He lit a smoke and tossed it near the monster's soiled feet, "Didn't anybody tell ya smokin's bad for ya, Jimbo?" Jimbo picked it up and grunted something Smith interpreted as thanks. It amazed Smith Jimbo wanted to communicate. All this time, he assumed the monsters' brains were fried beyond hope. Here was Jimbo begging smokes. Smith wondered how he'd react to a joint.

He glanced around the area and saw no one. It would be okay to fire up a doobie. Just for the hell of it, he removed one of the three he had stashed in his shirt pocket and lit it. He held in the first drag and then the second. It was good weed; the second drag already gave him a little buzz.

Jimbo sniffed the weed smoke as it drifted toward him. He eyed Smith expectantly and gestured for it.

"Thought you'd want it." Smith neared him and took a third drag. He considered it was too good to waste on the Already Wasted. Through a held breath, he grunted to Jimbo, "You gotta wait until I'm ready."

Jimbo offered to trade the cigarette.

"No comparison," Smith told him. "You wait a while." He inhaled a long fourth drag and held it in.

Jimbo beat on the bars and snarled. His teeth were a mess and had decaying human flesh stuck in the spaces between.

"You need to floss, Jimbo," Smith wisecracked. "Does that French pervert taste good? Bet he does. Clausberg's keepin' him fresh just for you."

A scream emitted from the tiny jail. Jimbo jumped and sniffed the air for the origin of the noise. It seemed to Smith the sound of the scream whetted the monster's appetite.

"Speak of the devil!" Smith chuckled. "Say, Jimbo! That your dinner callin'?" He took another drag off the joint, choked and coughed. "Shit! Say, Jimbo... If I give you this, it'll just give you the munchies. *Like you need to get the munchies.*"

Jimbo threw the cigarette out of his cage and reached for the joint.

Smith eyed Jimbo's three remaining cage mates. Acne Boy was masturbating in a corner; Don't Take My Glasses Guy was gnawing on what remained of one of the French guy's femurs; and Miss Pregnant Teen USA was sucking on the Frenchman's half-eaten foot. None of them displayed any interest in Smith. Only Jimbo seemed intent on social interaction.

"Bet you were a hardy party guy in your time," Smith remarked to him.

Jimbo snarled and banged on the bars. He growled at Smith and reached out, demanded the joint.

"What the fuck..." Buzzed enough, Smith took one more drag and tossed the reefer to Jimbo.

Jimbo retrieved it off the concrete floor and smoked it. When it got too short to smoke without burning his fingers, he popped the thing into his mouth and swallowed it.

Smith sat on the gravel and waited to see the results.

MITCHELL LISTENED WITH great interest to the chatter coming over his revamped radio. From what he could gather so far, a horde of mords invaded the rescue camp outside Reyton. The things had gathered en masse out of nowhere and had worked together to bring down the gates and the fence. According to the sporadic conversations between the soldiers and their leaders, the mordants outnumbered the unprepared soldiers. Some civilians and soldiers escaped the bloodbath by fleeing toward the hills. The order came over the radio to execute all deserters, even if they were civilians.

As that horror unfolded, the troops out in Bonito Valle alerted to the situation set up camp in town at The Blue River Hotel, the new housing complex for both military personnel and the highly skilled civilians who had been recruited for reconstruction duty.

The monitors in front of Glenda displayed the newest Army of Christ troops nearing the refuge. Their logo, a cross of two swords and the title *Army of Christ* in yellow, was clearly visible on their vehicles. The troops themselves wore vests sporting patches with the logo. They weaved through the route along the eastern ridge. It was a good route, wide enough to accommodate their jeeps, trucks and tanks, and well hidden from the skies within the forest of tall old pines.

"Looks like a hundred or so," Glenda estimated.

"Montana Moses?" Mitchell assumed.

"Most likely." She punched in James's number. "We need you up here."

James rushed into the room and made a beeline for the monitors. He grinned widely and clapped his hands together. "Thank you, Jesus!" To Glenda, he said, "Round up the entire team for rendezvous. Page Joe and Suzanne. Tell 'em all *stat*, no lollygaggin'."

MORRIS PEEKED IN ON Guffy and Isabelle through the two-way mirror. Guffy was in the rocking chair and it appeared Isabelle was asleep on his lap. Clausberg had told him about the Mario incident, and he felt pity for the child.

Out of the corner of his eye, he watched Clausberg step out for a smoke and a drink at the only bar in town. Clausberg had been on edge over the last couple of days, and she had been drunk most of the night before. She knew her little army in Baker Creek had dwindled down to only a handful of loyalists and her remaining sparse collection of mordants were slowly dying off. The puzzling fact of Isabelle's defeat of the virus also added to her troubles. Now that the little girl was lucid and healthy, she was tougher to handle and tougher to fool than when she was sick. It meant Clausberg had to come up with a whole new strategy for dealing with the kid. It meant she would have to be nice to her and win her trust, an almost impossible task.

While Clausberg numbed her sorrows with scotch, Morris took the opportunity to download all the footage of Isabelle, and all the information about the UEF on disk. He planned to turn it over to the *Army of Christ* as soon as he, Guffy and the kid could get free of this place. It was impossible for him to return to the Mohave Cross complex. Morris heard refugees from the major twin earthquakes that rattled southern California overran the Mohave refuge, and then the mordants overtook it. Communication ceased. However, Morris knew the Alpha Base was alive and well just up the mountain on the eastern side of the peak. This is where he would go.

Guffy drew his index finger to his lips when Morris entered.

"She asleep?" Morris whispered.

"Finally," Guffy whispered back. He rose slowly and carried Isabelle to her bed. He laid her there gently and carefully so as not to awaken her, and covered her with the blanket. As an afterthought, he tucked Teddy under her arm. He gestured for Morris to join him at the little table. They sat, and Guffy poured them each a cup of coffee from the thermal carafe. "The poor thing's a basket case. Seein' her brother like that really did a number on her."

"I heard about it," Morris said softly. "Say... I got us a VW, found it sitting in a garage at one of the houses. Found the key on a peg over the light switch. I checked it out last night. The thing runs. The engine's in great shape. Guess the guy had just finished restoring it. It's got a full tank of gas. We can use it to get out."

Guffy leaned forward and sipped his coffee. "When are we goin'?"

"Tomorrow afternoon." He nodded his head toward Isabelle, "I want to get one more blood sample from her just to be sure she's clear."

"Man, I hate to wake her up."

"I can do it while she's sleeping." He produced a blood-draw set-up from his pocket. "I only need one vial. I can test it while Clausberg's still out at the bar. She's spending more time getting whacked with the boys these days. I don't expect her back for an hour. Maybe two if she gets lucky with Smitty."

"Smitty?"

"You didn't know?"

"Know what?"

"She and Smitty have been servicing each other for months! You didn't know that?"

"Uh-uh...!" Guffy's eyes were wide with disbelief.

Morris chuckled softly, "She may be a cold old bitch, but Smitty says she gives good head. At least she's good for something, huh?"

Guffy was still amazed. "No shit?"

Morris laughed quietly as he said, "Who'd a thunk it?"

Guffy responded to this by making all kinds of faces that mirrored his many different reactions to this news. He could not picture Clausberg having sex of any kind, and if he could picture it, the image would fill him with revulsion.

Morris stood. "Let me get the blood test."

Guffy walked with him to the bed. Morris performed the blood draw like the pro he was, and Isabelle did not stir. He hid the vial in his pocket and went back to the table to finish his coffee. Guffy bent and kissed Isabelle's forehead. She was his daughter now, and would be forever.

Morris slugged down his coffee and stood as Guffy approached him. "We'll leave around three tomorrow, just before the soldiers change shifts. I'll get back to you in a half hour with the results of the test. Keep your fingers crossed."

"What if she's still infected?" Guffy hated to consider it, but he wanted to be prepared.

Morris paused uncomfortably. The only solution would break Guffy's heart, and his own, too. "We can't take her with us. We'll have to... put her to sleep."

"Put her to sleep?"

"An overdose of barbiturates." The tears in Guffy's eyes tore at him, "What else can we do? We can't leave her here! What the hell, Guff, it's better than a bullet to the brain. This way she'll just fall asleep and not wake up. No pain, nothing."

Guffy's face scrunched up and tears ran down his cheeks, "She's just a little girl. Can't we give it a little more time? Wait another week?"

"Aw, Guffy... Let's hope it doesn't come to that." It made him feel worse when Guffy kept crying. "Look, Guff. We're in danger here. There's no doubt some of our soldiers joined up with the UEF's army. By now, they know all about us. They're gonna show up any day now and blow this place all to hell. We don't have time. We've got to get out of here as soon as possible."

Guffy sniffled. "She's my little girl. She trusts me. She got no one but me."

He took Guffy's hands. "Let's pray for her. Okay? Let's pray."

"You're a believer?"

"I always have been. I had to hide it." He sat down and urged Guffy to do so. "Let's pray for her... and us."

"Ain't Clausberg gonna see it on the disk?"

"I shut off the disk and the mics. She won't know." He squeezed Guffy's chubby hand, "I gotta hurry up and do that test. Let's pray, Guffy."

SMITH'S LEGS HURT FROM sitting in the gravel. He had been watching Jimbo for twenty minutes. Jimbo was feeling the effects of the pot and toppled into a sitting position on the floor of the cage. For the past five minutes, he and Smith were having a staring contest. Smith was getting bored with it.

"Hey, Jimbo!"

Jimbo blinked his eyes and opened them wide. He grunted.

Smith stuck out his tongue, inserted his thumbs in his ears and waved his fingers at the monster.

Jimbo laughed loudly and collapsed into a fit of giggling. The others crawled over to him and sniffed him. They did not know what to make of this, and the odor on his skin was strange to them. After about a minute observing and examining him, they broke into laughter as well. They were giggling idiots, and Smith laughed with them.

INSIDE THE BAR, SOMEONE had slipped a drug into Clausberg's drink. By the time she slugged down her third scotch and soda, the drug took effect. She flopped over on her side on the bench in the booth, dead to the world.

The five soldiers wandered over and hovered around the unconscious woman. One of them removed her shoes. The men exchanged glances. The soldier who removed her shoes grinned at the others, pulled off her pants and underwear and deposited them on the table. Two of the men dragged her off the bench to the wood floor. These same two pulled her legs up and held them apart for the first assailant.

They all took turns with her. When they finished, one of the soldiers wiped away most of the evidence and dressed her.

CHAPTER 22

When Coltan awoke that night, Natalie was already up and cooking at the portable propane stove. He could smell beef and spices, and the aroma whetted his appetite.

Even though her back was turned to him, Natalie sensed he was awake. She lowered the heat on the two burners and poured broth into a mug from the thermal carafe on the table. She brought the steaming mug to him and sat with him on his mattress.

She offered him the broth. "Drink this slowly." After he took the mug from her, she selected a hand-full of vitamins and antibiotics and offered them to him. "Take these." He obeyed gratefully and downed them with a long sip of beef broth. "I'm making us noodles with our last can of roast beef. I think we should load up on carbs and protein before we leave. Do you think you'll be able to keep it down?"

"I should." The stomach medicine had tamed that problem. "I know I'm really hungry. That's a good sign, right?"

She nodded. "I hope it stays down. You need the nourishment." She rubbed his belly, "What's up with your stomach, anyway? Is it from the bites? Is that what did it?"

Matter-of-factly he answered, "I have ulcers."

"For how long?"

"Since I was a kid. I'm used to it. It doesn't bother me that often anymore."

"No wonder." Natalie sighed remorsefully. "Here I was loading you down with codeine. No wonder you were barfing blood!"

"You didn't know."

"You should've told me."

"I didn't know the codeine would bother it. I don't know anything about stuff like that." He sipped the broth and shifted into a more comfortable sitting position. The vertigo started again, and he rested against the pillows while it passed. "Everything goes to my gut. I get a head cold; it goes to my gut. It's always been that way."

She detected a glaze of pain in his eyes. "How's your pain level right now?"

"I'm okay." His entire body felt squeezed in a vise, and he was suffering the worst headache he had ever had in his life. He didn't tell her because she would worry. She had enough to worry her.

He was being Mister Tough Guy again and she knew it. "How about a small dose of morphine to take the edge off?"

Coltan thought about it. He wanted to be alert once they got on the road. He considered a small dose would not induce sleepiness. "How about a very, very small amount?"

"That's a good compromise." She reached into the med kit and found the vial.

"After this would you hand me my tablet from the table?"

"Sure. You're not planning on writing your will, are you?"

He chuckled softly, "Not a chance, babe! I'm gonna make a list of everything we need to pack."

"You and Mom... list makers."

"I'll forget stuff if I don't write it down."

She brought him the tablet and a pen while he finished the broth. He handed her the empty mug as he took the tablet and pen from her. "More broth?" she asked.

"Please." He stopped her from getting up. "Hey... did you get some sleep?"

"About six hours."

Coltan knew she had slept only sporadically all week. The fatigue still showed in her face. He wanted her to be rested and alert for their journey. "Try for a nap after dinner. I'll wake you after two hours or so. How's that sound?"

"Sounds good. And, then we'll pack."

The thought of the hardship of the road and the fact he still felt puny filled him with apprehension. He concealed this from her. "Yeah. We'll pack."

MORRIS STUFFED TWO duffle bags with medical supplies and diagnostic lab equipment and snuck out the back door. As he rounded the corner of the clinic, he saw Smith lying on his back in the gravel in the dim light from a nearby streetlamp. At first, he was concerned, but his concern lifted when he saw Smith light a cigarette. The soldier was only taking it easy, stargazing, making the most of this night's clear and moonless sky. The mords were unusually docile. He wondered if Smith had slipped them some drugs or something.

Clausberg had not returned to the clinic, and Morris assumed she was drunk again. He hoped she had passed out for the rest of the night. Loud rock music thumped from the jukebox inside the bar. The soldiers were partying away their boredom. Their drunken apathy would make it easier for him to finish his preparations in secrecy.

He entered the garage through the back yard door of the little house, and popped the trunk at the front of the Volkswagen Beetle. The two duffle bags took up a good deal of room in the small space. However, every item inside those bags was items Alpha Base would need. In addition to the standard diagnostic tools and equipment was the special solution he used to verify the existence of the mord virus in the blood. He fully doubted Alpha Base had that on hand.

On his way back to the clinic, he heard faint moans from the back of the tiny police station. The sound drifted through the window of a holding cell in the rear of the building. Morris knew it was the child molester; he was still clinging to his miserable life. The moaning tortured Morris's conscience. He vacillated between playing God and ending the man's life with drugs, or playing Judge and allowing the suffering to continue. As he hesitated under the window, he asked God to tell him what to do. He felt a strong urge to load the man up with a mega-dose of barbiturates and morphine. So, with that as his next task, Morris continued toward the clinic.

As he entered through the rear door of the clinic Morris saw Guffy stash a loaded kid-size backpack with his under a desk there.

"Seen Doctor Mean?" Guffy asked him.

"I think she's still at the bar." Morris brushed past him and entered the smaller lab one room over. He loaded a syringe with a mix of downers and morphine.

Guffy followed and watched him. He inquired anxiously, "What's that for?"

"The child molester." He turned to Guffy, his eyes troubled and sympathetic. "The bastard's still alive."

"How's he still alive after all this?"

"I think Clausberg's still got him on fluids. She's probably tied off all his arteries to keep him from bleeding to death." He capped the needle and put it in his jacket pocket.

Guffy suggested, "You oughta make up one of those for *her*."

He peered sideways at Guffy, surprised Guffy would want that, and then he wondered why that should surprise him. The old bat gave them all nothing but grief since this whole thing began. Guffy took the brunt of it, and now had the child to protect. Morris seriously considered the idea. It would be easy to get her while she was drunk. It would be nice and quiet, and the soldiers would never know.

Only God would know.

Morris said ruefully to Guffy, "That would be premeditated murder. You know how God feels about that."

Guffy's eyes narrowed and projected an uncharacteristic glint of meanness. "The bitch deserves it."

"Yes, she does."

"But it's okay to snuff the pervert?"

"That's a mercy killing."

Guffy rejected the difference. "Bull..."

"Look, Guff... You tend to the kid. I'll take care of everything else." He returned to the door. "You got her packed up?"

"Yeah."

"Are *you* packed up?"

"Yeah."

"Give me your stuff and I'll stash it in the car now. That'll save us time tomorrow."

Guffy gave him the two backpacks. "Where are we goin'?"

"There's a safe place up on the mountain. Don't worry about it." He opened the door and turned back to Guffy, "Keep the kid safe. Keep her alive. That's your job." Morris did not wait for a response.

After he stowed the packs in the trunk of the Beetle, he started over to the sheriff station. He spotted Clausberg sitting on the front steps under the light as he neared the entrance. Even from a distance, she appeared disheveled. Morris anticipated her mood would be surly; she got that way when she was drinking. As he drew closer, she saw him and lit a cigarette.

She asked lightly, "What are you up to?"

"Thought I heard something," he replied.

"I didn't hear anything," she said. "You're imagining shit."

He joined her at the steps and sat with her. "You look tired."

"Don't bullshit me, Morris. I look drunk. Drunk! Can't a lady have a drink?" She grinned at him childishly.

He looked across and down the street. Smith was still on his back stargazing and smoking. He nodded at Smith. "Looks like Smitty's on break."

"He works hard." She called across to him, "Hey, Smitty! Have you fed the kids, yet?"

Smith did not bother to raise his head. He hollered back, "Two hours ago."

"Are they behaving themselves?"

"Hell, yeah!" There was laughter in his voice. "Where's my replacement?"

"Passed out drunk." She giggled. "Sorry, Smitty. You're pulling a double."

"Just my fuckin' luck..." he replied lazily.

Clausberg elbowed Morris as she slurred, "I need some coffee. You're gonna make it for me, because I'm a little disabled at the moment."

"You ought to go to bed." It would only make things much easier.

"I wanna keep an eye on the little Mexican."

"She's sleeping."

"I wanna keep an eye on Guffy, too."

"I thought you trusted Guffy."

"Guffy's a fool!" She stood clumsily and reached down for Morris's hand. "Come on, Morris. You're the coffee guy tonight. I have elected you King of the European Roast!"

When she stood he heard a jingling, noticed the collection of keys clipped on her belt. Some of the keys belonged to the sheriff station. He had forgotten she kept it locked. Putting the Frenchman out of his misery would have to wait until he could get the keys from her. Maybe the bastard would not last that long.

Morris took her hand and stood. After he delivered a benign smile her way, he slipped his arm across her shoulders and escorted her back to the lab. As they strolled together, he reconsidered injecting her with the death juice intended for the Frenchman.

IT WAS WELL AFTER MIDNIGHT and Dillon could not sleep. He was feeling better, thanks to the triple drug cocktail, and most of his bruises were beginning to fade. However, his legs ached. He pressed the nurse call button and tried to be patient.

Familiar footsteps neared the doorway. They were too heavy to belong to a nurse, and he knew without a doubt Trevor was on his way in. His heart leapt in his chest. He had not seen Trevor all day, and he missed him.

"Still awake?" Trevor inquired softly.

"My legs hurt."

Trevor stepped back out into the hallway and eyed the illuminated call light over the doorway. He continued into the room and took a seat next to the bed. "They should be here soon, lad. They've been busy with some wounded."

Dillon had heard nothing all day from anyone. Not that he cared much what went on outside his room. "Was there a battle?"

"The arrival of more troops. Some had bullet wounds. A little skirmish along the way."

"Are they gonna die?"

"No. They'll be fine." Trevor leaned forward and stroked what remained of Dillon's messy blond hair, some of which came off in his fingers. Trevor casually dropped the strands to the floor. "You're lookin' brighter, lad."

"I've been pukin' all day!" He laughed weakly at Trevor's attempt to encourage him. He turned over on his side and faced Trevor. "My legs—they hurt bad."

"Be patient."

"I missed you today, Trev."

That pleased Trevor. All his efforts to befriend the boy were finally paying off. "I couldn't get away. I thought of you."

He smiled subtly. "Really?"

"I also prayed for you."

"That's a waste..."

"You still believe God hates you?"

"Yeah. He hates me big time." After a dour pause, he said, "If He even exists, which I doubt."

"We all have our moments of doubt," Trevor stated. "Even I."

Dillon found this interesting. "When?"

"When our bus was attacked by the diseased ones, most of the boys I tried to protect were devoured alive before my eyes. I couldn't reach them. I was too busy trying to fight off the ones who had me. We were trapped. I recall Ian desperately fussing with the rear door to force it open so we could escape. The diseased had filled the aisle, blocking the children in their seats. Their screams... their screams were... I still dream about it, lad." Trevor stared downward. This was only the second time he had discussed it with anyone, and the pain was just as severe as it had been in those terrible moments in the minibus.

"How'd you get out?" Dillon asked.

"Little Ian... he somehow... he pushed the door open. As I fought for my life, he stood there, grabbed the nearest boys and flung them out. To this day, I don't know where he found the strength. It was some time during that when the soldiers entered and began firing at all of us. There was no discrimination. I somehow managed to kick the rest of the beasts off, and Ian seized my arm and flung me out. We fell together onto the road. He would not let go of me. The boys ahead of us were runnin', runnin' for their lives. We caught up to them. We saw more soldiers comin', shootin', shootin' everyone. They shot some of my boys. They went down. I panicked..." He became silent. The recollection of what he considered his cowardice filled him with shame. "I stepped on one of 'em when I began to run. God forgive me, I trampled one of 'em! I heard him scream. Then one of the boys runnin' shouted to head for the forest. An' that's what we did. We dodged bullets and the diseased ones... and we kept runnin'. Ian... he couldn't keep up. He was the smallest of 'em them. I was draggin' him, shoutin' at him, beggin' him to keep up. I don't know how he made it. But we made it. We hid like frightened kittens."

"How many of you were left by then?"

"Five... no... six of us, I think." His eyes filled with tears. As he continued, his accent became more pronounced with his emotion, the years of practicing proper English to hide his lower class roots abandoned for the moment. "We 'id in the woods and listened to the screams and the gunfire. The interstate became a giant snake of black smoke below us. That's 'ow one of the boys described it... a big snake made of smoke. That poor lad was the first to succumb to his bites. We didn't 'ave a medical kit. We had nothin'. We used clothin' for tourniquets to stem the bleedin'. There was nothin' else we could do. The others fell sick one by one. Ian was the only one of 'em who knew what was happenin'; he'd seen the footage on the telly at the restaurant with me. I swore 'im to secrecy so as not to worry them all. The two of us... we knew what would happen once they awakened from their slumbers. We knew. I strangled each one as they slept. Choked 'em to death with me bare hands. Killed 'em before they could kill us. It was just me an' little Ian left." He paused to wipe the tears from his face. "That was when I questioned the existence of God. How could God exist in the presence of such evil?"

For once, Dillon felt compassion for someone else. "How'd you get back your faith?"

"Some men on their way here came across us. God answered our prayers."

"How'd you know they weren't soldiers and they weren't gonna kill you?"

"Their first words to us was 'Praise God!' No one else would dare to utter those words if they wasn't one of God's own. That's how I knew." He wiped the rest of his tears away, sniffed and wiped his nose with the back of his hand. For the first time since he had met Dillon, he saw compassion in the boy's eyes. "God forgave me for killin' those boys. God forgave me my cowardice. Why should God not forgive you, Dillon? Tell me. What is it makes you so unforgivable?"

"I took money for it. And I liked it. I still like it."

"Do you feel guilt?"

"Some."

"Do you think you were doin' wrong in God's eyes?"

"Yeah. But this is the way I was born. I've known it since I was a kid. If God exists, why did He make me like this?"

"I cannot answer for Him, lad."

"That brings us back where we started, Trev." He considered Trevor's devastating experience. Dillon could not imagine what he would do if faced with the same situation. On further consideration, he concluded he would have run; he would have run to save himself—to hell with everyone else. To Trevor's credit, he had done his best to save those in his charge. That counted for something. "I'm sorry about those kids dying. It sounds to me like you did all you could."

"T'will never be enough."

Dillon considered the one surviving child, pictured a very young child, based on Trevor's brief description of him. "What happened to Ian?"

"He's well. It took a long time." Trevor shook off the memory of it all and redirected his attention to Dillon. "I would like you to pray with me, Dillon."

Dillon hardened up at the thought. "I ain't prayin'. Fuck that!"

Trevor smiled wryly. "You're a little potty mouth..."

Dillon knew it and didn't care.

"How old were you when your mother died?"

"I was six or seven. I don't know. My cancer had been in

remission for about a year. Then hers came back and there was nothin' anyone could do."

"Any brothers?"

"Sisters. One older, one younger." He grinned at a sudden memory that made him proud. He also found it humorous. "I fucked my older sister's boyfriend before she did."

This didn't shock Trevor; he had heard similar stories from similar boys. "How old were you when you did this?"

"Fourteen."

"Was he your first?"

"He was my fifth."

Again, Trevor wasn't shocked. "Who was your first?"

"A guy who worked for my dad. He was seventeen. He taught me everything." The memory was bittersweet for Dillon. "He was good to me. He liked me."

"Why do you think he liked you?"

"He kissed me like he meant it. He never hurt me. Not like those old fucks that came up for the weekend with their fat wives and fat little brats. Evan loved me. He told me so."

"How did it come about to start making money with it?"

"That's how Evan made extra money. He cut me in on it."

"He pimped you out?"

"I wanted the money."

"Do you believe someone who loved you would encourage you to sell your body? Do you really believe that?"

Months ago, Dillon had vaguely asked himself that same question. However, he had shut down in the aftermath of the incident that served as the catalyst. It was too much trauma at one time. Now, Trevor reintroduced the subject in stark black and white. Dillon realized then his immaturity, his desire for acceptance and his painful loneliness blinded him to Evan's callous manipulation. The realization hurt. The devastation showed on his face.

Trevor leaned back in his chair. This same conversation had taken place many times with many boys and girls in many shelters and churches all over his native England. The sexual exploitation of these children was an international pestilence that stole away the innocence of the most vulnerable.

Dillon pulled the covers up and avoided eye contact with Trevor. He'd briefly forgotten about the pain in his legs, and now it seemed the pain screamed for attention. He said angrily, "Where's the fucking nurse? My legs are killing me!"

"I'll find her, lad." Trevor knew the boy was not acting. He left hurriedly to locate a nurse.

Dillon was glad for the moment of privacy. It seemed to him his life held nothing to ease his pain, not the physical pain, and certainly not the pain in his soul. There had never been anything, not even from his family. It always seemed all they wanted was to escape each other and escape their empty lives. His dad escaped through work and drink, his sisters through friends, and Dillon himself through drugs, booze, and a series of perverted sexual escapades. Escape had certainly been the goal of his life, and denial the panacea. Tonight he realized there was no escape, and denial was ultimately useless. He turned away from the door and cried bitterly and silently.

COLTAN STACKED THE four backpacks on the rear rack of the Harley and secured them with bungee chords. The extra weight would be hard on the bike, but they needed to bring as much as they could carry, not only for their own needs, but also for those at the refuge. One of the backpacks contained medical supplies, and one other contained small firearms and ammunition. He and Natalie each had one bug-out bag stuffed with batteries, a change of clothing, their Bibles, vegetable seeds and other small items. The saddlebags were bulging with what little food and water they could carry. At this moment, Natalie was gathering their rifles and sleeping bags. On her way out, she would secure the attic access and the rest of the house.

He felt dizzy again and sat down on a folding camp chair. The preparations and packing took what little energy he had stored. His body was already beginning to tremble with exhaustion, and he could feel a fever coming on. The small amount of morphine he had injected earlier was beginning to wear off. Natalie had given him more antibiotics and vitamins only an hour ago. He wondered if it was too soon to add some morphine to the mix. Without it, the journey ahead would be absolute hell.

Natalie had prepared a few pre-loaded syringes for him and had placed them in his backpack's front compartment at the top of the stack for easy access. He decided to go for it and, a minute later injected the medication. His pain slowly began to subside. While the pain subsided, his fever and exhaustion increased. He rested there on the camp chair with the exposed needle in one hand and the cap in the other. He closed his eyes wearily.

This is how Natalie found him when she returned to the garage. He heard her, and opened his eyes and raised his head to look at her. She noticed the uncapped syringe in his hand and observed him worriedly, which made him feel strangely remorseful at being *caught* imbibing something forbidden, although they both knew the drug was necessary to control his pain.

She set the sleeping bags and rifles on the floor and relieved him of the syringe and cap. "Do you really think you can make this, Colt?"

"The angel said..." Coltan replied.

"What angel?"

"God sent it."

She thought he was hallucinating. "Huh?"

"It's the same one." To him it made perfect sense. "The one that broke my fall!"

"What fall?"

"From the bridge!" It finally dawned on him he had never told her about it. "Aw... forget it, Nat."

"You have an angel..."

"So do you!"

"Have you seen mine?"

"Uh-uh. I *felt* it. I felt it that day your mom died. It stayed with us all that night." He realized he had never told her about that, either.

"How come I never felt it?"

"I don't know." He leaned forward from his sitting position and picked up both of the rifles. He slung them over his right shoulder. A wave of vertigo rolled through his head. He did his best to conceal it from Natalie. "Let's get this show on the road."

"Your eyes look funny," she said. "You're dizzy again."

"I sat up too fast."

She planted herself before him and took his face in her hands. She looked sternly, yet lovingly, into his eyes, "Tell our angels there will be no coffee breaks or manna breaks, or whatever kind of breaks."

"They're already ahead of us." The dizziness ended. He smiled up at her, suddenly confident. "How about a kiss for the road, gorgeous?"

She could feel the heat of his skin in her hands and noticed the pink flushing on his cheeks and forehead. She knew what that meant. "You've got a fever."

"I'm probably contagious, huh?" This bothered him. What if he had inadvertently infected her with whatever disease was ravaging him?

She kissed his forehead and hugged him tightly. "I love you so much, Colt. I do. I really do. I love you."

He returned her embrace and wished they could stay that way a while longer. Unfortunately, time was passing and the sun was rising behind the mountain. "I promise we'll be okay. You've gotta believe me, Nat. God will get us there."

Natalie released him and secured the sleeping bags on the bike. She took her rifle from Coltan and slung it over her shoulder while he boarded the Harley. She switched off the lantern and slowly raised the big door as he started the engine. He cleared the door and waited in the driveway as she closed the door. When she got on behind him, he handed her her helmet and put his own on. With a last glance at her, he flicked down his face shield and pulled out onto the street.

He slowed to a stop in front of the Spencer house. He lifted his face shield for one last look. Natalie did the same. Their flag fluttered on the pole in the light breeze. It was faded, soiled and tattered.

Natalie asked over the engine noise, "Will we ever have America back?"

"God willing." Coltan flipped down his face shield and waited for Natalie to do so.

She put down her shield. Coltan would never see the tears that spilled down her face, or know how difficult it was for her not to look back at the only home she had ever known.

She unzipped her jacket to make certain her only remaining connection to home was secure. The weak scent of spent lilacs drifted from the small branch she had tucked down her sweater, the only reminder of this place she wanted to take with her. Maybe someday, its seeds would produce a new generation containing the spirit of the determined little girl who talked to it every summer and persistently encouraged it to blossom into winter.

The memory of helping her mother plant it in the yard provided a pleasant, although temporary, distraction from their current dilemma as Coltan accelerated the Harley toward the foothills.

CHAPTER 23

With a lot of help from amphetamines and a full pot of coffee, Clausberg spent the remainder of the night wide-awake. If she had discovered the evidence of rape before she had downed the pills, she would not have needed them to stay awake; her shame, resentment and rage at the violation would have done that.

She discovered the dried semen in her underwear during her first trip to the toilet, and the amount of semen told her more than one man assaulted her. She sat there on the toilet, her temper seething, and vainly attempted to recall the events of the evening. All she could remember was going over to the bar and having two drinks. There was no recollection of anything between the second drink and the moment she awakened still drunk in the booth. She was still so drunk then she had not noticed the physical sensation of the mess in her underwear.

She foggily recalled there were five soldiers at the bar, all young, and all high and boisterous. It could have been any of them; and it could have been all of them.

Regardless as to the identity of the culprits, she felt humiliated and dirty. She spent a good fifteen minutes washing the violated area with antibiotic soap and hot water. The entire time she scrubbed, she scolded herself and thought she deserved what she got for her carelessness. By the time she dried herself and tossed the soiled underwear into the trashcan, she was considering revenge on all five, no matter which of the five had been the actual assailants. In her opinion, they should all pay. How they should pay would take up the bulk of her attention for the rest of the night and, by morning, she still had not decided on a plan of action.

She watched Morris as he slept in a chair in the reception area. Although certain he had not been a party to the rape and probably did not even know about it, she sensed something going on within him. He frowned and seemed preoccupied with his thoughts as he prepared her coffee earlier when they returned from the sheriff's station. He smiled and shrugged as he nonchalantly answered her question with a vague statement about being overtired and that he had a headache. For the remainder of the night, she kept a wary eye on him. Although he hid it well, she knew he was up to something. By sunrise, she still had not solved the mystery.

Clausberg left him slumbering and entered the break room. From the fridge, she removed the zip top plastic bag that held the remainder of her latest harvest from the child molester. Later on, she would visit him and carve out a little more. As for now, there was enough in the bag to satisfy her caged research subjects. She vented the bag and microwaved it on *defrost* to warm it just enough to bring it to normal body temperature. The mords insisted on warm flesh; no cold stuff would do.

She had to yell at Smith over the radio to wake him. He finally wandered in after the meat cooled to below normal. She microwaved it a second time and handed the bag to the barely awake Smith. "Make sure the pimply-faced kid gets some this time. He's getting too skinny."

"Will do." The odor of the meat drifted up from the vented bag. Smith almost gagged.

"They were awfully quiet last night."

"They ate good." He remembered something as he started out with the bag. "Have you checked on the pervert this morning? I haven't heard him."

"I'll see him later. Don't concern yourself." She suspected Smith knew about the assault, might have even participated. However, their relationship had been strictly sex, and he never had to beg her for it. On reconsideration, she could find no reason why he would violate her. In addition, there was nothing in his behavior to suggest he knew anything about it. She dismissively shoved him toward the door. "Go feed the kids."

After pouring a fresh cup of coffee, she went through the big lab and into the second observation room where the two-way mirror afforded a view of Guffy and Isabelle. She noticed the mic and the video feed were off. Her immediate suspect in this crime was Morris. What was he hiding? Pissed, she powered up the equipment, listened and watched.

Guffy was in the rocker, the kid on his lap. Isabelle was sipping Kool-Aid while Guffy read nursery rhymes to her. With Guffy in his long-sleeved plaid shirt, and Isabelle barefooted in a ruffled blue dress, they were the picture of innocence and idyllic Americana. Only a woman in a frilly apron serving them apple pie would complete the picture.

Clausberg scowled. Even with the equipment powered up, she could only barely hear Guffy's voice. The bugged bear had not worked, and she guessed the device was dead. Or... Guffy had found it and removed it from the toy. That would not surprise her in the least. He had become fiercely protective of the conniving little Mexican bitch.

For that reason, Guffy had taken up permanent residence with the child, and they were only apart when either of them showered. She would have to wait for that opportunity to slip Guffy a lethal injection without the kid seeing it.

She pressed the button and spoke into the mic, "Good morning, Guffy. Good morning, Isabelle."

Guffy stopped reading and Isabelle looked up. Their voices harmonized as they both replied, "Good morning" at the same time. Isabelle giggled. Guffy grinned down at her. He resumed reading aloud.

Clausberg narrowed her eyes at the child's image on the monitor. *Let's hear how much you giggle once Guffy's dead.*

OUTSIDE, SMITH APPROACHED the cage. The mords recognized the plastic bag and the contents. They smelled the odor of the meat. Smith waited for them to stand and approach the bars with their filthy hands out. He glanced at Acne Boy; he would feed him last to assure the punk a meal while the others greedily chowed down their own portions.

Jimbo grunted and kicked the bars as he stuck out his hand. He always wanted to be first, and he always got his way.

"Top of the mornin', Jimbo!" Smith said as he tossed a butchered body part to him. He went down the line and fed Acne Boy last. The kid seemed grateful; Smith could swear he saw it in his eyes. He watched as the unfortunate boy shoved the entire thing into his mouth. No one would take it from him this time.

The crunch of splintering bone created its own bizarre music in the still morning air. Smith had gotten used to the noise. He tossed the plastic bag with its remnants of blood and lit a cigarette.

Jimbo lay down on his back and began to kick at the locked gate. He did this every morning after breakfast.

Smith drawled, "Gettin' your exercise, Jimbo?" He was used to this, too.

However, this time Don't Take My Glasses Guy joined him in this endeavor.

"What the hell..." Smith laughed. "Mord Aerobics..." He shouted at them, "You want some music with that?"

Jimbo and Don't Take My Glasses Guy grunted with each kick. They ignored Smith. The cage clanged and vibrated in response to the assault. After a while, they tired of it and settled down.

Miss Pregnant Teen U.S.A. suddenly shrieked, groaned painfully and squatted in a corner. A torrent of blood gushed from her vagina and splattered onto the concrete. Acne Boy approached and sniffed the mess. He began to lick at it. She shrieked again as a blue premature fetus dropped onto Acne Boy's head and bounced with a sickening *thwack* onto the puddle on the concrete. The girl backed away from the thing that fell out of her, inadvertently dragging it with her by the umbilical cord leaving a smeared bloody trail behind it. She lifted the cord and bit through it, and then she stared terrified at the dead creature before her.

Acne Boy seized the feast and hurried into a corner with it. The other men saw and pounced on him to get it away from him. He stubbornly hung on to it and tried to stuff it into his mouth as they pounded him and tore at him. They got it from him, each man tugging at it, attempting to establish ownership. Jimbo won. He devoured the prize triumphantly as the other three shrieked at him fiercely.

Smith spit and walked away. This was more than he could stomach. He decided to take a break from the monsters and enjoy a beer or two across the street. Reporting the incident to Clausberg could wait.

NATALIE AND COLTAN had just made it into the center of the foothills when Coltan felt the sickness overwhelm him. He pulled off the road and shut off the Harley. For a moment, he sat there waiting for the vertigo to subside so he could make it into the bushes without collapsing.

Natalie lifted her face shield, "Are you okay?"

He pulled off his helmet and hung it from the handlebar. In the next second, he set down the kickstand. The bike teetered and rested sideways. His vertigo slowly eased. "I gotta puke." He rushed behind the nearest bush and fell to his knees.

Natalie heard the wrenching sound of his vomiting. She knew he wanted privacy, but at the same time, she wanted to be certain he was not throwing up blood. Braced for the inevitable scolding from him, she approached and knelt beside him. A mixture of fresh and old blood accompanied the remnants of last night's dinner. She closed her eyes despairingly.

He yelled at her between heaves. "Get away!"

She waited for him at the bike.

He didn't make it that far. He stumbled and collapsed at the side of the road, his face pasty white. Sweating and trying to catch his breath, he sat there brokenly, resting his throbbing head in his hands, his body trembling from the surge.

Natalie brought him water. He swished it in his mouth and spit it out, and then he took a drink. She hesitated to speak until he had somewhat recovered. "There was blood."

He replied weakly and a bit irritated with her, "I didn't want you to see that."

She said it more as a pessimistic statement than a question. "How are we gonna make this?"

His expression was one of determination. "Prayer."

AFTER FINDING MORRIS still asleep in the reception room, Clausberg gathered her bucket, scalpel, and a fresh IV fluid bag. She took the rear exit and the shortcut to the police station. The street was deserted. Rap music from the bar overwhelmed the pleasant songs of the birds in the trees. The angry monotonous staccato ranting was only noise to her, and it annoyed her to no end as she passed by the establishment.

She knew all the soldiers remained the night there. None of them bothered with their jobs anymore. They spent most of their time drunk or stoned. Because of this, they were useless as protection. This was something else she would have to confront.

The mordants imprisoned in the bear cage were unusually agitated. They beat against the bars and stomped around inside the cage like children having a tantrum. She thought at first Smitty had not fed them yet, but then she noticed the empty plastic bag dancing down the street in the breeze. She decided she would discuss it with Smitty and Morris later on.

The child molester was still barely alive on the cot in his cell. Clausberg unlocked the door and propped it open. Richard heard the clinking of the key in the lock and the grind of the hinges. Inwardly he cringed and shuddered. As she dropped the bucket on the floor next to the cot, the echoing hollow noise made his body jump uncontrollably.

She leaned her face over his and grinned widely. "Good morning, little boy toy!"

His tears ran down his temples and spilled onto the already damp pillow. He begged pathetically, "Kill me!"

"Not yet," she replied gently. "I want you to tell me something. Was it only boys, or did you do some little girls, too? Huh? Were little girls on the menu?"

Maybe his honesty would finally win some points with her. Maybe she would finally kill him and end his agony. His voice came weakly, sincerely, "Boys... Boys only."

"You're a very dirty, evil little man..."

He gasped, "Yes..."

She shifted her gaze from him to the empty IV bag on the aluminum pole near the cot. "Poor baby. All out of foo-foo water. Can't have that. I have to keep you fresh and juicy." She straightened and began to replace the empty bag with the full bag. As she did this, she continued to speak to him. "Tell me, little man... Do you ever have nightmares about the little boys you ruined?"

Richard stared at her, his voice trapped in his arid throat.

She persisted, "Do you ever think of those poor little boys?"

He wanted to tell her he did think of them, but his voice lodged in his throat.

This time, she raised one eyebrow when she looked at him. "Did you have a favorite? Some poor, unfortunate pretty thing you just could not get enough of?"

The word "pretty" evoked his memories of Coltan.

Clausberg could tell by the faraway glaze in his eyes, there had indeed been a favorite, and the *motherfuckerbabyraper* seemed to relish the memory.

Her rage at this was so great she delivered the statement to him in a dread-inducing growl. "You are an evil bastard!" The pupils of her eyes seared into his as if they were burning spears. "Do you know what we do with evil? We *cut it away!*" The burning spears traveled down to his genitals and then swept back to his eyes where they seared into him again. She raised the scalpel within his range of vision, enough within range to compel him to dart his eyes to see it. "*Cut it away!*" She paused long enough to let the message sink in as she savored the terror in his face.

His screams carried over the music and into the bar. Every soldier startled into abrupt silence. Even when the jukebox delivered its final drumbeat, the screams sang on. The harrowing siren call of the most wretched among them continued non-stop for an estimated ten minutes. Not a one of the men dared to move, dared to speak. Through a collective instinct, they visualized the heinous torture behind the screams; there was no wondering or guessing. They knew.

A soldier acting as bartender broke the silence and poured them all another round.

Twenty minutes later, Clausberg stormed into the bar. She planted herself firmly at the entrance. They stared at the bucket in her left hand and the bloody scalpel in her right hand. With a thud, she let the half-full bucket drop to the wooden floor, and she convicted each individual soldier with her flaming eyes. Satisfied she had their full attention she bent and fished something out of the bucket. Her fingers dripped blood. They could not discern the item in her hand until after she flung it across the floor. All eyes followed the course of the thing and its bloody trail as it skimmed the polished wood and finally came to rest.

After she retrieved the bucket and dramatically stalked back to the clinic, Smith kicked the amputated penis out the door. Someone yelled, "Goal!" and everybody laughed. One of the other soldiers then fed money into the jukebox. Their revelry resumed.

LOUD COUNTRY MUSIC and the heavy thumps of bass filled the air around the bar across from the bear cage at the abandoned wild animal sanctuary.

Jimbo resumed kicking at the gate of the cage with both feet. He paused only long enough to invite Don't Take My Glasses Guy to join in. With the Asian's assistance, the old welded bolt pocket began to weaken and split from the frame. They heard the cracking sound. Encouraged, Jimbo kicked harder and relentlessly. When he felt it weaken further, he decided it was time for an all-out attack. The big man stood and slammed his hefty body weight against the gate repeatedly.

The frame finally groaned loudly, the bolt pocket cracked free at its seam along the frame, and the gate flung open. Jimbo flew out with it when he gave it his final body slam, and he tumbled onto the pavement. He sat up and shook his head dumbly. His eyes met those of his cage mates. Jimbo laughed as if it was the most hilarious thing in the whole world.

His companions inched to the open gateway, apprehensive at first. Jimbo stood proudly on his muscular tattooed legs and grunted to them. They exchanged hesitant glances, as if each looked to the other for the final decision. Acne Boy took the plunge first. The others followed immediately after. For a minute, they huddled close together while they surveyed the surroundings.

The small group zeroed in on the music, the muffled laughter and drunken voices from the bar across the street.

Jimbo growled and bared his teeth. He lifted his head and sniffed the air, ran his foul dry tongue over his lips and growled again. The prey smelled delicious, and the others agreed with him. They followed him as he strode silently and purposefully toward the prize.

MORRIS HAD JUST FINISHED his coffee when he heard the gate crash open. He hurried to a side window and saw the mords on the sidewalk outside the animal sanctuary. His first concern was his own safety. Concern for Guffy and Isabelle's safety followed.

Guffy was reaching for another book and Isabelle was pouring a second glass of Kool-Aid when Morris rushed into the room.

He saw the child was barefooted. "Isabelle! Put on your shoes and socks right now!"

"How come, Unkabowis?"

"We gotta go!"

Isabelle said, "Huh?" and Guffy shouted, "What's goin' on?" at the same time.

"The mords are loose!"

Guffy ran and picked up Isabelle and carried her to her bed. He tossed her sneakers and socks in her lap. "Hurry, Isa. Do it now!" She hesitated and cast him a confused expression. He took her socks and hastily put them on her feet.

She tried to put one shoe on and struggled with the laces, "Can't make bow!"

Morris grabbed the shoe from her and roughly crammed it onto her foot and tied the lace while Guffy took care of the other one. Guffy lifted her and turned to head for the rear exit.

"Teddy!" Isabelle shouted. She tried to wrestle out of Guffy's arms to reach for it.

Morris seized the stuffed bear and placed it into her hands. "There you go..."

Guffy carrying Isabelle raced ahead of him down the hallway. Isabelle became frightened and rattled off ten questions all at once. Because of her speech impediment, most of her words made no sense to either man.

Morris pictured Guffy opening the door to the pack of mords. He intercepted him and blocked the door. "Wait! They might be out there!" He put up his hands as a way to tell them to stay put, and then he went into the small lab and returned to them with a pistol.

Clausberg's voice put shivers up their spines. "What do you think you're doing?" She caught up with them before they could open the door.

"They're loose!" Morris yelled at her.

"Stay in here!" She yelled back at him. "We're safe in here!" Her eyes fell on Guffy. "Guffy! Put the kid down!"

The crisis of the moment caused her to forget about the pervert's blood on her lab coat and hands, and she was completely unaware of the blood streaks in her hair.

Isabelle stared terrified at the doctor. She clung to Guffy in response to Clausberg's gory appearance. "No, Unka! No!"

Guffy protectively tightened his embrace.

Morris stepped forward. "They can smell us! They'll get in here!"

"What?" Clausberg placed her hands on her hips. "You think they have keys?"

"They'll bust in the windows!" He planted himself between Guffy and the doctor. "They won't quit until they get us!"

"Nonsense! They're too weak." She was truly unconcerned and confident. On her tiptoes and over Morris's shoulder, she told Guffy, "For crying out loud... Put the kid down."

"No!" Guffy replied. Isabelle wrapped her arms around his neck and hid her face in his shoulder. He stroked her hair in an effort to calm her. "She stays with me."

Clausberg was undaunted. "You're going to take her outside and risk them getting her? Think about it, Guff. They'll rip her out of your weak little arms and have her for brunch. They'll have you for brunch, too!"

"Thought you said she was still infected," he countered. "They wouldn't want her if she was infected." His eyes bore into hers. "Would they, Doctor?"

"Smitty has seen them eat their own. Read his reports if you don't believe me." To Morris, she ordered sweetly, "Give me the gun. You know you're a crappy shot."

Morris pointed it at her. "I can't miss from here."

She smirked condescendingly. "Really, Morris. You intend to shoot me? Really?"

The bullet penetrated the top edge of her heart. She remained on her feet and gazed at him with an unhappily surprised expression. A spurt of blood bathed her neck and spattered her chin and the left side of her jaw. She collapsed. Her breath came in short bursts as she lied there half on her side and half on her back. Her eyes seemed dead when she looked again at Morris, "Traitor!"

He knelt beside her, just as amazed and disbelieving at his action as she. "I once trusted you, Renée. There was a time when I believed we could defeat the disease and defeat the evil, as well. You let the evil devour you like a parasite. You let the evil win."

She coughed up a mouthful of blood. Her chest fell flat with her final breath. Her vacant eyes stared at him.

Morris closed her eyes. He silently prayed for her soul and his own. He was remorseful, but he also considered the outcome if he had not killed her. He hoped God would view it as a case of justifiable homicide as he confessed and begged forgiveness.

Isabelle remarked with a sigh of relief, "*Ella es muerto*. Go wiff Deezus, Dockitew."

"Yeah..." Guffy barely whispered.

Screams, growls, shrieks and shouts accompanied by gunshots and rifle fire drifted to them from the tavern.

"We can make it," Morris stated. "Sounds like they're occupied over at the bar. We can slip right past them."

Guffy was nowhere near as certain as Morris.

Isabelle patted his trembling shoulder, "Don't be cawood, Unka. Deezus hep us."

Isabelle's confidence was enough to stem the torrent of fear rushing through him, and he ducked out the back door behind Morris.

As they passed by the rear of the tavern, Morris sensed Guffy was lagging behind. He looked back and saw Guffy was already out of breath and weakening. Morris had forgotten Guffy was in bad health, and having to carry the child only made things worse. He paused running only long enough to take Isabelle from Guffy. This helped Guffy, and he was able to keep up.

The terrible and desperate sounds from the tavern came muffled through the old timber wall and into the rear parking lot. The two men and the little girl did not have to try to imagine the scene inside; the noises poured the visualizations into their brains.

As she clutched Teddy to her chest, Isabelle gazed around wide-eyed over Morris's shoulder. She expected a bloodied victim or one of the cannibals to crash out the rear door at any moment in pursuit. At the same time, she noticed Guffy begin to lag behind again. She waved him forward and urged him on over the noise in her high-pitched and frantic Isabellespeak. Guffy waved back at her and ran faster.

They made it to the house where the VW Bug waited in the garage. Morris set Isabelle down, opened the passenger door and flipped the backrest down and the front seat forward. Without a word, he lifted the little girl behind the seat into the back seat and then flung the front seat backrest up for Guffy. As Guffy got in, he went around the other side, hurried in and started the car. It turned over on the first try, a prayer on the run answered. As the Bug puttered and warmed up, he got out and lifted the garage door.

A glance in all directions indicated the narrow street was empty. Morris knew that could change in a second. He rushed back to the car and threw it into gear. The vehicle lunged and coughed a gray smoke cloud through the tailpipe as Morris floored it toward the main highway.

CHAPTER 24

In the foothills just west of Baker Creek, Natalie sat on the side of the road with Coltan. They had both decided to break for a cigarette while Coltan recovered from his latest bout of nausea. The cigarette only made him feel sicker, and he snuffed it out in the dirt. His rising fever had begun to make his body ache, and the unrelenting sharp pains in his gut added to his misery.

Natalie draped one arm across his shoulders. "Morphine?"

He sniffed at the pollen in the breeze before he gave in and nodded. At this rate, it would take much longer to reach the refuge, and the thought of it frustrated him. More than anything, he wanted out of the sun and into a nice comfy bed.

She retrieved the syringe from his backpack and injected the drug into his arm. "It won't be long now." She capped the needle and tossed the syringe behind a bush. When she looked into his face, she saw he was not looking at her, but looking past her. His expression was one of dread and alarm. Out of the corner of her eye, she caught sight of his hand extracting Clyde from his waistband.

He stood slowly, his eyes still riveted to a target behind her. He pushed her flat onto the dirt, aimed and fired.

Natalie rolled over onto her stomach. As her ears rang from the gunshot, she lifted her head to see the threat ahead of them. She had not expected this, not so long after the initial pandemic, and certainly not so soon after the freezing cold of winter.

A middle-aged man with a full beard and a crown of thinning blond hair collapsed face down on the blacktop. A company of two women and four children followed beside and behind him. The children, three boys and one girl ranged in age from six to twelve or so, by Natalie's estimate. It was plain by their wounds they all had the mord virus. The lightly damaged, although bloody, condition of their clothing indicated they fell victim to the mords and turned recently. The group stared intently at her and Coltan. As if sharing one mind, they started forward together.

She sat up, swung her rifle down from her shoulder and checked the safety. It was unlocked. She observed her targets. The children seemed to move faster than the two women. She aimed at the largest child, a boy, and shot him expertly through the center of his forehead. He dropped and partially blocked the path of those behind him. With the largest boy down, Natalie got a clear sight of her next target. The second oldest boy was cupping his spilled intestines in his hands. She noted the shock in his eyes as he peered at her. Natalie envisioned one of the mords had ripped him open. She felt compassion for him and wondered if he was conscious of any pain. For this reason, she chose to kill him next, to end his suffering quickly. Her perfectly aimed shot to his forehead ended his torment.

When he hit the blacktop, the little girl tripped over him and fell on her extended hands. The sound of bones breaking with her impact popped loudly into the air. Coltan shot her. The bullet hit her right shoulder. He paused only long enough to scold himself. As Brian had taught him, he took a breath and held it as he aimed and took a second shot. This one hit her heart, and she fell dead on her face.

Natalie heard him whisper, "I'm sorry."

"I'll take the other kid and the red-haired woman," Natalie said. She shot the kid first, and then the woman. Her accurate shots killed both instantly.

They stared at the victims. Each said a silent prayer.

Coltan scanned the road in each direction. It appeared clear to him until he heard and then saw the bushes rustle where the road curved ahead. He prepared for the inevitable.

Natalie also watched and aimed. She tensed. How many more would there be?

A policeman stumbled from the bushes to the blacktop. Blood had traveled down from the many wounds on his torso and had dried at the hem of his pants. Some of the blood had pooled on his socks and onto his polished black shoes. A month's worth of facial hair indicated how long he was infected. Only Natalie considered this. She considered it because the Bonito Valle Police Department officers did not grow beards unless they were serving undercover in the Narcotics Task Force. This man was uniformed, a patrol cop. His duty belt was missing.

Natalie froze at first. Shortly in shock, she lowered her weapon and began to walk toward him. The man stumbling closer was her father.

Coltan pulled her back, "What are you doing?"

She stared at the Bonito Valle Police Department uniform. "Dad? Dad..."

Coltan's voice seemed far away, "No, Natalie!"

She tried to pull out of his grip. "Dad..."

Coltan cast her to his side, released her and aimed for the officer. It only took one shot to the heart.

Natalie spun and struck his arm with her fist, "You just killed Dad! Why? Why, Colt? Why?"

He ignored the pain from her fist and stared at her incredulously. She had lost it. All she could see was the uniform and the false image of her father within it. He turned her to look again at the man. "That's not your father! Look at him!"

His insistence was enough to jar her out of her spell. She looked and saw the reality before her. At once, her heart leapt and sank.

Coltan stood in front of her and blocked her view. "Your father is dead, Natalie! He's been dead for months!"

"I saw him..." she replied dazedly.

"You saw a wish."

Two miles up the road, they spotted the patrol car and an antique minibus in a ditch. Deep dents and scratches on the minibus's roof and sides indicated the vehicle had rolled a few times before it came to rest in the ditch. The patrol car had landed in a partially upright position against the far wall of the ditch, the passenger side imbedded in the trunk of an oak tree.

Coltan slowed the Harley when they came across the wreck. After a quick survey of the mess that included five dead mords, he engaged the throttle and sped on toward their destination.

The morphine had dulled his pain, but it also blurred his vision. He blinked repeatedly to clear his sight. Natalie's arms tight around his waist irritated the pain in his abdomen. He wanted to tell her to ease her embrace but, at the same time, took into account her safety. Her safety won out, and he gritted his teeth and endured the pain in hopes the morphine would kick-in and relieve the torment in his gut as it had relieved his pain everywhere else.

IN THE VW, ISABELLE rocked Teddy in her arms, "Don't cwy, Teddy. Wew thafe." She shifted to the center of the seat and leaned forward into the space between Morris and Guffy. The road became increasingly curvy as it ascended the mountain. Morris was still recovering from his panic, and Guffy was clenching the grab bar on the dash before him. She could plainly see the whiteness of his knuckles. The girl felt a need to comfort the men. She patted Morris's shoulder, "Sow down, Bowis. Wew okay now. Sow down."

Morris did not reply, but he did ease off the accelerator.

She leaned up and put her arm around Guffy's shoulder. In the same movement, she thrust Teddy in front of him. "Hode Teddy fow me, Unkaduffy. You hodim."

Guffy looked to his side at her. She was trying to comfort him, and the thought of it endeared her even more to him. He could not resist grinning at her. He accepted her offer of the little stuffed bear, "Thank you, Isa."

She appreciably glanced around at the scenery. "Pitty up hew..."

CHAPTER 25

Coltan braked at the triple junction. An overwhelming urge to detour into Baker Creek caused him to reconsider taking the center route over the summit.

"What are you doing?" Natalie hollered over the engine noise.

He did not answer. The memories of his few friends at Baker Creek absorbed all his attention. He thought of Wilford, recalled the old man's laid-back humor. Wilford was one of only a few people Coltan had come to trust back in the waning period of his Days of Rage when he most needed to escape the world. The old guy had never pressed him for details; he seemed to understand the disheveled boy who camped at the river was only seeking refuge from his demons. Coltan had been grateful for his compassion and patient support. Then there was Riley the Sheriff who once gave Coltan a place to sleep when he arrived drunk one rainy night. Riley had never cited him for the DUI, but released him in the morning with only a stern warning and an order to get a free breakfast at the café and stay in town while he got his head together. He thought also of Shirley, the old gal who ran the café. Shirley always made sure he had food and never asked him to pay for it. One day he stashed a pile of fifties and twenties behind the bundled paper napkins under the counter where she would be sure to find it. When she discovered the money, she tried to return it to him and he refused to accept it. She gave it as a donation to the animal refuge in town and told him it was his tithe toward God's creatures.

At this moment with all the memories flooding in, he felt strong concern for them. He decided right then a quick side trip into Baker

Creek was in order, no matter how much time it added to their journey or how miserable his health.

Natalie's voice again, louder. "Colt! What are you doing? Let's go!"

He wanted to rescue them, wanted to get them out of there and lead them to safety. The need to detour into the little burg was stronger than anything he had ever felt in his entire life. Coltan felt his shoulders slump forward in surrender.

He leaned his head to one side and reclined so Natalie could hear him. "We have to go to Baker Creek!"

Her voice came back filled with fear and dread, "Oh no, we don't!"

"There's people I need to check on! We can lead them to the refuge."

"You're insane! We can't do it!"

He revved the engine and took the road into Baker Creek.

"Shit!" Natalie spat.

All the way into town, Coltan wondered what he would find. He recalled the military aircraft over the town's airspace, feared there would be roadblocks and checkpoints. Coltan wondered what he would do and say when he and Natalie encountered the soldiers. How would he explain their arrival? Would the soldiers scan them for chips? Would they arrest them as spies? Could there be a way around the roadblocks, a way to slip into the town undetected?

He considered pulling over in a safe area and ordering Natalie to wait for him. At the same time, he had no idea what area was safe. Neither he nor Natalie had any idea how many mords were lurking about in the mountains, or if the soldiers had eliminated them all. To add to his concern was the likely fact some of the soldiers had gone a.w.o.l. and were hiding in the dense cover of trees and brush. They posed as great a danger as the mords to Natalie.

No, Coltan decided, he would not leave her out there alone.

More than likely, she would flatly refuse the idea of it, anyway. She was not one of those who would be satisfied with sitting and waiting passively.

He reminded himself the angels had promised to protect them.

Coltan slowed the Harley as soon as they approached the first homes and cabins at the outskirts. Dusty cars in some of the gravel driveways were the only outward sign of humanity. The apparent emptiness and stillness in the heart of the tiny downtown struck him as oppressive. The roadblocks and checkpoints he anticipated did not exist. This made him wonder if there was hidden surveillance equipment. If that was the case, it was too late to turn back now.

He pulled over in front of the cafe, shut off the engine and dropped the kickstand. The restaurant's smashed front windows and wide open door told a tragic story he tried not to imagine. From what he could see, there was no one inside.

Natalie gaped disbelievingly at the damage. "Oh shit... Colt." She angrily removed her helmet. "What the hell are we doing here?"

He took off his helmet and, as always, hung it on the handlebar. As he dismounted, he took a good look around at the absence of signs of life. His heart fell with the suspicion his friends had either fled or been killed. A second later, the hope they were simply hiding brought him a brief glimmer of determination to find them and get them out of here. He replied to Natalie matter-of-factly, "The only right thing if they're still here."

Natalie complained, "Well, there's a good answer..."

"I have to do something..." He was thinking aloud, trying to make sense of the senseless.

"You have to get your ass back on this bike and get us the hell out of here!" She glanced around, certain someone was watching them. It made her even more nervous.

Coltan listened closely for any signs of life. There was nothing, not even the chirp of a bird. The silence weighed ominously. A stagnant heaviness replaced the energy of people, animals and everything else that should be there. It was eerie.

Another stabbing pain in his stomach reminded him he should be on the road to the refuge and not here in this godforsaken place.

"Let's go!" Natalie insisted.

He replied sharply, "Shut your trap and listen!"

"Listen for what?"

"Listen!"

"For what?" She said it loudly and with much frustration.

He was as frustrated as Natalie. "Be quiet!"

She lowered her voice, "Colt, we're probably being watched. Let's go!"

He checked the magazine in his rifle and found it almost spent. He took a second magazine out of the saddlebag and tucked it into his jacket pocket. He reloaded Clyde and took up surveillance on the wooden porch of the café. Something was going to happen. He felt it as sure as the pain in his gut.

Natalie dismounted the bike and set her helmet on the seat. She checked and readied her weapons. "What are we doing here?" she asked softly.

"I told you."

"What?"

"We gotta help them."

Her response came as a sigh of resignation. Once Coltan made up his mind, there was no swaying him.

She shook her head from side to side. "If you get us killed, I'm gonna kick your ass."

He smiled at her intentionally silly threat.

Someone laughed. The laughter came from the town square a short distance away from them.

Something else drifted on the air. Coltan smelled it immediately, and he inhaled a breath of it. Marijuana. He pictured Richard kicked back under a tree, casually smoking a joint. As that picture faded, he wondered why he thought of Richard.

Natalie observed him. "What?"

"Don't you smell that?"

"Smell what?"

"Weed."

She sniffed the air and came up empty. "No."

Coltan stepped off the porch and followed the scent to a grove of trees in the little park along the creek across from the clinic. Natalie tailed him, her rifle ready.

SMITH HAD HEARD THE Harley and then their voices when the bike went silent. By their voices, he could tell the visitors were young, and they were one male and one female. He listened with curious anticipation when their footsteps on the gravel drew closer to him. When they finally reached him, Smith grinned and acknowledged them with a lazy, half-assed salute. He was sitting under a pine tree enjoying a toke. Blood dripped from his throat and wetted his uniform. He no longer felt the pain.

At his side, Jimbo bit into a human leg he twisted off at the knee of his victim. He held it and bit into it like one would a barbequed pork rib. The foot was still wearing a black sock. As Jimbo lifted the extremity to take another bite, he unintentionally waved the foot toward Smith's face.

Smith shoved the foot away. "For cryin' aloud, Jimbo! Get that putrid smellin' foot outa my face!"

Jimbo paused in mid-bite and gazed at him inquisitively. As if he finally understood, he flipped the leg around and relieved Smith of the intrusion.

Natalie and Coltan stopped in the middle of the dirt path and stared at the wounded soldier and his extremely dangerous but currently docile companion. They were both amazed the mord understood the soldier's words and seemed to have no interest in him as a meal.

Smith greeted them, "Whuzzup, man?"

Natalie pointed her weapon at Jimbo while Coltan inquired, "Why aren't you afraid of him? He bit you, didn't he?"

"Naw..." Smith took a puff before he continued. "Little Acne Boy got me." He laughed as he added, "Jimbo here kicked his ass."

Coltan was amazed at this. "What? He tried to save you?"

Smith cast a disgusted glance at Jimbo who was preoccupied with his meal. Smith looked back at Coltan. "Maybe he tried to save me for *dessert*." He shrugged uncaringly. "For now, he's happy. What the fuck..." Smith addressed Natalie directly, "Say, girlie... don't shoot him yet. Let him enjoy one last meal. Hell, even the guys on death row get one last meal."

Natalie stepped closer and aimed. Jimbo made eye contact with her and growled through the bone he was stripping.

Smith took another puff of weed and held it for a long moment before he exhaled it. Smoke accompanied his words, "He's docile right now. He ain't gonna hurt ya."

"Where's everybody else?" Coltan asked.

"Dead. I finished off the ones that didn't die right away. They woulda wanted that." He offered the joint to Coltan, "Toke?"

"No thanks." He glanced around. There was only one military vehicle, a dented jeep with two flat tires. He had expected to see helicopters and tanks. "Where's all the whirlybirds and tanks and stuff?"

"We never had any tanks," Smith answered. "As for the birds, the first wave of deserters commandeered those; the jeeps, too. They left me with that piece of shit over there." He pointed to the dented jeep with the two flat tires.

Coltan stepped closer. "What happened to all the townspeople?"

The soldier smirked ruefully, "You don't wanna know, man."

"I had friends here," Coltan said.

"Your friends are all dead."

"From the mords or your army?"

"Both."

This angered Coltan. He dropped his rifle from his shoulder and aimed it at the soldier. "Why? Tell me! What were they doing here?"

"Hell if I know, man. I was just followin' orders!" Smith leaned forward as he stated plaintively, "Go ahead and kill me. You'll be doin' me a favor."

Coltan relaxed and slung the rifle over his shoulder again. "I don't do favors for murderers."

"What the hell," Natalie piped-up and stepped forward. "I'll shoot him."

"Don't waste your ammo," Coltan stated.

"Well, I'm gonna shoot his buddy, anyway." She tightened her finger around the trigger, and aimed instead at the eating machine. "One less mord."

Jimbo chewed and, while he chewed, he watched Natalie. He paused chewing and raised his head, sniffed her scent in the air. The scent pleased him. He moaned and bared his teeth at her. There came a desire for her in his eyes.

Coltan noticed. "Natalie... Back off."

Smith observed Jimbo, took note of the desire in his eyes. To Coltan, he remarked, "Looks like he's taken a shine to your little girlfriend, dude."

Coltan turned to Natalie. "I mean it. Back off. Way off."

She replied stubbornly, "After I shoot him."

"Not yet."

"Why?"

"I want to observe him."

"Get real, Colt!" She did not move.

Coltan waved his hand in front of the monster to divert his attention away from Natalie. Jimbo looked him in the eye, smiled and grunted. Coltan found that curious. In the next moment, the big mord nudged Smith and gestured for the joint. Smith gave it to him, and he took a puff.

Coltan almost laughed. "No wonder he likes you."

Smith cracked a wide grin, and gestured to Jimbo to return the joint. Jimbo hung on to it. He told the monster, "Don't be selfish, now."

Jimbo grinned back at him and offered the leg to him.

"I don't want that!" Smith sneered, "Gimme back my reefer, asshole!"

Jimbo chuckled playfully and gave it to him.

Coltan stated with unrestrained astonishment, "Now, I've seen everything."

Jimbo grinned and laughed at Coltan. As his laughter died down, he resumed his meal.

"He don't seem to have no interest in you," Smith considered. "Why is that?"

Natalie took the shot. Jimbo fell forward. His bleeding head rested limply on his knees. His final meal dropped to the grass with a dull thud beside him.

"What the fuck..." Smith mused, "He was dyin', anyway." To Natalie, he said disdainfully, "You just couldn't wait, could you?" He then addressed Coltan, "What's with this bitch? Don't tell me. PMS. Guns and PMS don't mix, man. What the..." he trailed off and took another hit off the reefer. After a moment of thought, he pointed his finger at Coltan. "Jimbo seemed to like *you*, kid."

Coltan had an inkling why Jimbo had no interest in him as food. He did not want to discuss this in earshot of Natalie. "Natalie, why don't you cool off across the way over there?"

"Why?"

"Because I asked. I need you to watch my back. No telling what's wandering around. Do it for me, okay?"

She took her time. She knew Colt was hiding something, and she suspected the nature of that something. In her heart, she avoided the truth of it. Maybe he knew she was not ready to face it. Wordlessly, she backed off and waited for him at the steps of the clinic. She watched him converse with Smith, although she could not hear the conversation.

"Why her and not me?" Coltan asked him.

Smith sat forward and finished the joint. "You're infected."

"I was attacked by dogs, not them."

"The dogs were infected. You're fucked, dude." He shifted and reached behind him. "I've got my gun here. I ain't gonna use it on you. I'm gonna use it on me." He slowly exposed the gun and held it benignly in his lap. "I suggest you get that girl to safety before you turn."

"I would've turned by now if it was the virus."

"You look sick, dude. One foot in the grave and the other on a banana peel sick." His wry smile denoted compassion. "Hell if I know why you ain't turned yet."

"I don't have any symptoms of the mord virus."

"Suit yourself, man." He cocked the gun and poised the point of the barrel under his chin. As he did this, he remembered something and brought the gun down a ways. He told Coltan. "Say, dude. I forgot to do somethin'. There's a guy locked up at the jail. He's dyin' slow. Not the virus. He's sufferin', man. Sufferin' like no one deserves. Finish him off for me."

"Why's he in jail?"

"Molested some kid."

Coltan felt his stomach twist. "Who's the guy?"

"I don't know, man. Some French guy."

A chill ran up his spine. He thought it could not possibly be true, yet every cell in his brain screamed otherwise. "French?"

"Somethin' like that. Clausberg was carvin' him up to feed the mords. She was keepin' him alive just for that. The last time I heard him scream was about a half hour ago."

Coltan shuddered at the soldier's explanation. He could not ignore the picture of it in his mind. As much as he hated Richard, Coltan did not wish such suffering on even the Devil himself. He vocalized his distress at this in a horrified whisper, "Shit..."

"That's all I know." Smith pushed the point of the gun into the space below his chin. "Finish him off for me. Okay, dude? I'd do it myself, but I can't walk no more."

"Accept Jesus Christ as your Savior." The command spilled out of Coltan at the urging of the Holy Spirit.

"What the fuck, dude! You want me to do *that* before you go off the bastard?"

"Christ died for all of us."

"So I heard."

"Do you believe it?"

"I don't believe nothin' no more." He pulled the trigger.

Coltan prayed for the soldier and the unfortunate mord. In conclusion, and as added insurance for their souls, he made the Sign of the Cross over them.

Natalie watched this from across the street, cynically amused by Colt's attempt to play clergyman and perform Last Rights for those she considered already damned. She remarked as he approached her, "Gave them Last Rites, huh, Pastor Coltan?"

"He committed suicide." He took her hand and led her down the steps with him. "We have to go to the jail."

"What for?"

"To finish the business that brought me here."

FINDING THE PLACE LOCKED, they shot out the large window at the front and gained access that way. They readied their weapons as they entered and surveyed the front office. No one responded to the intrusion. After a sweep of the room, Coltan opened the door that led down the hall to the offices and beyond that, the narrow block of four holding cells. Natalie found all the office doors locked. The only open door led to the weapons room, and all the weapons were gone.

"Hello?" Coltan shouted.

In response came a muffled whimper from inside the cellblock. Coltan slowly pushed open the door and aimed his rifle. The hallway was dark. Natalie felt for a light switch. She found it and turned on the overhead fluorescent lights.

Seeing the hallway was empty, Coltan called again. "Hello?"

The whimpering came again, a little louder this time.

They checked each cell as they passed. The fourth cell at the end of the hallway housed the lone prisoner. The door to that cell had been propped open with a large cement block. Natalie and Coltan were glad they would not have to go in search of a key.

A weak voice familiar to Coltan called out. "Please..."

The sound of Richard's voice tore at Coltan's heart. At once, Coltan wanted to flee, and he wanted to end his former tormentor's suffering.

He turned to Natalie. "I need to go in alone."

"Why?" She strained to get a look. "Who is it?"

Shakily, he answered sadly, "It's Richard."

"Don't tell me you want to rescue him. Not after everything he's done to you."

"He's dying."

"So what?"

Richard's voice came weakly, pathetically. "Coltan…?"

Coltan avoided looking at him. "Yeah. It's me."

He whined child-like, "Help me…"

Natalie yelled angrily at him, "Go to hell!"

Coltan told her sternly, "This *is* Hell!" He took a step into the cell and briefly turned back to her. "Stay out here. I have to do this myself."

Natalie understood, but she did not agree. In her opinion, the sadistic pervert deserved no sympathy and certainly did not deserve rescue. However, Colt, the rescuer personality, was committed to this mission. She decided to stand guard at the cell entrance while he entered the cell and approached the wretched prisoner.

Coltan stood at the side of the bed and observed Richard. The man was strapped securely to the bed frame. Blood saturated the mattress. Blood-soiled bandages covered his many wounds. Tourniquets on each severed limb prevented him from bleeding to death. The IV tube fed fluids into what remained of his right arm.

Not prepared for this horror, Coltan turned away from the sight. He expected Richard would interpret his avoidance as more sissy behavior. A real man would swallow his disgust and trepidation. Considering that, Coltan summoned all his courage to look again and deal bravely with the sickening reality of it.

Richard's face was almost as ashen as the sweat-stained pillowcase. He looked up at Coltan with dull, desperately pleading eyes. His voice came weakly and starved for breath, *"Coltan! Mon Coltan! Miséricorde! Coltan… Grâce!"*

Coltan's memories of Richard's brutal treatment flooded through him. Yet, Coltan took no pleasure in the sight of his torturer undergoing an even more hideous and agonizing torture. He wanted with everything in him to end the man's torment. At the same time, Coltan's resentment and virulent rage towards him boiled to the surface. Those feelings overpowered everything else for the moment.

Coltan bent and leaned his face close to Richard's. "When did you ever show *me* mercy?"

"Mon Coltan! Grâce à moi!"

"Speak English!" Coltan demanded.

"Please... my sweet boy! Kill me! End this! I beg you!"

"Your sweet boy?" Coltan questioned. "That sweet little boy who wanted nothing from you but acceptance? That sweet little boy you tortured?"

"Ah... Coltan." He gasped for his next breath. "My pretty..."

"No!" He shouted in his face. "No pretty! You almost destroyed me!"

From the cell door, Natalie yelled, "Just kill him, Colt. Get this over with!"

Coltan ignored her. To Richard, he demanded, "Tell me you're sorry!"

"Yes...," he sobbed. "I am sorry. My poor boy. My good boy."

"Why did you do it? What made you think I deserved it?" Coltan was near tears, and he stubbornly held them back.

Richard had only one answer, and it did not qualify as an answer, but an excuse. "So pretty... little, pretty, sweet boy..."

His gut stabbed pain, and he felt nauseous again. He furiously rejected Richard's attempt to place the blame on him. Coltan fought back. "Are you blaming *me*?"

He gazed up at Coltan, defeated. "No. The blame is mine."

"Apologize to God."

"Why?"

"I belong to God."

"No." It was too late. He fully expected God would send him to Hell regardless of his apology.

Coltan pointed his gun at him. "Ask God to forgive you. Tell Him you're sorry."

Richard laughed weakly. "Or, what, my pretty boy? You will

shoot me? Please... shoot me. Do it!"

Coltan lowered the weapon, "I can leave you here to die slowly if that's what you want. It's your choice. At least, I'm giving you a choice. That's more than you ever gave me."

Natalie wanted out of this town, and she was well out of patience. She pointed her rifle at Richard's head. "Finish him off, Colt! Finish him now, or I'll do it for you."

Coltan glared resentfully at her. "Stay out of it!"

He looked back at Richard's face, and then he slowly performed a visual examination of the man's exposed naked body. Besides the amputated sections of limbs and excised squares of flesh, Coltan discovered something else. That discovery produced in him a mixture of satisfaction and sympathy. He felt satisfaction because it was a fitting punishment and sympathy because it had undoubtedly been excruciating to experience.

His bitterness swallowed his feelings of sympathy. "Well, well, well!" He taunted Richard cruelly, "I see they've cut off your weapon of childhood destruction! Talk about the punishment fitting the crime!" Once again, he hovered over Richard and bent his face close to his. He snarled and growled slowly through gritted teeth, "Do you have any idea how many times I wanted to do that?"

Richard met this with knowing silence.

Natalie had never before heard such malevolence in Coltan's voice. She had never before seen him display such complete and unrestrained hatred as he poured onto Richard. His behavior frightened her. "Colt, please..." Natalie pleaded.

Coltan felt empowered and satisfied. He stood up straight. His anger gradually dissipated. For a few moments, Coltan felt nothing. It was a strange sensation to be empty of emotions.

Richard gazed at him with tear-filled, begging eyes, the eyes of a terrified child; a child brutalized beyond his capacity to sanely endure more.

Natalie said, "Let's get this over and get out of here!"

Coltan did not hear her. He could only hear the hard, frantic beating of his own heart and the raspy, laborious breaths of his dying tormentor. The Tormentor was now the Tormented, and Coltan realized Richard had probably been beleaguered all his life. Compassion and absolution filled him. He wished to end the misery for Richard as well as for himself.

"I forgive you, Richard." He said it with heartfelt sincerity. "I pray God forgives you, too."

With tears streaming down his face, he aimed at Richard's forehead and pulled the trigger.

CHAPTER 26

There was no conversation between them as they exited the sheriff's station. Coltan felt completely drained mentally and physically and shell-shocked by his experience with Richard in the jail cell. His stomach burned and cramped with pain, and the nausea began to return. Natalie saw it in his face and in his self-protective posture when she joined him in the shade on the top step outside the station.

Natalie considered Coltan's condition. She returned to the Harley and went over their supply of medications in their packs. The antacid liquid was almost gone, as were the tablets. There was also the matter of morphine. Only one vial remained, and they could use some extra syringes. They were out of vitamin water, too. The clinic across the road and a short distance up from the station caught her eye. It was a good opportunity to stock up on more medical supplies while they were still in town.

She rejoined Coltan at the steps. "I'm going over to the clinic for meds."

He sat there cradling his head in his hands. He did not seem to hear her.

She tried again, and this time she gently nudged his shoulder to get his attention. "I'm gonna get us more meds."

He closed his eyes for a moment, and then he sunk forward and clutched his gut. The expression on his face told her what was coming. She stepped back while he rolled over on his side and scrambled in a semi-crawl to the bushes along the railing. He bent and vomited a mixture of old blood and fresh blood. This time,

Natalie stayed put and simply watched him from a distance and waited for him to be done.

When it was finally over, Coltan reclined against the wall, totally spent. "Forget it," he said softly. "Let's get outa here."

"We need meds."

"You packed enough. We got enough."

"There's only one vial of morphine left," she persisted. "It'll take me five minutes."

"Forget it." He coughed and cleared his throat, gazed vacantly at her.

"You can't possibly drive the bike yet." She kneeled in front of him and looked into his eyes, tried to diagnose the severity of his condition, tried to detect the telling signs of vertigo, anemia and early-stage liver damage. All were readily apparent. "I'll go over and get the meds while you rest. You have the gun and the rifle. You'll be safe until I get back." He said nothing in response. She cupped his chin in her hand, "Right, Colt?"

"Do you think God's mad at me?"

"For what? Killing Richard?"

"Yeah."

"Isn't that what you were sent here to do?"

"I'm not sure."

"You and Richard made peace with each other. And, you ended his suffering."

"I should've waited for him to apologize to God. If only..."

"He's had plenty of time to do that, long before you got here. I'm sure he spent a lot of time talking to God about everything. I'm sure he confessed things no one will ever know about except God. You gave him the two things he wanted: mercy and release. Maybe God kept Richard alive long enough for you to resolve the past with him. Maybe he needed to resolve it as much as you. Who knows? I don't think God will fault you for being compassionate."

Coltan jerked his head up and peered into the sky. "What's that?"

"Huh?"

"That noise." He sniffed the air like a dog. "Fuel. Chemicals..."

"Colt, I don't hear or smell anything."

No sooner had she spoke, an earth-shaking rumble from a distance came to her ears. She searched the sky, unsure of the direction. In a few moments, drab gray military planes soared over the horizon above the bank of hilltops in the west. There were six of them, and they were making a rapid beeline for Baker Creek.

"Aw, shit...!" Coltan's eyes grew big, and he rose weakly to his feet. "We gotta get outa here. We gotta go now!"

She stood up and steadied him. "Can you make it?"

"I have to!" He slung his rifle over his shoulder and took her hand. "Run!"

He had parked the Harley one-quarter mile away in front of the café. Natalie took note of the distance and doubted Coltan could make it that far, running, in his condition. Yet, he ran. He ran and pulled her along by her hand, his expression desperate and determined.

The first two of the group entered the burg's airspace. They fired missiles. The first missile slammed into the clinic and blew it to pieces. What little remained of the building burst instantly into an inferno.

When Natalie looked back and saw this, the realization of how close to death she had come hit her with numbing clarity. If Coltan had not delayed her, she would have been inside the clinic, and she would have been dead.

She quickened her pace and came up beside him. She wrapped her arms around his waist and supported his body as he frantically stumbled toward the Harley.

Missiles struck around them in all directions. The noise deafened them. Smoke, dust and a sticky shower of unidentifiable chemical soup danced and swirled through the air. The toxic rain burned their eyes, nostrils and lungs. Fragments of trees, buildings and cars flew; projectiles they had to dodge.

Something hit Natalie's back in the space between her shoulder blades. The impact threw her flat to the dirt, and it knocked the air out of her. Stunned, she laid spread eagle on her belly, her head vibrating from the sudden assault. Coltan grabbed her from behind and pulled her up on her feet. He both dragged and carried her to the Harley where he hoisted her onto the two-up seat in a sitting position. In the next move, he retrieved her helmet from the ground and hastily dropped it over her head and flipped down the face shield. The chemical rain burned her eyes. She closed her eyes to get relief from the pain. During that moment, she felt Coltan's weight shake the bike as he mounted the seat. The next thing she felt was the bike shuddering as he started it up. She could not hear it over the noise of explosions.

The rest of the aircraft arrived by this time, and they joined the first two in their mission to destroy the little town. More tree parts, flora and building materials went flying, much of it on fire.

Coltan fastened his helmet and flipped down the shield. He tore out of the lot and sped onto the road leading back to the main road. He could barely see ahead, but that was the least of his worries. The chemical-laced smoke was his main concern; he was certain the smoke was poisonous, and he feared it would kill them before any flying debris did it. They had to get out of this tiny valley and up into the mountains to avoid the toxic fumes. With this as his primary intention, he took the narrow winding road at the highest speed he could safely manage, and only slowed when they reached the triple junction at higher ground.

Down in Baker Creek, the destruction continued.

Coltan headed up the center road toward the summit. After they had cleared a few miles and reached a higher, safer elevation, he slowed and pulled over at the side of the road. From that vantage point, he and Natalie could view the ongoing destruction.

"Let's keep going." Natalie urged.

"No. Wait." He noticed a stream a few feet below the shoulder of the road. His eyes and skin were still burning from the toxic soup the aircraft dropped on them. They needed to wash it off quickly or pay the consequences. He shut off the engine and engaged the kickstand. "We gotta wash off in that stream. We gotta do it now."

Her eyes still burned and she could barely see. "There's a stream?"

He took off his helmet and dismounted the bike. When he looked at her, he saw the chemicals from the airstrike left a mist on her face shield. He lifted the face shield. "Is that better?"

She could see. "Yeah."

"C'mon, Nat. We gotta wash." He carried his helmet and added, "We gotta wash our helmets and jackets, too. No telling what kind of poison they dumped on us!"

She laboriously climbed off the seat. Her head ached, and she felt slightly dizzy. The space between her shoulder blades stung and felt wet under her jacket. She decided not to mention it to Coltan.

When they reached the bank of the stream, Coltan removed his jacket, shirt and undershirt. He tossed the undershirt to Natalie, "We'll use this to clean the helmets and jackets."

She noticed his skin had taken on a yellowish tone, and the many stitched dog bites had developed bruises. Her first intention was to wash his skin. She dipped his undershirt into the icy water and bathed him as he bent to wash his face and hair.

"It's freezing!" He exclaimed. After a moment, he paused and told her, "Don't worry about me. Wash yourself—especially your face and hair."

She stubbornly continued to bathe him, "In a minute."

Miffed, he turned and snatched the undershirt from her. "Do it now, Natalie!" Her hurt expression exasperated him further. "Look," he explained, "I don't mean to yell at you. The longer that stuff's on you, the more time it has to sink into your skin. From there, it'll go into your system. I don't want anything to happen to you. Please do what I tell you. Please!" He resumed washing himself. "I can take care of this myself. For once, take care of *you!*"

Without argument, she removed her jacket and set it aside, and then she removed her sweater. The little branch of lilacs was still secure in the vee of her bra. She extracted it carefully and set it on the dirt at her side.

Coltan saw the lilac branch. "You brought some along!"

She shivered in the cold. "Yeah. I thought maybe I could plant the seeds some day."

That struck him as quite optimistic of her. It also did not get by him it was her way of bringing a memory of home along, a little something that held the promise of a new beginning from an old foundation. "That's a good idea. We could plant a whole orchard of them. *Natalie's lilac orchard.*"

Natalie offered no reply. It was a nice dream, a dream that would simmer on the back burner until the world regained sanity and life was worth living again.

She bent over the stream and began to rinse her face. The frigid water soothed the burning. She did not mind her hands were quickly going numb. A sudden freezing cold burst of water rushed over and into her hair. She felt Coltan's hands push her head down closer to the water. He gathered handfuls of water and dumped them over her head. The iciness of it caused her to shiver violently. Her headache became an all-out assault of sharp stabbing pains through her skull. Even her eyes suffered.

"Stop!" She reached to push his hands away.

"You're bleeding!" Coltan told her in a startled tone of voice. "Where?"

"The back of your head." He gently pressed the area at the base of her skull, "Right here." It hurt precisely at that spot when he did that. She yelped. He began to part her hair, "Let me see."

She tried to bring her head up, but Coltan held her down. "It's just a scratch." She protested, "Something hit me, grazed me. It's nothing to worry about."

"Stay still," he ordered gently. As he investigated the wound, he discovered something embedded there. This was probably the reason it had not bled profusely; the foreign matter was plugging it up. If he attempted to remove the object, the removal could make matters worse. He opted to leave it alone until they could get medical help. He decided not to tell her what he found. "Yeah, it's a cut. It's not bleeding much. You'll be okay."

"Told you," she replied.

However, he noticed she had another wound between her shoulder blades, a large purple bruise scarred with skid marks of small lacerations in the center of it. The lacerations had bled slowly, but the blood had begun to coagulate over the wounds. Blood stained the rear band of her bra. He lightly touched the wounds. She arched her back and pulled away.

"Did that hurt?" It was a dumb question, only one of a zillion dumb questions he had asked in his lifetime.

"It's a little sore."

Her reaction told him it was more than a little sore. He knew she did not want to add to his worries. He downplayed the severity of the injury, just to make it easier on her. "You got a bruise there."

She noticed he was shivering, "Get dressed before you freeze to death. I'll wash the helmets and jackets. You take it easy."

He tossed her his thick cotton over-shirt, "Dry your hair."

She caught it. "Then you'll have to wear a wet shirt."

"I'll survive." He massaged his upper arms with his hands.

She tossed the shirt back to him. "No way! You're too sick. You need to stay warm." He gave her *that look*, to which she responded, "Don't argue!"

The valley below became quickly silent. For a few moments, the stillness rivaled the stillness of death. Natalie and Coltan looked out and searched the valley in which Baker Creek once thrived. Black smoke blanketed Baker Creek. A strong chemical odor accompanied the scent of burning wood products. They heard the sound of the aircraft engines, strong at first, and then saw the crafts circle above the tree line and veer west, away from them. They listened, shivering in the coolness, as the noise diminished with the distance.

AT THE REFUGE, MITCHELL, Glenda and Roger had picked up a transmission from Bonito Valle early that morning. The transmission was scratchy and full of dropouts, but their ears pricked up when they understood plainly the words, "loaded missiles" and "Baker Creek." They alerted James to their anticipation of an attack on the little burg. It was late in the morning when they watched the demolition of Baker Creek via satellite on their monitors.

The three of them were discussing the strike when something new came over their perimeter monitors. Roger shouted at them to turn and look as the VW shot under the first camera at the south entrance and then the second and third at high speed. The way the vehicle shot up the narrow dirt road and almost missed a curve told them the driver was close to panic, or at least in a very big hurry.

"SOW DOWN, BOWIS!" ISABELLE pleaded. "Don't dwive so fast. Make me frow up!"

"Aw, no..." Guffy told her. "Don't do that, honey." He clung to the grab bar on the dash. He had been clutching it since they left Baker Creek.

She ignored him, "Bowis! Sow down!"

"Alright, sweetie." Morris took a deep breath, eased off the gas and switched gears. The only thing on his mind had been reaching the refuge and the safety it would provide them. During their entire time on the road, he had been haunted with the feeling something evil was chasing them. As the refuge loomed nearer, he felt the evil back off until it was far, far behind.

Now that he finally took the time to breathe and gather his thoughts, a feeling nagged him he had forgotten something. The image came to him of the pervert down in Baker Creek. Morris silently chided himself for forgetting the man in their rush to escape. He remorsefully accepted the fact he could now do nothing to end the man's suffering. He recalled the syringe full of death juice in his pocket. Morris knew the Alpha security would search him upon arrival and he did not want the hassle once they discovered it. He slowed the car further and casually rolled down the window and tossed the useless thing into the brush.

Isabelle took a deep breath of the pine-scented air, felt the VW slow. "Dat's bettew!"

Amused by her tone of voice, Morris eyed Isabelle through the rear view mirror. "Say, Isa?"

"What, Unkabowis?"

"When you get married, are you gonna let your husband drive?"

She grinned and laughed. "Uh-uh! No way!"

CHAPTER 27

There was still snow on the ground at two thousand feet elevation. This was a bad portent. The road would only get worse the higher they climbed. Coltan pulled over and shut off the Harley.

He lifted his face shield and said, "I need the map."

Natalie hopped off and unzipped the front pocket of Coltan's backpack. "Are we gonna need to turn back?"

"I hope not!" He set the kickstand and dismounted slowly to avoid an attack of vertigo. His fever had risen still higher, and his body was painful. He knew he was becoming weaker with each passing hour. If they had to double back, there was a good chance he would not survive the journey.

Natalie spread the map open on the seat. "I don't even know where we are."

"I do." He stated confidently.

"Are we close?"

"Halfway, maybe."

With his attention fully engaged reading and tracing the map, Natalie studied his face and his posture. His face was a pasty ashen color, and he was sweating. The whites of his eyes had turned yellow. Even his lips had paled and had taken on a yellowish tinge. He stood hunched over while he studied the map, but she saw he was cradling his belly with his left arm. His legs were trembling, and so were his hands. The realization he was dying drifted through her. She pushed the thought away as if she could will him back to health simply by denial.

Coltan nodded to himself and then said, "If we go back half a mile, there's an old fire trail that hooks up with the south side route. We'll drop a little in elevation, but there won't be as much snow. It's a little longer, but it's safer. I think, even though it's longer, it'll take us less time because we won't be having to slow down as much for snow and hazards." He paused and thought for a few moments, recalling his ordeal on that rainy night on the south route not so long ago. "There was a rockslide out that way, but I think we're already past it. If there's no more slides, we should be okay."

She put her arm around him, "It's your choice, Colt."

He faced her with eyes full of confidence. "The southern route." He wiped sweat from above his lip.

"How are you feeling?"

"I'll make it." He began to neatly fold the map as he added, "We got angels."

"It'd be nice if they sent us a limo."

He grinned and chuckled, "You don't like my Harley anymore?"

"I love your Harley!" She kissed his cheek. "It's just so damned cold out here!" His skin felt frigid and damp as she brushed her cheek against his. She could feel him trembling. She could hear his quick, shallow breathing. "Do you need a break? Maybe some water? Meds?"

"Water."

"Would you like to stretch out for a few minutes? I can put a sleeping bag down."

Coltan knew if he stretched out and rested for a while, he would likely fall asleep. "We have to keep going, Nat."

"Five minutes. A smoke break."

"You can smoke."

She untied one sleeping bag and opened it over a sunny, relatively dry spot on the road. He eased himself down on it reluctantly. His belly hurt again, and he doubled over and hugged it with both arms.

Natalie handed him a bottle of water and a roll of antacids. She removed the medical kit from the saddlebag. "I'd like to check your temp before you drink."

He dismissed the idea. He did not want to know. "That's okay."

She joined him on the bag with the kit, "Please?"

He knew she would not give up. "Shit..."

His temperature was 103.

She opened the water for him and offered it to him, "Drink up." To remind him, she added, "Slowly."

It was like ice water. He took sips of it, longed for something hot and comforting. She noticed his jacket was open below his neck. Without a word, she reached for the zipper and drew it up to close the jacket completely. He had not been aware of the chill on his neck until he felt the warmth of the jacket around his skin.

"Better?" Natalie asked.

He nodded. She appeared pale to him. It made him think about the injury to her head. He reached for her and pulled her close against him. "Let me check the back of your head."

"I'm okay." The headache was no worse and no better. She considered no change was a good thing. She let him examine the injury.

It had stopped bleeding. He was relieved. "Well... Your head's not bleeding anymore."

"That's good." She smoked and worried about him.

He chewed four antacid tablets and drank a little more water. A minute later, he felt like heaving again. He rose slowly and made for the nearest bush.

Natalie did not follow him. She sat and smoked. She wiped tears so he would not see them when he returned.

IN THE PROCESSING ROOM, Morris handed James the disks from the lab at Baker Creek. "These will answer most of your questions." The Security Team had examined their vehicle, luggage and other belongings outside the perimeter over an hour before. As soon as they deemed everything clear and safe, two soldiers brought the bags to the Processing Room and declared all items passed Security. Morris emptied the bag containing his medical and diagnostic equipment and set it all on the table. "Your hospital will need these items. I'm sure you don't have the diagnostic solution that identifies the mord virus, but here it is. As you may recall, James, I'm a pathologist, and I've had extensive medical training. Do you have a pathologist on staff?"

James grinned at Morris, "We do now!" He had no qualms about welcoming Morris onboard. They had kept in touch over the years after their first meeting at an Army of Christ planning event. He had given Morris up for dead eight months ago when he learned the fate of the Mohave Cross Base. He rejoiced at this reunion with his old friend.

The two men shook hands and briefly hugged. Morris then remembered Guffy, who was standing silently at his side. "This is Guffy. He has a lot to tell you. Without him, that little girl over there would be dead."

Despite James's trust in Morris, it dismayed Trevor no one had noticed or even thought to examine the child's stuffed toy bear. Something that innocent was the perfect vehicle for a bomb or a surveillance device. He had already scanned it for a chip and found it clean. He pulled Franks aside and ordered him to check the stuffed bear for any surprises.

Franks squatted in front of Isabelle. "Can I see your teddy bear, darlin'?"

His face seemed kind enough to her, but she was reluctant to surrender Teddy to anyone except Unkaduffy or Unkabowis. Her dark eyebrows met at the bridge of her nose as she regarded Franks's request with suspicion. "How come?"

"To make sure he's okay." He reached out his hand to her. "I bet you took good care of him, huh? What's his name?"

"Teddy." She still would not let go.

"Let me check him out, okay?"

She glanced at Unkaduffy and Unkabowis. They were talking with the big black man and the soldier guy with the funny accent. She could not get their attention to seek their guidance on the matter. Better safe than sorry, she told Franks, "No. I keep."

A tall man in a set of blue scrubs entered the room as she began her stalemate with Franks. She studied this new person, noted his uniform and the stethoscope hanging from his neck. He looked like a doctor, and she did not trust doctors. Yet, like Franks, he had a kind face and kind blue eyes.

Franks reached again for Teddy, ever patient when it came to kids. "Please, Isa?"

She shook her head, "No."

The doctor-type man squatted in front of her. He had perfect teeth, and his smile reminded her of Mario. He spoke to her in an upbeat, cartoonish tone of voice. "My name is Joe. What's yours?"

"Isa." She sucked in her lips over her teeth before she asked him, "Aw you a Dockitew?"

"No, sweetie. I'm an emergency medical technician. Have you ever seen an ambulance?"

Her eyes got round with the memories of her old neighborhood. "Lotsa times!"

"I'm the guy in the ambulance that helps people."

That was okay. At least he was not a doctor. "Oh."

Joe patted Franks's shoulder, "This is Franks, Isa. He's got a little girl younger than you. And I've got a little girl just your age. She's here with her mom and brothers. I bet she'd love to meet you."

"What hoo name?"

"Rebecca," Joe answered. "Would you like to meet her in a couple of days?"

"You want Teddy fo' hoo?"

"No, honey." Franks interjected, "I'll give Teddy back to you right away."

"Why you wannim?"

"To make sure he's okay." Franks again reached for it. Isabelle pulled it out of his reach. He dropped his hand in a frustrated manner. "Look, kid. I'm not gonna hurt it."

Joe said softly to Franks, "Bugs and bombs?"

Franks nodded. "Yeah. Standard procedure."

Joe plugged the stethoscope into his ears and said to Isabelle, "How about if I listen to Teddy's heart? Bet he's tired and scared from all you've been through. I can listen to your heart, too."

"No needews?"

"No needles." He extended his hands for the bear. When she pulled away, he lifted the stethoscope off his chest and nested it in the palm of his hand. "Just listening. You've seen a stethoscope before, right?"

"Uh-huh..."

"It's for listening to your heart."

"I know dat." She said it as if she was insulted.

Joe continued, "How about I listen to Teddy's heart?"

She reluctantly handed him over to Joe. "You gibbim back wite away!"

"I will." Joe took the stuffed bear and listened to his "heart," while Isabelle hovered and watched with grave concern. He smiled at Isabelle. "His heart's fine. Good and strong. I'm gonna listen to his tummy now." He moved the stethoscope over the toy and listened for ticking. At the same time, he searched with his fingers for hard spots and hidden internal foreign objects. When he was satisfied the toy was safe, he nodded and smiled at Isabelle. He returned Teddy to her. "He's in fine shape!"

"All good?" Franks asked Joe.

"All good!" Joe said. "Did they scan it for a chip yet?"

"Trevor did—from a distance. It's clear."

"Nothing to worry about, then." He patted Isabelle's head, "Where did you come from, little lady?"

"Da mean dockitew pace."

Joe referred this puzzle to Franks, "The mean doctor place?"

"Baker Creek. They set up a research lab there."

Joe remained squatted before Isabelle, "Did someone hurt you there?"

"When I had biting sick." Her eyes became sad.

Joe thought it could not be true. "You had the virus?"

She nodded. "Aw bettew now. No mo' bite. No peep fing."

Joe and Franks looked to each other, completely confused. Franks addressed the question to Isabelle, "What's peep fing?"

She thought they were stupid to not know what peep fing was. "Peep fing! Peep fing fo' eat. *Peep fing!*"

Her voice and those words carried over to Guffy and Morris. They both abandoned James and Trevor in mid-sentence and rushed to her. It was bad enough they had to reveal Isabelle had once suffered from the mord virus. They had spent the last five minutes trying to convince the men at Alpha Base that Isabelle was not a threat. Now, Isabelle inadvertently revealed the *peep fing* business. It was too soon to talk about the hideous menu at Clausberg's Café.

"Isa, honey..." Guffy picked her up and cuddled her. He stammered and told Franks and Joe, "She just loves hamburgers."

Isabelle scrunched her face at Guffy. "Day don't know peep—"

"I'll explain it to you guys later," Morris offered.

"Explain it now!" Franks demanded.

"Watch the disks with James," Morris replied. "It explains

everything."

Franks pointed at Isabelle, "Is she sick?"

Morris stated positively, "No!"

Trevor had been watching and listening with James. Both of them were ninety percent certain the three new arrivals posed no danger. The ten percent left over was their concern about Isabelle. Even though Morris promised to remain vigilant and perform weekly blood tests on her, he couldn't rule out the possibility of her relapsing. This is why Trevor had paged Joe into the Processing Room. He wanted Joe to work with Morris monitoring Isabelle's condition. He also wanted Morris to teach all the medical personnel how to diagnose the mordant virus, both by sight and through laboratory tests. Of all the people who had arrived at the refuge, Morris was the only one who had extensive experience and knowledge about the mords and the mord virus.

Trevor stepped in to calm the waters. "We'll keep the girl in isolation in the Infirmary for observation, Franks. Will that be good enough?"

Before Franks could answer, Isabelle questioned worriedly, "What icelation? What Infoomy? Is dat dale?"

"No, Isa," Guffy soothed her, "It's not jail. It's a special room at the hospital where the doctors and nurses watch over you for a few days to make sure you're well."

She trembled at the thought. "*Dockitews?*"

Trevor told her, "We have nice doctors here. No one will hurt you, luv."

Her eyes filled with frightened tears. "Unkaduffy tay wiff me?"

Trevor had no answer for her. None of them had considered Guffy or the little girl's dependence on him.

Joe asked Guffy, "How long have you been taking care of her?"

"Months," Guffy answered. "It's all recorded on the disks. Everything's there." He cuddled Isabelle a bit tighter. "Look, man...

she's got no one else. If you put her alone in a room, she ain't gonna handle it. Let me stay with her. You got a double room, right?"

Trevor was not comfortable with that idea. He knew nothing about Guffy, knew nothing about the true nature of his relationship with Isabelle. It was highly unusual for a man to be so protective of a child who was not his own. His thoughts drifted to all his encounters with the Dillons of the world, the children exploited by seemingly benign men such as Guffy. Trevor hated suspecting Guffy, but he only had his past experiences on which to base this.

Trevor turned to James, who had been listening with unusual patience and restraint. "What say, James? Perhaps a room nearby each other? Observe them both?"

"Tay wiff Unkaduffy!" Isabelle insisted tearfully. "Unkabowis, too!"

Morris assured her, "I'll be working there every day. I'll see you every day."

Isabelle buried her face in Guffy's shoulder. "Unkaduffy!"

Guffy knew what this was about. "It's all on the disks, man! She's like a daughter to me! Watch the disks! I got nothin' to hide!"

James stepped forward. "Chill, dude. You'll stay together for now. Considering you've been exposed to the virus through her, that makes the best sense for now. We gotta observe both of you to be sure." He eyed the rest of the men in the room. "How's that set with the rest of y'all?"

Only Trevor had reservations. Still, he agreed reluctantly, inwardly planning to keep a close eye on Guffy in order to protect the child. He knew the isolation rooms were under twenty-four hour camera surveillance.

THE MUD SPATTERED HARLEY reached the better road at the

south face where there was no snow on the ground. The dappled sunlight did little to warm them as they sped onward against the cold air. Natalie was glad she had put her trust in Coltan's instincts. They had encountered no hazardous conditions, and they were making good time. In fact, the tiny valley in which the refuge hid unfolded before them.

Coltan slowed and paid close attention to the little hiking trails leading off the road. He recalled the wide trail that led to the south entrance of the valley was approximately twelve miles from the junction of the fire trail and the main road. He had reset the trip odometer to zero when he reached the fire trail/main road junction so he could anticipate the twelfth mile and find the wide trail on the right easily. As of that moment, the trip odometer rolled over to ten.

Over the last twenty minutes, he had been in agony from his stomach and the steadily rising fever, which produced not only body aches, but also a horrible pounding headache. Foul sweat soaked his body, and it became an ordeal to maintain control of the bike with his wet hands. To add to his misery, a moist rattling cough that had begun in Baker Creek developed into a chronic symptom. With every coughing spell, he tasted and swallowed blood.

Natalie could not hear the rattling of his lungs with each cough, but she could feel the rattling through his ribs as she embraced him. She was unaware of his sweat-drenched body because she could not feel it through his leather jacket. Although he seemed to be managing well, she still worried about him.

Her headache remained at the same intensity since they entered the fire trail way back at the summit route. She considered the fact it had not worsened a good sign. However, her upper mid-back was another matter; her pain had increased there, and her sweater under her jacket felt glued to the spot.

The trip odometer rolled to twelve. Coltan slowed the Harley to almost a snail's pace. He spotted the trail at the right and eased to the side of the road. He stopped the motorcycle at the top of the trail where he evaluated the difficulty of the terrain. The trail was wide enough to accommodate the bike, but it was going to be a rough ride. Small rocks and pits peppered the firm mud, and he could see overgrown trees and foliage that would slap them as they passed through.

From here, it would be five miles to the location of the refuge—five miles of bouncing and flogging, and maybe even a flat tire. Coltan reset the trip odometer to zero.

He trembled with exhaustion. He felt dizzy and feared he would pass out. Another coughing spell gripped him which made the vertigo worsen. This time, he saw flying pinpricks of stars before his eyes along with the vertigo. He sucked in a slow, deep breath after the coughing fit ceased.

"Are you okay?" Natalie asked, hollering over the engine noise.

"Yeah." ...*Liar, liar*...

"Is this the right trail?"

"Uh-huh."

"Are you sure?"

"Positive!" He revved the engine, leaned his head back against her shoulder and shouted to her, "Hold on!"

It was now or never. He mumbled a plea to God, and started down the path.

As he expected, the ride was akin to roller-skating on a cobblestone walkway. The foliage slapped them as they passed. They ducked below overhanging pine tree limbs and jostled in their seats around every sharp curve. For Coltan, it was pure torment. Every bump, every turn, caused his body to scream in painful protest and made his brain swirl in his head like a washer drum set at high-speed spin cycle.

Now and then, he glanced at the trip odometer. Two miles, three miles, four... It would not be long, now. He thought they would make it.

He never saw the odometer roll to five.

Natalie fell forward with him when he collapsed on his chest over the gas tank. The bike slowed and wavered as his hands dropped limply from the handlebars and the controls. She screamed and attempted to reach over him to grab the handlebars. The bike popped over a rock and teetered to the right. The force sent Natalie tumbling off the left side of the bike. She hit the ground at full force on her left side. She felt the bones crack and break in her left arm, felt the painful twist of her left ankle as it met the rocky mud. Her body rolled uncontrollably down the embankment and finally came to rest against the trunk of a pine tree.

She lay stunned for a few minutes, and in those minutes she heard the bike crash, heard the engine continue to hum and sputter. It was only her concern for Coltan that brought her back to full consciousness. After she removed her helmet, she tried to stand, but her broken ankle protested and crumpled under her weight. This caused her to crash down onto her broken arm. The pain was something she could never imagine, and she almost fainted. She cried out and began to crawl up the embankment toward the trail.

Coltan sprawled in the center of the trail. His upper body lay flat on his back, and his lower half lay twisted in a skewed position off to one side. A short distance beyond him, the Harley was on its side, the engine still engaged and emitting puffs of pale gray smoke.

Natalie did not care about the motorcycle; Colt was all that mattered. She dragged herself over the rocks and mud, stubbornly intent to reach him. She called out his name when she came upon him. He did not respond. Fearing the worst, she cautiously and gently supported his neck with her leg as she slowly removed his helmet with her one usable hand. Now she could see his face. His skin was pale as an eggshell and moist with beads of sweat. She bent and listened to hear him breathe. She could not hear any breath sounds or feel his breath on her skin. Her search for a pulse also came up negative.

Dazed, Natalie could only stare into his lifeless face. She caressed the cold, damp contours, swept his wet hair away from his peaceful, closed eyes, the delicate lids shut forever. How she would miss the deep, dark blue of those beautiful eyes! How she would miss his voice, his touch and his kiss! She wanted to never forget him, to never forget his face. Serenity replaced the suffering she had seen there over the many days past. This was only a small comfort to her; she was glad for him his suffering had ended. His face was now the face of a peacefully sleeping child. This is how she would remember him.

There would be no peace for her, not for a long time. He was all she had left, and now he was gone forever. At this moment, she could not imagine continuing her life without him. She could not imagine any reason to go on. There was no reason.

It was so unfair, so wrong. Where were those angels he said were protecting them? They didn't exist—that's what; and God didn't exist, either.

She screamed despairingly at the wretched hopelessness of it all. She screamed and screamed, and she cried hot, bitter tears for the loss of her beloved, precious Coltan.

All the sounds around her fled away. All the light fled away.

The darkness devoured her.

CHAPTER 28

O ne week later.
Mitchell gently squeezed her hand and looked up at Joe. "Why won't she wake up?"

Joe adjusted the pillows along the railing at the left side of the bed. He and Ian had placed them there to protect her from further injury.

"The doctors think it's emotional trauma," he answered.

"You sure she's not in a coma?"

"They're sure." Joe took a seat at the left side. He leaned forward, stroked her hair and pushed the overgrown bangs away from her eyes. Her face remained frozen in a morose expression since they wheeled her in from recovery. During his days caring for her, he observed the movement of her eyes under the closed lids and other unmistakable signs of normal brain activity. She dreamed often. She sometimes whimpered. Once, she had cried. Other times, she changed positions, and she appeared to be aware of her injuries whenever she moved. Yet, through all of that, she had not awakened.

"You want my personal opinion?" Joe asked Mitchell.

"Go ahead."

"She don't wanna wake up."

Mitchell sat back in the chair and ran his hand over his mustache and his mouth. He figured Brian and Beverly had died, or they would have been with her. Long ago, Mitchell had promised Brian if anything happened to him and Beverly, he would take care of Natalie. Now, he was at her side keeping his promise, and he never felt so helpless in his life.

He rose, bent over her and kissed her forehead. "I gotta get back to work." In a way, he said it to both Natalie and Joe, and he said it apologetically. Directly to Joe, he said, "Send word to me if anything changes."

"I will." Joe doubted it would be anytime soon.

JAMES, FRANKS, TREVOR and Suzanne finished watching the final disk recording of Isabelle's amazing transformation from mordant to normal child. The first disk contained the recording of Clausberg's initial attempts to tame the infected little girl. This footage included the horrifying cattle prod incidents. James, Suzanne, Franks and Trevor found the punishment extremely disturbing. Suzanne and Franks cried and had to turn away from the screen. As for their opinion of Morris's participation in the routine use of electrical shocks to control the mordants, once they reflected on their anger at him, they realized he had to participate in order to maintain his cover. To Morris's credit, it was clear he did not enjoy witnessing the torture of fellow human beings, and had attempted to prevent the incidences many times.

The next two of the four disks followed Guffy's work with Isabelle. Guffy's patience and persistence with the child impressed them. They even chuckled sympathetically a few times during the early phases when Guffy was frightened of her, and laughed uproariously at Isabelle's consonant-mangling conversations with him. It was impossible for the four of them not to fall in love with the remarkable little girl.

Even Trevor, who at first had serious reservations about Guffy and Isabelle, softened at the authenticity of their friendship. He relaxed further when Isabelle's lab work from that morning revealed she was still free of the virus. Guffy's and Morris's lab work also came back negative, which proved the mord virus was not airborne.

"That child is a miracle," Suzanne remarked as James shut off the machine. "I'd like to hear from her what she remembers about the period when she was fully infected. She could tell us a lot about how the virus affects the brain."

"If she remembers anything," Trevor said.

Suzanne had already considered it. "Yeah…"

DILLON WAS NEARING the end of another round of powerful medications. The intravenous drug treatments always left him exhausted, and he invariably ended-up taking a nap while the bag emptied into his ravaged system.

In all the time he had been at the refuge, he never had to share his hospital room. He liked it that way. He relished the privacy, relished the solitude. If the Leukemia Monster decided to live in him for the rest of his life, he would not mind. Chronic illness and a weakened immune system would guarantee him a private room and a good excuse not to go out and mingle with the Bible Bangers outside his door. Dillon was content to spend his time reading while the doctors and nurses poked him with needles and got him high on drugs. Trevor's visits eased his loneliness. He decided his semi-solitary life here was not so bad.

A sudden, vague sensation he was no longer alone began to stir him from his slumber. As always, his sense of smell was his first conscious awareness. A distinct aroma had come to rest at his bedside. It reminded him of freshly mowed grass and the raw soil of the forest behind his childhood home, the identical scent his younger sister carried after a day playing outside. The stronger it grew the more apprehensive and curious he began to feel, for it was alien to his current environment.

He weakly opened his eyes and squinted at his intruder.

She stood alongside the bed in a ruffled blue dress. Her shoulder length hair was dark and wavy. Thick dark eyebrows framed her serious brown eyes. She had a small round mouth with full lips, a cleft in her chin. Around her neck, she wore a toy stethoscope as if it was a necklace. She crooked her head to one side as her eyes met his.

"What do you want?" he asked gruffly.

"I gotta wissen to yo' hot," she said concernedly. With that, she placed the earbuds in her ears and the stethoscope to his chest.

Her speech impediment amused him. "Well... If you wanna listen to my *hot*, you gotta put that a lot lower."

Her eyebrows came together as one curvy line. "Huh?"

"Get outa here, rug rat!"

"Wet me wissen to yo' hot!" she insisted.

He took the stethoscope up to his mouth and gently blew into it. His breath traveled up the tubes and tickled her ears.

She drew back and laughed. "Dat tikkoos!"

Dillon tried to conceal his amusement. "Okay, now. Get outta here."

She pointed to his bald head. "Wew yo' haihw?"

"The monster stole it."

"Why?"

"He's gonna build a nest with it. Like a giant bird."

She thought he was serious. "Is da monstew in hew?"

"Yeah. He lives under the bed." He was certain that would scare her off.

After what she had been through, a measly, hair-stealing monster was nothing to fear. Curious to see what it looked like, she dropped to her knees and searched under the bed. All she discovered there was a discarded cotton ball. She stood and informed him, "Dew's no monstew unda deh."

"He probably went to lunch." He yawned and pulled the pillow to a more comfortable position under his head. "Go find someone else to torment."

"Tow-men?"

"Bother."

"Aw you biting sick?"

"No." He lifted his head and leaned his face close to hers. "But I will bite *you* if you don't leave me alone!"

His threat frightened her. She stepped away from him and decided to let him sleep. Like most grown-ups, he was terminally grouchy. "Okay." From the doorway, she told him, "I hope you get bettew soon."

When he awakened late that night, he found a red lollipop on his nightstand.

Mitchell smoked his pipe outside in the smoking section off the gardens. As he took another puff, he stared up into the starry night sky and wondered about death, God, and purpose. In all his life, through his one failed and childless marriage, through his tours of duty in the Marines, and through the months of therapy after a roadside bomb fractured his skull and damaged his brain, he had never felt the presence of God or anything supernatural.

He considered the vast universe above him and all around him; it could not have come about by accident. Even the sun, the moon, the stars, the novas, the black holes up there served a purpose. Those mysteries kept everything in balance, kept the earth turning reliably every twenty-four hours, all to sustain life on this one fragile planet with its equally fragile inhabitants. Even the tiniest microbes, even the frigging mord virus, had their purpose in the universe.

Under this infinite, nocturnal blanket of extraordinary creation, Mitchell sat and pondered these things. He could not understand why his destiny had so far been intangible and even more mysterious than the secrets of the universe.

Brian had spoken endlessly and enthusiastically about God, about Jesus, about every human life having a divine purpose. Mitchell had studied sporadically with Brian over the years and had come to believe in God. Yet, he still could not ascertain God's purpose for his life. This was the stumbling block in his faith. Although his life had been interesting, even exciting at times, it all felt empty and meaningless. He thought surely his expertise with electronics and technology was not enough to make him useful to God. There had to be something else.

He thought about the Danburys again. Now, there was an example of purpose fulfilled. They had brought many to Jesus. Heck—Brian had even managed to bring that smart-mouthed, sullen what's-his-name-kid to Jesus. He had even managed to assume the role of father figure to the punk. That had been a miracle all by itself.

His thoughts led him back to the present, to Natalie. Mitchell remembered he had held her a month after she was born. He only held her for a minute; he was afraid he would drop her, or hug her too tight or something, and he had been only too happy to return her to Beverly's arms. When she was younger, she called him Uncle Mitchell. That ended around the time she entered puberty. Nowadays, he was simply Mitchell or Mitch to her, and he was more comfortable with that than the title of Uncle.

He was not surprised when the team brought her in a week ago. Somehow, he felt strongly she was alive. He had also expected her parents to live through this, as well. Were they still out there? Were they searching for her and her for them? How had she survived all this time on the road? He would not know the answers until Natalie decided she wanted to wake up and live again. He wondered why she refused to awaken. What had happened to her that would make her resist a return to reality?

Above all this, Mitchell wondered, *What can I do for her through all of this? What can I do? How can I take care of her when she won't even talk to me?*

He barely heard the refuge's camouflaged door open, and he turned to see Joe's lanky form silhouetted in the brief shaft of light before the door closed. Joe lingered near the door while he lit a cigarette.

"Any word?" Mitchell called to him.

Joe ambled over. "She's still asleep."

"Sleeping Beauty, uh?" He bent and tapped the spent ashes out of his pipe. "Are they sure there's nothin' else wrong with her?"

"They've tested her for everything, Mitch." Joe took the chair next to him with a tired groan. "The kid don't wanna wake up. It's as simple as that." The cigarette trembled between his fingers and his thumb. He had been going on caffeine and adrenaline the last twelve hours. "Even Carolyn tried. She shook her and yelled at her. You know what Natalie did?"

"What?"

"She backhanded that poor girl. Sent her flying backwards onto the floor. Ian just about had a shit fit."

"You mean she woke up for a minute?"

Joe shook his head and wrinkled his face, thinking about it as he glanced up at the stars. "I don't know, man. It was hard to tell. After she decked poor Carolyn—her best friend, I might add—she simply laid back down and started snoozing again like nothin' had happened. We don't know what to make of it."

"Is Carolyn alright?"

"Oh, yeah. She got a big bruise on her cheekbone, that's all. Ian was more upset than she was."

"Maybe Ian should go back to working at the library."

"He's wasted at the library." Joe pointed his finger at Mitchell, and Mitchell pulled back from the lit cigarette between his fingers, "Ian's a natural for the medical profession. He knows it. He asked for the transfer, and I'm more than happy to train him."

"He's a good kid."

"Yeah." Joe sat back, relaxed for the first time all day. "He's keeping an eye on Natalie right now. He's been talkin' to her, tryin' to get her to talk back to him. So far, no luck." Joe stood and stretched out his back, shook out his arms to relax the kinks and the tension from so many hours on duty. Finally, he asked, "Did you get a load of that little girl that came in?"

"Isabelle?"

"Yeah. What a character! Cute little bugger."

"Her and Guffy still together?"

"For now. Suzanne thinks she should be placed with a family."

"Why?"

"To get her back to interacting with other kids."

"How's Guffy feel about that?"

"No one's brought it up yet. We gotta give it some time."

"How'd she beat the virus? Anyone know?"

"Morris is still workin' on it." Just then, his radio beeped. He answered a call from ICU and promised he would be right there. Mitchell heard the brief conversation, but Joe told him, anyway. "We got a transfer out of ICU"

Mitchell's memory stirred at the mention of ICU As far as he knew, there had been only one patient in Intensive Care, and that had been a week ago. He thought the kid had died. He stood up and began to accompany Joe to the door, "The boy?"

"Yep. Maybe he can wake her up."

*J*ames and Trevor burned the midnight oil at the computer in James's office. They looked over the list of names and vital statistics of the head honchos of the United Earth Federation.

"Bankers, energy resource industry execs, software conglomerates, politicians..." James pursed his lips and blew out a stream of breath. "This is amazing! These people are from every continent!"

Trevor pointed out a few that jumped out at him, "Look at all the heads of social science organizations, leading psychologists, medical doctors, specialists. Yegad! Look at all the names from DataTrack!"

"That's the chip conglomerate, isn't it?"

"Yeah! Look who's on their Board of Directors!"

James quickly scanned the list, "Senators, congressmen, governors, five past presidents... bigwigs from the whole dang North American Union; From Europe—Sorry, Trev—your Prime Minister, see?" He pointed to the name on the screen. After Trevor acknowledged with a disappointed sigh, James continued, "Heads of State—Great Britain, Belgium, Italy—damn... the bulk of the European Union! Look at this! Asia, Russia, some Middle Eastern countries—the one's that aren't trying to nuke each other and us—Say, China's got a big piece of this, too!" He darted his eyes from the screen to Trevor, "This is a worldwide endeavor!"

"Who's the leader?" Trevor strained to read through the hundreds of names. There was no indication which individual led the UEF. However, they had twelve more disks to examine. "God help us, James. This will take us months! Let's hope they don't bother with us in the meantime, ay?"

"I can tell you one thing," James said. "There's one name missing that you'd expect to be there."

"Who?"

"President Alderton, our current President of the United States. He's not here."

"Didn't he die during the mords siege?"

"Conveniently!" There was a knowing gleam in James's eyes. "Someone used the crisis to conveniently snuff his ass. He didn't die. He was murdered! As far as Vice President Tewly goes, I wouldn't trust that snake as far as I could spit!"

"Look for Tewly on the list." Trevor suggested.

James put in a search for Tewly, and the two of them waited. Tewly's name popped up as a member of the Board of Directors of DataTrack, and as a consultant to Social Innovations Corporation, a human behavior research organization.

"Sonofagun..." James whistled. "We missed it the first time."

"I wonder if the Royal Family has a hand in this. I doubt it, but I'd like to check." Trevor scooted closer to the keyboard and began to type in names on the search command. The results were a relief to him. Trevor wearily leaned his elbow on the desk and rested his chin in his hand, "Oi!" He nodded. "The Royal Family's not here. God, please save them... and the rest of us with 'em. God help us all..."

CHAPTER 29

J oe and Ian maneuvered the gurney into Natalie's room from the ICU. Due to the seriousness of his condition the doctors gave orders to park this patient in the bed nearest the door. The space there was bigger, which meant plenty of room for the monitoring equipment and all the bells and whistles that went with it.

They pulled the gurney next to the bed, and together they lifted the patient into the bed. Joe began to untangle all the tubes and chords and connect them to the host machines.

"May I 'elp with 'at?" Ian offered.

"Hang up the IV bag. Don't forget the second bag for later."

"Will do." Ian hung the bags and rechecked the tubing for unimpeded flow. When he was done, he watched Joe tend to the rest of the monitoring equipment. Ian knew he was not ready for that responsibility yet, but Joe would teach him soon.

The patient coughed. It was a hollow, rattling sound.

Joe glanced at the patient, and then looked at Ian. "Oxygen."

Ian connected the mask and placed it over the patient's nose and mouth while Joe turned the button for the oxygen. "We 'aven't used these kind in years." Ian remarked about the oxygen equipment.

"Everything here is fifth-hand salvage or auction, even the beds." Joe replied. "They had to buy everything off the grid to keep it secret."

"I see."

Joe continued, "I guess you noticed a lot of our blood pressure equipment is the old-fashion manual type. You know why I prefer it? I prefer it because the battery-powered ones are useless when we run out of batteries—which we will someday. The same for the thermometers."

"That's quite sensible." Ian pushed the gurney to the other side of the room. He retrieved the patient's chart folder from the mattress and set it in the pocket at the foot of the bed.

Joe completed the connections. "Let me see his chart."

Ian lifted it and read the name, "Allen, Charles Coltan. Is that correct?"

"That's the one." He took the chart from Ian and looked inside. "Next vitals due in two hours."

"I can do that." Ian said. "Your eyes are lookin' a bit red, Joe."

"So are yours," Joe replied. He rechecked the monitors and all the connections. Everything was fine. The young man's skin was warm and his coloring had improved. His eyes were half-open, but not focused on anything, and Joe attributed that to the medications. Joe patted his shoulder comfortingly and said, "Hey, buddy." Coltan responded with a soft grunt beneath the oxygen mask. Joe considered Coltan's brief response a positive sign. He confessed to Ian as he brought the blanket under Coltan's neck, "I could use a cup of coffee."

Ian nodded. "Go ahead, Joe. I'll buzz ya if I need."

"If it's urgent, grab Sharon first and then page me."

"Roger that." Ian pulled up a chair at the bedside and watched Joe leave the room. After five days of tending to patients, he was more confident in his ability to provide basic care. Apparently, Joe had confidence in him, too, or he would not have left him there to solo.

Coltan weakly mumbled something. Ian returned his attention to his patient. As he looked into the young man's face, Ian got the eerie sensation he had seen this stranger before. After many moments researching his memory, fragmented images of the *where* and the *how* sparked forth. At first, he thought it could not be possible, not be true. Yet, his affinity for this ragged refugee grew stronger. He decided to keep the revelation to himself; otherwise, they would all consider him batty. Coltan mumbled a second time and his voice returned Ian fully to the present. "What is it?" Ian asked softly.

"Froid!" Coltan whispered. "J'ai très froid."

Ian was surprised to hear him speak French. "You're cold?"

Coltan opened his eyes and looked up at Ian. He had expected to see an adult, not a boy. However, the boy's face was gentle and his eyes seemed mature with the wisdom of ages, full of compassion. Coltan immediately trusted him. "Yeah... cold. What did I say?"

"You said, 'froid.'"

He could not understand why he uttered his first words in French. "I meant 'cold.'"

"I'll get you another blanket." He returned a few minutes later with a twin size blue comforter from the linen closet. He draped it over him and tucked down the foot and the sides, "This is lighter and warmer. Will it do?"

"Thank you." Coltan found it difficult to speak. The infection and the virus debilitated him. He felt pain everywhere. The medications made him woozy, and it was a challenge to see anything clearly. "Is this a hospital?"

"Yes."

He said with trepidation in his voice, "Bonito Valle?"

"No, sir. Army of Christ."

Coltan smiled. "We made it."

"Yes. You're safe here."

"Natalie... Where's Natalie?"

"In the next bed. She's sleepin'."

"Is she okay?" He tried to turn his head to steal a look at her.

"She has some injuries. Nothin' that won't heal. She's gettin' well." He noticed Coltan swallowed hard, winced as if it hurt or his throat was dry. "They said you can 'ave water now. Would you like some?" Coltan nodded, and Ian poured a small amount into a plastic cup from the bedside pitcher. "Would you like to sit up?" Again, Coltan nodded. Ian placed the bed control panel into his hand, "Push the top button to bring the head of the bed up."

Coltan was all too familiar with hospital beds. It dismayed him to be flat on his back again. He pressed the button and raised the head to a reclining position. He did not anticipate the pain that shot through his abdomen, and he grimaced.

Ian set down the water and rose quickly. "Ho, there. I should give you somethin'." He hurried to the closet and brought down an extra pillow. He returned to the bed with it, folded down the comforter and blanket and gingerly set the pillow upon Coltan's abdomen. He placed Coltan's arm over the pillow and brought up the covers. "Keep it there, sir. It 'elps with the pain." After a thought, he added, "Especially when you must cough or sneeze."

Coltan accepted it gratefully, "Good idea. Thanks." He intended to ask the boy his name and to inquire about his accent, but the combination of medication and fatigue caused him to doze off for a few seconds. He forced himself awake and removed the oxygen mask.

Ian held the cup of water to his mouth. "There you are. Take sips. Gotta take it slow."

Coltan sipped the water slowly. It felt good in his parched throat. When he had enough, he brushed Ian's hand with the cup away. He strained to look over at Natalie. She was still and silent; he could not hear her breathing. "Are you sure she's okay?"

"She's sleepin'."

"You said she was hurt."

"You crashed your motorcycle."

Based on his own condition, he feared the worst for her. "Was she hurt bad?"

"A broken arm and a broken ankle."

He hazily recalled being wet and shivering along the banks of a stream—or was it the river? He imagined he had crashed the Harley into the river. A quip blip of an image showed him Natalie's back and head were bleeding, and he remembered finding something small and hard in her scalp. "What about her back and her head? There was something stuck in the base of her skull. Did they find it?"

"It was only a small pebble of cement. They removed it. She's fine."

Coltan had no distinct recollection of the crash. "Does she remember what happened?"

Ian hesitated to answer. It was a tricky subject. How could he tell Coltan Natalie had not awakened in a week's time? "She's been sleepin', mostly. She hasn't spoken about what 'appened."

Coltan found this suspicious. "Has anyone asked her?"

He did not know what to say. Ian was not one to tell lies, even if it meant protecting someone from the truth. He opted for honesty. "She does not seem to want to awaken, sir."

Coltan wanted to escape the bed and rush to her side. "What the hell does that mean?"

"We think it's depression. Trauma. When they brought her in she was unconscious, the same as you. Joe noticed her face was still wet with tears. She has wept a little since. Otherwise, she's been quiet." He regarded Coltan sympathetically. "Per'aps she'll awaken soon. We all spend time with 'er, talkin' to 'er, encouragin' 'er. We expect she'll come 'round."

He reclined tiredly into the pillow. He thought over how he could comfort her. An idea came to him. "Could you roll her bed next to mine, so I can be with her?"

Ian was unsure if it would be against the rules. In this case, it seemed wise to break the rules. He thought it would help the girl and the young man. What harm could there be in moving their beds together? "I could do that." He rose and went to Natalie's bed. He transferred the IV bag to the holder at the head of the bed frame, unplugged and rolled the bed next to Coltan's. Before he moved the bed flush, he lowered the railings on both beds so the two of them could snuggle unimpeded. The task completed and the wheels locked, he told Coltan, "There you are." He retreated to the other end of the room and observed them from there to give them a small measure of privacy.

Coltan powered his headrest down almost flat. He turned over slowly and immediately took Natalie's hand. "We're okay, Nat."

She slept obliviously.

He caressed her cheek. "Natalie?"

She made a soft noise, a non-descript comment that at least indicated she could hear him. Her hand closed around his.

"We're both okay. Can you hear me?"

Natalie seemed confused. She whispered, "Colt?"

"Yeah, hon. It's me. I'm here." He squeezed her hand. "Open your eyes."

She began to cry silently. After a few moments, she said, "You're dead. Colt's dead. They're all dead."

It broke his heart to hear this. He leaned painfully closer to her and turned her face to see him. "I'm here, Natalie. Open your eyes and look at me!"

"No... I can't... You're not real."

"Mon belle ange!" He hoped this would convince her. He often called her his *beautiful angel* in French. She loved to hear it.

Could it really be Colt? Had he returned from the dead to console her? "Colt...?"

"Je t'aime!" How many times had he professed his love to her? How many more times would she need to hear it to be convinced he was there at her side? *"Natalie... Je t'aime."*

She finally stirred, slowly turned over on her side and tightened her grip on his hand, "Colt...?"

"Natalie... I'm here. Look at me."

His voice settled into her as a warm and comforting tonic. Her heart leapt with the realization. Yet, she feared it was all imagination, a ghostly manifestation of her impossible hope he had not actually left her, but had only been sleeping.

He persisted. "Natalie... I love you. I'm here with you."

If she had imagined him, she could close her eyes again and remain asleep until she died. She braced for her feared disappointment as she opened her eyes and looked for him.

He smiled at her, his eyes bright and deep blue and full of love for her. "My angel," he whispered, relieved and happy.

Her eyes filled with ecstatic tears, and her voice came weakly yet joyfully, "Colt?"

He laughed softly. "Alive and relatively well."

She nestled into him, rested her head on his shoulder. "I thought you died! Oh! Thank God. Thank you, God!"

Coltan held her tightly and rested his cheek against her forehead. "Yeah..." he murmured, "Thank you, Father. Thank you." Lulled then by the medications and the comforting rhythm of her warm breath upon his neck, he closed his eyes and drifted easily into peaceful slumber.

For the first time in months, they felt hopeful.

THE PAIN IN DILLON'S bones invaded his sleep. In his dream, he pressed the nurse call button. A petite, small-framed young woman appeared instantly at his bedside. He stared at her in the dim light, amazed and stunned by her beauty and the quiet confidence in her face, the love and tenderness in her eyes. When she bent and gently stroked his cheek, her long black hair fell in soft waves upon his neck and chest, and the pain in his bones subsided.

She spoke to him in a whisper, her voice deeper than he would have expected from such a sprite. Yet, her words drifted in and away and in again as if carried upon a shifting wind:

"...*my side ...sword ...pure and true.*"

As she straightened, he dimly perceived she wore a military uniform that seemed pieced together out of the remnants of many old uniforms. He wanted to ask her about it, but he could not summon his voice. She smiled warmly, regarded him as if he was the most precious creature in the whole world. Then, after another moment, she bent and pursed her full round lips, placed the gentlest kiss upon his brow. She exuded the sweet scent of the forest as she did this, and her scent covered him, caused his heart to bask in the spreading warmth of ecstasy.

The intoxication of that moment lulled him into a deeper sleep, a slumber so unfathomable it was beyond the realm of dreams.

At his bedside, little Isabelle quietly watched over him. She silently prayed for him, asked her beloved *Deezus* to lift the sickness from his body and replace it with strength and serenity. Deezus must have heard her prayer, for she observed the transformation on Dillon's face, the pain, anger and sadness replaced by profound peace.

She placed a tiny stuffed white angel bear on his nightstand and tiptoed out of the room.

END OF BOOK 2

Thank you for reading, "*Claiming Destination Book 2: Flight of the Destined.*"
Independent authors rely on reviews to spread the word about their works.
If you enjoyed this book (or hated it), please leave an online review where your book was purchased.

THINGS GET CRAZY AND downright dangerous for our friends as their story continues while the entire planet descends into madness in the remaining five books of this series:

Book 3: Isa

Book 4: The Bitter Fruit

Book 5: To Move a Mountain

Book 6: Mister Death Shadow

Book 7: Desitus